More praise for
Another Song About the King

"This mother/daughter novel, which moves back and forth in time between Silvie's childhood and her present-day life in Manhattan will move you tender . . . and then some."

—*Mademoiselle*

"Though we empathize with Silvie's every wound at Simone's hands, the author forces us to take this mother to our hearts, with a writerly compassion so honest we can cringe but not look away. . . . While [this] may be Kathryn Stern's first hit, it will not be her only."

—JACQUELYN MITCHARD

"Stern handles the love/hate relationship between mothers and daughters with skill and understanding, making this more than just another novel about an often-explored theme."

—*Booklist*

"This tale of mothers, daughters and the King is gently told and heartfelt."

—*Publishers Weekly*

"An insightful, well-written look at a difficult mother-daughter relationship."

—*Library Journal*

Another Song About the King

Kathryn Stern

Ballantine Books • New York

For my mother,
who filled us
with color
and light.

And for Jim,
who taught me
about finishing
the hat.

The thing about darkness

is how it lets you see.

—ADRIENNE RICH

ANOTHER

SONG

ABOUT

THE KING

PROLOGUE

*M*y hands are calm. I put in, take out, take my time. I'm standing inside my closet, filling my honeymoon suitcase. Three o'clock in the morning. I can't sleep. Sunglasses. Hat. Lingerie. Bathing suit, jeans, sneakers. Outside my bedroom window, light swallows darkness until, gradually, morning will come, my wedding day. I start humming a Dylan song, "Visions of Johanna," our song, Scottie's—my fiancé's —and mine, and fold a nightgown my mother might have bought me if she were here, for my trousseau.

I slip into one of my mother's favorite songs, "All Shook Up," picking up the pace a little, the Elvis rhythm. Tuck the sunscreen and my sketchbook in the corner of my suitcase until suddenly I'm bent over, unable to move as my mind races back, remembering.

◆ ◆ ◆

"You were named for Elvis," my mother says calmly, as if she's telling me we've run out of milk or bread or juice. Theo's not born yet, so I must be four, almost five. It is my first real memory, and we are in the kitchen in our small house in Michigan. It is 1966. When my father is out of town, we spend a lot of time in the kitchen, at the round Formica table—me with my coloring book, my mother heating leftovers. She cuts corners when he's away. And she sews. The tiny square of brown linoleum floor becomes a place where outfits get made and tales get spun. Alone with me, my mother can transform herself from an ordinary wife and mother into someone capable of greatness.

I look up from the house I'm coloring without saying a word. And so she lowers her sewing and repeats, in her pretty southern accent, "Darlin', did you hear me? You were named for Elvis Presley. Not even your father knows that. Wouldn't you like to share a secret, just you and me?" My mother and I have never shared a secret before, and I'm flattered and shy and resistant all at once, as if she is taking me somewhere I'm not sure I want to go.

"But my name is Silvie, not Elvis!" I say, thrusting out my lip, looking at her. When I was older, I thought my mother had a stern and noisy beauty, a high forehead and long, oval face that, to me, suggested the nobility she longed for. Her large nose had a bump that only made her more beautiful, along with the thick straight hair the color of warm toast and the lips red with lipstick. But on this day in the kitchen, she frightens me—there is too much to see in her face, and I look down at the house I'm coloring, purse my lips, let my fingers graze over the shiny points of my new box of sixty-four Crayola crayons.

"*Silvie* backwards spells *Elvis*," my mother says. "Roughly speaking, of course. The exact backwards is *Sivle,* but I didn't want to get too carried away." She laughs brightly. I feel somehow ashamed. I thought I had my own name.

"It's an anagram," my mother says, and I hold my sky-blue crayon tightly; I've been coloring the sky above the house and I don't want to stop.

All my pictures are the same: a burnt-sienna house with a chimney, a green tree, green grass with a red tulip, and sky, sky, sky, all around and above. I love the sky, because it takes a long time to color, although, really, it's nothing, just color layered upon color.

"An anagram is letters all scrambled up that make different words. If you take your name, Silvie, and move the letters around, you get Elvis."

"Oh," I say, and concentrate harder on my coloring, hooking my feet around the legs of my chair.

"You know who Elvis Presley is, don't you?"

"Sure. The guy on the record." I am coloring faster, only now I'm thinking of the dark-haired man with the buttery voice who my mother listens to almost every day, biting her lip and closing her eyes. A net of butterflies unfastens inside my stomach. I don't want to be named after him—after anybody. Where's Daddy?

She smiles. "You know those songs we play? And sometimes we dance?"

"In our pajamas?"

She frowns. "Well, yes. 'Blue Suede Shoes,' 'Hound Dog,' 'Jailhouse Rock?' Those songs are his, and they've made him famous. Do you know what famous means?" Her eyes lift, bright and soft at the same time, like when she straps on the shoes and dances away from me. I don't feel like answering.

"Yes." I stop coloring and stare down at my half-finished sky.

"What?" she asks.

"I don't know."

"Famous," my mother says, "is when everyone knows who you are."

"Everyone in the whole world?" I ask, lifting my eyes from my picture. Sometimes, even when I squint my eyes and look right at her, I have trouble seeing her face. With my father, I can stand right up close and see him; he's just there, himself.

"In the case of Elvis, yes. He's the most famous—and the greatest—singer who ever lived. Some people might say it's Frank Sinatra, but they would be wrong. They don't call Frank Sinatra the King, do they?" She stabs at crumbs on the place mat, bringing her finger to her lips to taste each one. Then she leans close and her voice drops. "Silvie, I went out with Elvis once. We had a date."

I don't say a word. I feel her waiting for me to say something, but I don't like this conversation. I begin to peel the paper off my crayon, so it's smooth, naked.

"Before I was married, when I was a teenager, in Biloxi, Mississippi. M-I-S-S-I-S-S-I-P-P-I." She smiles. "You know, I wasn't always a suburban nobody driving around in a white station wagon."

A nobody? I didn't understand. She was a *mother.*

She sweeps the crumbs into a tiny pile, smiles. "We had to sneak into the back booth in the restaurant so no one would bother us or ask for his autograph." She looks at me. "That's when someone famous writes their name and gives it to you."

"I can write my name." I write my name below the picture I'm coloring. Slowly. Carefully. *Silvie Page. Silvie Page. My* name. When I look up, my mother is lost in memory.

"He had the most beautiful blue eyes always folded up in that squint, as if he didn't trust just anyone with his heart. And his voice, even just talking, was so pretty. Just a caramel-coated drawl that made you feel he had never told anyone even one of the things he was telling you. He wore a gold ring from his mama, and his hands . . . well, his hands were soft as rain. He touched my hand before we ate—a piece of fisherman's wharf pie, that sublime pie that isn't exactly apple but has cinnamon and nutmeg. And we shared a tall glass of milk with a straw. The strangest coincidence was that he liked ice cubes in his milk. Just like me." Her remembering voice is quiet, slow, like a music box winding down. "There's something so romantic about sharing food."

"You didn't have a chocolate soda?"

"No, but the milk was very cold, and they were famous for that pie, so warm and spicy and . . . well, it was delicious."

"I would get a chocolate soda."

Now my mother gazes toward the window above the sink. "Not many girls can say they were named after a king."

I follow her eyes, but it's dark now and there's not much to see out the window, just a vague impression of our small yard in this suburb of Detroit, the last of winter's snow baked on the grass like piecrust, the black expanse of driveway faded into the dark horizon; beyond that, the curb where our station wagon sits, along with the other station wagons parked on this quiet street in this quiet subdivision.

My mother looks at me, suddenly annoyed. "You will be proud of this, Silvie. Someday."

I don't say anything. I bite my lip and look back at my coloring, but that record cover won't leave my mind: Elvis, in a green satin shirt and a nubby sport coat, leaning back into that smile.

"His smile is kind of limp-sided." I squirm a little as I say this. I raise my eyes to hers, then back down.

"Oh! You mean lopsided! A half smile, as if he knows a secret. Enchanting, isn't it?" Her eyes drill holes into me, but I don't look up. Dimly, I know I should, but I can't. Or I won't. The power of her need frightens me, silences me. A minute later, she rises from her chair and, with a sigh, starts poking around inside the refrigerator, and I try to finish but never do finish my sky because, suddenly, she's beside me and music is coming from the record player in the living room, one of the slow songs she loves—"Any Way You Want Me."

"Let's dance," she says, taking my hands in hers, tugging me out of my chair.

I let her pull me up. Her perfume envelops me—magnolia blossoms—a strong flower, she's told me. On her, the scent is more than scent; it's an emotion that wafts out, humid as the Biloxi air, soft yet fierce, like the first breath of a hurricane wind. "Now, remember what I taught you?" she says.

I stand on tippy-toe, put my right hand in hers, the way I've been told. I'm still holding the blue crayon. Now I reach up and place my left hand on her shoulder just the way she showed me. I don't see how I could be a very good dance partner with my head barely reaching her waist, but she seems to be happy.

" 'I'll be as tame as a baby, or wild as the raging sea,' " she sings in a pretty voice, full of vigor. " 'Any way you want me, well, that's how I will be.' " She sings with her mouth wide open, her whole face bright with teeth.

I press my head into her stomach, tighten my grip on her hand. My feet feel heavy as bricks. Her red turtleneck feels scratchy, and the old scuffed flats she wouldn't be caught dead in outside the house make a shuffling noise across the floor.

Her palm heavy on my back, she guides me in circles around the kitchen, singing away as around we go. She leads; I try to follow. " 'In your hands, my heart is clay, to take and hold as you may. I'm what you make me, you've only to take me, and in your arms I will stay-ay-ay. Ooh-ooh.' "

I hear the faint delicate rumblings of her stomach; I hear her gather the air she needs to sing. " '. . . Any way you wa-a-a-ant me that's how I will be, I will be-e-e . . .' "

And we dance on into the night, being who we are at that time, my mother and I, she with her head full of dreams, me with my hands full of sky.

◆ ◆ ◆

Elvis hung over us, a specter, a ghost of Mimi's glorious past, filling our house with hope. I loved my mother and wanted to believe her; I was drawn again and again to the power of her vision, to the gauzy web of mystery she wove around us. And to the question:

Does every story we tell about ourselves contain both the truth and the lie?

◆ ◆ ◆

For nine months, I imagine now, my twenty-year-old mother put her hands on the baby growing in the globe of her belly and pressed into me, with her hands and her heart, her hunger to be somebody. I was successful in the womb—obedient and nimble, turning somersaults in those jelly seas of color and sleep. She was so sure I was a boy that she painted the small baby's room blue, and for the whole nine months, a list of robin's-egg names lifted off her lips: Michael, Stephen, David.

The moment I was born, I believe, I began to disappoint her. According to my father, the nurse lay me on my mother's chest and my mother took one look and said, "A girl?" She handed me to my father and went to sleep, and I gripped his pinkie finger and yawned my eyes into the milky slits of a newborn kitten.

My father wanted to name me Elizabeth, for his mother, but he folded his hands quietly over the blue Air Force hat in his lap, his mouth impassive, a sour taste of surprise on his tongue when he heard that his firstborn would be named Silvie. By then, my mother's indomitable spirit had already snagged his gentle one, creating a tiny tear that one day years later would cause the long fabric between them to unravel.

I think about how they must have filled out a form with their new daughter's name, my mother light in her bones for the first time in nine months, wondering how quickly she could get her shape back. Was she excited then, looking down at me, a real baby, flesh and bones in her arms, a being who owed her already? I imagine her picking me up, her hands heavy with the realization that from that moment on, she was a *mother,* bound to the ordinary things she'd claimed she wanted—a husband, a child, a harvest-gold refrigerator.

I imagine her holding me tighter, thinking, I could be someone, little girl, I could do things, go places, but now I have *you*. And how that thought could lead to another—that she could hurt me, stick me with a diaper pin, turn her back on me in the bath, forget to test the milk's temperature in the crook of her arm; and there was power in this, that she could be everything to someone, and hurt her. I wonder now how power felt to her, why she needed it so. Did she bite into it and taste blood—not just hers alone but ours, everything together? Maybe she grew ravenous then, gripping me even more tightly, holding me higher, murmuring, "Silvie, eat *now; do as I say now,*" a round, hot, ravenous *now*. I'm told I howled a lot, red-faced, and rejected her milk. She had to throw the nursing bras away and make soy bottles.

The only way I slept at first, my father says, was on his shoulder, and this surely must have made her want to grab me, hold on to me tighter.

She loves me; she loves me not. For years, I played this game with flowers, revolving doors, sidewalks: Step on a crack, break your mama's back. I love her; I love her not.

◆ ◆ ◆

When I was older, in school, what I focused on about my mother, to justify my worries that she wasn't right, were her shoes. She had too many pairs. The shiny, unscuffed heels lay curved together in boxes in her closet, each pair giving her some idea of herself that my father, brother, and I could not give her, as if in each of the narrow size 7 boats she could one day sail away. She came by her affection for shoes naturally: Her father, Leon, whom we called Paw Paw, made his fortune from a shoe store in the small town of Biloxi, Mississippi. He fell in love with my grandmother, Nora, or Granny, the minute he plucked her away from where she stood with her nose pressed to the store window, looking longingly at a pair of pumps she couldn't afford, and gave her a job. In a gesture typical of their odd blend of whimsy and narcissism, they named each of their four children after shoes—Connie; then my mother, who was Simone; then Shelby; and last, Sweet Nina Baby.

My mother's favorites were the blue suede pumps with rounded toes and ankle straps atop chunky three-inch heels. She'd found them in New Orleans, and even though they were expensive, she'd snatched them right up. They were tap shoes without the tap, she said, and *that* she would supply herself. They were her most glamorous pair, and whenever she put them on, she had to jump up and dance around to Elvis on the stereo.

Even when she was pregnant with my brother, Theo, who was born when I was five, my mother would pinch her swollen feet into those blue suede shoes and play the Elvis ballads, the slow songs, "Love Me Tender" and "Treat Me Like a Fool," swaying in front of the stove in the kitchen while she made dinner, going back to that younger, freer self, the one she might have become. I wanted to ask my father what he thought when he saw those blue suede shoes on her feet night after night, but I said nothing, and he came home and left again in his cycle of days, a husband, a father, a traveling salesman who tucked his feelings inside his briefcase and under his hat.

◆ ◆ ◆

When I was nine or ten, it started—my bizarre taste for bland. I plotted makeovers—or, rather, make*unders*—ways to make myself disappear. And my mother, too—to drain her of color, tone her down. I drew her with crayons, a silhouette, a faded paper doll.

More than once I wished her gone.

And yet, with another breath, I clung to her—to the good side of Simone: the ripe, boisterous flare of her cheekbones, her manic love, her quick laugh, the high music of her anger, her lies. I needed our shrill, expensive battles, fevers raging in the one skin that held us together.

Queen of weather, my mother—foul weather that stripped leaves off the trees, that whipped your self away and left just your body standing there, a tree shorn, nothing but a few bare branches and a fistful of shaky hope. She erased you until you erased yourself.

And so where I learned to exist was in my art, safe in that silence of color, of light and shadow. I made sure I wasn't very good—not good enough to stand out—but I lived there.

Once, I painted her smiling, in a blue silk jacket, one eye cocked to heaven, a blue kite soaring from her head. In her hands, more kites, stacked one on top of the other, lifting up and away in a powerful gust, but fragile.

"No," Theo said, studying my efforts later, when it was all over. What did he know that I didn't? "You've got her all wrong."

I never could get her right.

CHAPTER I

When I was little, my mother and I, after putting Theo to bed, would sit in the dim living room, the lamp low, she at her sewing machine and me curled up underneath her desk, watching her feet move up and down on the pedal she sometimes called a treadle. I was five, six, seven. My father had a new job selling adding and accounting machines for Sperry Rand and was gone half-weeks. It seemed it was just us two mostly. Tonight, he was in some midwestern state that started with *I*, Illinois or Indiana or Iowa.

"Pain in the you know what, tacking these seams," my mother murmured, hunched over a difficult one. She was making fancy draperies for the living room, heavy pleated ones that weren't easy. I watched her calves and feet awhile, crossed gracefully underneath the wooden dining room chair, one of six sent from my grandfather's furniture store.

She smoothed the wide cloth under the teeth of her handsome

black Singer sewing machine, pumping the pedal with her bare foot. From time to time, she strained to look out the window above her desk, as if checking to see whether something she had left out in the night was still there. In our neighborhood, the small houses were so close together they seemed threaded like beads on a string. My mother didn't like it that all the houses looked alike and that it was April and the trees were still just skinny sticks wearing a wig. She said they reminded her of the witch in *The Wizard of Oz*.

"Hey, sugar pie, whatcha doin' down there?" Her voice smiled; her drawl lifted certain words and stretched others, into a song.

"I'm watching your feet," I said. They were pretty feet, long, in skin-colored stockings, with fire-engine-red toes.

"Well, that can't be much fun," she said, humming to our new *Camelot* record. I'd rather have had *The Sound of Music,* but at least *Camelot* wasn't Elvis. Her feet moved in perfect rhythm to "I Wonder What the King Is Doing Tonight."

I crawled out from beneath the desk, watching her hands. I believed my mother's hands could do anything: install zippers and flat-felled seams, make all our dresses match: summer shifts in orange cotton, polka-dot jumpers, a pink sundress with daisies—all with button straps. In the winter, plaid wool skirts. I loved it when she sewed—even her complaints had a lilt to them. Sewing was focused activity, a discipline, a gift, really, handed down to all the girls in my mother's family—not just from Granny, but from Paw Paw's mother, my great-grandmother Henriette, who at Auschwitz had her name taken off the death list because, so the legend went, her needle's speed and precision made her too valuable to kill. Sewing became equated with strength, with sanity, one shimmering bubble that each of us tried to live inside. There were times, much later, when my mother would renounce sewing altogether, forgetting how the small, cold glint of the needle had shaped her happiest afternoons, how the industrious whir of the machine had structured her nights.

She sighed down at the material in her hands and said, more to herself than to me: "You know, it's nice when Dan goes away for a few days. I mean, I get more done. I really do." Her nod was a small gesture, chin close to her chest, one part of her agreeing with the other.

Hearing her talk about my father always made me fidget. "Mom, I'm bored. What can I do?" I didn't want to bake another tiny pie in my Easy-Bake oven or build another rickety Lincoln Logs cabin or send a Slinky down the stairs. I didn't even want to take Barbie swimming in a cake pan filled with water.

Her foot stopped, moving off the pedal and becoming too still, poised. It was the same stillness I'd observed lately in the kitchen, always followed by sudden movement.

Sure enough, she jumped up, darted to the coffee table. "I've got it!" she said. "Did I show you what Helen, that sweetie at the sewing shop, saved for me?" I crawled out from under the desk and sat up, eager to see what she had in her hands: huge books with the names Butterick, Simplicity, and Vogue in large letters. She went to the kitchen, came back with a pencil and paper, sat down cross-legged near the sewing machine's pedal, and patted the speckled linoleum. She wanted carpet in the living room, wall-to-wall. That was why my father worked so hard, she explained, so someday we could buy carpet, a bigger house, a better life. "I'll set you up right here by me."

Nestling close, I watched as she spread the Butterick book open over our laps and tore from a tablet a piece of the thinnest paper I'd ever seen.

"It's onionskin paper. The best for tracing."

My eyes grew wide. "The paper's made of onion?"

"No, it's just thin as an onion's skin." She held it over a picture of a little girl in a pretty flowered dress, pattern #8117, and traced its outline with a fat pencil in slow, careful strokes. "Now, you try. When you're done, you can color in the pretty dresses. Design them. They don't have to match the ones in the book. We can make them any color we want."

I stuck out my lower lip. "I want them to match the book."

"Fine. Whatever is most fun, that's what you should do."

I loved it when my mother was like this—calm, happy, a friend whose lips curved in a sweet smile. I got up on my knees and quickly turned several pages until I found a picture I liked, of a small brown-haired girl holding hands with her mother, a tiny black dog prancing at their feet. They wore matching outfits—even the dog wore a little jacket from the same plaid fabric. Pattern #9219, the book said. I clutched the pencil so tightly that I almost broke it in two, trying to guide my lines to be as graceful as hers.

The pencil marks smudged easily on the strange paper, but I didn't mind. Soon I was lost in a new world of drawing, of pretty girls in pretty clothes living inside this grand make-believe coloring book, my mother's foot dancing on the pedal beside me.

After a while, I noticed an absence of sound and I looked up. Her foot had stopped and she was inspecting her work so closely that she seemed to be in a different room.

"Mom?" I said, and she glanced up distractedly, biting off a length of thread with her teeth.

"I'm bored. I want to sew, too."

"Well then, sugar pie, why don't you rummage through here and find me some olive-green thread?"

I loved my mother's sewing kit. It seemed to me that the whole universe was contained there, that my mother's happy life was inside a black wicker basket lined with flowered fabric that she'd had ever since I could remember, and to be part of it, of her, you only had to lift the lid. Inside, hundreds of pins, some with bright red heads, dozens of needles of various sizes, tiny scissors, at least three rippers, a small metal ruler to make straight hems, a pair of shearing scissors with a heavy black handle and ferocious jagged teeth.

"I know you miss Daddy, Silvie," she said without looking up from her work. "But aren't you happy with just the two of us here?"

Something open, expectant in her face, and inside me a vague notion stirred—to make her happy, I would have to lie. But I hadn't learned how; not yet. "I like you both here," I said.

Her hands flashed; the needle sped over the fabric, darting and jumping like a fish. I looked from her small wrists to mine, liking how similar they were, the pale skin, the veins on the translucent underside milky blue as moonlight.

"But we have fun, just us two, don't we?"

Something in her tone made me angry, and I opened and closed the sewing box lid. It had a little hinge that looked like a strawberry. Didn't she miss him too? On the day he came home from a trip, she always wore a pretty dress and heels that weren't the blue suede, and she checked her lipstick in the mirror before lifting the curtain to peek out the window.

"Silvie, don't we have fun? Sewing together, listening to music . . ." She looked up, a hint of glitter there.

"Yes, Mommy." I watched her lips for a smile. But she could turn, she could. I didn't know when to trust her lately. Something in the way she looked at me—or didn't quite anymore.

That thread. I wanted to find it for her. Olive green.

My mother put her needle down. "Silvie, you're quite a big girl now, aren't you?"

I nodded, trying to guess the answer she wanted. In my stomach, a knot tied all by itself.

"If you help me with that thread, I'll show you a surprise."

My pulse quickened. I nodded, barely able to speak. My fingers scurried over spools and little silver bobbins of white, brown, yellow, blue—maybe we'd get a puppy, with a tail that wagged when I called his name—and I seized upon the perfect color. I lifted it triumphantly.

But she shook her head. "That's lime, sugar."

My mind filled with green, raced with green, until I wasn't sure I knew green at all. In the sewing box, so much thread, all the colors of the rainbow, and a ripe red sand-filled tomato pincushion with a green-felt stem and a leaf at its crown, every inch stuck with pins and a few needles, waiting patiently, small lengths of thread strung expectantly through their eyes. I loved that soggy, faded tomato, thinking for a long time that it was just hers alone. When I grew older, I found that a lot of mothers had the same little red tomato, and that made me like it even more. I always wanted us to be like everyone else.

"Olive green is more—you just need some reminding. Come with me." She held out her hand, and we tiptoed to my room and stood in front of my metal-framed dollhouse, open on one side to reveal several rooms, miniature beds, assorted tables and lamps, and a little doll family of four—a father, mother, little girl, and little boy, just like us. She'd decorated it for months, sometimes changing a room three times to get it exactly right, cutting colored squares of felt for carpeting, tiny swatches of brocade for tie-back drapes trimmed with a thumbnail strip of jingle-ball fringe. For the parents' room, she had stuffed cotton balls in leftover scraps of crimson velvet to make a puffy bedspread and matching bolster, mounting painted Q-Tips above the windows, from which she hung the diminutive drapes. From pipe cleaners, she made accessories—umbrellas, a birdcage. One day, when we had a big house, she said, she wanted it to look just like this one. Then it seemed as if the dollhouse were really more my mother's than mine.

"This is olive green!" She pointed to the carpet in the doll parents' bedroom. "Very chic, very fresh, deeper and darker than a true grass green. More sophisticated. On every page of *House Beautiful*. Do you like it?"

I nodded. "Yes."

"I thought you would. Now, your father, he likes plain old green. He doesn't go for anything too modern."

I blinked. "He doesn't?"

"He's a Republican!" She laughed, and the night seemed enormous and strangely beautiful. "I'm positive I bought olive thread. Let's check again." She took a last glance at the dollhouse, and we walked to the living room.

"Mommy, are we Republican too?"

"Oh, sugar, no. We're Democrats, like Jacqueline Kennedy."

"We're not the same as Daddy?"

"No, we're different. We have flair. We could go places."

Part of me wanted to be like Daddy, but I held on to her hand, an odd sound in her voice leading us back to our places by the sewing machine, where I reached into the sewing box and put my hand right away on the olive-green thread. I held it out to her proudly, shyness giving way to breathless joy.

She smiled, taking it from me and planting a kiss on my hand. "Remember, Silvie, when I told you that you were named after Elvis?"

Then she led me into her bedroom, where she slowly opened the lid of her jewelry box and, like a magician, reached in and, out of thin air, conjured up a silver charm on a long chain. "This was his good-luck charm. Saint somebody or other engraved right here." She held it high, and I watched it sway back and forth between us. "See, it's really a locket." She opened it and held it out to me.

I peered closely at the silver piece, the size of a half dollar. In the tiny picture were two miniature people. My mother reached back into the jewelry box and pulled out a snapshot. "Here's the same picture but bigger."

In that one, I saw a chaise longue in front of a swimming pool. On the ground, a boy in a striped bathing suit, arms looped casu-

ally around his knees, dark hair swept back, maybe this same necklace around his bare chest, and a pretty girl beside him, sitting up
on her knees, her face eager, even surprised.

"That was the bluest water I ever saw," my mother said, gazing at
the snapshot. "You know who these people are, don't you?"

I peered closely. "Mommy, is that you?"

She nodded, running her thumbnail across the image. "That's
me with Elvis Presley. I like to think he came to me near water because water is what dreams are made of."

She touched the chain with her fingertip to stop its motion and
glanced down at me, lowering her voice. "Someday I'll tell you
even more about it. But for now, this can be our secret."

I wondered what my father thought about all this, or if he knew
at all, my father with his strong chin and even features, short curly
brown hair, handsome mouth, and a space above his eyes that
seemed to shine and go on shining all the way up to his hair. He
wasn't tall, but he seemed tall to me, and when he spoke, I felt he
pulled each word up from some deep, true place in the earth. I
began to twist my hair around my finger, then to suck it, a nervous
habit I would later find hard to break. I wondered where Daddy
was. He had told me what state. I wished I could remember.

Gently, my mother placed the locket back in the jewelry box. I
felt hot and dizzy. She looked at me. I looked at my shoes.

"Well." She snapped the box shut, and I followed her to the
kitchen, where she set out crackers and Brie, a cheese my father
said we could afford only on special occasions. Standing up, she ate
a few crackers, then moved to the freezer, took out the chocolate
ice cream, and filled two bowls. Something had changed; I felt it.
She was edgy now, bored in her skin.

We sat down. She beat her ice cream into a smooth mash with a
spoon and quietly we ate small bites. The room seemed too bright.

My mother leaned on her elbow, licked ice cream off her spoon.
"Silvie, passion is . . . feeling things very deeply. Having the capac-

ity for deep emotion. Don't just think with your head and hold things in. Think with your heart. You probably have the *potential* for deep feeling. You just have to learn to use it."

She carried our bowls to the sink and returned to the table with a sponge, wiping our place mats, scrubbing around a bowl of waxed fruit in the center of the wooden table. I sat very still as she cleaned my place, moving my hands to my lap, holding them quietly, thinking, But I *do* feel things very deeply. Just too many things. Or the wrong things. I felt confused.

My mother plucked up a glossy red apple from the fruit bowl, perfect as one in a magazine, held it by the stem, the way she had held the Elvis necklace. Suddenly, she brought the apple to her face, crunched her teeth into the shiny red fruit, and slumped over onto the linoleum until she lay with her arms and legs akimbo, her neck as loose as one of my floppy dolls.

I waited, expecting her to jump up, finish the story, take a bow—something—but she didn't budge. Trembling, I stood over her body.

"Mommy?" I peered down at her, said, "Mommy?" again, in a tentative voice that curled higher and higher, like smoke. Cold seeped all the way into my bones, a ridge of ice hardening underneath my skin. My breath came in sharp gasps that hurt like a stomachache.

Just when I felt my knees going soft as Jell-O, she sprang to her feet like a jack-in-the-box and pulled me into a rough hug. Her laugh sounded mean, with an air of victory about it.

"I'm not dead, silly! It was just a joke, a little trick. To make you feel something, to feel *passion*."

Iowa, I remember thinking. Iowa was where Daddy might be.

She brought the apple out from behind her back with a flourish and held it out for me to examine, revolving the perfect wax orb slowly, pointing to its dull shine, its faintly freckled skin, intact everywhere, no bite missing. "Sugar, this apple is fake. I couldn't take a bite out of a plastic apple if I wanted to." She hugged me, but I stood stiff and unyielding, my arms behind my back.

Her smile faded. "I can see we have to work on your sense of humor, too," she said. "You barely even cried, and you thought I could be sick, or dead."

"I knew you weren't!" I burst out. "I don't like this game!"

She was speaking softly now, pulling me to her, and I buried my face in her shoulder. I felt my head go soft, felt myself spin off into my own galaxy.

I felt frightened, and also embarrassed, humiliated. She had fooled me. This notion drifted over me, the light coming down from above the table not kitchen-bright or -cheerful, just a weary, sour blue, like spoiled milk. I wanted to bite her soft flesh and leave teeth marks. I wanted to hit her, to hurt her. I hated her.

I'd show her who had passion. Glancing up, I tried to meet her gaze, but my eyes flew right back down to my socks. My scratched Stride Rites looked odd and familiar at the same time on the scuffed kitchen floor. I felt dizzy. I wanted to get away. Indiana. It came to me. Indiana. That was it. I could see my father then, smiling, driving, calm, far away, the way I wanted to be, in a state where I had never been, folding his clothes in the hotel room, his mystery book on the nightstand. A king.

CHAPTER 2

It was at least twenty years since she had bitten into that apple and transferred to me my first taste of knowledge—knowledge of who she was, who she was capable of being, and, inevitably, who *I* was capable of becoming. The fantasy of leaving mesmerized me and I brought it out from time to time, just as my mother did the Elvis necklace, to gaze at, to reckon with.

I finally did get away, not counting the escapes into my art and the fits and starts that characterized my college career. Now, at twenty-four, I was moving to Manhattan, and my mother had given me three months' rent money to prove to her that I could do it alone. I had hundreds of dreams drifting around in my head like balloons. The problem was plucking one from all the others and holding on to the string.

New York City—elegant in old movies that flickered across our television screen, exotic in films, and, most important, hundreds of miles away. I'd dreamed of the New York City of artists like Andy Warhol, Jackson Pollock, Man Ray, Picasso, of eccentrics like Holden Caulfield, Dorothy Parker, Woody Allen, and, yes, Eloise. I'd dreamed of wandering the museums and the Soho galleries, sitting in Central Park on the weekends with my Black Warrior 372 pencil and drawing pad, sketching away. I'd come to lose my mother and find myself, to put some distance between her dreams and mine. I'd come, full of hope, buoyed up by the encouragement of my best friend, Martine. And I'd come, as so many dreamers do, full of the conviction that in the huge heart of the city I could vanish and reemerge, reach in and pluck out a life, a *self.*

I found a small studio apartment in the West Eighties that I could afford. I liked that there was no room for visitors, for my mother to stay. She'd offered to help me find an apartment and set it up, but I knew all too well how she took over, how I got confused and caved in, rather than find my own way. No, my space had to be *mine.* Now I was here, where the only sound of breathing was my own, a breath in, a breath out, *my* breath, filling the air with my own giddy hope.

"I'll pay three months' rent and moving costs," my mother, whom I'd taken to calling Mimi when I was young, had said before I left. We had more money since my parents' divorce—money from my grandparents, now dead, and money from Henry, my mother's second husband—and my mother used it like a lasso. "You'll need good skin care in a city," she said. "I'll throw in skin-care products."

I was dreaming of coffeehouses, crowded subways, *freedom,* and here was my mother, saying good-bye to me at the airport and presenting me with a complete set of Erno Laszlo face treatments, and a warning: "You have to walk around in that skin for a lifetime, you know."

And a lifetime was what it seemed to take to get away. I'd gone not to one but to two colleges, having quit once, filled with self-doubt, only to restart a few miles from home. With my parents newly divorced and my brother and mother so close by, I found myself spending all my free time at Mimi's kitchen table, hearing her talk about why she'd left my father and how she resented that I'd gone off and left her despite her suffering, so raw, so fresh. She hadn't wanted me to leave—either to go to college or to move to New York. Just because she'd up and left my father didn't mean she expected to be *alone*. Defying her took energy, but I knew if I didn't get away, I'd fold up inside myself, like a collapsible cup.

In college, I performed below my potential, especially in art, my major. Mimi drew, too, and we'd always navigated this terrain awkwardly. I recognized my ability as a gift she'd given me, and I felt traitorous taking my talents further than she had. The biggest event of my college career was the senior exhibition. People came from all over the state, and much of my final year was spent preparing. When the big night came, Mimi stepped out of a limo in one of her creations, a three-piece white pantsuit, with a vest, long jacket, and flowing pants. She wore huge sunglasses, a wide-brim hat, and dark lipstick. She looked like Sophia Loren at Cannes. No one could find me to talk about my work. I hid behind the wine-and-cheese table, watching Mimi gush and flirt as if it were her show and not mine.

Now, the night before I was to start my first day of work in New York—I'd signed on as a Kelly Services temp, setting aside four years of college education to bestow upon the world typing skills I'd learned at sixteen—I stood barefoot in cutoffs and a T-shirt, unpacking my books on the side of the room that I called the living room, an area two or three steps away from the foot of my bed. Bloomingdale's had delivered a queen-size mattress that swallowed up the whole room and a flowery Laura Ashley comforter in shades of pink and red. From Mimi.

I'd set up my stereo and easel first, saving the books for last so that I could savor each one. I might not have much time to read now that I would be working, and I wanted any extra time to go to drawing and painting. I didn't know exactly how to become an artist, but Professor Bouchard at college had said, "You do it by doing it." The idea of all that discipline made my knees weak. Maybe I could be an artist partly by osmosis, by being in New York, the way you could learn French by living in Paris.

A breeze lifted the white curtains at my window; the selling point of my tiny apartment had been its slice of a view of Riverside Park. I sat in the old rocking chair that I'd found on the curb of Ninety-first Street and lugged home, and watched the joggers, dog walkers, and people sitting on a bench, who fanned out their newspapers and waited for the bus. Then I slit open a carton of books with a knife and began placing them on the shelf in alphabetical order.

Bonnard, Raoul Dufy, a poster book of the wonderfully elongated Gustav Klimt women, my beloved Matisse and Picasso, Georgia O'Keeffe, Helen Frankenthaler, a few photography books —I was especially fond of the weird, startling work of Diane Arbus—and my textbooks from college—*Figure Drawing, Landscapes and Still Lifes, Watercolor, Working in Oil, Illustrating Children's Books.* Kindred spirits, my books, lending me strength.

That I'd gotten from Michigan to New York, entirely on my own, stunned me. I guess I'd been propelled by a desire so powerful that, like a strong gust of wind, it picked me up and set me down in an entirely different world. It helped that Martine LaRue, my best friend, had left Michigan, too, moved to Chicago with her Yorkshire terrier, Twyla Tharp. Now we tracked each other's progress in our separate cities on the phone every night, like an airplane's flight pattern in an old movie, the red line moving up and down as our small triumphs and despairs waxed and waned.

That night, as I unpacked box after box, the phone rang. I hoped it was Martine, but it was Mimi's code—two rings, a hang-up, two more rings. It was our college calling system, and it meant I should answer even if I was running out the door.

"Good luck tomorrow, sugar," she said. She could be so *jaunty*. "Wear the red suit, red's a power color. Your first day, you want people to notice you."

Actually, I didn't, but saying so would just create another discussion. "Okay," I said.

"And, honey, your hair. Are you sure you have the face for a bob? Blow it dry or something. Otherwise it *hangs*. You're splashing, aren't you? You have to splash twenty times after the sea-mud soap . . ."

"You told me."

"This will be a big day for you. I'm so proud. I would have loved Manhattan. I didn't have that opportunity, you know. I had responsibilities. I was going to be . . ."—she hesitated—". . . a teacher."

"I never knew that."

"Absolutely. I was ambitious. I had plans. I was going to go back to school after I married your father, get my degree."

"So what happened?"

"I got pregnant with you."

"Ouch."

"Did I tell you about my new art class? My teacher, Dominick, is fabulous. You could really learn something. If you'd stayed here, we could have taken the class together."

"I don't think so."

"I hope red's not too strong a color for you. Oh, Silvie, your first night in New York. I should be there. I remember your first day of kindergarten, how you cried. You've always had a hard time with change. You've never had my strength. Well, you can always come home."

"I'm not coming home."

"I'm just saying you could if . . ."

"I'm not coming home."

"If I was there, we could have a little slumber party . . ."

"Mimi, I'm fine." My apartment felt hot. And small. The bed

seemed to be growing, taking over the room, pushing against all four walls until it broke clean through the plaster, and I imagined my mother and me, heads sharing one pillow, feet tangling, hurled into the sky, floating above the twinkling lights of Manhattan at midnight, clutching our Erno Laszlo tubes and bottles. We said good-bye, hung up. The phone rang again.

"Hi," Martine said.

"Thank God it's you," I said, exhaling deeply.

"So who else would it be?"

"Mimi. Morning, noon, and night."

"Ah, yes. What are you doing?" she asked.

"Unpacking boxes, my books. Wishing I'd moved to Chicago with you."

"Silvie, New York is the greatest city in the world. Especially for an artist. Maybe next year I'll come there." But I knew she wouldn't. Martine's mother had died when Martine was in second grade. Vivian had been an actress and dancer in Chicago, and Martine planned to follow in her footsteps. Now Martine's voice was stern. "You have to embrace your new life. *I* am."

Martine had landed an internship at the Body Politic Theatre in Lincoln Park and, her first week at work, had flipped for a director named Brent. Next week, she had an audition for the part of Amy in the Full Moon Theatre's revival of *Company*.

"Marty, I'm embracing my new life. Come on, I'm a Kelly Girl, right? Well, they don't call us that anymore, but, God, a Kelly Girl. I should have a uniform."

"Green with kneesocks?"

"And a beanie."

"A beret. And a sash with badges."

We both laughed. "Maybe I should have let Mr. Bouchard help me get an internship on an art magazine."

Martine laughed. "Hot Lips Bouchard would have had his

tongue halfway down your throat if you'd have said yes. Anyway, that was college. Another lifetime ago. How's your father?"

"He thinks moving to New York is—how did he put it?—'a little half-baked.' He said I needed a plan."

"Like a 401(k) or something?"

"Yeah. Right now, he's on Theo about dropping out of college to start a band."

"Look, temping can lead to something permanent. Go for it."

"How's Brent?"

"He's just the perfect man, is all. Handsome, a director—Silvie, he's *thirty-eight*. Isn't that just so . . ."

"Old?"

"No! *Alluring*. He thinks I'm gifted and beautiful, and he laughs at my jokes."

I answered with glum silence.

"Any guys in your building?" Martine asked.

"There's a drummer above me who wears a diamond-stud earring and has a ponytail. Does that count?"

"Ponytails are good. We like ponytails. Introduce yourself."

"Yeah, right."

"Silvie, you can't just sit around with your sketch pad and wait for life to knock on your door. You have to chase after it. What are you going to do without me? You're as insecure as a, a Volkswagen at a Rolls-Royce convention."

When we had stopped laughing and said good-bye, I pried open one last carton, the skin-care box from Mimi, and spent the next fifteen minutes lining my sink with bottles identical to the ones I'd seen in Mimi's bathroom for years, small bottles with pink labels: OIL, TONER, MOISTURIZER DAY, MOISTURIZER NIGHT. The very bottles I'd been scheming to escape now stood between us in this new world where I lived, where I prayed that something—anything— would happen to me, while Mimi, I knew, prayed it wouldn't.

◆ ◆ ◆

The next morning, my first day of work, I found myself riding the subway. I made my way onto the number 1 train, comparing every stop with the map for fear I'd end up in a deserted section of Brooklyn. When I finally relaxed, I noted people's shoes as they boarded the train—heavy white sneakers with a maze of laces; black, thick-soled East Village shoes; three-inch stilettos—everyone moving from one point to another en masse, like one enormous well-heeled body, looking for work, fun, love, a man, a woman, a home. I wanted to paint those shoes and all they stood for.

I possessed a bizarre typing gift, averaging over ninety words a minute, so Rhoda Ricklin, my "career" counselor at the temp agency, was able to land me a plum assignment—typing letters all day for three literary agents at International Creative Management. Typing was just the kind of thing Mimi liked me to be good at—girlish, not threatening, miles away from my aspiration to be an artist. ICM was one of the biggest talent agencies in the country and the place was constantly abuzz with deals being struck, competitors being screwed. In the morning the whir was exciting, but by afternoon I grew tired of smiling and my shoulders ached with fatigue. I felt anonymous. During my lunch hour—which I took late, because that made the afternoon go faster—I ate a yogurt and a bag of peanut M&M's at my desk and called my mother long-distance for free, feeling a strange, anxious thumping in my chest, as if I'd dived into deep water but couldn't swim. One lazy afternoon, I made a trip to the storeroom and stole a small notepad with the ICM logo.

On the subway home, as the mosaic tiles at the Fifty-ninth Street station rushed by, I basked in the glow of my first day of work in New York City. I loved the democracy of the subway: the woman in a fur coat sitting next to the man with tattered sneakers and no coat. I pulled out the notepad, feeling silly for wanting to draw

shoes. But the long row of feet mesmerized me, tugged my eyes
downward, and I stared, remembering Mimi's tale about being
pregnant with me and sitting in a department store watching the
feet on the escalator going up, up, up, thinking about Granny and
Paw Paw naming her for shoes. Soon, my sketch pad was filled with
drawings of shoes—a huge pair of shoes, inside of which stood a
tiny woman. Then one of a woman with shoes coming out of her
head and another, of a woman holding an enormous bouquet of
shoes that covered her face, titled *How She Sees the World*. I was obsessed. This hunger would never leave me. Like an addict, I would
dig and dig for twigs and branches, dirt and berries, even poison, to
fill the hole.

Climbing out of the subway, I got a jolt. There, in the middle of
Eighty-sixth Street, was a pair of ladies' shoes, worn black pumps, a
million stories stuck to their soles. My fingers itched to draw that
scene, the pedestrians' faces barely registering the odd sight, a few
cars trying in vain to avoid the shoes, then a taxicab barreling right
over them, sending one shoe flying onto the sidewalk. I pulled the
sketch pad out right there on the street and began to draw.

◆ ◆ ◆

On Friday, I left work congratulating myself. I'd made it through a
week. One whole week. Monday, I'd have a new assignment. The
next week, the agency placed me at a perfume company called International Flavors and Fragrances. The halls smelled wonderful,
each floor with a distinct scent: hyacinth, musk, sweet tea-rose. In
the ladies' room, sandalwood soap squirted out of a shell-shaped
dispenser, all gold-colored and creamy. When I rattled the metal
paper-towel container, a scent like vanilla, but spicier, wafted up.
Still, it was getting to me, eight hours alone at another person's
desk, sipping cups of coffee, ripping open envelopes not addressed
to me, staring at framed pictures of strangers.

A week there, and then on to Monahan Music Management

and the Benson and Levin Advertising Agency. I usually answered
phones and typed, chin pinned to my chest. At lunchtime, I called
Martine. Then, my afternoon sojourn to the storeroom, where I
stole more notepads. The jobs were hard to remember otherwise:
always a desk, a phone, harsh fluorescent lights, a receptionist with
blue eye shadow who filed her nails and read *Cosmopolitan* during
long lunch hours and offered to French-braid my hair in the slow
afternoon time.

I'd asked Rhoda Ricklin to try to get me work in an art gallery,
and after two weeks, she did, at the Jessica Wells Gallery in Soho: a
three-day assignment. I'd heard of Jessica, a pioneer of the Soho
gallery movement, and I was excited to meet her. I promised myself I'd be the best temp they ever had, and at night I fantasized
about the artists I'd meet, the technique I'd absorb. But when I arrived on my first day, the walls of the gallery were bare; they were
having a *situation* with an artist who wouldn't let go of his work.
A week before the scheduled opening, not one painting was hung.

Instead of typing, I was a glorified delivery girl, forced to work
with a guy named Bram, who dressed in all black and called me
Dorothy, as if Michigan and Kansas were the same state. As for Jessica Wells, she never came out of her office. Never did I see the
whole woman; I only caught glimpses of an armful of bracelets,
long red nails on tapered fingers clutching a phone. Once, I made
out a blunt line of dark, chin-length hair, a curve of cat's-eye
glasses, and lips pressed against the phone. She remained, the few
days I was under her employ, a disembodied voice, pleading with
Johann, the troubled artist, to share his brilliance with the world.

When they finally got him to sign, I was given the distasteful assignment of picking up the contract from the artist himself. I rode
the subway uptown to his building. My timid knock on his door
was answered with heavy breathing and the sound of many locks
and bolts clicking, chains sliding. The door opened an inch. In the
crack appeared an unshaven face and a set of very crooked, yellow

teeth. A curl of cigarette smoke escaped through the small opening.
A gravelly voice: "Here it is. Signed. Fucking *shit*." But he didn't
hand me the contract; he slammed the door and burst into tears.
Then a lot of ranting and raving, the sound of breaking glass, the
thud of a heavy object overturning, all above Johann Schneider's
low, keening wail. If I had been walking down the hall, I might
have thought it was a woman in labor. So this is what it is to be a
New York artist, I thought.

I stood by the door, not knowing what to do, barely breathing. I
looked at my watch. Bram had said to get that piece of paper back
"tout de suite." Finally, I knocked again. "Mr. Schneider, Jessica is
waiting. Please. Can I take the contract?"

"I don't *care* about Jessica Wells. It is *my work*." I heard a thumping sound that must have been his fist beating against the door.
"Oh, just take it," he screamed suddenly. "Now, go." He shoved a
sheaf of papers through the crack in the door, and I bolted, clutching them for dear life.

Back at the gallery, Bram met me at the door. "Hey, Dorothy,
didn't I tell you to follow the yellow brick road?"

"I'm sorry. It took a while. He . . ."

"I trust you got it?"

I handed it to him, triumphant, certain they'd ask me to stay on
permanently.

"Good work, Dorothy." He gave me a tight-lipped smile.
"Didn't even stop at Bloomingdale's, did you?"

I lifted my chin. I wasn't about to let these black-clad New York-
ers intimidate me. "Resisted the temptation."

I was rewarded for my successful mission not with a job offer but
with an invitation to the gala opening, whenever that would be.
After three days, the job was over and I was back on the streets. I
swallowed my disappointment, reminding myself that New York
wasn't supposed to be easy right away.

◆ ◆ ◆

Monday morning, I sat across from Rhoda Ricklin, who said, "I have an amazing assignment for you." A bulky woman with a sloping chest and bold eyeliner, she tugged on her short skirt, her long fingernails snagging on her nylons. She riffled through a file box and pulled out an index card. "*Country House* magazine. Editorial assistant is pregnant and on bed rest. Art background preferred. Could turn permanent. Editor is desperate." She lowered the card and looked at me, her long earrings swinging. "If she likes you, she just might hire you on the spot. Hurry, you can get there by ten-thirty. I'll call her and tell her you're coming."

To my astonishment, Florence Harper liked me, on the spot. At *Country House* magazine, where I was given a permanent position, I was saddled with my first official title, editorial assistant, which a thrilled Mimi quickly recast as assistant to the editor. Those two little words puffed it up a little, allowing her to brag to friends. Someday my name might be on the masthead—just think. I had hoped to start in the art department, but this was all that was available and Florence had guaranteed me mobility.

Florence Harper was a tall, thin, fiftyish woman with a blunt New York accent whose sharp brown eyes, beaky nose, and firm mouth suggested a steely resolve. Her gray hair stuck out in a triangle around her face, just like Ramona's in the *Ramona* books I'd read as a child. She wore expensive suits, and, on Fridays, long skirts with sweaters and boots. This pattern never varied. Her outfits were always monochromatic—black, navy, rust, charcoal gray, or plum. She was beautiful and ugly and imposing all at once. She intimidated me—not because she alone had created the magazine, but because she seemed to be in full possession of the best parts of herself, as if she'd walked around a long time in her skin and was comfortable there.

My first day, Florence called me into her office and handed me a

folder overflowing with letters written in her tiny, precise scrawl.
"Type these," she said curtly. "Please." I already appreciated the
magazine's calm compared to the chaos of the Jessica Wells Gallery.
A magazine might be a good place for me. I'd taken several
graphic-arts classes at college and was good at layout, stuff like that.
Longingly, I stole a glance at the slides of all the beautiful homes
and gardens spread over her desk. She caught my eye and said in her
clipped tone, "Possible covers for the January issue."

"January?"

"We work months in advance around here. It's like being in a
time warp." She lifted the magnifying loupe and studied the slides.

I stood frozen, fingering the too-long sleeve of my dress, which
Mimi had sent to "fortify" my wardrobe, and tried to think of
something brilliant to say.

"Let's get those letters started," Florence said brusquely.

I blinked. "Yes," I said, and beat a hasty retreat.

◆ ◆ ◆

During my lunch hour, I found the storeroom and took some small
notepads that said COUNTRY HOUSE and a few pencils decorated
with a row of tiny houses that reminded me of my old dollhouse. I
thought of the energy my mother had put into each room. How
ironic that I'd find myself working at a home-design magazine. At
the end of the day, I sat with my stash safe in my purse and waited
for Florence to tell me I could go.

For a week, I typed Florence's backlog of letters and filed a
mountain of paper. She thanked me curtly and shut her door.

One afternoon I took out my sketch pad and quickly, lightly,
began to work on the sketch I'd started of the disembodied shoes in
the street. Just an easy sketch, really, light strokes, but with depth;
perspective mattered—the huge, hulking cars, the tiny pair of
shoes. I sat in my cubicle at my wooden desk, the tall wooden file
cabinet with the overgrown ivy plant sitting on top, but I might

have been anywhere. Vaguely, I noticed Florence walking around the corner, a stack of papers in her hand. I was lost in the work, lost in my head, in that wonderful place behind the eyes that I wondered whether other people had access to. While I drew, I listened to the quiet. It always struck me at the end of the day, after everyone had gone home except Florence and me—the silence, the massive silence, the whole guts of the office spilled out into the city and just the bare ribs of machines left behind, machines that by day made the whole place hum and were now quiet.

I hadn't meant to draw my boss, but there she was, appearing in front of my eyes like magic, the only pedestrian in my drawing who had stopped to look at the shoes, as if she alone understood their wanton flight.

Suddenly, I felt someone behind me. I whirled around and there stood Florence.

"Ahem. Sorry to interrupt," she said dryly. "Stick these in the mailbox on your way out, please." She handed me a stack of envelopes.

"Sure." I took them.

She glanced down at my paper. "Nice work. But my face is longer than that; my eyes are closer together. The secret is in the eyes. And let's be honest about the nose. Proportion is everything."

I felt myself blush, but before I could speak, she was standing over me, picking up my pencil, adding a line here and there, lightly correcting my work. "There," she said. And with a flounce of her skirt, she was gone.

◆ ◆ ◆

One day, after she had caught me drawing several times, Florence called me into her office. I knew it was coming. The job was good, but I had trouble concentrating. Always, I held something back, while the leaves rustled outside the window, while, underneath the fluorescent light, I typed and filed and watched the hours fall away.

"I sense you're not completely happy here." Florence was wearing a forest-green suit, green stockings, and brown shoes. She looked beautiful.

"No, I, I just . . ." I stared down at the carpet.

"We had an agreement, did we not, when I hired you? I was under the impression that you wanted to work for me."

"I did. I mean, I do . . ."

"We're getting nowhere fast. Silvie," she said, her mouth firm. "May I ask you a question?"

I nodded.

"What brings you here?"

"To the magazine? Or to New York?"

"Both." She wasn't smiling, but her eyes were soft and I felt rather than saw a flicker of compassion.

Caught offguard, I froze, unable to think of a thing to say. Several seconds ticked by.

Finally, she laced her fingers together and leaned back in her chair. "Okay, let me ask it this way: What do you want? Let's talk about something you want in your life."

I blinked. How often my mother had steered me along, her finger against my spine, telling me how to feel. Nobody had ever taught me that I could ask for what I wanted, which might have something to do with why I had so little ability to know what I wanted, much less stick to it.

Tears welled up in my eyes. Florence handed me a tissue and I noticed for the first time that her well-manicured hands were flecked with what looked like blue paint. I stared at them a second, trying to figure out whose hands they reminded me of. Mine.

"That's the problem. I don't know." I was looking down at my lap.

"I've never understood this world," my boss said in a brisk voice. "It's no place for artists, who bend and mold but never fit. Of course, if they fit, there would be no art. Artists see stars when the rest of us see a dark sky. A delicate enterprise, not always compatible with reality."

I raised my head. Florence was staring into the distance.

"Well," she said. "That's my speech for today." Now she was smiling—a gentle, rueful smile that I hadn't seen before.

I realized she was a kind woman. Underneath her crusty shell was a kind of bruised tenderness, as if she'd been wounded in some profound way. For a second she seemed like Mimi, or what Mimi might have been.

"Well, Silvie Page, I was young once too. I had dreams. In fact, I still have dreams—this is just my day job."

"It is?" I was surprised, eager to hear more.

"Yes. I was—I *am*—an artist. But when my husband walked out on me and our children, I went full tilt into a career. That's a long story, for another day." A musical laugh rippled out. "I saw your drawing. You're good. You've got talent. You have to develop it. Yet here you are typing letters. You're bored, for one thing. That's not the only problem in your life, but it's one we can address. Maybe I can ease you into the art department. Mindy Carson lays out the booklet section, but she's always swamped. You could look over her shoulder a bit this month, help her out. If you do a good job, you can help with the spring layout." She put her hand up. "This is not to say you won't have to keep up with the typing and filing."

"Oh yes," I said, jittery with excitement. "Thank you. I don't mind the typing. And I can bring you coffee in the morning."

She smiled serenely. "That's not in the job description, Silvie. I can handle that myself."

◆ ◆ ◆

I liked Florence Harper and I vowed to make her proud of me. With gritty resolve, I focused on my work. At night I lay awake, listening to the city's strange symphony of horns, sirens, and car alarms, and stared at the ceiling, turning the cracks into shapes, clouds, animals; but by day, I smiled, acted successful, if weary, with pale blue moons under my eyes. I grew to like typing until my hands cramped, filing until my heels ached, grew to value the rhythm of everyday life. I especially liked helping Mindy with layout. Soon, I felt I was getting somewhere.

I was not so proud of my personal life. I had few friends, except for Martine, whom I talked to endlessly. But while Martine and Brent were pirouetting across the stage holding hands, I, so far, stood outside the door of love.

Vanessa, a girl Martine and I had known in college, invited me to a party in her Tribeca apartment, with lots of wine and cheese and marijuana. A photographer, she framed her black-and-whites in huge Lucite box frames and hung them floor-to-ceiling behind her sofa. Vanessa herself was tiny, with short, spiky black hair and huge brown eyes that ate up her whole face. She introduced me to a guy named Evan, cute, a writer, but I broke out in a sweat and croaked out a "Hello" and he drifted off to talk to someone else.

That same night I met Jeffrey, a quiet, nasal pessimist who worked in insurance and sent me daisies that wouldn't die. Every day, the daisies lost a petal or two and grew browner around the edges, but they refused to die. They just sat on the table, their dry heads slumped so far over that they brushed the tabletop, making my heart grow a little harder by the hour. With certain men, my shyness made me act haughty, superior.

After Jeffrey, I met Paul, a student at Columbia Business School, who had gelled hair, ate his steak bloody, and did not believe in the minimum wage. And Hilton, the musician with the ponytail, who, at Martine's urging, I had finally approached in the laundry room and who, to my dismay, had turned down my shy invitation to go for coffee.

At parties, I tried to be light, frivolous, to flirt, but I felt weighed down with darkness. Here were my mother's sorrow-edged prayers, made up of emptiness and longing, etched upon my skin like a curse.

She sent me a white-noise machine, a basket of Sleepy Nights herbal tea, a book called *How to Get the One You Love to Love You Back,* and a manila envelope full of perfume samples she'd torn from magazines. I shoved the gifts under my bed. She knew I hated perfume.

CHAPTER 3

*I*n our kitchen in Michigan, that day when I was five and my mother had pretended to eat an apple and die, I stopped calling her Mom. I didn't call her Mommy or Mama or Mother, either. Most of the time, I called my mother nothing, by no name at all. This was my declaration of something—not of independence, not yet, but of a flicker of awareness that our relationship had shifted, the way the deep earth settles after a quake. I was changed. I'd never trust her in the same way again. Now my love was tinged with fear.

◆ ◆ ◆

Theo came home from the hospital in a blue blanket. I pinched his skin, disappointed because he wasn't a sister.

"Lift him slowly," my mother admonished, putting his soft new bones in my hands. "Now you can be Mommy's good helper!" I grabbed hold of her hospital voice, so soft and sweet, thinking that she must have gone there and fetched not just the new baby but the nice mother, the mother who didn't dream about Elvis.

She showed me how to hold the bottle and draped a folded diaper over my shoulder so I could burp him. I liked helping, because it pleased her to have me doing what she was doing. But I worried that she loved him more, the way she was gentle and soft with him, singing in his ear, whispering in his belly button small bubbles of sound when she changed his diaper. And he wasn't named after a rock-and-roll star but after her father, Leon Theodore.

One day, when Theo was very small, close to one but not yet one, I tickled him, and he began to gasp and struggle but my fingers wouldn't stop, not even when a faint blue appeared under his eyes and around his mouth and he stopped gasping. Alarmed, I pulled my hand back, thinking for a second that I'd killed him. Then he laughed his baby gurgle and everything was all right—but not the same, because then I knew that the meanness inside my mother lived inside me too.

Besides a real brother, I got from my mother a brother doll for my dollhouse. I also got a baby doll, a girl baby, so I could take care of my baby while my mother took care of hers. My doll had a soft body and fabric arms, a rubber face and neck, and short brown hair, flat against her head like a real baby's. Her eyelids opened and closed, and if you fed her water from her tiny plastic bottle, you had to put a diaper on her quick, because she would tinkle it out. Drink and Wet Bess, she was called, my mother said. She let out a little cry when you tipped her, but later I wonder if I only imagined that part, that sob, sudden and high, more like a yelp than a cry, a startled whimper. I liked the name Bess, but my mother, who loved big names and had named our tiny black poodle Wolfie, called her Lady Jane Grey. She sewed Lady Jane an entire wardrobe, little dresses edged in lace and rickrack, summer playsuits with tiny matching sun hats, a terry-cloth bathrobe with a hood. Even a stretchy swimsuit.

My brother was an affectionate child and beautiful, with brown hair the color of a caramel apple and round blue eyes—and, my mother said, Paw Paw's delicately humped nose, to a T. He was all Reisman, she said. One day she could look at him and see her father; the next, her brother, Shelby; the next, Sweet Nina Baby; another time, her own oval face. I looked like my father, she said.

I thought my mother smiled more with Theo than she did with me, and I understood that it had something to do with the fact that he was a boy. He was born easy, free of competition, not having to apologize for being female.

◆ ◆ ◆

That summer, on our annual visit to Biloxi, I found and promptly stole a picture of my mother and me from Granny's old shoe box of photographs. I was small, red-faced, two weeks old but as wrinkled as an old man—no hair, no teeth, no defenses against her arms, thin with me in them. She was kneeling on the lawn outside the brick apartment building where we lived, holding out a blanket-wrapped bundle, me, not humbly but with triumph's high, shimmering heat, her waist thin, her stomach flat, her body miraculously freed of any hint of pregnancy. She would turn twenty-one in three months.

At night, in bed, I studied the picture until I heard my mother coming in to give me a kiss, then I slipped it under my pillow, remembering how she had stolen Granny's lipstick and kept it under *her* pillow when she was young. Now I wonder if all daughters hide something from their mothers under their pillows to help them grow up.

After she left, I examined my mother's face in the picture again until a delicious, sleepy warmth spread over me and I was happy, admiring the smile the camera had caught, the lipstick a strong red, a little crooked, sure she had loved me. How she clung to me, protecting me from the other side of her, every feature on my small baby face scrunched, my pink lips gathered like a flower, my nose and eyelids squinted shut against the bright sunlight.

I carried the picture around in the pocket of my jumper, even to school. First grade was a haven: a whole day where I could read and draw. I loved forming the letters of the alphabet, such calm and pretty shapes, and then making them into words, sounding out the letters. Now that pencils were officially for something more than drawing, I devoured the woodsy smell, the sharp tang from touching the tip of the lead to my tongue, the pink rubber eraser ash I brushed gently off my paper. And I fell in love with the whiteness of blank paper, ready for pictures or letters or numbers. Oh, and numbers, what a perfect kind of sense they made, one following another, in order, growing into something bigger or smaller, adding up to a meaning I hoped I'd someday find in the world.

A calm settled over me when Miss Shane handed out the writing paper with the blue lines where we had to print our capitals and smalls and our numbers, one to ten. It was like drawing, only easier, because there were Miss Shane's letters and numbers right up on the board, and ours were supposed to match. I liked that every time I wrote an *a* or an *s* or a *z,* it always turned out pretty much the same. The world as it should be, predictable and fat and happy, a clock's tick.

C-A-T spells *cat.* D-O-G spells *dog. Hello,* said Dick. *Come play with me, Jane. See Spot run.* And in second grade, the story problems, the picture of the plate with six cupcakes.

How many?
6.
Take away 1.
How many left?
5.

I chewed on my pencil, content. I could do this. This, I could do.

◆ ◆ ◆

By the time I was seven or eight, I understood that my mother was too changeable to be trusted, more driven, more complicated than other mothers. My relationship with her felt heavy, confusing, like some of her fabrics—what looked like tiny flowers from a distance were just squiggly lines up close. I grew quiet and keenly observant, and later I would wonder if this habit of scrutiny, especially of my mother, was the only talent I had or would ever have. She pulled me in and pushed me away, and to my chagrin, she used any excuse at all, any mood, any whim, to play those Elvis records and to tell me her story, over and over, until it became a legend, usually when my father was gone and Theo was asleep.

One night my mother, father, and I were watching the Jerry Lewis telethon when a boy came on, no older than ten, in bell-bottoms and a huge belt buckle, belting out "Hound Dog," gyrating his small hips.

"What a weak imitation," my mother sniffed, jumping off into the story of how she happened to be lying by the pool at the hotel Paw Paw owned, sunning herself, when Elvis sauntered over, opened those bee-stung lips, and talked. To her. She said she'd have fallen off her towel if she hadn't been lying flat on the hard cement. There she was in a sleek black tank suit, her face clean of makeup except for bright red lipstick, her hair slicked back, just like Elvis's, and there he was, standing over her, eclipsing the sun. He asked her to go out with him, and sure enough, they went out to eat and he drove her home and she stood with Elvis on her front porch and he had that jet-black hair falling over one eye and she looked down at her new red shoes, running a finger over her lips to keep them quiet, a funny tingling there because that's where people kissed.

As she talked, my father, who had looked young and carefree in his easy chair, legs stretched out and one knee up, grew tense, his jaw clenched as tightly as a kid's wind-up toy. "A load of horseshit, Simone," he said, rolling *Time* magazine into a cylinder and hitting it against his leg.

But she went on, about how Paw Paw was waiting for her on the porch when she got home, how he slung his arm over Elvis's shoulder and walked him in little circles on the porch, discussing his success and asking him if he had a backup plan. My mother would giggle then, showing her perfect white teeth. "I blushed a hundred colors. Can you imagine? Telling Elvis Presley that he needed a backup plan?"

I tried to focus on the TV, where an old man with a small dog on his head swung a Hula Hoop around his waist. Boy, I thought, she could pick you up like the wind picked up Dorothy's house in *The Wizard of Oz* and set you back down again in a different part of the night.

She continued in a gruff, grandfatherly voice. " 'Son, the dogs are eatin' it now, but they'll turn away and sniff at somethin' else. That's a fickle business you're in.' 'Oh, yessir,' Elvis said politely. He was always polite. Elvis wanted to kiss me good night, but Paw Paw said no and so he kissed my hand." She held up her left hand and wiggled her fingers. "I haven't washed this one itsy-bitsy spot. See, Silvie?"

"That's a mole," I said wisely.

My father leaned over and ruffled my hair.

Suddenly, I didn't want to be sensible. I wanted to be a teenager, to wear red lipstick, to drink milk with ice cubes with Elvis, my gut filled with my mother's wildness, not my father's deep calm.

"So what does all this prove, Simone?" my father asked.

"That I had options. You know what I mean." She squinted at something far off in the future or the past, and I could tell that the story was unraveling. Whether they ever kissed, really kissed, or even went out again would be shrouded in mystery.

"Options? Why don't you give Elvis a call? I'm sure he'd love to hear from you. You can rekindle old times, have a mint julep." My father folded his arms across his chest and burrowed deeper into his chair.

I looked from one scowling parent to the other, hardly breathing, a hard bead forming in my stomach, threatening to rise up and choke me.

My mother moved to the edge of the couch so that she was only inches away from my father, her face at once earnest and sarcastic. "I didn't marry Elvis, I married you. And as for Silvie and Theo, maybe I just want them to know that there's more to life than . . . than . . . *this.*" She waved her hand around our small family room, but I could see only the kitchen, with its brown appliances and floor, the aqua Formica partly visible through the doorway, the scratched kidney-shaped coffee table in front of us, the bunched rug under our feet, her sewing machine quiet on the desk in the dark corner.

My father regarded her mildly, but his eyes narrowed to slits that gave him away. "I was your ticket up and out of that mess of a family of yours." He ran a hand through his thick curly hair, his cheeks pink and healthy, young. "I'm the best goddamn thing that ever happened to you." I watched, incredulous, as my father stood, tucked his shirt into his chinos, gathered his magazines and newspapers, and headed toward the door.

"How *dare* you just walk away?" my mother sputtered, the blue in her eyes turning as gray and cold and sharp as the sky on all the winter days that would follow that autumn.

Grabbing a pillow from the couch, I held it against my chest, squeezing its soft middle, wishing I could disappear.

Suddenly, my mother swayed to her feet, lifted the nail-polish bottle off the table, and sent it flying across the room. It hit the fireplace hearth, where it shattered and oozed red along the brick. She regarded it coolly, gathered herself up, and stalked out of the room. Even furious, she had a regal grace.

My father stood with his head bowed, pressing two fingers against his forehead.

Stunned and shaking, I scooted away to my room, where I sat on the floor in front of my dollhouse, with its chic olive-green felt carpet, petting Wolfie's soft fur, her heart beating a hard *thump thump* against my hand. Something came clear to me: I liked plain green, too, like my father.

I heard her raging: "I have nothing up here. I'm a nobody." Her footsteps pounded past my room, and then the door to her bedroom slammed shut.

Slowly, I moved the father, mother, daughter, and son dolls to the couch in the miniature living room. A terrifying new feeling vaulted up from my heart: relief. She was gone; we were safe. I imagined my father folding himself back into his chair, staring glumly at the TV.

Maybe my parents would get divorced, like Stephanie Listfield's parents. Her father didn't live in their house anymore, but every Saturday he took her to IHOP for pancakes, just the two of them. That one part sounded okay.

But my mother loved my father, didn't she? Yes, she did, because when he returned from a trip, my parents would hug in the middle of the kitchen on the square rug smack underneath the light, a globe that gave the ceiling purpose, symmetry. Their bodies made a triangle, and they would ask, "Silvie, want to join in?" laughing together. And I would scamper between them, hugging their legs, looking up into the apex of their bodies, at their young, beautiful, trusting faces, foreheads pressed together, limbs mashed. As if in blessing, they would both place their hands on my head at the same time, and like that, in their tepee of faces, arms, and legs, I stood safe in the world.

The mother doll sprang up from the porch swing and threw herself on the father. They tussled a minute, then pressed together, lip to lip, in a long kiss. *Don't worry,* the mother doll said. *It's just a dumb story. I never kissed Elvis. Yours is the only kiss for me.*

Just look at this dollhouse she'd made—a porch swing, for goodness' sake, crafted out of toothpicks and hanging from paper clips. My mother could be very nice. She helped me pick out books at the bookmobile, made cupcakes with sprinkles. She filled a blue bowl with water and a sponge and let me paste the S&H Green Stamps into a book. Also, she was very clean, and so was I. I helped her vacuum and dust and scour the sinks with blue powder, but she said you didn't need to wash bath towels every week, because you used them after a shower and so they were clean. She was careful too: She flossed every night so her teeth wouldn't fall out, and she never went into the sun without a hat, because that made your lids freckle. And every few months she took us to Farrell's and we pretended it was her birthday and got a free sundae. There was a lot about my mother to love.

Sometimes she cried into my hair, whispering, "Poor Silvie. She has a young mother, all knotted up inside with her own needs." She called me Sugar Pie, or just Pie. "Pie, I'm so, so sorry. I was only twenty when I had you." Then she waved her hand vaguely to swat away her bad temper. I knew she was trying hard to love me and that I must be very hard to love. I must try very hard to love back.

After a minute or so, I let the dolls drop to my side. Suddenly, my dollhouse looked different, silly, just a metal box on a floor smelling of lemon wax, the sky above just the ordinary air of my bedroom. Inside were dolls, just dolls, with scrawny rubber faces, the mother with painted-on curls and a set of stupid painted pearls around her neck, as much a mystery to me as my own mother, whose stories and fierce longings lay jumbled in my head like an angry puzzle. At that moment, I came to the conclusion that my mother was lying, that she'd never even met Elvis. And I didn't care whether she ever had or not.

◆ ◆ ◆

The year I was in third grade, my mother sewed herself a red cape. She wore it to PTA meetings; she wore it to pick me up from school. Most mothers wore navy peacoats or car coats in harvest gold or olive green, colors you saw in their tidy kitchens on dishwashers, stoves, refrigerator doors. The cape buttoned in one dramatic brass button under her throat and billowed out and down, hovering somewhere around her ankles.

At night, my mother strutted back and forth in front of the mirror in her room while I sat on my parents' bed, memorizing the multiplication tables. "Silvie, know what? Jackie Kennedy wore a cape like this to hear Pablo Casals play cello at the White House."

"So?" I didn't hesitate to roll my eyes; I'd just hit the age of sass—eight, on the cusp of nine. *Three times three equals nine; three times four equals twelve.*

"This cape's gorgeous, miss. Pure alpaca wool. I worked hard on it. But only a strong woman can wear bright red."

"Uh-huh."

"You don't care now, but you'll want the really good things someday."

"Will not."

"Will."

Four times four equals sixteen; four times five equals twenty. The work was easy. It was the rest of the school day I had a problem with.

I was shy at school, always standing on the side, watching. I didn't have any real friends. My mother didn't like me to have friends besides her, and even if she had wanted me to, the girls intimidated me. The boys were loud, funny, obvious. You knew just what they'd do next—make goofy racing car noises or press their open mouths to their arms to make farting noises. They didn't scare me; they were harmless. Even when Jonathan Rose threw my Brownie cap in the boys' bathroom every day until he got bored, I just trudged in and retrieved it. But around the girls, I whispered and smiled nice, too nice. I was aware that I tried too hard, and that only made me more clumsy and awkward. The red cape wasn't helping matters.

Neither had it helped that on an otherwise ordinary day in second grade, I'd climbed into the wrong mother's car, and sat mute in the back, afraid to speak up, all the way to Beth Cady's house, where Mrs. Bird, thinking I was Beth, tried to deposit me. Since that day, my mother had insisted on picking me up from school. Whether my action had been deliberate or not, I wasn't sure, but I was aware that I'd been drawn to Mrs. Bird's dumpy figure, her stretch pants and ordinary saddle shoes, her beauty-shop hair, the curls bouncy and softer than my mother's latest style—gamine short spikes. How comforting, how ordinary, was Mrs. Bird's old peacoat, pilled, with a large pin of a magenta-and-lime-green bird on the collar. I didn't mind her soft, doughy hand landing on my shoulder, giving me a shove, herding me into her car.

Sitting in the backseat of Mrs. Bird's station wagon, I clutched my drawing of a two-story house with brown brick and lots of windows and a chimney billowing perfectly round coins of smoke, different from our own white ranch. I twisted my hands, huddled there in my coat, trying to gather my thoughts into a straight line. On a giant blackboard in my head, words wrote themselves, one letter at a time: SAY YOU'RE NOT BETH. SAY THIS IS THE WRONG CAR. SHE'S THE WRONG MOTHER. But I couldn't speak. I just looked out the window, panic sloshing inside me.

And when Mrs. Bird stopped in front of a brick house with white pillars and a large chimney, the trees on the lawn green and full, I wanted it to be my house. I wanted a woman wearing a soft skirt and an apron to open the door and be my mother, a normal mom, and I would run out of the car and into her arms and she would kiss me, just like other kids' mothers did. Mrs. Bird took a long look at me and, realizing I wasn't Beth, gunned the gas, spitting gravel, and sped back to school, where, in the parking lot, I saw my mother's car, the gold finish seeming to shimmer and shake with anger. Then I saw her dragging Theo up the concrete steps to the school, her cape billowing out behind her.

My mind soared and dipped and filled with terror. When I stumbled out of the car, my mother seized me by the shoulders and knelt, pulling my wrists toward her, holding them so tight that my fingers tingled. "I was so worried." But, more than worried, I knew she was furious.

Mrs. Bird emerged from the driver's seat, her lower lip trembling. She gestured toward the car as if it were the car's fault. "Well, gee, she climbed right in with the other kids. I thought she was Beth Cady . . . I didn't even look . . ."

"*Obviously*, you didn't look."

"That child didn't say a word," Mrs. Bird said shrilly. "She could have spoken up."

My mother straightened up and fixed her gaze on Mrs. Bird, eyes narrowing into slits at the sight of the pink-and-green-bird pin on the collar of her heavy, dull coat. "Is that a bird on your collar?"

Mrs. Bird's hand fluttered up to her pin. She gave a small tight-lipped nod.

My mother gave her a withering look. "Charming."

"Well, for Pete's sake . . ." Mrs. Bird clutched her throat with shaky fingers.

"Let's go home," my mother said, yanking me toward the car. She was silent until we hit a red light. Then, whipping around, she said, "Why didn't you say something? You knew you weren't Beth! I don't know what is wrong with you, letting that idiot of a woman drive you halfway to Kalamazoo."

Now, every day, my mother, afraid I'd run off again, appeared in front of the school early, in her "brand spanking new" gold Cutlass with its white vinyl top and white interior, in her cape, calling,

"Silvie, over here!" Theo, smiling at me from the backseat, called it the blond car, as if the car and my mother were the same.

Today, she seemed to levitate out of the driver's seat. She was wearing blue tights and tall black boots, and when she lifted her arms, the red wool cape, stiff and full, rose like bat wings.

I ran my tongue over my last loose tooth. My mother didn't know about it. I liked having a secret from her. A steady trickle of kids flowed out the school door and into cars, their mothers kneeling down to straighten the younger ones' collars and scoop them up into a hug. I always felt something else behind my mother's swoop down to gather me up, a flicker of insincerity, a moment of doubt before she crushed me into an embrace.

"Silvie, it's me, Mommy," she called, waving.

Mommy? I was in third grade; I wasn't a baby. I lowered my head and trudged on.

"Silvie, it's me, Mommy," Margo Meliani mimicked, charging past me, glancing in frank astonishment at the shiny car, the ridiculous cape. Margo was a hall monitor. I was afraid of her height, the fast balls she kicked in gym, how she climbed the rope faster than any of the boys, all the way to the top.

I plodded through the crunchy leaves, kicking at brown whirlybirds with the toes of my penny loafers. I loved the fact that loafers were more grown-up than Buster Browns, and I didn't mind a bit that the stiff leather bit into my heels.

"Is that your mom?" Libby Mandell sidled up to me, eyes wide and envious. I liked Libby, but I didn't feel like talking. "She looks like a movie star," she said.

"Uh-huh," I said, running the tip of my tongue over my chapped lips, shrinking further into my ordinary wool jacket, trudging on, the car glittering in the distance. Jeffrey Quackenbush's head popped up from a mound of leaves long enough for him to steal a quick peek in my mother's direction. He whistled, loud enough for the other, older boys to hear. "Hey, shrimp, your mom is a *fox*! What happened to you?" Then his head disappeared under the leaves, and the rest of them howled and made smacking noises with their lips.

I saw myself as they did, some dopey third-grader, making small, noisy craters through a high crust of mud, the ends of my limp brown hair sticking out of the scratchy over-the-head-and-ears hat I had to wear before winter even came, to prevent my frequent sore throats, the oversize hood on my jacket flopping on my back like a dead animal.

I glanced at my mother's car. Good. She had settled back inside, her shoulders curled tensely over the steering wheel. I could see Theo in the back, waving a small Tonka truck. Soon I would be inside the car and we would drive home to our curtained house, where no one would see us.

I ducked behind a tree and stood still as stone, basking in the warm sun left over from summer, admiring my new penny loafers, the red-brown leather so shiny that I could almost see my face reflected. I flexed my toes and the bright penny embedded in the slot, for good luck, seemed to jump up and twinkle.

"Silvie darlin', I'm here." I stole a backward glance. My feet wouldn't move. I stood there for what felt like a full minute, stealing furtive glances at the car.

There was my mother's wave, amplified and gigantic, nothing like Jacqueline Kennedy's delicate, ladylike wave, her other hand resting on the poor, fatherless shoulders of Caroline and John-John. When I thought of my mother, I thought of size. Immense space, volume, dimension. "Silvie, over here, sugar," she called.

Sighing, I made my feet move. I shuffled, slow and heavy, toward the car and got in. What else could I do? I belonged to her; she belonged to me.

In the car, we drove along for a few minutes in tense silence. Several times, my mother glanced over at me, brow furrowed. "You can forget going to the bookmobile today."

My window was half open and the air outside smelled like leaves, dry and smoky. Nervously, I poked at my wobbly tooth with my tongue.

"Open up," she demanded. With one hand, she turned my chin in her palm, right and left. "Is that ol' tooth still loose?"

I shrugged her off; her hands were always hovering—fastening a button, looping an itchy wool scarf, straightening the hem of my skirt. Sometimes she followed me with scissors to cut off a dangling thread I couldn't see. Now, she snapped my jaw closed. "Didn't you see me? Didn't you hear me calling you?"

"No." Outside my window, the road rushed by in a blur of subdivisions, strip malls, a gas station, a 7-Eleven. The sky was a harsh blue; the trees were losing leaves. It was too cold in Michigan, those afternoons. Those afternoons. My heart was a hard little seed.

I felt her soften, like icing on a picnic cake. "Well okay, honey. How was art?" she asked in a silky tone I didn't trust.

I didn't answer. She always asked about art, but something in her voice seemed to say, *I'm* the artist in the family.

"What did you make?"

"String art."

"String art?"

"It's just string that you dip in glue and twirl into circle designs." I was embarrassed by how much I liked winding string around an orange juice can and calling it a pencil holder.

"What's this?" My mother pulled a loose paper from my reading book, where I'd stuffed it out of sight.

"A contest," I said reluctantly. "At school."

At the light, she read out loud. " 'Boys and Girls—Help Hill Elementary Welcome in a New Decade! Create a Poster.' "

"I don't want to do it."

"You're a good drawer," Theo said from the back.

"Oh, Silvie! The theme is 'Our Country's Heroes.' I was just saying about the Kennedys and Martin Luther King . . ."

I folded my arms across my chest. In spite of myself, I felt a spark of something ignite inside me. She could energize me this way.

She looked at me. "It's a wonderful opportunity."

Some tiny voice in me shouted, "No."

We drove to the market in silence, and to the cleaners and the drugstore. A telephone wire stretched against the horizon, a long rope of black licorice, dozens of birds perched there like black question marks. Soon, we'd learned in science, they would fly south for the winter.

Finally, I spoke. "I'm sorry I . . ." What had I done, exactly? I wasn't sure, but I felt guilty, assuming that anything in her repertoire was also in mine, that on one ordinary fall day the tables would turn and one of her tricks would bloom inside me.

My mother looked over at me curiously, her brow knitted, her face softening, her mouth settling into a crooked line. "Maybe we can find the bookmobile after all. He's usually on Ironwood by now."

"Goody," Theo cried.

We zipped down a few streets, and soon we were parked across from the bookmobile. We got out of the car. "Silvie, shall we skip? Theo, let's all hold hands and skip."

We managed to skip all the way to the steps of the bookmobile. Theo wanted *Mike Mulligan and His Steam Shovel*. Again. I, having discovered biographies, wanted *Madame Curie* and *Susan B. Anthony: Suffragette*.

CHAPTER 4

The opening at the Jessica Wells Gallery, delayed for months, was a catered affair, with tiny rolls of sushi that I at first thought were pinwheel cookies. Men in black turtlenecks passed around silver trays holding little globs of what looked like green paste. Then more sushi, slabs of raw fish draped over a bed of rice, which everyone dipped into the green gook, looking pleased with themselves. Johann, the artiste, wore dark glasses and stood in the corner glaring at the floor. Jessica and Bram flitted about.

I'd barely made it to the opening, barely managed to pull on a short black skirt over black leggings, an olive-green sweater, and black boots. I walked from my apartment to the subway, huddled into my coat, wishing I'd stayed home and worked on my drawings. It was a raw March night, and the city seemed unbearably cold and damp, the streets cramped and more narrow, the frigid no-end-to-winter air rising from the concrete as resolutely as heat in summer.

As it turned out—and I found it hilarious—Johann's work was miniature: tiny paintings you had to stand right up close to see. No detail, just small splashes of color. The one called *Woman,* where Johann had apparently thrown an egg in the center, featured what looked like a tiny womb with a splash of yellow. A man was pressed up against it with a magnifying glass. I surveyed the crowd. Mostly, people wore black and cultivated a bored yet appreciative look while gobbling down raw fish. There were few men, at least few available-looking men.

Mimi had recently pointed out that I hadn't had a real boyfriend since high school. "Not since Eddie Cullum—and he was no prize. He used to follow my every move with that moony gaze. What was that all about?"

I had an idea what it was about, but I held my tongue.

"Anyway, you gained weight after the divorce, before college. You've had to work your way back. Thank God you got those contact lenses early."

When I was fourteen, Mimi had taken me to get contact lenses. Afterward, over tea at the Maple House, she'd said, "Now that you've got your period, sugar, *and* contact lenses, I feel so *close* to you. We can talk now, really talk, woman to woman."

The spunk and fizz in her voice made me nervous. "Eventually, you know, you'll have a boyfriend," she'd said, laughing. "You're young, you have energy, you have contact lenses."

I knuckled my burning, watery eyes with a clenched fist. Contact lenses: my only hope. She thought being pretty would solve everything.

"You do have beautiful eyes, even Dr. Baum said so, and think of how many eyes he sees *every day.* And with these new lenses, lots of boys will find you attractive."

"Yeah, right." The late-afternoon sun fell across our table, forming a large warm square. In a little game with myself, I thrust my hand into the sunlight, then snatched it back.

"Whenever, um, whoever, I hope it will be a good experience for you, sugar." She took a long swallow of tea, considered something, and cleared her throat. "When the time comes, several years from now, let's say, I'll take you to get reliable birth control. I'd rather have you come to me than keep it a secret because you feel you're doing something wrong. Yes." She nodded, pleased with her decision.

"Now, about dating," she continued. "It's important that you keep your options open, Silvie, meet all the nice boys, date *around*. Don't marry the first person whose blue eyes knock your socks off."

"Is that what happened with Dad?"

She nodded. "Not that your father isn't a wonderful man. But he hasn't turned out to be as ambitious as I'd hoped. Remember, Silvie, you don't have to settle. And you don't have to settle just to have sex."

My mind did gymnastics: me having sex; Mimi having sex.

Mimi lit a cigarette—she allowed herself one in the afternoon and one in the evening, her two "hungry" times—and her eyes seemed to ignite, too. "It's beautiful when you find the right man. I did. I found the right man."

I held a wet napkin to each eye, hoping she was talking about my father.

"Silvie, if I had played my cards right, who knows what might have happened? With Elvis, I mean. A woman knows these things. I just have a feeling . . ." Her voice trailed off, her eyes wandering to a spot on the wood-paneled walls of the Maple House. "If I had been born in the sixties, like you, I would have had more options. Elvis and I might have eloped. I could have been *someone*." She exhaled and clutched the mug, bringing it to her face, warming her cheeks, even though the tea must have been cold.

"It's funny," she said quietly after a minute. "What I remember most is his hands. He had the softest hands. And he cared, honey, he really cared. You can't underestimate that with a man. Some men in his situation wouldn't have, but he did. He wanted me to feel special." She blotted her lips with a napkin and went on. "That's a big thing in a woman's life. It is, sweetie. You'll see. When the time comes, you'll understand. I just hope you'll find the perfect recipe . . . sex, yes, but blended with *love.*"

A few years later, when I brought home my first boyfriend, Eddie Cullum, my mother sashayed out to the porch, holding out a cake on a foil-covered cookie sheet. Her black mules made her tall and a trifle unsteady on her feet. She wore her red wool beret, even though it was July, and she posed in her wobbly heels, a white apron tied over her black cigarette pants and red flowered blouse, a strange cross between Marilyn Monroe and Betty Crocker. After sizing up Eddie with a lengthy appraising stare, she situated herself between us on the back step and regaled us with one of her stories, until night gathered. Then, she leaned back against the step, her red beret a little crooked, her legs crossed, and dangled one mule off her bare foot. In her hand was a long cigarette holder. Every few seconds she tipped her head back, inhaled deeply, and exhaled upward. On Eddie's face was a strange mixture of lust and bewilderment, and before the moon was fully visible in the night sky, he bolted. He called again and our relationship gathered speed and Mimi lost interest in being our chaperon, but whenever I was with Eddie, I was plagued with the notion that he was looking over his shoulder, waiting for my mother to reappear.

◆ ◆ ◆

Since college, I'd felt I'd met them all—the thinking ones, the feeling ones, the sporty ones who threw the remote control across the room when someone didn't tackle someone else. I'd met the amateur comedians, who cracked jokes like eggs in a skillet, until my brain was the thing scrambled; the stockbrokers in rumpled shirts, who took me to dinner, loosened their ties, and gazed into my eyes as they rolled their gum out from behind their tongues and stuck it on the lip of the ashtray before digging into the pasta. I'd met the salesmen, who talked fast, with their mouths full, and the arty ones, who wore black baseball caps and used words like *gosh* and *swell* and said wholesome, cynical things like "Having lost interest in life and wanting to see if I could retrieve it, I called you tonight. Busy?"

I'd even met Tokey Lane, an amiable ex-pothead whose real name was Thomas, and Marshall Sloves, who, when he told me his last name, added, "That's *love* with an *s* on either end."

But now, at the Jessica Wells Gallery, after a stretch when my mother clipped and sent a forest's worth of articles about women who choose unavailable men, I was standing by one of Johann's paintings, chatting with Dr. Scottie Perlman, a tall, skinny guy dressed in a burgundy cotton shirt, who talked too loud and leaned in too close, whose long face and cap of dark, curly hair reminded me of an overgrown sunflower, its stem bent from the weight of its textured head. His bright smile invaded my space. I hadn't come to New York to meet a burgundy golf shirt. I had come for the slovenly intellectual, the unshaven poet in torn Levi's and fetid sweatshirt, ravenous not for food or for money but for metaphors, the kind of guy you'd meet at a gallery opening.

I asked Scottie what he thought of Johann's work, and he said he thought "little" of it, and we both laughed, and then he was asking me about my job and telling me about his residency in the ER and wait, what was this? He was reaching into the pocket of his jeans and pulling out a . . . *coin.* This guy with a lopsided smile the size of a circus now held out *money*—a quarter. Then, as if reading my thoughts, he flipped it. It spiraled high in the air, landing expertly in the flat of his palm, where, like a good conjurer, he made it disappear.

"Heads or tails?"

I eyed him suspiciously, folding my arms. "Um, tails."

He shook his head and, without saying a word, flipped another one, easy as a pancake. He turned on me a level gaze, his brown eyes so dark they looked black. He curled the coin into his fist and held it there a dramatic second.

I jumped in, "Heads!"

"Sure you wanna do that?" Nice teeth, damnit. White as the bones he was born with.

"Heads," I repeated. "I've got a feeling."

"Ah, *gut instinct*. Everything depends on it." He tossed the coin high in the air. "Tails. But they're yours anyway." He plunked the two coins into my palm.

I protested, trying to return them. Our eyes met and locked.

He didn't look away. "A souvenir," he insisted, curling my fingers around them.

Ka-ching.

For a week afterward, the quarters sat on my desk next to my drawing pencils and paintbrushes. *Gut instinct.* I was sure he'd call. But the following week, when he hadn't, I spent the quarters in a crunch, doing laundry.

◆ ◆ ◆

Now I sat at work wondering if Scottie Perlman would ever call, wanting him to, wanting to call him, but I called Martine instead. I asked her to please explain what, exactly, love was.

There was silence on Martine's end of the line until, finally, she snapped. "Look, I just don't know, Silvie. Brent and I just moved in together. Twice already he taped a Bulls game over my shows." Her shows, I knew, were PBS programs about dance. "Love—it comes and it goes."

"That's the best you can say?"

"It waxes and wanes, like the moon," she said. I imagined her hands fluttering around her face, as they did when she talked, like butterflies. "All right, Silvie," she said, resuming her normal tone. "Here's my wisdom for the afternoon. Then I'm getting off the phone and I'm going to entice my boyfriend with this stupid sheer-pink teddy that's crawling up my ass. We both took a personal day to have sex, and what's he doing? Playing a computer game."

"You took a personal day to have sex?"

"Well, yes. We've both been so busy."

"Wow. So, like, your co-workers think you're waiting for the plumber or renewing your passport or going to the dentist . . ."

"Shut up, Silvie, and listen before I attack the man in my living room, who's battling the evil sorcerer in *Zork*." She took a deep breath, one of the loaded ones she'd learned long ago in acting class. "Love is knowing you can't have it all but opting for it anyway, because the alternative is just too grim. Okay?"

"That's it? You're saying it's better than being alone?"

"I'm sorry to be the one to tell you."

"I can't accept that," I said.

She sighed, sounding nearly as dramatic, I realized, as my mother. "Neither could I."

◆ ◆ ◆

As Mimi would say, it was the long part of a minute before Dr. Perlman called, but then he called three times in one week, during downtime in the emergency room of his Brooklyn hospital, before a teenager had jumped or been shot, before a kid darted in front of a car to retrieve a Frisbee, before the neighbor discovered that the old woman living in 4B had died of an aneurysm (the arteriosclerosis kind) in the bathtub and brought her in for an autopsy. We talked in low voices, the intermittent music of sirens in the background, while he taught me about head trauma and eclampsia and

AIDS. Talking to Scottie was like watching one of my old favorites—*Marcus Welby, M.D.* or *Emergency!*—but being able to ask questions.

I learned about melanoma and subdural hematoma, alcoholic gastritis, mitral valve prolapse, kidney stones, fractures, concussions, things that pose as fainting or nausea or headache but are indications of something worse. I learned about gunshot wounds, about manic depression and hysteria, and about paranoid schizophrenics, who wait and wait for something to happen that never will.

"I thought about you on the subway," Scottie said on the phone one day. "I bought the *Post* and read your horoscope. I want to see you tonight. I want you to want to see me tonight." Pausing dramatically, he lowered his voice. "In fact, I miss you."

"How can you miss me? We haven't even seen each other since the night we met." Cool. Nonchalant. Martine had trained me. But my heart speeded up.

"That is about to change. Anyway, as I was saying: I get to the hospital, don my scrubs, eat a chocolate doughnut that Trudy the fat nurse sets out for me, lather my hands, and think about your horoscope instead of the old geezer with the chest pains lying on the gurney who fears it's his heart when it's actually gas."

"Gas?" I said, frowning. "I don't like the direction this conversation is taking."

"For instance, I'm thinking about your horoscope right this minute on my five-minute break with an appendicitis waiting in surgery."

"Acute?"

"Sub," he said. "About tonight? Dinner?"

"Okay." The casual okay, though my insides were shouting, *Yes!* I hung up and went to work on the layout for "Feel-Good Kitchens, Fresh and Functional"—limited, small in scope, demanding little artistic ability, but I enjoyed it. I dreamed of the time

I'd move up the ladder to "Bathrooms and Other Small Spaces," and of more immediate, achievable, delicious goals, such as a date that night with a nice guy.

◆ ◆ ◆

That night, Scottie and I saw *Rain Man,* with Dustin Hoffman and Tom Cruise. I showed up in a long skirt, relishing the warm spring air on my legs. During the movie, Scottie took my hand. I didn't try to take it back. I was pretending to be a girl without a battery of inner doubts, a girl who liked a guy who was comfortable in his skin, a girl with a voice, a girl who could *trust.*

On the way home, we strolled through the Upper West Side, the gray sky stretched tight as a balloon filled with water—it would rain and turn cool, pushing spring back a while. We were talking softly, about the film, about our jobs, when suddenly a car screeched to a halt, an inch away from the truck in front of it. I jumped about a foot in the air, but Scottie just looked at me, eyes wide, and said, "I-I-I'm an excellent driver," in perfect mimic of Hoffman. My easy laughter sounded like the laugh of another girl—confident, sexy, strong.

Outside my apartment, I hesitated. The protocol—never invite a man upstairs on the first date—danced in my head, but I couldn't help but admire the fact that he was climbing the steps ahead of me as if it had never occurred to him that he *wouldn't* come inside. "I see you know where you're going."

"I-I-I'm an excellent driver."

I laughed and led him into my one room.

"Nice," he said. "Big." Now we both laughed.

I watched his eyes roam around the tiny space, resting, at least in my imagination, on my bed, looming huge and florid.

"These yours?" To my chagrin, he was moving straight toward the drawings and paintings I'd hung on the wall with masking tape.

I was shy about my art and rarely showed it to anyone except Martine and Theo. I don't think I'd shown my mother even one drawing I'd done as an adult.

Now, here were my pictures, fluttering in the breeze of the radiator, doing a strange kind of ghostly dance, as if my hidden self, my alter ego, had come out to play.

"You're really good."

"You think?" I blushed, and then blushed at the thought that I was blushing. And there were so many of them—appalling, like a rash that had grown out of control. I drew all the time now, on park benches, buses, while standing in a long line for a movie at the Lincoln Plaza. Lately, I drew only two things—faces pressed up against faces, and feet.

"Yes, really. Didn't your mother ever hang your drawings on the refrigerator?"

"Are you kidding? *She's* the artiste in the family."

"Oh, I get it. Only room for one, huh? So you couldn't be better. You know, my father came to the United States from Lithuania with only a high school education. He became a butcher . . ."

"Really? A butcher?"

"Yeah, Meaty Mel. And he wanted me to be a butcher."

"They called your father Meaty Mel?"

He nodded solemnly. "I grew up obsessed with rump roasts and pork loins and nice chicken gizzards." I couldn't tell if he was teasing or not.

"By the time I was in high school, it was all heart valves, frontal lobes, and baboon lungs. And that's how I made the transition from budding butcher to doctor. You'd think he'd be proud to have a doctor in the family, but no. He's famous for giving me a dog-eyed look and saying, 'Sure could use another pair of hands good with a knife around here.' " He grinned.

Before I knew it, I was showing him my sketch pad, lifting the pages, my fingers light as the wind. Subway riders' faces flew by—tired, angry, bored, empty; only a few serene, calm, eager.

Scottie's face grew serious. "You've got something here. You should push yourself."

"Oh, anyone can draw."

"That's what talented people say to us losers who can't."

I pulled my lips into Mimi's pouty smile, one I didn't know I had in me.

"Seriously, there's real feeling in these faces." Scottie riffled through the sketch pad. "Look at this guy here, Julian—"

"Julian? You know him?"

"Sure. So do you." He squinted. "He's definitely a Julian. Too sensitive; can't take a joke." He pointed to another one. "This must be Marisa, with the sad eyes. Kinko's is closed and she's trying to get her poems into a contest at the *Black Rose* literary journal."

"The deadline's tomorrow," I offered.

He grinned as I joined in his game. "And this kid, Kevin. That vacant stare, man—he just ingested an ounce of ganja brownies and he's on the up elevator."

Scottie turned to another page, a drawing of shoes. His gaze shifted downward. "Here's Tess. She hasn't read a book in a long time."

I suppressed a smile.

"Has a bad stereo and listens to Michael Bolton. And this must be Gwen—she's a loner. Stays up late reading *War and Peace,* which she never finishes. Works in a bookstore, sneaks *People* magazine on her lunch hour. Curly hair like a mop."

I stared at him, remembering the girl in the black lace-up boots. "She did have curly hair!"

"And here's Kim. Validated through money. Expensive mules, gold ankle bracelet. Major sorority girl. And Brenda. Plays volleyball. Does something pharmaceutical. Here in the white shoes is

Consuela, a nurse in urology who calls the old men "dearie" and says "anyhoo."

I was bent over double, laughing. "How did you see all that?"

"You made them come alive." He tilted his head so his eyes met mine.

When he leaned close to me, I didn't pull away. We kissed, and I would carry that kiss around for a week, like a balloon, a prayer, draped around my body like shelter.

◆ ◆ ◆

Six dozen roses, red, arrived at my desk. Six. Dozen. They just kept coming, each dozen wrapped separately, in flowered paper. I guess that being a doctor, Scottie prescribed flowers. Lots of them.

"I haven't seen this many roses since my uncle Lester died." This from Julie Myerson, a fact checker with a year-round tan and rigid posture, who, on every break, it seemed, plucked her eyebrows in the ladies' room. "Do you like him?" blinked pale vegetarian Kate Belden, who wore Birkenstocks with socks on Fridays and littered the office refrigerator with sandwich bags full of tofu and bean sprouts. Did I like him? No. Yes. I didn't know. All I knew was that under New York's frantic sky, I'd found a face.

◆ ◆ ◆

Scottie and I were sitting on a bench in Riverside Park early one Sunday morning, drinking coffee from paper cups that said I LOVE NEW YORK. It was late April; the air was warm and sultry, the trees, green and lush. We'd just gone out for breakfast. In the last few weeks, we'd talked on the phone every day at work, seen several movies, been to one basketball game at Madison Square Garden, and shared sushi, but just that one kiss. Our slow pace had its own felicitous rhythm, which suited me fine.

Scottie leaned back against the bench, stretched his legs out in front of him, and said, "We need to spend the day together."

"We do?" My arms were crossed. I unfolded them. I drew a shuddering breath. I was afraid. Afraid he'd leave, afraid he'd stay.

"Yes. A whole day." He finished his coffee with a gulp, got up, threw the cup in a garbage can, and returned, stretching out his legs again.

"Why a whole day?"

"We have to see how we do." His voice was grave.

"How we do?"

"As a couple. How we do."

My throat loosened a little and I laughed. "Oh."

"Don't you want to?" He looked down at his hands, but I caught a glimpse of eagerness on his face.

"What?" *Cute; sweet.* He was all those words that I'd vowed never to use; his words made my spine tingle.

"Spend the day with me. The whole day, I mean. And night."

"Do I want to spend the night with you?" I laughed again and felt bad for laughing; he looked so solemn.

"No! I mean spend the day and go *into* the night together, I don't know, have dinner, see a movie. The whole day but not the whole night."

"So you don't want to spend the night together?" Opening my eyes very wide and serious.

"No, I mean yes. Well, that's why we should spend the whole day. To see if we want to spend the whole night."

"Oh, I get it."

He leaned toward me. Suddenly I pulled away, words tumbling out, "I'd like to draw a picture of you. Where's my drawing pad?" I fumbled in my backpack.

"But I was about to, I mean, do you have to draw right now? When the sun's shining on the Hudson and we're discussing our future?"

I smiled apologetically. "I've got the urge."

"So this is what it's like being with an artist. All the obsessiveness.

Silvie, do you think you could be avoiding, like, um . . . I mean I was trying to kiss you."

"You were?"

"Yeah."

"I didn't know. You can." Silly, but my heart was galloping.

"I can what?"

"Kiss me."

"Thank you." And we kissed, right there in Riverside Park, on a bench, underneath a lacy veil of leaves.

◆ ◆ ◆

"Oh, Silvie, a doctor!" Mimi said. Our phone calls were less frequent lately, and I hadn't been home in over two months. "I dated a doctor once," she went on. "At Ole Miss. A surgeon . . ." I held the phone about a foot away from my ear, marveling at her narcissism. She was as contained as one of those snow globes in a souvenir shop, so pleased with itself, the whole little world there poised on the lip of transformation every time you shook it, the same veil of snow fluttering down prettily.

As for Scottie's phone calls, even Florence had been tolerant; she'd seen the roses. She'd shaken her head, saying in her clipped tone, "I must say, a gesture that extravagant is absolutely irresistible."

One day she walked by my desk and leaned down to whisper in my ear. I assumed that one of her gentle reprimands was coming, but she said, "There's a wonderful show at the MoMA. A must-see. Take your new beau." I did, and as things developed with Scottie, Florence pushed me harder at work, giving me more responsibility, urging me to bring in the book of drawings I'd once mentioned shyly. Sometimes I felt as if she were grooming me for something—not her job, no, something more subtle than that. Success in work, and in love. Or maybe she was simply revealing the secret of her wisdom so that I could one day be happy.

◆ ◆ ◆

A while after meeting Scottie, I came to work armed with a series of sketches I called "Lost in the City"—subway stuff, park benches, buildings, crowds, and, of course, the shoe drawings. Florence leaned back in her chair, gazing very seriously at the pages I'd stapled together. She rocked back and forth as she looked at the pictures, her face expressionless.

Finally, she shut the book. "Well, Silvie," she said, her voice cheerful. "I must tell you, you can do better."

My mouth went dry; I leaped up, reaching for my work. "It's not ready. I need more time . . ."

Florence put up her hand. "It's not untalented, you understand, but it's all over the map. You must find your . . . voice, your signature style. You need more discipline, training. If you mean this to be a book, it must cohere. You start lush, but by the middle of the book, you've become Salvador Dalí."

Above Florence's desk was a painting of a little girl standing in front of a cottage. The painting always startled me, because the girl had the face of an old woman.

"There's a good series of classes at the New School—a fine woman who handles illustration, and there's also a gem of a man who teaches painting."

I swallowed hard. "I don't know. I—"

"I wouldn't push you if I didn't think you were good. You have talent. Now, learn to use it. Sign up."

"Do you have the number?" Instantly, I saw something in the painting of the girl I'd never seen before—a signature: Florence Harper.

"This is New York City!" she said, grinning. "Get out the phone book."

◆ ◆ ◆

The phone was ringing when I got home. Despite the fact that my sore throat was becoming a full-fledged cold, I was whistling on my way home from work, happy on a glorious day late in May. I'd been in New York for almost two years. My life was good. Work was going well, and I'd signed up that day for the art class. I had a date that night with Scottie, who was calling before I was even in the door. Lately, Mimi had seemed genuinely pleased about Scottie; she hadn't even mentioned skin care once. Maybe we were outgrowing the old ways of being mother and daughter; maybe we were on the verge of a new, smooth rhythm.

But it wasn't Scottie on the phone.

"Do you have a cold?" My mother's greeting. "You sound stuffed up."

"Just a little one," I said. A lie. At work, my scratchy throat had turned vicious, heading straight for my chest, knives sharpened.

"Did you take . . ."

"Uh-huh, a thousand milligrams this morning. And the zinc."

"If you'd come home, if you weren't so busy with What's-his-name, I have this new vaporizer right here for you . . ."

"Scottie. His name is—"

"I know his name. You're a little preoccupied, you know. Normal, I suppose. Do you still use that small hairbrush I gave you for your purse?" She didn't wait for me to affirm. "Soak it in ammonia. You should do that every two weeks. I bet your hairbrush looks like something the cat dragged in . . ."

My sneeze drowned her out. I grabbed a tissue from a box on the nightstand. "We have a date tonight."

"Wear something bright for a change."

There was something tight in her voice, like sunburned skin. "What's up?" I said. Tucking the phone under my ear, I plucked another tissue and folded it into an accordion.

"My test results came back today."

"What test results?"

"I have cancer. They think it originated in my uterus. Remember that Pap smear?"

"Cancer?" My chest felt constricted. "Pap smear?" I tried to fan away the sudden heat flushing my face and neck.

"I didn't tell you?" she said. "I thought I did."

I cradled the phone and rubbed my bare arms. "You didn't."

"Well, it's cancer and it's already spread to my lymph nodes." Her voice was losing steam, like a balloon losing air, just as I felt. "Dr. Tilden said it's rare for uterine cancer to spread so quickly." She sounded almost proud.

I sat down on my bed. "You didn't tell me about a Pap smear or about tests . . ." I was stuck there, on the fact that she had never told me.

"I didn't want you to worry."

"What are you going to do?"

"Chemotherapy. Once a month for six months. There goes my hair! I'll get some wigs, different colors and styles. Keep everybody fascinated."

It occurred to me that she could be inflating this, and I even prayed: Please, God, let her be exaggerating. But I didn't really think she was.

Mimi broke the silence, her voice thin but determined. "I'm going to beat this, Silvie. It's going to be a battle. But I know how to fight, and I can win."

I was numb, but I wanted to ask about chances, statistics. "Have you told Theo? What about Dad? Have you told Dad?"

"Not yet." A long pause. "I love you."

"Why don't I fly home for the weekend?" I couldn't say "I love you," not even then.

"No, stay there, don't fly with that cold."

"I have a date tonight."

"Well, bundle up and go. Flirt a little." I heard some of her old energy surging back. "Men like a feminine girl. Don't come on too strong. Wait till they know you. Oh, and wear something bright. Men prefer bright."

I thought of my black jeans and black turtleneck, and my eyes flooded with tears. "Okay," I said, my anger gone. "I'll wear something bright."

We said good-bye. I walked to the bathroom, where I brushed my teeth and hair. That morning, I had arranged a long row of bras and panties over the shower rod to dry and they looked frozen there, in awkward shapes, like shriveled ghosts. I thought of Martine, who in college used to wash her panties in mixing bowls, white underwear in one bowl, black in another, the water reflecting back a pale pink.

In the mirror, I looked at my face: startled, pale, my eyes red-rimmed, watery. I parted my hair a tad off the middle and ran a slow brush through my bangs. Mimi insisted that men liked long hair, so I had worn mine short for a long time. Once, she had suggested I wouldn't have a boyfriend until I grew it back. A tremendous wave of feeling gripped me. Anguish. I was almost dizzy with it.

Well, I had a boyfriend, and for him—no, for *her*—I was putting on the purple top she'd sent me, the brightest thing I owned. This was my summer to fall in love. And now my mother had cancer.

♦ ♦ ♦

"How's that soup?" Scottie asked, his voice a low, sweet hum. "Can you taste anything at all with that cold?"

I sat across from him, unable to get the words out, wearing my purple sweater, at Hunan Balcony, Ninety-eighth and Broadway. We sat by the window watching a steady stream of people move by, but I didn't see faces, only accessories, a blur of hats, briefcases, umbrellas under a cloudy sky. My skin felt so tightly stretched over my jaws that I could hardly talk. I was trying to push away thoughts of my mother, but her voice kept nudging me, whispering in my ear: *cancer*.

"Today I saw a little kid with progeria," Scottie was saying.

The disease where you age at a furious rate. Normally, I'd be eager for details, but now I couldn't concentrate. As hard as I tried to listen, thoughts of my mother kept stealing in, taking my ears, my tongue. Why couldn't I say something? "My mother has cancer," I blurted out.

"Oh God," Scottie said. "When? What?"

"I just found out." I looked down with sudden distaste at the table, crowded with plates of sesame noodles, dumplings, spicy ginger prawns.

"She's young, isn't she?" Scottie said.

"Forty-six. It's cancer of the uterus, but it's already in her lymph nodes."

He just looked at me.

Tears sprang to my eyes, and as I shifted food around on my plate, I thought that life wasn't fair—not to Mimi, who would suffer, and not to me. I'd just wanted to get away, to have my own life. It seemed impossible. And now Scottie would need a warning: *Damaged goods. Date at your own risk.* Then the guilt came flooding in, because I was thinking of myself.

I swallowed hard. "She's going to fight it." Just then my cold came alive; my nose dripped, and I sniffled. The tissues collected in my lap like snowballs.

"Of course," he said as I cracked open a fortune cookie.

Scottie exchanged his cookie with me, so that I read his and he read mine. "Opportunity knocks on strange doors." "A life lived in fear is a life half lived."

We left the restaurant, holding hands all the way home, down the quiet, rainy Manhattan streets, hearing the wet slap of taxi wheels as they drove over slick pavement.

Scottie had walked me home many nights, and we'd parted at the door, with maybe a quick peck, murmuring a casual "'Bye" over our shoulders. But tonight he invited me over, and we ended up in his tiny apartment, moving to the bed like siblings, not even kissing, just listening to each other's cautious breath. Then we were kissing and touching, until I pushed him away, afraid of some deep place, now crowded with mother, sickness, fear. Lying side by side would have to be enough for now.

I lay transfixed, watching Scottie's profile, the hard, shadowed space around his features, and in one split second I knew—not that Mimi would leave me, but that I was on the edge of something powerful, something I deserved, and that I had to jump in. After years of insomnia, I fell asleep, against his back, my cheek pressed against the hard ridge of his shoulder blade, my knees hiked up to the base of his spine.

He turned and placed his cheek against mine. "Face," he said. And that's what we called it from then on when we lay so close, breathing each other's breath. Face.

♦ ♦ ♦

I dreamed that Mimi and I were on the subway, the number 1 train, riding downtown to the Village. She was wearing her red beret, but I didn't mind it in New York the way I'd minded it in Michigan. We were admiring a very old woman's fire-engine-red shoes when we heard rattling underneath the tracks and felt the swaying of the subway car. The old lady just went on clutching her matching red purse, her face a web of wrinkles. Suddenly, our subway car broke off from the rest and hurtled forward into a place we didn't recognize, rushing pell-mell past graffitied tunnels, past tall-windowed buildings dark gray against a slice of white sky, past throngs of people hurrying through the streets, through a veil of snow, and we realized it was no longer summer and there was no more city outside, only fields, miles and miles of open fields, white with mounds of snow, a snowy desert, what I imagined Siberia must look like, not a tree or a person in sight, and then there were no more windows, and we were outside the train. We were hurtling forward through the air like bullets, just our bodies, surrounded by nothing, no ceiling, no walls, nothing except ice and snow, and it was cold, bitterly cold, like a fierce Michigan winter. Again we stopped, with a jolt, and it was just us standing side by side in the knee-deep snow, holding hands. Now Mimi's body went rigid with terror, and she was crying, her words stumbling out, disjointed, unintelligible. I grabbed her shoulders, begging her to hold on to me, to let me hold her, but she just circled around and around, like a dog looking for a place to rest. I reached for her. My arms reached and reached but floated right through her, as though we were both made only of air. I felt for her heart, and my hand brushed something hard, and I knew it was not the real heart but a false one, made up of old songs, silver lockets, blue suede shoes. I wondered if this was what had made her sick—those bad dreams, secrets, lies, the false values, her heart given to the wrong things, things she could never have. I longed to pluck it out, this false heart, this liar's heart, throw it far away from us and everyone. I longed to stroke her real heart, make it beat again, but I couldn't; I never could. I could not grasp my mother, yet there it was—I felt it—my mother's love, but I could not curl my fingers around it and in a flash it vanished, as quickly as it had come, and something else became clear: I saw that she was leaving me, just as I had tried to leave her, over and over again, all those many years before, and now.

CHAPTER 5

The bookmobile was more than a small white trailer with OAKLAND COUNTY PUBLIC LIBRARY printed on the side; it was a sanctuary. Crowded on low shelves, the books beckoned, the air silky with the smell of soft paper and dust, a place where I could turn away from my mother and myself and toward something else. Reading was my most profound freedom, and I lived to disappear inside those words and pictures, to be anyone I wanted to be. We went there once a week.

You could set your watch by the bookmobile if Victor was driving, but with Billy, four o'clock was more like four-fifteen. Billy always thought my mother was my sister. My mother blushed and giggled at this, saying, "Well, I sew our clothes to match. That helps." Up three little stairs you went until you were inside the white trailer. In the center were a wooden table and chairs, which Theo called the Three Little Bears' table. My mother, who wasn't tall, had to stoop and fold until she fit in one of the little chairs.

Even I felt as huge as Alice in Wonderland after she'd swallowed the Drink Me potion, and babyish at the same time, wearing a jumper in the same fabric as my mother's skirt.

I'd added *All-of-a-Kind Family* and *Helen Keller* to my pile. Theo had already dragged *Green Eggs and Ham* off the shelf and was jumping out of his chair and shouting "Sam I Am" over and over again until my mother shushed him. We were at different stages of book worship. While I read everything I could get my hands on, he asked for the same books over and over, until he knew the sound of every word.

My mother pulled *Edie Changes Her Mind* off the shelf and held it out for me. I shook my head; I was too old for that. I was aware by now that she didn't want me to be smarter than she, yet she picked out books for me, sometimes ten at a time. She chose girlish books—*Betsy, Tacy, and Tib*, *Ramona the Pest*, *The Saturdays*, *Little House on the Prairie*, *Charlotte's Web*, *Little Women*—domestic books, books about families, houses, dolls, girls who stirred up harmless mischief. If I pulled out a book about presidents or astronauts, war or science, she eased it out of my hands and placed it back on the shelf.

My mother was sitting with Theo nestled in the crook of her arm reading *The Cat in the Hat Comes Back*. After a while, she looked up and said to me with a firmness that made me listen, "We're going to learn to draw."

"I know how to draw," I said, not lifting my eyes from my book. My mother tolerated biographies about women and had even checked out one on Lady Jane Grey and Anne Boleyn for herself. I'd devoured ones about Madame Curie, Clara Barton, Florence Nightingale, Jenny Lind, the "Swedish Songbird," and Elizabeth Blackwell, "Lady Doctor."

"Practice makes perfect," my mother said. "We need to focus on the illustrations in a way we never have before. We must *concentrate*, not just with our eyes."

"Cinchy," I said with a shrug. I focused on the illustrations naturally, without thinking; my eye just went to the pictures all by itself.

"Get you ready for that contest."

"I'm not entering the contest."

Theo tugged her arm. "Mom, read."

I'd learned a thing or two about siblings. Just when you'd gotten past the fact that brothers peed in your eye when you changed their diapers, they started flying your Liddle Kiddles through the air or using your kaleidoscope for a gun, yelling, "Pow! Pow!" and landing in a heap on the floor. Still, Theo was useful for certain things, such as interrupting my mother at exactly the right time.

At home, my mother began to practice drawing. Theo was now taking a nap every other day, and on those afternoons, my mother opened a book she'd checked out, *The Lonely Doll,* a book I'd loved in kindergarten. In it, the doll, Edith, was wearing a checked dress with an elaborate collar over a petticoat. "I can draw this," she said, pointing to the doll's dress. "And if I draw it enough, I can move on to drawing my own clothes. Clothes for the whole family."

"Great." I sighed, fingering the lace and rickrack and jingle-ball fringe on my jumper. I wanted plain.

"Sewing from patterns just isn't enough for me anymore," she went on. "I want to design. And this is one way to start."

She made a dress just like Edith's from bits of leftover fabric. We renewed *The Lonely Doll* three times before she got the petticoat right. Over the petticoat went several different pieces of her own design—a light gingham jumper; a heavy velvet smock. She called the outfits "frocks." For once, I didn't mind dressing Lady Jane in them. I realized my mother was breathing her whole heart and soul into those clothes.

Her enthusiasm was infectious. Soon, I was racing home from school to copy illustrations. What I loved most was how a book's pictures so perfectly explained the words. I thought of the boy's chocolate skin and the bright blocks of color in *The Snowy Day,* the thin, squiggly lines in *The Cat in the Hat,* which reminded me of comic strips in the funny pages, how in *Goodnight Moon,* the old lady whispered "hush" first in black and white, then in blooming color. And those were just Theo's books.

"We're copycats," my mother said. "But good ones. With *ambition.* We're trying to get ahead."

I sat by the coffee table, my books piled high and the onionskin tracing paper spread out before me. My fingers clutched the pencil, formed the lines, the shapes, and it came to me that I could illustrate children's books when I got older, and I felt infinitely relieved, as if I'd been worried about something I didn't know I was worried about. But good illustrations, like the ones in *Alice in Wonderland,* required skill, and that took practice. I didn't tell my mother about my lofty goals. She thought I was just imitating her, teaching myself the fundamentals so that I could design clothes too.

My mother moved on to *Glamour, Vogue,* and *Harper's Bazaar,* sketching dresses, skirts, jackets, and pants. Her fingers gripped the pencil, her eyes glazed over, and her jaw clamped shut. I realized I'd never seen her concentrate this hard before.

I'd asked my father if I had to make a poster for the contest, and he'd told me it was required of all third-graders. "It doesn't matter if you win, honey," my father said. "Just do your best." But I was sure I would lose, and winning, I knew in my bones, would raise the stakes with my mother in a game I didn't want to play.

I worked with pencil first, on the poster board my mother bought me for the contest, sketching my design. I was filling up with ideas in spite of myself.

While I sketched, my mother peered over my shoulder, licked her index finger, and reached. "That's nice, but I want to show you . . ."

I pulled my paper away. "I want to do it myself."

"Just how to smudge your line. It softens . . ."

"I hate soft!"

"It provides contrast. See?"

I glared. Didn't her offers to help always have a knife's edge?

"I guess you don't really want to win," she said. "Well, have it your way."

I finished the poster while she was making dinner and hid it under my bed. The next morning, pulling it out, it looked silly to me, unfinished, in babyish lines and too-bright colors. At the top of the cardboard, I'd painted a sky and written OUR HEROES, in letters made of twinkly blue stars. Underneath that, on a bed of clouds, I drew the back of three men's heads as they tilted up to read my words. Underneath them, I drew a little girl holding a flower that said PEACE, rain falling around her.

I tried to get out of the house without my mother seeing my work, but she called out, "Where's the masterpiece?" I had no choice but to show her.

Her pride seemed genuine, almost shy. "Silvie, how did you dream this up? It's so imaginative. Look, that's Kennedy, and Kennedy and King. And that little girl holding out a flower, her peace offering. The rain is her tears. Dan, you've got to see this."

My father came around the corner tying his tie, a fleck of shaving cream on his chin and an absentminded look in his eyes.

I held it out to him with a faint apologetic smile.

He studied it for a while, then reached to kiss me. "Honey, this is terrific."

I was proud inside, where no one could see, until my mother snatched the poster back and studied it again. "Silvie, I swear I saw a picture like this in the 'Weekend' section of last Sunday's newspaper. You know the one I mean, don't you, Dan?"

My father looked at her blankly.

"Yes, in the 'Weekend' section. I'm sure of it."

I didn't remember such a picture, and I waited for my father to say he didn't remember, either, but he didn't. He just turned to the mirror and straightened his tie.

I took the poster back from her and looked at it. It seemed different then. The perspective was all wrong. Nothing was the same.

♦ ♦ ♦

As it turned out, I won the contest. I felt nothing about winning except burdened—it was one more thing I wanted to hide from my mother. But I couldn't hide getting first place; a letter was sent home. And a prize, a book called *Beginning Drawing: Technique,* which I shoved underneath my bed. Cynthia Mullen won second place with a design, my mother later said, she must have had help with. Todd Brenner won third. Our posters would be on display in the auditorium and a special assembly was planned. The winners would have to stand up.

At dinner that night, Theo clapped and said, "Da-da," and my father said, "We have an artist in our midst!" My mother echoed his praise, but there was something tense and hollow in her voice, and as we ate, she grew quieter. I fed chunks of beef stew to Wolfie under the table. It was my mother's stage and I'd walked across it, stepped into her spotlight. I was afraid of what she might do; I was afraid of her, plain and simple.

♦ ♦ ♦

For Halloween, when I was nine and Theo was four, Theo wanted to be an astronaut. In July we'd all sat glued to the TV watching Neil Armstrong walk on the moon. I had stopped making suggestions for my costume; my mother always had something up her sleeve grander than anything I could dream up. I'd been a pumpkin, a Gypsy, Little Bo Peep, and Cinderella, among other things. Now, on a crisp October afternoon, we were on our way to see Helen at the sewing store so that my mother could begin designing our costumes.

"You know, Silvie, since Theo's going to be an astronaut, you could be the moon. We can make you something white and shiny . . ."

She looked at me; I nodded. I hadn't even put up a fight. Since the contest, I hadn't done much drawing. My mother, however, had been spurred on to higher goals.

A Stitch in Time wasn't big, but it had long aisles like a grocery store and was stacked with bolts and bolts of fabric—velvets, satins, cottons, and the scratchy wool plaids my mother used for our miniskirts. Against one wall in the back, all the pattern books sat jumbled on a long counter, under which were flowered stools that spun around. That's where my mother used to sit before she became a designer. She'd jot down her pattern numbers, and then Helen would go to the back room and bring out the corresponding patterns in their envelopes.

Helen had beautiful silver hair and dark brown eyes, and although she wasn't wrinkled or shrunken, she still seemed old to me, because she spoke softly and had in her eyes a great well of organized calm, as if every morning she laid it out along with her clothes and stepped into it for the day. I liked Helen; I may even have loved her. I felt she knew that going into that store every week and poring over patterns and fabrics, threads and buttons, gave my mother's life some order it might not otherwise have had. And I think Helen saw that underneath my mother's giddy energy, she had talent.

Usually, as soon as Theo and I walked into the store, we made a beeline for the velvets, where we ran our hands back and forth against the plush, leaving little tracks. But today Theo marched directly to the front counter and waited by the cash register for someone to lift him up so that he could sift through a big shoe box full of buttons, which sold for a quarter a scoop, like candy.

"Helen," my mother said. "I need at least two yards of something silver, something with a little shine. Theo's going to be Neil Armstrong, and Silvie's going to be the moon."

Helen took her cue. "My, but you are clever, Simone." She walked directly to a fabric that looked shiny and thick, almost like rubber. "How about this?"

"Hmmm. Interesting." My mother knitted her brows.

Helen lifted more fabrics to show my mother, all silver and silky. "What do you think of this lamé?"

"The lamé just might be the answer."

"How inspired, an astronaut and a moon," Helen said, her eyes twinkling.

Theo called out, "I'm Neil Armstrong, astronaut." And off he went in a slow circle through the store, lifting his feet in exaggerated steps, as if a string of taffy were stuck to his shoes.

"You never use the patterns anymore, Simone, and I think it's wonderful," Helen said. "So creative; you have the feel. Have you seen this announcement? A sewing contest, sponsored by *Notions* magazine."

" 'A New Decade New You sewing contest,' " my mother read out loud. " 'Design and sew a winter/summer ensemble to help the new woman usher in the seventies.' " My mother's cheeks flushed pink with excitement. She shot a glance my way. Helen, I noticed, was watching my mother closely. "I never knew the end of a decade brought so much *activity*."

"There you go." Helen smiled, and her wrinkles jumped out of hiding like little animals.

Theo was now on tiptoes trying to see the buttons. I found a stool and he jumped up and we both sifted through the box.

"First place is a brand-new Singer sewing machine," Helen said. "And your designs published in the magazine."

My mother said, "Who can enter? Is it national?"

"Oh, heavens no, just local, but still, you never know until you try. Do you have a scoop of buttons, Theo? How about you, Silvie?"

We gave her our buttons and she put them in a small brown bag.

"You know, Helen, I won a sewing contest once in high school," my mother said. "I made a poodle skirt and I won first place. My father was so proud." She smiled wistfully. "And Silvie won first place in an art contest at her school. Her design just knocked everyone out."

I cringed. Since the contest, my mother, despite her jealousy, had used every opportunity to brag about my winning.

"Marvelous," Helen said, ringing up our purchases. "It runs in the family. Have fun. That's what counts."

We left the store with that little piece of paper fluttering in my mother's hand and the silver fabric for our costumes.

Dutifully, my mother finished our costumes, and on Halloween, Theo and I were the talk of the neighborhood. A delighted Theo wore a silver padded jumpsuit. My mother had covered a helmet and his rain boots with foil. Miss Moon, far less enthusiastic, shuffled along in a white turtleneck and tights and a crescent-shaped cardboard covered with shimmery white lamé.

Before Theo and I had spread our bags of candy on the floor and started trading the Almond Joy bars for the Snickers, my mother had moved her makeup mirror off the kitchen table and begun working on her designs for the contest. My father, who grumbled every Halloween about all the sugar, snitched the rejected Almond Joy bars and Raisinets, then fled.

In the afternoons, as we ate our candy unobserved, my mother sat, her sketches spread out around her, the oven timer for the meat loaf ticking like a metronome. When it rang, she jumped up to check on dinner. To keep us quiet, she gave us a wad of S&H Green Stamps and a wet sponge so we could stick them in books. I loved gluing them in, filling a whole book, that feeling of completion, of anticipation—what could we get? Best was looking through the catalogs, counting the books to see if we had enough for a new coffeepot or a toaster oven or a life-size doll with real hair. Theo wanted a huge stuffed llama. We liked to go to the redemption center on Wednesdays, double-stamp day. I loved our mother's exuberance those days, the way she led us to the car, wearing makeup, rings, jaunty sunglasses, the day full of possibility. The excessive energy she put into household matters made me feel secure, like a baby bird whose mama was flying back to the nest with the best bits of seed in her beak. She said you had to work to find real quality, but she liked the hunt. Check for flaws, she said, holding up a china teapot; heft its weight in your hand. Best, though, was that it was free.

"Not exactly," my father said. "You paid for the groceries at Kroger, didn't you?" My mother and I gave him a blank look, but Theo pointed out that it *felt* free. Over the years, we had traded our books for a percolator, a Corningware chafing dish, grapefruit spoons, various toys, and sleeping bags—stars and planets for Theo, Flower Power for me.

One day, when we'd made our way through the shoe box of tangled Green Stamps, my mother announced: "My portfolio!"

At the dinner table, she held up a drawing of a maxi-dress over patent-leather boots. "What do you think, Dan?"

My father looked hard at the picture, taking a bite of his Shake 'N Bake chicken. "Nice. Good chicken, too."

" 'It's Shake 'N Bake and I helped,' " Theo quoted in a hokey southern accent. At four, he could do TV—theme songs, commercials, entire skits with Ernie and Bert, Big Bird, Oscar.

Next, my mother displayed a drawing of a striped pantsuit with a feather boa. "This? Or this?" She showed us a belted tunic top over flared pants.

"The last one's nice."

"Dan," she cried. "That's the most boring one. Although if I used a deep multicolored swirl, in vinyl . . ."

"Honey, aren't they a little much? I mean, where would you wear any one of those outfits?"

"For Halloween?" Theo asked. He could say stuff like that and she wouldn't even blink.

"To pick me up from school?" I ventured, waiting for the volcano to erupt. But Mimi was too stirred up to scold. "I'd wear any of these to a party," she said.

"Not around here, you couldn't," my father said. "Who are you designing for? Know your client. Is she a New York fashion model, or is she an ordinary housewife who wants to knock out her friends at the neighborhood bash?"

My mother frowned. "I don't want ordinary."

"Ordinary doesn't have to mean boring," my father said. "You'd have a better chance of winning if you could be more practical. Come up with some outfit a woman could wear with confidence in her everyday life."

My mother was nodding, and that nod was gathering speed. "Know your client," she mused, picking at her mashed potatoes. "Maybe you're right."

My father helped himself to more potatoes.

"I've got an idea!" she said, her face a shiny pink, like the inside of a shell. "My focus could be to, to . . . *transform* the housewife, someone like me, who, for the past decade, stood on the outside looking in."

My father dipped a bite of chicken into his creamed corn and chewed. "It's just a sewing contest, Simone. You're not running for the Senate.

"The war, civil rights, women's lib." My mother spoke haltingly at first, gaining confidence as she went along. "The sixties has been a decade that's changed the world, and women like me have watched it from their homes while the work they're doing is being devalued—taking care of babies and making dinner. My design could be a signal for women to say, 'Hey, we're interesting too! America, here we come!' " She jabbed her fist in the air.

I ate my Shake 'N Bake, catching her excitement. I had to admit she was luminous at times, her zeal winking like Christmas tree lights, all extravagant shine and color. I loved her like this, expansive, like a little girl in her mother's high heels. There was something contagious in her exhilaration, and something sad underneath that made you want to protect her.

She held her paper at arm's length and frowned. "My design must reflect both strength and femininity, the delicate balance that the modern woman strives for."

She made trips to the sewing store, discussing with Helen fabrics, buttons, and trims. One night she sat down at her sewing machine, but not to sew Theo his latest heart's desire—a Batman costume he could sleep in—or to hem my father's pants or to make our matching skirts and jumpers. No, tonight she sat with a stately calm, starting up the Singer's gentle purr, her skin taking on a sheen. She plucked pins from the red tomato, from its plush heart, holding them between her lips, wiping away a line of sweat above her lip with her pinkie. I noticed that *Elvis' Golden Records,* usually an accompaniment to her sewing, lay in its jacket.

Night after night, she crossed her legs, licked the thread, and pushed it through the needle's blue eye. Watching her, I realized that Helen had given my mother something none of us could—a chance to channel her energies and talent, to make something of herself, to still her unquiet heart.

She finished the night before the deadline. Although it was past our bedtime, she lined us up on the couch next to our father and modeled her outfits. Wolfie sat on Theo's lap, her pink tongue hanging out, watching my mother with a regal and expectant air, as if the outfits might be for her.

"Ta-da," my mother said, parading across the family room, hand on hip. With a little hip thrust, she stopped in front of us in a crushed-velvet jumpsuit. Red. On one finger, she hooked a matching jacket over her shoulder, like the models in *Vogue*. She twirled once, then deftly slipped the jacket on.

The three of us, even Theo, sat gaping.

"A wonderful option for a winter look—a jumpsuit," she said. "Nothing like a jumpsuit to create a long, lean line, a clean look for the modern woman. The crushed velvet is very new, very fresh, and the jacket is long here, a classy touch."

"What did you call that? A jumpsuit? Very pretty," my father said, one finger propping up his cheek.

I sat very still, stunned to see those many pencil sketches come so blazingly alive. "Pretty," I stammered. The jumpsuit *was* pretty but bright, a fire-engine red.

My mother looked at us. "You don't like it."

"The design and the work are lovely," my father said. "But isn't the red a little . . . vibrant?"

My mother's lip trembled. "Color is an important part of the overall design. Color is the soul's way of saying hello. I am not just handy with a needle; I have the spirit of an artist. In my own way, I'm a Rembrandt or a Picasso." She thought a minute. "With a little touch of Warhol. By not taking me seriously, you're trying to silence my gift."

"I am taking you seriously," my father said. "Now, turn." He nodded. "It's an eye-catcher."

"You really like it?" Her eyes were shining.

Wolfie barked, and we all laughed.

"Okay, I'll be back," my mother said. "And while I'm gone, start pretending it's spring." She dashed upstairs and came back a few minutes later, accompanied by the sound of tinkling bells. She rotated slowly. This time, the fabric was a sunny yellow chiffon, a sleeveless top and matching flared miniskirt, over a pair of matching yellow tights. Little silver bells trimmed the edge of the top and the hem of the skirt.

"I return to the mini here because there's nothing like it to symbolize the freedom of the sixties. The mood in summer is lighter, more carefree, and a woman wants a chance to show a little leg."

"Hear, hear," my father said.

"Of course, the icing on the cake is the bells." She lifted her skirt so they jingled. "Not only do they ring in a new era, they allow the woman to announce herself, to enter a room boldly, *be herself.*" She spun around, bringing on a mad tinkle of bells.

"Well, Simone, when it comes to creativity, you're unbeatable."

"Oh, Danny, do you really think so?" She was glowing now.

"I really do."

"You're gonna win, Mom." Theo threw his arms around her waist, and as usual, I envied him his easy affection.

But, somehow, I knew in a flash that while her designs and sewing were good, her bright colors were too jolting. And those bells—they pushed the whole thing too far. I hoped I was wrong; I wanted desperately for her to win. Please, God, I thought, let her win.

"Just think. We could have two contest winners in one house!" she was saying. "I just have to call Mama and Daddy and tell them." She ran to the phone in the kitchen and in a minute was chattering gaily to Granny and Paw Paw, sharing with them the details of the New Decade New You sewing contest. After we'd all had a chance to say hello, she hung up the phone, her lips pressed together, saying, "Well, Mama, true to form, said that designing your own clothes is a waste of time when there are perfectly good patterns out there by Butterick and Simplicity. And Daddy, you know Daddy. He said, 'Simone, you know what I always tell Shelby? "If you ask a girl for a kiss, you'll get a lot of slaps in the face, but you just might get a kiss." In the game of life, there are winners and losers. Winning is one way of getting ahead. Now, go out there and show the world you're not a nobody, you're a Reisman.' " She turned to my father, the excitement drained from her face and an anxiety creeping in.

"Simone," my father said, pulling her into his arms. "Forget it. Don't let them poison this. You've already accomplished something just by setting a goal and creating such beautiful designs." He kissed her forehead. "Finishing the race is the goal. You can't control what other people think."

My mother pulled away from him with a pout. "You don't think I'll win."

"I think you *should*."

"I'm just a housewife in a Yankee suburb . . ."

"Don't start, Simone. If I were a betting man, I'd say you could walk away with this whole thing."

She looked at him. I'd seen that hope before—on Theo's face when he asked if Batman was real, wanting to believe but knowing the truth.

The results were announced the third week in January, on a cold day under a gunmetal sky which threatened a snowfall that could exceed the sixteen inches Chicago had seen in 1967. In fact, the new decade had blown in with blustery winds and the coldest temperatures since some long-ago year before my father was born. Nineteen seventy, the year *Sesame Street* would celebrate its first birthday and Nixon would send U.S. troops into Cambodia.

Before my mother could drive down to A Stitch in Time that Saturday, Helen called. My mother hadn't won first place. She didn't win the sewing machine or the publication of her designs. But she did win second, with its promise of fifty yards of fabric and a pair of books, *Haute Couture* and *Sewing with Elegance and Ease*. She put her hand over the mouthpiece to tell us, and my father whooped and cheered, "Yay! Sweetheart, I'm so proud."

When my mother hung up the phone, her jaw was locked. A

second later, she burst into noisy tears. My father gathered her into his arms and Theo stood beside her, patting her leg. I hovered around stupidly, unable to think of anything consoling to say.

"I'm crushed, just crushed," she sobbed. "Helen said that Diane Dover won, with a more mainstream design, a wool coatdress and a jersey day dress. The judges said it was a tough choice, that I got many favorable comments about my designs and technique, but that my color choices were not subtle enough. They had to pick one, Helen said. She would have picked me, but . . ."

"It's a crapshoot," my father said. "Any contest is. Anyway, second place! And all those entries!"

Mimi raised her chin defiantly. "This is what the public wants— a day dress? Can you believe it? I bet Diane Dover didn't have a whole political theory behind her designs. I just don't fit in."

She had deserved to win first, I thought. Maybe in a bigger place, New York or California, she would have won.

For the rest of the day, my mother moped while Theo and I played Go Fish. She sat on the sofa, her hands curled in her lap. We ate an odd dinner that night, pizza my father had ordered and left-over baked potatoes with sour cream. The phone interrupted us.

"Well?" Paw Paw boomed over the line. His voice sounded so loud, we all heard him. "You win the sewing machine?"

"Well, I . . . I," my mother stammered.

We got up from the table and formed a little circle around her. "Tell him you won second place," my father whispered.

"That's really good, Mom," Theo said.

"I won second place, Daddy." My mother twisted the phone cord around her hand. "I know, but I learned a lot from this contest. I grew. I mean, I changed. It was fun. I know, but you know what Dan says. It's about finishing the race . . . yes, well, I did my best, Daddy. I love you too. Put Mama on."

"That's not it, Mama," my mother said on the phone. "I'm not trying to sell anything. Never mind. I like designing clothes, and . . . and, I'm good at it. Listen, is Shelby starting that job? Didn't you say Daddy was going to talk to Sanford Harmon at People's Bank? He won't go? Well, he's a musician, Mama. Banking is not his . . . okay, well. Can I speak to him? He's asleep? It's the middle of the afternoon. How about Nina? Okay. When she gets home, give her a kiss for me."

After she hung up the phone, she said, "I should have known better than to tell them at all. Nothing is ever good enough."

"You know how they are," my father said in a soothing voice. "That's why I brought you way up here, remember?"

Taking no solace in his words, my mother began clearing the dishes from the table.

Theo looked up, apprehension on his face. "Mom?"

"Just leave me alone, Theo," she mumbled. Her skin looked pasty now, and her hair had a wild, uncombed look.

"Hey, guys, let's cheer Mommy up." My father pushed his chair back from the table and pulled both of us into his lap, although I was far too big for that now.

My father began to sing, his clear tenor soaring. Outside, the last bits of sunshine, gilded and edgy, played in shadows around our backyard, but all his tunes wore jaunty hats.

Her arms dripping with soapy water, my mother turned from the sink, where she was scrubbing the dishes, and said, "Jesus, Dan, not that old song."

My father went on singing, tipping first Theo, then me, down past his knee, and the three of us finished the song together.

My mother approached the table with the sponge, swatting away crumbs with short, hard strokes, her other hand cupped to collect them. Then her voice. Angry. "You know, I don't have to stand around listening to this, this, *performance,* while I clear the table, wash the dishes . . ."

"I was singing that song for you," my father said. "It's about optimism."

I remembered something my teacher had said. "Mrs. Patilla told us that second place means a person tried really, really hard . . ." As soon as the words were out of my mouth, I knew I was in for it.

"So this is what first place does to you! You think you're a big wheel now, do you?" My mother spun toward me and in one swift move turned the entire container of sour cream over on my head.

The cold, sticky goo spread slowly from my scalp to my ears and down my cheeks and neck. I was too astonished to move, to breathe, certainly to cry. Mimi's eyes widened, her hands flying to her mouth.

"Mom!" Theo cried.

My father, red in the face, jumped up, a muscle in his jaw doing an angry dance. "You're a child sometimes, Simone, you know that?"

"It was an accident!" Mimi said, bursting into tears. "I slipped." She covered her face with her hands and reached for Theo, who stood very still, his arms at his sides.

I stood still, too, the cold clump of sour cream feeling like the weight of a dull headache. I deserved it. I'd dared to win my contest while she hadn't won hers.

My father, still glowering, led me to the bathroom, where he wiped my head and face with a damp washcloth, a little clumsily; but I liked his gentle touch. "Sometimes there's not a thing I can do with her," he mumbled, shaking his head.

I nodded, blinking back tears.

"Don't worry, honey. Mom just got mad. You know how she is. When she gets like this, there's nothing we can do."

From the bathroom, I could see Theo sitting in his chair at the table and my mother next to him, dealing out graham crackers like cards, a blank look on her face. Theo ate them one by one, the same blank look on his.

"Daddy, why is Mommy so mean?" I wanted answers from his clear blue eyes, even though he'd said there was nothing we could do. But why? Why couldn't he do something?

"Honey, Mom's a little tangled up inside." He stopped and tried again, attempting a laugh. "She likes to be the queen, you know."

I nodded. "And she wishes she'd married the King."

My father looked at his hands. "Well, let's put it this way. She *thinks* she wishes that. But in reality . . . she's had a hard life. Her own mommy and daddy were . . . weren't . . . always nice. Sometimes, it's easier just to give in, to not fight back. Anyway, I'm going to have a talk with her tonight, and things are going to get better around here, I promise, pumpkin."

"Okay." I looked at his gleaming forehead, his even teeth; you could trust those teeth.

♦ ♦ ♦

That night, I lay in bed clutching Lady Jane. Lady Jane. What a stupid name. Beverly Bell, a girl down the street, had a Betsy Wetsy and a Chatty Cathy and I had Lady Jane Grey. I squinted at my doll in the dark, studying her straggly hair. It wasn't Lady Jane's fault. "From now on, I'm going to call you Sarah," I whispered. "Sarah Prudence. Your new secret name. Just between us."

That same night, I created a new name for my mother, a name that came from her name, Simone, but was not her name. It lived in my head until one day, a few weeks later, it popped out of my mouth: *Mimi.* When my mother heard it, she cocked her head as though appraising a garment of the finest silk, decided it was a loving nickname, and declared she liked it; she seemed dazzled with the idea that I was praising her. But it wasn't praise; it was my way of saying we no longer lived under one skin in two different bodies. We no longer coexisted like paper dolls connected at the hip and holding hands. This, I was trying to say, is where you end and I begin.

CHAPTER 6

I woke at six to the sound of sirens on the streets of New York. I lay in a cold sweat, sick with a horrible guilt I couldn't shake, my nightmare clammy on my skin. Scottie was still sleeping. Stumbling out of bed and into the shower, I dressed in the same clothes I'd worn the day before, left his apartment, and went to work, turning sideways to squeeze onto the subway car. And all that time anger, in a hard bead inside me, stole my breath. Anger at my mother, who was once again taking over. Her life for mine; that had always been the deal.

By nine, the office was humming—phones ringing, copy machines buzzing, people eating bagels, drinking coffee, me with the dream still playing in my head. How many years had I spent leaving my mother, taking baby steps away, two forward, one back? And, still, she carried me with her always, a daughter in a tiny box. When she turned the key, I called. When she lifted the lid, I danced. When she got sick . . . well, I didn't know what I was supposed to do. I'd always coped with her tricks before, but cancer was something new.

All day, I did everything I could think of except work—sipped coffee, read my horoscope—and while I was avoiding work, Scottie called. He was at home, chipper, full of how light the world could be, free of illness and mishap. He'd already pushed my mother's trouble down underneath his skin. He hadn't met her yet. To him, she was just a statistic, another cancer statistic.

"Hi!" he said in his big, jovial voice. "How are you? Guess what I'm working on? Anatomy. I bought an anatomically correct model of a man."

"Don't you get enough of people's anatomy?"

"This is a whole different view. If I hadn't gone to medical school, I might have been a sculptor. Do you sculpt?"

"Sometimes. What body part are you on?" I found myself laughing. It felt good to laugh.

"Ah, I just finished the heart."

"How about the penis? Have you assembled the penis yet?"

He laughed. "No."

"Well, this is splendid. A new hobby."

"Yes. After I put it all together, I'll paint it."

"The heart?"

"Well . . ."

"The penis?"

"Silvie!"

"Gotta go." There was Florence, looking spiffy in a cinnamon-colored suit, in her hand a color copy of an enclave of compact, affordable gems in Bucks County, Pennsylvania. I hadn't told her yet about Mimi's illness.

An hour later, I called Scottie back. "Hi," I said, feeling weak-kneed and sad.

"I was just getting ready to call you," he said.

"Is my mother going to die?"

"I don't know, Silvie," he said soberly. There was the sound of a siren far off.

"A sad sound," I said quietly.

"It doesn't have to be," he said. "The person's getting help." He sounded calm, wise.

"So much happened between us. It's hard to know where to put it all now."

"Maybe it's time to forgive."

"You're going to tell me to go home, resolve all our issues. My life is here!"

"It's not for me to say, Silvie. I've seen people who don't attempt to work stuff out. They live to regret it. I don't want to see that happen to you."

"You know," I said, "you're the kind of person who sees a moth and calls it a butterfly."

"I am." His voice was even, filled with the steady beat of power—to restore, to heal. I couldn't help but think: How different the sound when the siren is for you.

◆ ◆ ◆

In the days and weeks after Mimi told me about her illness, I felt myself crack open, just a little, and felt all the hard work I'd done to leave her trickle out of me, drop by drop. Mimi had always been strong. Call her crazy, but she had the strength of a mother lion. I counted on that. Without it to pull against, I'd come unhinged. I was trying to go on with my life, but I was listless, scared. When my mother and I talked, it was only for a minute or two, and she ignored my questions, saying things were fine. But one night she surprised me.

"What do you want for Christmas?" Mimi said, her voice sounding small and far away.

"Mimi, it's Halloween." I flopped down on my bed. Something was up; she never shopped until the last minute.

"I know that," Mimi said in a clipped tone, with a trace of her southern drawl. "But one can never shop too early." Strange; she never said "one." "I'd like to get you what you really want. Theo has rattled off his usual baffling string of electronic equipment, which I cannot pronounce much less purchase with any amount of discernment, and now I'm calling, dear, to query you, knowing that you, my only daughter, will include items I understand, like, uh, for instance, a Big Wave Crimper. Not that I'll have hair much longer, but I do, of course, still have an affinity for the desire to curl one's hair and I'd like to get you one if you still want it." She paused to catch her breath.

Discernment? *Query*? Who was this person? "Big Wave what?" I managed weakly, completely unnerved.

"Big Wave Crimper. Good. I'll write that down."

Sounds of scribbling and rustling paper. I saw an image of her hands—pale, slow, fumbling.

"What else? Earrings, or nice keepsake jewelry? We haven't added to the collection I started for you on your sweet sixteen."

I barely remembered the "collection," which consisted of two gold rings with diamonds she'd gotten on sale. One looked exactly like an engagement ring, and every time I wore it, people asked, much to my embarrassment, when the wedding was.

"Okay, a camera," I said impulsively, not even knowing whether I wanted one.

"You lose cameras, dear. How about a string of pearls with matching earrings? Something you'll have forever."

Matching earrings? She sounded like an alien in a gleaming kitchen turning out sheet after sheet of perfectly round cookies. "You never call me dear," I said.

"Can't a mother call her daughter dear?"

"I guess so." More scratching. She must be doodling with the flat side of a pencil or with the new green pen my stepfather, Henry, had given her, sketching her first initial over and over, the *S* slithering and darkening like a snake.

"Fine, dear. Matching pearl earrings." Scratch, scratch.

"Christmas is weeks away . . ."

"Yep. That's why I'm starting now. Anyway, I *like* making lists. Now, for Scottie. Well, I haven't even met him. Is he one of those men who wear running shoes?" She laughed. "You know, one foot out the door?"

"Actually, he's not."

When she spoke again, her voice was different, harsher, full of tentacles, reaching for me and pushing me away at the same time. "You're all wrapped up with this boy, aren't you?"

"Yes," I answered, swallowing a bitter taste in my throat. Guilt.

"As it should be, I suppose. It wouldn't hurt for him to see where you come from. Why don't you bring him home for Thanksgiving?"

"Thanksgiving? That's too soon."

She drew a sharp breath. "Silvie, you're embarrassed, aren't you? That's it, isn't it? You always hated it when I dressed nice. You despised the red cape and my darling beret, and now that I'm almost bald . . ."

I swallowed hard. "Mimi, no . . ."

"I don't blame you, sugar. Rilly, I don't." She slurred the last words a little, like a drunk just getting started.

"Are you okay?" I clutched the receiver. She had assured me that except for a day or two after chemo, she didn't feel bad at all. But tonight she was scaring me.

"How do you like the blazer I sent you?"

"What blazer—oh, the blazer. I love it." She had sent it three months ago.

"Don't I take good care of you? Here I am dying, worrying about whether you're wearing the sleeves turned up or did you get them hemmed like I told you to?"

"Turned up," I mumbled, sitting up straight on the bed. She'd never said anything about dying; she always talked about beating cancer, meeting the wild animal eye to eye and wrestling it down.

"Lazy, lazy, lazy." Again, her words came out garbled. "Bring the boy here Thanksgivin', along with the blazer. I'll hem it for you." Her accent had grown as thick as charred marshmallow. Now she gave a low, throaty laugh I didn't understand. "But no sewing now. No. I'm too drunk."

"Drunk?" I repeated. The Dilaudid sometimes made her groggy, but she'd always made sense. "Mimi, I'll take it to the tailor here, on Broadway . . ."

"Not once has he done a decent job on sleeves!" Her voice had built to a low roar.

I laughed uncertainly. She'd never used my tailor.

"No laughing please!"

"You're funny," I admitted. "I'm sorry."

"Bring that jacket here. I'm in the mood for a little hand work. Tell me about the asparagus before we hang up."

"What asparagus?"

"Oh, I'm really out of it. Must be the corn. I mean the walnuts. Or maybe the Sustacal."

"What's Sustacal?" My fingers gripped the edge of the bed. "Mimi, what's going on?"

"Sustacal is liquid food that comes in chocolate, vanilla, eggnog, and strawberry. It's all I eat now. Now, you wear that blazer to meet Scottie's parents, you hear?"

"I've met his parents, Mimi, remember?"

"Wear the damn thing here then, when I meet him. I am going to meet him, aren't I?"

"Of course," I said slowly.

"Well, hurry it up."

Limp after our conversation, I stood in front of my stereo, chest tight, staring at the titles of my cassettes. I chose something blindly, slipped it in, and turned the volume up until the music was blaring. Five stories above Riverside Park, lit block by block by dim street lamps, I stood at the window, staring at a thin man in pants that were ripped along the seams of both legs. Last night, I'd seen a woman sleeping on a garbage bag. The man rummaged through a metal trash can, came out empty-handed, kicked it, and walked on. If no one knows you're missing, I wondered, are you lost?

The music swelled inside me, rich and full. I broke into a dance, arms flailing and feet splayed, my head bent, eyes closed. I whirled around and around until I was dizzy, reeling, but I didn't stop. I moved faster, faster, muttering the lyrics between jagged breaths, moving toward the mirror out of habit, to dance in front of it; but tonight I didn't see myself. I wanted to leave her behind, shake her off, but it was beginning to feel as if she was the child and I the mother, and what kind of person leaves a child?

Arms above my head, I twisted my hips and shoulders, snapping my fingers, but I wasn't dancing so much as staggering, reeling, and my knees grazed the table edge. The table wobbled, and I screamed, reaching out as the lamp crashed to the floor, scattering large pieces of broken pottery at my bare feet.

As I gazed at my face in the mirror, a phrase of college French floated in my head: *La mer s'est elevée avec les pleurs.* "The sea has risen with tears."

◆ ◆ ◆

I called my father, who also lived in Michigan. When Theo and I had told him that Mimi was sick, he'd stopped talking and sat very quietly for several minutes. "I'm stunned," he said. "I don't know what to say." And he bowed his head, hands folded in his lap, as if he were praying.

Now, on the phone, he started our conversation with, "The ex-husband is in a strange position. I feel helpless. What can I do? Seventeen years you live with someone and, boom, they get sick. You want to do something, but she has Henry now. There's no place for me."

"There's a place for you." But I didn't know where it was.

"You know, when my mother died, I was in Japan on business, teaching a seminar. Imagine walking out of a four-hour class and getting a note that your wife has called from America to say your mother is dead. Heart attack. I rushed out of that hotel and boarded a train at the base of Mount Fujiyama. When I looked out the window, the businessmen from my class, about ten or fifteen of them, had all followed me there, and they stood by the window of the train waving good-bye. One man, I'll never forget, got on the train with me, tears running down his cheeks. He sat down next to me and said, 'This will be the longest day of your life.' "

"I never knew that . . ." I eased myself down on my bed.

"There's a lot you don't know." And we sat for a second with the truth of that: how little most daughters know about their fathers, and vice versa.

"What I regret most was never saying good-bye. I flew all the way home from Japan to Baltimore for the funeral, but I was too late to say good-bye."

His voice was thick with unshed tears. "So what I'm getting at is, make sure you tell your mother everything you want to say. Don't leave things unfinished. Forgive her everything so she can move on, and so you can, too."

"You sound like she's going to die!"

"You have to face that possibility."

I was quiet.

"She needs your forgiveness," he said. "Mine too." The startled tone of his voice told me he'd just now figured that out.

Next, I called Theo, who lived in Ann Arbor. "Mimi talks like she's on acid," I said. Theo was twenty, working at Schoolkids Records.

"Heavy-duty, isn't it? Didn't she tell you? She's on morphine, Silvie. For the pain. This is happening pretty fast."

She had shown me only her smile, wide and easy, camera-ready makeup, purse matching the shoes, no hint of a shadow hovering outside the frame.

"She told me she was scared," Theo said.

"Really?"

"She said having cancer's like falling on your back into snow and she wants to make snow angels but she can't, 'cause she'd never seen snow until she was twenty and married."

Theo went on to tell me he'd dyed his hair—lavender, like an Easter egg. He assured me that it wouldn't necessarily stay that color for long. Tomorrow it might be a darker purple, next week aqua or coal black. He hadn't said a word about brown, the color we were both born with. I remembered my mother dyeing her hair blond after Paw Paw died. Perhaps that was the way our family responded to crises—we altered ourselves, created visible evidence. Maybe it was just that word: *dye*. And Theo had gotten a tattoo, courtesy of his new girlfriend, Claire, who had a nose ring, which, he said, Mimi didn't know whether to fret over or admire.

"I look forward to meeting her," I said, sounding stiff, but I was scared. Everything was changing, falling apart.

"Thanksgiving. Ditto for Scottie?"

"We'll be there." I'd invited him to Michigan for the holiday and he'd said yes.

"See ya in a couple weeks."

I hung up the phone, my hands trembling with the truth of it: my brother with purple hair and a tattoo; my mother on morphine.

CHAPTER 7

After my mother lost the New Decade New You contest, I began lying on tests. I didn't plan to, not exactly, but it had come to me that if I was careful not to outshine Mimi in any way, I would be safer and she would like me better. She had begun checking out art books, tracing paintings by Rembrandt, Renoir, Matisse. I had a sinking feeling that she knew I was a better artist than she and was checkmating me. The Elvis records were back on the stereo, as if she needed them again to pump herself up, to transport herself back to a time when she had felt special.

One day near the end of fifth grade, Mrs. Chenowith announced the Iowa Basics test for all fifth-graders. On the day of the test, I felt almost sick. I leaned over my paper, the instructions seeming to swim in front of my eyes, my fingers pressed on the pencil, knuckles white. They'd given us sharp new pencils with

smooth pink erasers, and I just kept looking at mine, pressing the
eraser against my lips.

First question. I circled C, which I knew was correct. Second
question. Harder. I circled A. Correct. I answered the next few
questions quickly. But then my mind began to race and at the same
time to feel heavy, dull. I fidgeted; I couldn't sit still. I circled answers—B, C, all of the above—but I wasn't sure anymore if my answers were right, and I didn't care. Working through the fog in my
head, I began circling A or B, almost at random, making a pattern
on the page. My mouth was dry and my hand shook. I gripped the
pencil hard. Circles. Fog. Maybe I was sick. But it didn't feel exactly like sick.

When I looked up from my test, the rest of the kids were still
bent over their papers, looking tense. I bent over and tried to look
busy. I doodled in the air above the paper without letting my pencil touch, while the minutes ticked by on the round clock with the
blank white face and large easy-to-see numbers.

Finally, Debra Flores rose from her seat and walked to the front
of the class with her paper. Next, Martine LaRue and Wilson
Hegedus strolled up, then a few more kids, and now I was free to
stand, as long as I wasn't first. I gave my skirt a good tug—once I'd
left the bathroom with my skirt tucked into my tights and everyone
had laughed—and walked up to hand in my test full of what I was
pretty sure were wrong answers, my thighs rubbing against each
other in the thick, ribbed tights. Mrs. Chenowith gave me a thin
smile, her eyes, with their frosted-blue eye shadow, crinkling to
slits. She wore her dark brown hair in a complicated vertical hive,
stiff as stale marshmallows. Chip Gompert claimed he'd once
dropped his eraser in her hair and it never came back out.

When she got the results, Mrs. Chenowith called my parents and
me in at the end of a school day. We all sat across from her desk,
Mimi and my father wedged awkwardly into a couple of student

desks. Mrs. Chenowith studied me, not unkindly, and said, "I suspect that it takes someone very smart to get this many wrong." I
had been ranked in the fifth percentile; I had answered almost
every question wrong. I'd have to retake the test.

The next time, I started strong, but soon my brain fizzled out
and I struggled to understand the questions. Every time I circled
what I thought was the correct answer, it looked wrong and a fog
of confusion swirled around me and I circled anything, just to finish.

Fiftieth percentile. At home, the little white report trembled in
Mimi's hands. "Average," she said. "That's okay." I felt sodden with
relief.

That weekend, my father said, "I'm puzzled about your test
grade. You can do better."

I hung my head.

"Did you try your best? That's all I ask, that you try your best.
Did you?"

I shook my head and felt his gaze deepen.

"Did you try to do poorly, Silvie? You can tell me."

I nodded.

"Why?"

"She doesn't like me when I'm smart."

He raked his fingers through his hair and sighed. "Do me a
favor, honey. Don't hold yourself back, okay? Don't let her, or anyone, diminish you. Do your best. Do it for me, okay? It'll be our secret." He took my hand and I gripped his, a sudden panic choking
me. I nodded, not believing I would be able to do it but determined to try.

Over time I improved my test scores, and once, I made it all the
way to the statewide spelling competition, but there, onstage, I felt
the familiar panic rise inside me and I stumbled, spelling *squirrel*
with one *r*. I felt both furious and relieved. "Didn't win," I told

Mimi, and she patted my arm consolingly. At the next bee, I lost on *veterinarian*.

Every time I came close to winning, I felt the sting of Mimi's competitiveness. My father never said a word about my losses, but a look in his eye told me he felt I'd given in to her, gone toward the darkness instead of the light.

◆ ◆ ◆

In the first majestic burst of autumn, on a Sunday afternoon, Mimi rallied us into the car. We drove through a relatively hilly area for Michigan, gazing at the oaks and maples flaunting their vibrant orange and yellow hues.

"Danny," Mimi said, after a while. "Her nose has been in that book this whole time. If she's not looking at these beautiful autumn leaves, could you please tell me why we're in this car? Theo, you're looking, aren't you, sugar?"

"Yes," he said, without looking up from his Batman comic book. We were just beginning to be silent allies in the phenomenon that was our mother, although Theo could laugh her off more easily than I.

"Well, honey, she's always loved to read," my father said. "Don't forget she read all of *A Present for the Princess* at *four.*" I looked up, thinking back to how I'd followed Mimi's navigating finger and stuttered out each syllable. I remembered my father's mute surprise and my own cheeks stinging from pride as I read, thinking, Well, there's this, there's always *this*.

My father's hands were at precisely ten and two on the wheel. "Smart, both Silvie and Theo. Headed for college."

"I'm only ten," I informed them from the backseat. From my father's enthusiastic descriptions, I saw college as a sunny place, with lots of green grass and people riding bicycles, a four-year picnic featuring girls with cute haircuts and lipstick and stockings, who chewed two pieces of Doublemint gum at a time and flattened their enormous breasts with a mountain of books.

"I'm going," piped up Theo.

"I'm not," I said, loudly.

"See what you started?" Mimi said to my father. A small satisfied smile tilted the corners of her mouth. "Anyway, brains won't get you anywhere if you don't know how to drive." My mother giggled. "Drive—get it?"

My father slowed the car to a halt at the red light. "No," he said. "I don't get it. What do you mean?"

"Nothing," she murmured. She fumbled in her purse and, fishing out her compact, dusted rouge over her high cheekbones and across her nose, then snapped the compact shut. It sounded like the bite of a small animal.

"Children, you know that your Paw Paw was an immigrant?" Mimi told us. "He came over to this country from France before the war, a Jewish immigrant. His family stayed behind and his father and sister were killed in the camps. We weren't raised religious, because he wanted to assimilate, but how, I'd like to know, with a last name like Reisman, in Biloxi, Mississippi? Anyway, there he was, a fish out of water, living in a small southern town, where he bought and sold land. His dream was to own a small patch of America; he said you weren't a somebody unless you owned land."

"I knew this was coming." My father's hands twisted on the wheel.

"Even a company man can have the entrepreneurial spirit. You have to set your sights and set them high."

My father hit the brakes for a red light. "What is this? Improve Dan Day?"

"Yes!" Mimi inhaled deeply, her eyes filling with that preoccupied, searching look that meant she was revving her engines for a story or two.

Leaning my chin against the back of her seat, I listened.

"Paw Paw came here without even a penny. His first job was managing his uncle's shoe store, and as fate would have it, Paw Paw hired Nora. She sold more shoes in a week than the previous girl had in a month. And they fell in love." Mimi went on, shading and coloring the story like a picture in my coloring book, a little violet here, a little burnt umber there, gripping the crayon so hard that it broke.

"But managing that store wasn't enough for my daddy, no. Eventually, Paw Paw bought the ground underneath the shoe store, his first purchase, and he and Granny got married. Granny and Paw Paw's love began and ended in buying, in *owning*. All life's other pursuits—education, marriage, raising children, religion—were diminished next to the one goal—to own land and make money—which they believed made them somebody. A somebody made money, a name for himself. That's what a somebody did."

"Message received, Simone."

"I'm just saying, well, that store was so important to him that all us kids were named after *shoes*." She leaned her head back against the seat, bumping my hand. I moved; her head didn't budge.

"Is that why you love shoes, Mom?" Theo asked.

"I guess it is. All of us named for shoes. Connie, then me, Simone, then Shelby, the only son—boy, he never had a chance—and, last but not least, Sweet Nina Baby. We all called her Sweet Nina Baby right off the bat. 'Best mistake I ever made,' Mama used to say."

"Not such a bad bunch," my father pointed out, the muscles in his face relaxing now that Mimi had moved on to the subject of her family.

"Dan, my mother didn't know how to love!" Mimi turned on him. "Even now she tends everybody's backyard but neglects her own. She saves up all her kindness for *strangers*. But that's another story. As I was saying, here's my father, a poor immigrant who comes to this country with nothing, and you, Dan, with all the advantages . . ."

"All the advantages! My family was dirt-poor. I went to college on an Air Force scholarship." My father's voice was rising.

"Many men who come from nothing work a little harder. When I first met you, I looked into your eyes and knew I was safe. I knew you were going places. Me, down in little backwoods Biloxi, and you, from way up north, smart, full of potential."

"Simone, I'm at one of the finest computer companies in the country. Don't belittle . . ."

"Oh, Daniel, Daniel, it's not the place. It's what you *bring* to a place. The attitude, the spirit . . . for instance, it's high time you asked for a raise."

"Simone! I just got a raise." My father looked back over his shoulder, checking the open lane.

"But you deserved more! And you didn't fight for it. At Lazarus—kids, that's the department store where your daddy worked before he set his goals—I'd sit in the cafeteria all alone, eating an enormous lunch. Remember, Dan, you had a special employee card that gave us a discount? I was pregnant with Silvie and I'd sit and eat and eat, watching all the shoes on the feet on the escalator—sturdy loafers, dainty pumps, blocks of sneakers white as freshly painted houses. I guess it's in my blood to be obsessed with shoes. But it wasn't just the *shoes;* it was the feet inside them. Stepping out, going places! And I told myself, Don't worry, Simone. Dan'll be on that up escalator real soon." A wistful note crept into her voice. "You need to push ahead a little, bully your way to the front of the line. Be heard! Be noticed!" My mother's head bobbed up and down as she spoke; my father's was rigid, still.

"I am not your father, Simone. Or you, for that matter."

"Darlin', you're *you*. I know that. It's just . . . even way up here,

I'm under that spell, that dream, of being somebody, of getting away from my mama and daddy, the small town, everything. I didn't win the sewing contest, but like you and Helen said, at least I tried. Just say you'll try."

"That's all I can do."

Minutes passed, then suddenly Mimi said, "I've got it! We'll have a dinner party. For your boss. Invite a few other couples, eat, play music, you know, get to know each other as people."

My father frowned. "Roger's so stiff, Simone."

"We'll loosen him up! Dan, this is how people get ahead. And it's something I can do! They're gonna love me. I'll wear one of my own designs. Yes, a dinner party, with fresh flowers, and . . . and shrimp!"

"Shrimp?" My father frowned.

"Shrimp. Of course, you can't get the kind of shrimp we have in Biloxi way up here, but I can work with what we have." Mimi's hands were clasped beneath her chin. Her cheeks were pink.

"I don't know, Simone."

"I'm a great cook, am I not?"

"You are a good cook."

"Except when you're drawing," Theo said. "Then you sometimes burn . . ."

I giggled.

"Shush, you two. The other secret ingredient is atmosphere, and I'm great at creating atmosphere. Dan, with a dinner party, we'll rejuvenate your career."

"Who says my career needs rejuvenating?"

"A little something extra can't hurt." She clasped her hands together. "I take it that's a yes?"

My father laughed. "More like a maybe."

"Now, Dan, you know I never take maybe for an answer."

My father laughed again and we drove, a calm settling over the car as Mimi daydreamed, pointing out the bright orange and gold and cinnamon-colored leaves outside her window.

Later, as the sky turned a dusky blue and the air cooled, we stopped for gas. My father and Mimi and Theo went inside and Mimi returned with water and candy. She and I leaned against the car door, sipping from soggy cone-shaped paper cups, both of us wearing the matching lightweight jackets she'd made, hers unzipped.

She tilted a carton of malted milk balls into her palm, handing me one. "Don't you think this party's a great idea?"

"It's okay."

"Now, sugar, about college—it's too early to worry about it. We'll just have to see, that's all."

I desperately wanted to go to college yet desperately wanted to stay home.

A bite of chocolate shell snapped between my teeth, then the sweet malt spread over my tongue. The ride home went a little faster until, soon enough, we ended up back in our driveway, where we'd started from.

◆ ◆ ◆

That spring, eight people squeezed around our dining room table, including my father's boss, Roger Capell, and his wife, Tina. Larry Sloan was there, too, with his wife, Bev, and the O'Reillys, who lived next door. Mimi had spent an hour darkening the wicks of our new candles and filling little glass butterfly bowls I'd never seen before with black foil-wrapped candies. I figured the house had to be fancy and quiet because Mimi wanted to impress my father's boss, otherwise we could have waited until summer and had a barbecue in the backyard, with my father wearing the chef's apron and hat my mother had made him and poking at the charcoal with a long stick that looked like a back scratcher and everyone would have gotten corn stuck in their teeth and Mimi could have made her Mississippi Cajun hot fudge sauce with a dash of cinnamon and cayenne pepper.

My father hadn't wanted to include the O'Reillys, because, he said, they would stick out like a sore thumb, but Mimi had read an article in *House Beautiful* that said a sparkling dinner party depended on the blending of different minds and personalities. Besides, Betty O'Reilly, being from the South, was a friend, a kindred spirit. It didn't hurt that Jim O'Reilly had a good job at the bank and Mimi thought he might give us a home-improvement loan. I didn't know what she wanted to improve, but I did know that she wanted a new dining room table. She was embarrassed because ours seated only four. She could crowd in six if she was creative, but eight looked like we couldn't afford better. Another reason not to invite the O'Reillys, my father said, but Mimi insisted that having a southern girl there would make her feel less intimidated by the Yankee wives. And besides, Betty was pregnant with her third child and once that baby came along, there wouldn't be any chitchat over mint iced tea for a while.

So the O'Reillys were invited, and while Theo watched our Friday-night TV lineup upstairs, eating his Libbyland TV dinner on a tray, I was given the option to watch with him or stay in the kitchen. I could read or draw while I was eating, Mimi said. But I didn't read or draw, I just sat at the kitchen table, listening to the grown-ups talk, polishing off my tiny chicken drumstick, the leprechaun-size dollop of mashed potatoes and sprinkle of shiny green peas, the brownie, smaller than one of Theo's Matchbox cars.

Our guests' voices made a low drone, which was punctuated by clinking silverware and occasional gusts of laughter. Mimi's voice rose above the others', a little forced, overwrought. They were eating shrimp étouffé in little white casserole dishes that had emerged from the oven hot and bubbly and golden brown, and they were noisy about it. My father had worried that shrimp was too expensive, but Mimi had only rolled her eyes. "They're frozen, Dan."

Mimi had rung a small bell and I'd carried in a basket of soft rolls, little clouds, and everyone smiled and Betty exclaimed, "Oh, how cute! Thank you, honey."

"My little helper," Mimi said with a winsome smile. "Tina, how about a roll? More rice pilaf? Roger, how is the shrimp? I hope you're not a meat-and-potatoes man . . ."

"Well . . ." Roger started. Tina said quickly, "He likes seafood fine, don't you, dear?"

"Oh my," Mimi said, her voice giddy and high. "Dan, have we a steak for Roger?"

Have we a steak. Sad, how hard she was trying.

Twice my father came into the kitchen to get a bottle of wine from the refrigerator. Except on holidays, I'd never seen wine in our house. After a while, Mimi bustled into the kitchen, arms full of dishes. I looked up from my TV dinner and saw that every person had cleaned his or her plate. Running to her side, I whispered in her ear, "They liked the shrimp."

"Or else they were very hungry," she whispered back. "Even Roger, the old goat, gobbled his up."

My mother sparkled tonight; she'd flipped the ends of her golden-brown hair like Ann Marie on *That Girl* and it swung gently around her pretty face. She was wearing the jingle-bell miniskirt and top she'd sewn for the contest. Like most of her outfits, this one was too loud, too dramatic, but tonight she carried it off. The little bells made a tinkling sound when she walked.

"You can hear me coming a mile away," she'd said, laughing, when she put the outfit on. My father had looked as nervous as I felt. But at least she wasn't wearing the blue suede shoes. Because my father's boss was there, she said, pulling her mouth into a pretty pout, she had to be conservative. She was wearing bright yellow pumps.

On a tray, we arranged the coffee parfaits, made from melted marshmallows and coffee. Instant will do, she had said, although strong-brewed is better. She showed me how to spoon the coffee into glasses and top it off with real chocolate sprinkles—just shave a Hershey's bar with a butter knife, drizzle the shavings on a dollop of whipped cream, and it looked fancy. She whisked the tray out of my hand and waltzed back into the dining room, and I heard everyone *ooh* and *aah* and I was happy, because I knew Mimi's face was bright and shining.

The group was getting louder. Betty O'Reilly's laugh spilled out, a loud bark that sounded like a man's. I opened the kitchen door a crack and saw her pat the huge drum of her belly in rhythmic beats, as if the baby inside were responding with a kick that made her fingers jump. Jim O'Reilly stood behind her, holding her shoulders. At the end of every day, as I waited for my father at the foot of our driveway, I watched Mr. O'Reilly get out of his own car wearing a brown hat, which he removed outside his door and turned over and over in his hands before going inside. He was reed-thin, with smudged glasses; he had a quiet voice and a crease like a cross between the saddest eyes I'd ever seen. He smelled of mustard and mothballs and baby powder. With his bright white shirts and dark skinny ties, he seemed no match for Betty, who was always tossing a loose nest of black curls and popping her gum, her red lipstick even brighter than Mimi's. Betty made me jump, the way her voice could boom out, squashing mine quiet, and my feet would turn heavy as bricks, my hands hanging uselessly at my sides. And while I stood looking at my feet, Betty just laughed and called me bashful. When she was around, Mimi seemed far away from Theo and me, flushed and excited, words toppling out. Sometimes, when she leaned close to the fence that separated our yard from theirs, touching Betty's arm, her accent grew thicker by the minute to outdo her friend's drawl.

Now, my father was leading everyone to the living room and changing the record to one of his favorites, Barbra Streisand's "People." Mimi came back to the kitchen and scurried around getting coffee and tea, the little bells on her skirt jingling. She cocked her head. "Run upstairs, Silvie, and get Theo into bed. It's getting late. Go on, like a good girl." She blew me a kiss, which was my cue to sneak to the staircase landing, where I figured I could see without being seen.

Mimi bounded out of the kitchen with a coffeepot and stood right next to Roger—too close, I thought. "Coffee, Roger?" she said, smiling brightly.

"Still working on the real thing, Simone," Roger said, having exchanged his wine for "the real thing" several glasses ago.

"Chicory coffee, straight from the French Quarter," Mimi said, fixing her eyes on him with the intensity of brightly shining headlights.

"No thanks," Roger said, and reluctantly Mimi moved on, flitting about, pushing her chicory coffee.

The men stood in a little clump, clinking the watered-down drinks they'd brought from the table, chomping their jaws over dots of melting ice. My father was standing Air Force straight, his head tilted, listening very hard to Roger, a huge man with a face massive and pink as a ham, who rocked back on the balls of his feet as he spoke. He didn't seem very stiff to me—Mimi had told my father just to give him a few drinks and see if he wouldn't loosen up. Larry Sloan, a man with a stutter and no chin, held his glass by the rim down at his side, his eyes blinking steadily from behind thick black glasses. Skinny old Jim O'Reilly sipped his drink and observed the group thoughtfully, thin-lipped and gap-toothed, his shirt gleaming in the soft light.

But it was the women on the other side of the room that I wanted to listen to; they didn't jam their hands in their pockets as if they had something to hide. In fact, they hovered close to each other, touching each other's bare arms in their sleeveless dresses, laughing the way dolphins kissed, with their noses almost touching. Tina complimented Mimi's outfit and Mimi acknowledged the praise with vivacious grace and a modest disclosure that implied she'd won first place in the contest. Now Betty's voice swelled and dipped; she was giving advice about morning sickness to Bev Sloan and Tina Capell, whose coral lipstick exaggerated the lines of her lips.

"An old Irish trick—chocolate milk!" Betty grinned broadly, and Bev and Tina asked, almost in unison, "Chocolate milk?"

"Tastes better coming up than it does going down." The three women howled with laughter and Mimi flew in from the kitchen, skirt jingling. "It's true! I tried it!"

That made them laugh harder, and the men looked over and snorted, one of them asking, "What's so funny, dollfaces?"

"You wouldn't understand." Betty waved them away, and the three women doubled over again.

"Girl talk," Mimi said, bringing her skirt edge up to dry her eyes but lowering it hastily when she encountered a jingle bell. She stood still a moment, observing the group, then sidled up behind my father and put her arms around his neck.

"Dan, I love you, but what *is* this music?" He held her bare arms below the elbow and it seemed for one instant that his strong hands would pull her over his head and onto his lap, but they just held her still, until she jumped up and his hands fell away into air.

"How about some real music?" Mimi said, bustling around, putting a record on the stereo. On came "Jailhouse Rock," and Roger called out, "Heads up! Look alive!" and Mimi kicked off her yellow pumps and jitterbugged around the room. My father's shoulders tensed, but he relaxed when he saw Roger grab his wife and break into a vigorous dance, and he was not a bad dancer. My father grew more and more animated as he watched old boss Roger letting his hair down. Even Larry and Bev joined in—if you could call it dancing. They seemed to be doing some strange chicken-necked skip. Betty grabbed Jim's arm, and he put his hand on the small of her back, and bounced her stiffly to the wall, where they leaned along the console stereo, beaming and clapping. Betty reminded me of Theo's old round-middled clown, which bounded back when you punched him.

"Now *this* is music," Mimi cried, cheeks flushed, silver bells jingling. She pulled my father to the middle of the room, and I leaned so far forward on the steps that I almost toppled off. I had never seen my parents dance together. Mimi was clearly the leader, but my father followed in a very graceful, handsome way and he seemed to be having a good time. When that song was over, Mimi put on "All Shook Up," and then a slow one, "Are You Lonesome Tonight?" But my father, flushed and breathing hard, went off to mix another drink for Roger, and Mimi was left alone, head thrown back, swaying to the music.

When the music stopped, there was applause from Betty and Jim, while Bev and Tina fell on the sofa laughing, smoothing down their hair, touching their pearls. "Now, there's one southern boy who can sing! Not that you Yankees would understand," Betty said, still bobbing in place, and I wondered why she'd ever frightened me. Now she seemed big and slow and soft. "Nobody can make a girl swoon like old Swivel-Hips."

"He does have quite a voice," Tina chimed in, patting her hair. Frosted, and a pixie cut, Mimi had warned me.

"Like melted butter," Betty said.

"Especially the slow songs," Bev said, glancing at Tina, wanting, it seemed, the older woman to hear her.

"Nothin' but a pair of jelly hips and a microphone." Betty slapped her knee and howled with laughter.

"And blue suede shoes," Mimi said, beaming. Suddenly, she left the room, calling, "Be right back."

And then there she was, the blue suede shoes on her feet, her hand curled around something I couldn't see. "If you like this music, y'all, you'll love this." A wave kicked up in my stomach. When I saw my father's eyes move from Mimi's feet to her hands, his lips tightening, I began breathing hard.

"Now, I don't usually talk about this, but if we're going to be friends and share good times . . ."

"Simone." My father looked like he'd taken a big bite of something he couldn't swallow.

But moving gracefully to the center of the room, into an imaginary spotlight, my mother opened the locket, held it up, and with a push of her finger sent it into a gentle sway.

Betty marched up to have a look. "Darlin', that's you?"

Everyone stared, rapt.

"Yes, it's me. And Elvis." Mimi's hand fell to her side. "I dated the King."

There were open mouths and audible gasps, except for Roger, who peered closely at the picture and said, "Hey, Dan, you've put on a few."

My mother wagged a finger. "Roger, you must be blind as a bat. That's not Dan. That, my friends, is Elvis Presley."

"Simone, I don't think anyone's interested." My father's voice stretched tight.

"I am," said Betty, settling into a chair. "You dated Elvis?"

"You mean him?" Larry adjusted his glasses and held up an album cover.

"What other Elvis is there?" Bev said.

"Elvis the Pelvis?" Roger said, sounding jolly, gleeful, as if he were just now beginning to have a good time.

"Elvis Presley!" Betty said. "I'm fixin' to go into labor right here in the living room! What was he like?"

"Well, we went out to eat. We shared a piece of pie and a glass of milk with ice cubes." How proudly Mimi stood there, in an aura of devotion, the bells on her skirt jingling ever so slightly.

"Oh, I get it," Bev said. "We're playing something, like Truth or Dare. Was he nice?"

"Oh yes." Mimi's face glowed and her hands fluttered through the air. "He loved to talk about his mama. And how his music had a beat and . . . and I bet you didn't know that Elvis once worked in a furniture factory. In Tennessee. Before he became a star, I mean." My mother went on blithely talking, displaying the locket and the picture like a teacher pointing to a map in geography class.

Panic rising in my throat, I listened for the familiar rhythms of her tale, the beats and pauses I'd grown used to.

Roger and Tina stood poised, drinks midair. "Nothing but a fad," Roger said, dismissing the whole thing with a wave of his hand.

"Now, Roger," Mimi said. "Imagine it's nineteen fifty-six and on the hit parade you've got Doris Day singing 'Que Sera Sera' and Perry Como singing 'Hot Diggity' and along comes, Elvis singing 'Baby, Let's Play House.' Moving those hips."

"Just a fat boy dressed up in spangled . . ."

Mimi bristled. "Remember the 'sixty-eight–'sixty-nine comeback concert? Elvis was lean, passionate . . . *manly.* No one—not the Beatles, Mick Jagger, Bob Dylan—could replace him. He was still on top of the mountain."

Roger cocked an eyebrow and said, "And the Las Vegas Elvis? Sideburns. A jumpsuit with a high collar. For chrissakes, he wore a *cape.*"

"Yes!" Mimi said, triumphant. Her voice quavered with emotion. "We share a great fondness for capes."

Strained laughter welled up. A wary silence fell over the room. The longer she rhapsodized, the more the respectful faces of our guests seemed to cloud over with doubt, suspicion. Shame rose up inside me, like smoke from a fire you can't see. I felt sorry for my father, but at the same time I felt embarrassed for Mimi, trying so hard, pulling her story out of her pocket for people to admire and getting it all wrong.

"So you and Elvis Presley shared a fondness not only for capes but also for milk with ice cubes," Roger said, his face smug. Elvis came out as "Elvish" and everyone laughed. "Right. And Marilyn Monroe and I shared a fondness for . . ."

Tina jabbed him with her elbow. "My sister met Engelbert Humperdinck."

Mimi gave Tina a scornful look and turned her attention back to Roger. "Oh, Roger, I know the kind of man you are. You need *proof.* I respect that."

"Simone darlin', I can't believe you never told me something so . . . so . . . huge!" Betty said, struggling to her feet. Jim pulled her down.

"I wanted to!" Mimi said. "I just . . ."

"Maybe she thought it sounded a little half baked," Roger said. "But, hey, I've got a sense of humor, right, Larry?"

"Oh yes, sir, you do. A good one. I was just telling Bev, honey, wasn't I saying on the way over about the time . . ."

"Shut up, Larry," Roger said calmly, and I thought that those words probably had cause to come out of his mouth a hundred times a day. He grinned at Mimi. "So, Simone, what else did you share? Besides milk with ice cubes? I mean, how did it work? Elvis'd pick you up in his limo and you kids would take a spin around the block? You're what? Eighteen?"

"Sixteen. And we . . ." Now, under Roger's contemptuous gaze, Mimi seemed unsure, like a little kid on ice skates.

"You what?" Roger's eyes narrowed.

"Well, he drove me home and . . ."

"Simone." My poor father, red-faced, caught on top of a roller coaster waiting for the descent.

"Okay, well, the touch of his hand, the warmth, it was just . . ."

The very notion of Elvis's touch left Mimi breathless, a high rosy flush rising in her cheeks.

"She's something, Dan," Roger said. He seemed to be having trouble standing, and more than once, Tina reached out to steady him. "A real peach. Where did you find her? Alabama?"

"Mississippi," my father said, sounding tense.

"Now, sweetie pie," Roger said. "You leading us down a peach-tree path?"

Everyone studied Mimi curiously, shifting on their feet, an air of bafflement descending on the room. Tina played with her neck-lace; Bev bit her lip. Even Betty looked skeptical. "How many times did you go out with him?" she demanded, crossing her arms.

"A few," Mimi said, still standing in the middle of the room, de-flated now.

Roger hooked his arm around Tina's neck and pulled her close. "Let me get this straight. With old Swivel King you shared a glass of milk?"

"Well, we had pie too." Mimi licked her lips, her eyes darting nervously, like little fish scuttling off in different directions. One of her feet was turned in, like a child's. "Betty." She looked at her friend. "You believe me, don't you?"

"Well sure I do. But, honey, something this big, why didn't you tell me before?" Betty's eyes were full of hurt and pity, and I knew she didn't believe Mimi at all.

"You shared milk with ice cubes with Elvis but settled for a reg-ular guy like Dan?" Roger thundered.

"Dan's no regular guy," Mimi said, lifting her chin, looking at my father's face, which was very still. "He's salt of the earth."

"From Mr. Rock 'n' Roll to old salt-of-the-earth Sensible Shoes," Roger said.

Sure enough, there were my father's feet, in the brown suede Hush Puppies I'd always liked. His ears were crimson.

Roger clapped my father on the back. "You sure know how to

pick 'em, Dan." He winked, his florid face crumpling. "Will you bring your discriminating taste to our boardroom, I wonder?"

"Well, sir, I . . ." My father's words seemed to be knocking against each other, like bumper cars.

"He most certainly will," Mimi said, eyes flashing. "My husband is twice the man you'll ever be. He doesn't belittle, and he doesn't drink." The room filled with a stunned silence.

Bev coughed. Larry's hand shot into his pocket. Tina sighed and said, "Roger dear, it's time to go home."

"Yes, it's getting late, Larry," Bev said. "We should go."

"Oh, don't go," Mimi pleaded, her mouth puckered. "It's still early . . ."

"Actually, Simone," Betty said, her eyes fixed on her friend. "It's late." Her hand fluttered down to Simone's arm and away, as if she'd touched a hot stove.

"Did y'all know that Elvis dyed his hair? It wasn't naturally jet-black, it was a sandy brown. He dyed his eyebrows, too . . ."

The room took on the quiet of a library. Jim's low voice, sounding kind, broke the silence with the first words he'd said all evening. "Nice evening, Simone, Dan. I don't mind a story at all. An interesting life is made up of stories."

"Yes, every party needs a good tale or two," Larry said, placing his hand tentatively on Roger's shoulder.

Scowling, Roger swatted Larry's hand away. "Get your ass-kissing mitts off me."

That released a flurry of nods and general activity; people gathered their coats, thanked Mimi and my father, shuffled out, and said their good-byes, but with falsely cheerful tones.

I disappeared up the stairs before I got caught, but when I paused on the top step, I heard my mother's shrill voice. "Those people were animals. Not even a bone of decent kindness in their bodies. That Roger. What a boor. Why didn't you tell him to go to hell?"

"We threw this party for my career, remember?"

"I stuck up for you! I wasn't about to let anyone trample you. And those women—empty-headed. Not a bit stimulating. Just wives, Dan. I don't want that. I don't want to be just a wife!"

"I don't want to hear about you tonight, Simone."

"You're better than them all, Dan. You could be a great man, Like John F. Kennedy or Martin Luther King."

"Like Elvis?"

"You have the potential! You just need a little push."

"Oh, you pushed me all right. Right off a cliff. I can safely say you ruined my career. In your own inimitable style."

Mimi looked at my father as if for the first time that evening. Now she got weepy. "Oh, Dan, if anything, it will only be a tiny dent. I was trying to impress everybody. I thought I was helping."

"I don't need help," he said, and their voices trailed off.

I tiptoed to my room and sat down in front of my dollhouse thinking about Mimi and her story. It sure had power, but the wrong kind. It made my father's head hang low, as if he, in his Hush Puppies, wasn't enough. And weren't people funny? They'd do anything to stand next to a famous person, but say you'd shared pie and milk with one and they'd say you were lying. In her way, she'd been trying to help, to *decorate life*. I felt empty, sorry for both my parents, floundering in their roles, trying to please. But Mimi should have known better than to tell her story, tonight of all nights, and in a sudden longing that scared me, I wanted nothing to do with this grown-up world. And I wanted a different mother.

After a while, I got up, put on my nightgown, and tiptoed down the stairs, past the dishes piled high in the sink, the wine stain on the living room rug that Mimi would attack with a frenzy tomorrow. I slipped out the back door, stood outside on a patch of grass that Wolfie's chain had left flattened and brown. I'd never been outside alone at night before, and the effect was overwhelming: so much air, and the sky so dark it hurt my eyes, and so many clouds I couldn't find the moon. I remember being surprised that it was spring and that the breeze, which by day stirred the first green buds on every tree, was now eerily absent; there was only the soft chirping of crickets and the beckoning of the whole world beyond—the bike path where every summer I practiced riding with no hands, the neighborhood creek where Theo caught crayfish and snails in his red pail, the little wooden bridge that my mother liked to cross. Next door, along the Fishers' yard, the lacy heads of early lilacs nudged across the fence. The air smelled of rain, that springtime scent of fresh worms and wet dirt and cooked lettuce. Outside, I was calm, invisible, holding a part of myself away from my mother, opening myself to *possibility,* to something bigger than this house, this yard. As I stood there, a piece of me, the person I was, drifted up and out of me like breath, leaving only a shell of a girl behind, a shadow girl, dutiful, clean, and smiling, always smiling. My mother wouldn't even know I was gone.

CHAPTER 8

Thanksgiving Day dawned crisp and dry, the sky a bright, fearless blue, with only a few high, fluffy clouds. We stood on the porch of my mother's house, my hand above the knocker. I was ambivalent: Knock or run?

Scottie, seeing me hesitate, raised his hand to knock.

"Wait!" I said. I was nervous. "There are some things you should know."

"Like what?"

"My stepfather, Henry. He doesn't talk. He whispers. Waitresses are always bringing him the wrong order. And he has, like, a hundred cotton turtlenecks, all earth tones, which he wears even in summer, because he's allergic to fabric."

Scottie laughed. "Silvie, you're just nervous."

"I don't even have a key to my own house. I bet you think that's weird."

"I hadn't thought that, no."

"I don't have a key because it's not my house, it's my mother's house. I mean, I've never lived here. My father doesn't live here."

"Well, sure. Your parents are divorced. I wouldn't expect your father to live here."

"Right."

"Hey." Scottie squeezed my hand. "Calm down. I've met families before. All families are a little nuts."

"A family where the stepfather doesn't talk and the brother has purple hair and the daughter doesn't have a key?"

"Your brother has purple hair?"

"Um, lavender, actually."

"That's it, I'm outta here."

I grabbed his arm. "And—my mother's on morphine." I took a deep breath, shaking my head to compose myself.

Scottie's hand was poised above the knocker, but he didn't knock. "Hey, I know all this." He took my face in his hands. "I want to be here, okay? You do too." Pivoting my shoulders so that I faced the door, he curled my fingers over the brass knocker, the way you'd teach a child to knock. And I knocked.

◆ ◆ ◆

"Nice to meet you," Henry whispered, opening the door. Today, in a terra-cotta turtleneck, he kissed my cheek and extended his hand to Scottie. Mimi, who had once swept into a room, a glamorous peacock, now stood an uncharacteristic step behind him, looking pale and thin, her collarbone sharp and her face weathered, like the side of a house after a kid's been throwing a ball against it all summer. Without meaning to, I drew in a sharp breath. I realized how terrified I'd been to see what she looked like. Would she be thin, brittle? Would she break if I hugged her? She looked as if she could.

Under the brass light fixture, she seemed smaller than I remembered, opening her arms slowly to my hug. Life had shrunk her down to miniature size; we could carry her in our pockets, I thought. She wore a scarf on her head. A strange feeling spread over my skin: too many molecules of air to protect her from.

She smiled over my shoulder at Scottie, cooing, "You must be Scottie."

"And you must be Simone." He looked her straight in the eye, ever the doctor, radiating goodwill and connection.

"I am indeed." She inspected him, taking in his brown hair, the color of cola and curly, recently cut, a little short. "Theo," she called to my brother, who bounded around the corner, his hair leading the way like a flag. Purple, all right. The exact shade of a grape Popsicle.

Seeing Theo, Scottie thrust out his hand, a happy puppet springing from a box, big and floppy and safe as a winter glove. Theo shook it in his friendly, open manner. Three small silver hoops trembled on his right ear, tiny as dolls' earrings.

As Theo bent to give me a kiss, his other ear revealed a colony of little charms: a skull, a hammer, a dangling man—like the tiny playing pieces in Clue. "Hiya, Sil," he said.

I squeezed his hand, my eyes glued to Mimi, who had a ratty tissue balled in her fist. Her jaw seemed swollen, and there was a faint blue smudge around the bridge of her nose, which you see on newborn babies.

A click sounded down the hall and a door opened, spilling out a girl who could only have been Theo's girlfriend, Claire. Large brown eyes, alabaster skin, a mouth festooned with the blackest lipstick I'd ever seen. A black camisole and a black crinoline, combat boots, thick gray athletic socks cuffed at the ankle—she was a sight in monochrome, except for the hair, which was certainly green, as Theo had warned me, green as early June grass, fresh, lush, verdant, green-green: far from olive, and not calm, either. She was gripping a 7-Eleven Big Gulp, sucking on the straw with a swallow so healthy that her nose ring quivered.

Theo introduced us. I stared at the small hoop dangling from her left nostril and soon I was lost in a maze of speculation about sneezing, kissing.

Scottie nudged me. I stared at him, too, so that she would think staring was just something I did. "Hello," I said.

"Hello," Claire said, never taking the straw from her mouth.

"Now, Claire, don't drink too much Coke before dinner," Mimi warned, and I thought of all the times she'd said that to me.

For Mimi, Claire flashed a surprisingly easy, incongruous grin. "Okay."

I felt a little weak at the knees. Who was this girl, appropriating my mother? Who was this mother, thin as a pencil, tenuous as a cloud?

We walked toward the kitchen, Scottie hanging back in solidarity with my mother, bent toward her like a question mark, uncertain of what he, as a new acquaintance, could give her. I walked ahead, not yet part of Scottie, no longer part of her.

"Your stirrup pants are so slimming," Mimi said to me, stopping abruptly as the others moved on. Never once in our lives together had she been shy, and yet here she was ducking her head, her fingertips scurrying to tie her scarf's unraveled corners into small rabbit ears.

I turned and faced her squarely, placing both my hands on her shoulders, a thing I'd never done. I felt the way a new mother must feel: overwhelmed with love for someone I hardly knew.

Suddenly, she whipped the scarf off. "You like it?" she said, and I looked at her hair—straw-colored, straight, too shiny. Brittle.

"It's a wig. Exactly the color and style of my real hair."

"It looks great. I wouldn't even know."

She looked directly at me. "Didn't I teach you never to tell a lie?"

◆ ◆ ◆

In the white kitchen, we roasted a twenty-pound bird, made mashed potatoes, stuffing, creamed onions, green-bean casserole for Theo, tiny peas, cranberry sauce, and the old lime Jell-O salad that no one could give up. Mimi wouldn't allow her housekeeper, Letty, to help with the meal. She wanted to make the food herself. Her hand, shaky but determined, cracked a cardboard tube of Pillsbury crescent rolls against the counter until it sprang open, releasing white, rubbery circles. She scored frozen pumpkin and pecan pies with a knife and whipped up the cream. Then, clearly exhausted, she assigned me the potatoes and returned to her regal position at the table, directing traffic with her voice.

By three-thirty, we were seated at the table, which Letty had set, passing the food around wrong. Scottie asked for salt and got pepper; Theo wanted green beans and got creamed onions from Henry, who, noticing his mistake, looked down at his hand, startled, flexing it to be sure it was his. I overturned a basket of hot rolls into Henry's lap. No one said grace.

Mimi glanced at Theo and said, holding a bite of food in her mouth without chewing, "Theo, you don't eat meat anymore? Not even turkey?"

Theo paused, fork laden with mashed potatoes. "No."

"This is that vegetarian thing?" Mimi frowned. She put down the good silver fork and looked at him closely.

"Yes, it's that vegetarian thing. Don't spaz about it."

"I'm just asking." Mimi skated her fork around her plate, leaning her forehead against her palm, bangs pushed up.

There was a long space of silence, which Scottie filled by asking Henry to pass the cranberry sauce. Henry did, dribbling cranberries on the tablecloth, which bloomed into a large pink rose.

"I myself say you need a little brain food," Mimi said.

"Oh, don't worry, Simone. We do protein," Claire said.

Henry leaned over and patted Mimi's arm. "Baby, this is something he wants to try."

My mother scowled. "Well, here we are gathered around the table as one big, happy family and we haven't even asked Scottie to tell us what he does," she said, taking a small bite of turkey. "What kind of doctor are you?"

"ER," he said, taking off his glasses. "I just finished my residency. I started out in pediatrics, but the ER hooked me."

"It's nice to change your mind. Theo's changing his right now. About what, I'm not sure. Same with Silvie, something about her work. I guess all young people change their minds. It's a specialty of this house for sure."

Scottie laughed. "Good. I'll fit right in then." He was feeling at home, I could tell, a relaxed smile on his face, his hands sweeping expansively as he spoke. Of course. He was comfortable with the sick.

Without warning, Mimi pushed her chair back and stood up. Then she floated out of the room as if a magnet were pulling her.

A heavy silence fell over the table. We all averted our eyes, chewing solemnly until she returned a few minutes later with a box of pastels, and then we let out a collective sigh of relief. Standing behind her chair, she lifted the lid and showed us the crayons in a neat row of thirty-six shades. The sudden fan of color resembled a tiny, portable rainbow.

"I want to tell you, Scottie, about the cancer center Henry and I visited. They promote laughter and play. You know—*self-expression*. For healing. I'm even trying to keep a journal. Silvie's great at it, but she sure didn't get that from me. I write for a few days and then I lose interest."

What had I been doing the weekend she went to the cancer center? Eating out, doing a marathon movie session with Scottie, three in a night?

"What exactly do you do at the center?" Scottie blotted his lips on a napkin.

"Oh, Simone, show your pictures." Claire was now chewing the ice from her water glass, green hair glinting in the light.

Proudly, almost shyly, Mimi displayed a drawing of small, colorful flowers. "I draw in my journal more than write. As you can see." Peonies, dozens of peonies. Usually, she painted abstracts, bold ribbons of black or gray with streaks of red, and sometimes mixed in bits of fabric, creating a strange kind of collage. They looked like she'd analyzed her life and come to the conclusion that it lacked a design, was just color and texture filling space.

"Your old stuff was more interesting, Mom," Theo said.

"Well, look at this one." Mimi flipped the pages and, still standing, a little unsteady on her feet, held up another watercolor.

It really wasn't very good, I realized. My stuff was better. Thinking that made me nervous. I shoveled food into my mouth.

"Dr. Meyers gave us paper and a set of colored pencils and said, 'Draw a picture of yourself, your treatment, your disease, and the white blood cells eliminating the disease.' My mother spoke with the increasing fervor of someone trying to convince herself. "They say that one develops an illness when one tries to be who they are not. You must open to who you are. Like you, Theo. The vegetarian."

Theo raised an eyebrow.

"See, here's me and here's my heart." She pointed to her drawing of herself, thin in black palazzo pants, the blond wig perky, cute, her hands hidden behind her back. Through the blouse, a red heart, shaped like a Valentine's Day heart; another heart was lodged in the pelvis. "That's the cancer," she said. "Shaped like a heart, because I've loved too much." Connected to the two hearts was an IV with three hanging bottles, and daggers and arrows with more hearts flying out of them. "These hearts avenge the cancer," she explained. "Do you think that's crazy, Scottie?"

"Not at all. Think of Norman Cousins, who watched videotapes of comedies and laughed himself into health. It would be good to visualize that every day."

"Oh, I do!" Mimi's cheeks flushed with pleasure. "Get this—Dr. Meyers went around and looked at all our pictures, just like in an art class. He stopped behind my chair and said, 'Simone, where are your hands? In this wonderful picture you've drawn, you have no hands.'

"I looked down at my page and, sure enough, I hadn't drawn hands! 'Dr. Meyers,' I said. 'You're right. I haven't drawn hands. What does that mean?' He said, 'Well, people take care of themselves by using their hands. I would have to wonder, how are you going about getting your needs met?' I thought for a minute, but, well, that's not a question you can answer right away."

"No," Scottie said.

"Oh no," Henry chimed in, almost inaudibly.

"This guy's saying that if you get your needs met, you get better?" Theo asked.

Mimi nodded.

"Then the real question is, What are your needs?" Theo fixed his intense gaze on her.

"Yes," she said quietly. "That's it, isn't it. You have to have the courage to examine your life. 'Something else,' Dr. Meyers said. 'You have no feet.' I looked down again and, yessiree, I hadn't drawn feet."

We all peered at the long legs that ran off the page. No shoes; no feet. Simone, my mother, who had been named after shoes and had owned dozens of pairs, hadn't drawn them in her self-portrait.

"Dr. Meyers said, 'With no feet, I'd look at core beliefs, groundedness . . .' "

"Roots, foundations," Henry added.

"Exactly." Mimi looked down at her picture. "Whew. I guess my roots and foundations need work."

"A whole new way to look at disease," Henry commented, folding his napkin into a neat square. "A holistic approach. Ironically, exactly the paradigm I use in my dental practice: Look at the whole person to discover why the teeth aren't healthy."

"I don't get it," Theo said.

Mimi said, "If your ear hurts, you have to ask yourself what you don't want to hear." She smiled a radiant smile, and for a moment, with her watercolors and tablets and pictures a jumble in her arms, cancer seemed an accessory, like a new lipstick, something to try to enhance her beauty.

"That makes it your own fault," Theo said.

"Like you blame yourself . . ." I nodded, stabbing a piece of turkey I couldn't eat.

"Maybe I do," Mimi said. Clutching her journal to her thin chest, she sat down clumsily, almost missing her chair. I wanted to reach out across the table to her. The edge of the Groshong catheter peeked out of her blouse, the skin around it pink and swollen. In the sunlight's glare, a blotch of makeup Mimi had smeared, trying to cover the redness. I looked away, feeling frightened.

Claire's arm shot out past Theo to rub Mimi's back. Across from them, I frowned, envious that Claire could touch her so easily.

Mimi winced, her face ashen, and I realized she was in pain. Her bright red cardigan sweater and white blouse bunched up around her chest, the collar scraping her chin. Around her waist was the morphine pump, a small black box with white buttons.

"Speaking of small purses, Silvie, have I showed you this thing? Does everything but whistle Dixie." She sounded almost excited, crowing about her latest fashion find. "When I need to, I push a button and it spurts a bolus into my system."

"A bolus?"

"A dose of morphine." She hit the button. "There."

We'd all stopped eating, utensils poised, and now we resumed our meal just as Mimi's eyes fluttered and went soft. Her whole face seemed to melt; her giggle turning high, childish.

Letty had opened the curtains in the dining room and the late-afternoon sun made a circle of light on the pale carpeting. An orange ceramic bowl in the middle of the table seemed to hold not only grapes and pears and apples but a promise of growing families, future Thanksgivings.

Mimi's head drooped momentarily, then she snapped it back up and said in a thick voice, "Well, Scottie, I sure hope things work out with you and Silvie. She needs a good . . ."

Henry, who had been deep into a low-decibel conversation with Theo and Claire about the sanctity of combining legumes with a starch for complete protein, coughed loudly into his cloth napkin, the kind we used only on holidays.

Scottie's smile was too bright. My leg jumped under the table, and I kicked my brother.

"Ah, what the fuck was that?" he cried.

"No swearing on Thanksgiving!" Claire said slyly, tilting her green head back and slurping from the Big Gulp.

". . . man," Mimi finally finished.

Scottie gave me a steady look, amusement in his eyes. My family was still a game to him, like the models he liked to construct: Attach skull to spine, spine to pelvis; seal with glue.

"You play guitar, right, Theo?" Scottie said. "What's the name of your band?"

"Boy Toy," Claire said, chomping on an ice cube.

"I'm a feminist," Theo explained, both he and Claire bursting into laughter.

Scottie considered this and, after a polite minute, continued unfazed. "How did you two meet?"

"Claire asked *me* out," Theo said. "To a vivisection lecture. From there, things just . . . cooked."

Scottie spoke in a mock-serious voice. "Sure. I've found that seeing slides of quartered animals is a real turn-on . . ."

Theo grinned. "Yeah, well, we're both vegan now. No animal products at all. Not even honey."

"You can't just *be* a vegetarian," Mimi said. "You have to have a *plan.*"

"Scottie, you probably know that babies cannot eat honey until they're a year old," Henry said. "There's a certain kind of poison . . ."

"Botulism," Scottie said, nodding.

"So what do you think of Claire's nose ring?" Theo interrupted. "Awesome, huh?"

"I'd do mine if I could," Mimi said.

I looked at her.

"Oh shush, old Mrs. Grundy," she snapped.

"More potatoes?" Letty bustled in, her bronzed, chubby cheeks lifting in a shy smile, her dark almond eyes fixing on Mimi with their quiet strength.

Claire cleared her throat and tossed her green hair, nose ring dancing merrily in the waning afternoon light. "I'd like to make an announcement. In my family, on Thanksgiving, we play Go Around the Table. Sounds silly, I know, but it's cool."

Grateful as I was for a chance to lighten things up, the game sounded so feeble that I had to raise my eyebrows to Theo, who shrugged and echoed my thoughts cheerfully. "Sounds pretty lame to me," he said.

"Go around the table?" Henry asked gamely.

Claire nodded, the nose ring breaking into a merry frolic. "We go around the table and say what we're thankful for."

"Okay," Mimi said, voice girlish and high.

"Sounds Thanksgiving-ish," Scottie agreed.

Henry nodded. "I'm in."

"Oh, punkin, let's not and say we did," Theo said, reaching out to tickle Claire. She punched him, this time initiating a mock fist-fight.

"Claire wants to pierce her lip next," Theo said. "It's totally awesome now to pierce your lip or your eyebrow or your . . ."

"Navel," Scottie said.

"Exactly!" Theo said, looking at Scottie with new appreciation.

For the first time in what felt like forever, my mother and I shared a smile across the table.

Claire said, "I'll start. I'm thankful to be here with such a nice family." Her eyes grew misty. She adjusted the tiny hoop in her nose.

"Yeah, well, I'll be thankful if this is the last Thanksgiving we play fucking go around the table," Theo said.

"That's a lovely sentiment, Claire," Henry said, ignoring Theo. "We're happy to have you."

"I can't hear you, Henry," Mimi said loudly. "Why are you always whispering?"

"Right on, man," Theo muttered, flashing a smile of approval.

Henry rubbed his chin as if she'd given him a right hook. Mimi just pressed the fork to her lips and took a tiny bite, her voice turning syrupy-sweet. "Ummm, the stuffing is delicious, Henry." She glanced at me and lifted her eyebrows.

"Great, Henry," I piped up dutifully.

"Your turn, Theo," Claire said.

Absently, Theo began tapping his two index fingers on the table in a series of complicated rhythms. "Here goes," he said. "I'm not exactly thankful for anything but . . . well, Ma, I gotta tell you about something I got."

My foot groped wildly for his under the table. "It can wait, Theo," I said.

Mimi's hand froze, her glass halfway to her lips. Her mouth opened and closed like a wound. "Who'd you get it from?"

"Mom! It's a tattoo." Theo allowed his fingers an extravagant trot through his hair.

The word blinked out like a neon sign. Mimi's glass met the tablecloth with a thud. Scottie and I sipped coffee, busily adding sugar to the sugar we'd already added, stirring a tad too vigorously. Letty posed in the doorway, a pie in each hand, lips parted.

Theo stood up, announcing with a flourish, "No time like a family holiday to bare all!" And with that, he grinned, lifted his leg, and pulled up his jeans to his knee, revealing, on his ankle, a garish red-and-blue cartoon pig leaping through a flaming hoop.

All eyes turned to Mimi, who wiped a line of sweat from her upper lip. "Oh, son. I had hoped it would say MOM in a big red heart."

We all burst out laughing, Theo with the too-loud laughter of relief. "Next time it will, Mom, don't you worry."

"It better," she said, tossing her napkin on the table, touching the tip of her nose and both of her pale cheeks. "Now if y'all will excuse me, I have to go powder my nose."

I watched her stand, terrified she'd leave, terrified she'd stay. But she didn't leave. She just stood there, then lowered her body slowly, painfully back into her chair and stared distractedly, almost peacefully, into the candle flame, her expression grim, resigned. The worst part of dying must be looking down at the people you love, seeing what you think are their mistakes, seeing they'll go on without you. She lifted a spoon to point at Letty.

"Blow that out will you?" she said. Letty did, efficiently, and Mimi seemed on the verge of making a speech. In anticipation, Theo drummed on the tablecloth, like the steady beat of rain on hard-packed dirt.

Mimi leaned forward, her glasses slipping off her head and coming to a bumpy landing on her nose, where they wobbled and perched, slightly askew. When she raised her eyes, she seemed to be deciding something, and for a fleeting second, she looked young and pretty, her face small beneath the wig. "My turn."

Not one of us moved a muscle. I had a single thought: How easy could it be to feel thankful when you're full of morphine, when you're dying?

Quickly, Mimi slid her arms off the table and into her lap. "Mabel, Mabel, take your elbows off the table." She sat still as stone, staring at a wisp of smoke curling up from the candle. "I'm thankful for the night I spent with Elvis."

"Now, baby, you didn't really . . ." Henry started to object.

"Speak up, will you? I never had any trouble hearing Dan."

"You knew Elvis Presley?" Scottie's eyes were bright with interest. He turned to me. "You never told me."

"I was saving it for Christmas," I said dryly.

"These days, I carry all my memories in a jar," Mimi said. "Elvis loved his mama, Silvie. Remember that."

I fidgeted in my seat.

"Now, *you're* not Silvie's fiancé, are you?" Mimi looked at Scottie. "You can't be. I remember, he was taller."

"I'm the guy," Scottie said gently.

I touched his knee. "You don't have to say . . ."

"Sssh." He squeezed my hand under the table.

Mimi's eyes smoldered. "Silvie, you're not pregnant again, are you? Tell Mama the truth. You don't have to marry him just because you're pregnant. In my day you did, but there are options today."

I looked pleadingly at Scottie, who seemed to be calm as a winter lake. "Mimi, I'm not pregnant; I've never been pregnant. And I'm not getting married."

"Yet." Scottie looked at me.

"Well, congratulations, you two." Now her voice was higher, tiny and far away, as if it came from a TV in another room. "I wish for you as much happiness as Dan and I have."

Theo and I shared a glance. Henry, speechless, let out a dry cough.

"Do you do drugs, Scottie?" Mimi was on a roll.

"Do I . . ."

I massaged my temples, whispered to Scottie, "What are the symptoms of a migraine?"

"Don't beat around the bush, boy," Mimi said. "Theo's been stoned since grade school. Silvie would be too if she weren't worried about increasing her appetite. And Henry? Always swilling Chivas. And look at me, so high on morphine you could fly me to Chicago and wash the windows on the Sears Tower."

In spite of ourselves, we all laughed. The sky outside the windows had darkened while we ate; dusk was dissolving into night.

"Only the prescription kind, Simone. Sorry."

"Ah well. I'm so tired I feel like I died and forgot to drop." Mimi coughed once and didn't stop.

Trembling, my hand flew up to my own chest; I was gripped with a sudden cold.

"Have you had that cough looked at?" Scottie asked.

"A touch of pneumonia, I think." Mimi cupped a hand over her mouth and rubbed her chest, staring across the room and out the window. Abruptly, she got up, and we watched her drift from room to room, a thin, wraithlike figure pausing in each doorway.

The rest of us huddled forlornly around the table, studying a smattering of drops and dribbles that had stained the white tablecloth.

"It might be in her lungs," Henry said in a voice we had to strain to hear. "Don't say anything."

Hearing that death was inevitable jolted me. I had to haul my breath up from deep in my stomach. I should be preparing myself, but how?

"Why not?" Theo demanded. "Why not say something?"

"Because," Claire snapped, pushing back her chair and departing for the bathroom in a torrent of emotion, the way a teenager leaves home.

"Dr. Tilden says her cancer is progressing very fast," Henry said. "She's stopped all chemotherapy treatments. There will be a few more radiation treatments, but just for pain control."

"Just for pain control?" I said.

"There's nothing else they can do."

After this sank in, Scottie said gently, "There's another school of thought. And that is to always tell the truth. Patients deserve to be treated with respect."

"Exactly!" Theo said, but before Henry and I could respond, Mimi appeared at the table, now wearing a red fringed sweatshirt and red leggings, wig perfectly brushed and dark Coffee Bean lipstick heavy as chocolate on her chapped lips. Her eyes were wide and foggy; she wore a brilliant smile. I waited to hear what she'd say next, my heart rising to my throat. Stopping near Scottie's chair, she touched his arm. "You really are a long drink of water, aren't you?"

He smiled. "My mom says that."

"You know, I used to be the kind of woman who scrubbed the refrigerator with a toothbrush," she said apologetically, her voice thick and gummy. "Every corner of my house sparkled." She waved her hand around as if to say, *Everywhere.*

He reached up and patted her hand. "Looks great to me."

Walking slowly to the other side of the table, she eased herself back into her seat and lifted her mug to her chin, warming her jawline, eyes hot, feverish. Mimi curved her sad face toward me. "Silvie, I fear you won't be good at love, because I haven't been able to teach you how."

"She does just fine." Scottie touched my hand.

"So hurry the hell up. Go for it. Sometimes you have to wear big boots and jump right in."

My mouth opened and shut.

Scottie's face, to my surprise, shone bright.

"Although you should know what you're jumping into. Silvie's a deep lake. Muddy. High-maintenance, if you know what I mean. And you sure better make enough to hire a maid."

Stung, I bit the inside of my cheek. Scottie lowered his eyes.

"Mimi, let me get you more tea," I said weakly, practically wrenching the teacup from her hands.

She lurched upright and followed me into the kitchen. "You can't do that by yourself, can you?"

"I think I'm capable." I stood with my hand on the kettle, still reeling from her words, wanting to but unable to fight back.

Mimi sidled up next to me, the window above the sink dark, the spectacle at the table already a thing of the past. "I like him." She smiled.

"Great. Because he probably doesn't like me anymore."

"Oh, relax. You know what I always said. You get the guy, I'll get the dress."

She meant a dress for her—the mother-of-the-bride dress.

I had thought there was promise here, an opportunity to solve at least some of the mysteries from the past, that maybe, just maybe, real knowledge was within my reach. Now I wasn't so sure. What was she trying to prove—that even sick, she still had the power to crush me, to bring me to my knees?

I stood at the sink, turned on the water as hot as I could stand it, thrust my arms into it, let it course over my fingers, my wrists, up past my elbows. Along the night at the edge of the window, the small veins of a flowering plant. Outside, the stars just tiny lights pushing through the skin of sky. From the water, steam billowed up, and in the fog on the window I wrote my initials: S.P. S.P. S.P.P. Silvie Page Perlman. Then I smudged them out with my fist. I stared at my face in the glass. Behind me, the dark shadow of my mother's bent head. Then she turned and walked away and there was nothing left but my own reflection.

CHAPTER 9

My new friend in seventh grade, Martine LaRue, gave me courage. Martine was a spindly girl with curly pumpkin-colored hair, huge eyes the color of milk chocolate, skinny arms and legs, and no mother. Her mother had died when she was in second grade. The whole school knew her mother was dead, and that's how I knew Martine LaRue for years without really knowing her. Her father, Bernard, was a lawyer. She had no brothers or sisters. Every day, her father waited for her by the door of the elementary school wearing a suit. Rumor had it that he wouldn't let her take the bus and that after school, she went to his office and played underneath his desk. Once, a while after her mother had died, Mimi felt sorry for her and invited her to our house, but Martine wouldn't come.

Finally, five years later, I'd gone to her house. The LaRues had a Portuguese housekeeper, Carlota, who cooked and told Martine when to do her homework. But Martine didn't do homework. She played with Flatsy dolls, although she admitted she was too old for them. She had the whole collection, and also a Woodburning Kit, a Spirograph, a Magic 8 Ball, a Ouija board, all the *Little House* books, and a canopy bed *and* a chemistry set, something I longed for but Mimi thought was dangerous.

Martine wore velour skirts and matching tops, whose too-short sleeves she tugged down over her wrists—maroon velour, navy velour, striped velour, even flowered velour—and her tights always matched. She wore clunky brown leather tie-shoes every day. Mimi said one would think a mother was behind that velour, but those brown shoes were all man.

One weekend my mother, saying she wanted to give Martine the feel of a real home, invited her to stay at my house because her father was out of town. On Saturday afternoon, we were sitting at the table while my mother moved around the kitchen making lunch. My father was due home from a business trip any minute. Theo was studying the liner notes to *Jesus Christ Superstar,* his newest obsession. Lately, he was worrying my mother sick by walking around in her old white bathrobe and flip-flops.

Theo began to sing in a low voice: "Hosanna Heysanna Sanna Sanna Ho . . ."

I rolled my eyes, but Martine listened politely, and when he paused, she said, "I like musicals, too."

Theo studied her seriously, considering this affinity. "What's that?" he asked, pointing to Martine's wrist.

"It's an MIA bracelet my father got for me. To honor a soldier in Vietnam."

"Cool," I said. It was. Only a few kids at school had them.

"I know all about Vietnam," Theo was saying. "From *Hair.*"

"I love that show."

"Isn't that sweet?" Mimi floated from the stove to me, whispering in my ear. "They're getting along."

Frowning, I took Martine's elbow, gently, and led her away from my mother and brother. "This is my room," I said, uncurling Martine's fingers from where they clenched her suitcase handle. I set it down on my bed. It was a small suitcase, brown, worn, peeling in places. "You can unpack now." Opening a drawer, I pushed my socks and underwear to one side.

Martine plopped down on the edge of my bed, the tips of her shoes turned in and touching, the way Theo's feet had when he was born. She looked all around, her eyes skimming over the navy-blue-and-green-striped bedspread edged with olive-green fringe balls. Mimi had nixed pink and purple. Martine's gaze slowed down and fixed on the long bolster at the head of my bed, where most kids had pillows. Mimi had made it; sewed on the fringe balls herself. She said the look of a bolster was modern and contemporary and I should be proud to be the only one of all the kids in our neighborhood to have one.

"What's that?"

"A bolster."

"Oh."

"It's contemporary."

"It's kind of weird." Her eyes wandered to the fake window Mimi had painted on my wall because my room had no windows. "Who painted that?"

I whirled my head around and felt my cheeks flush. "My mom."

"She's a good artist."

"I guess so." Wanting to divert Martine's attention, I moved toward her suitcase, unfastening the brass buckles. "There," I said, satisfied at the loud noise they made.

But Martine's brown eyes only flickered from the suitcase before fixing on the window again.

"Oh," I said, startled. Inside her suitcase were a pair of thin white underpants folded in quarters and a faded pink nightgown, a line of ripped lace around the bottom. Another velour outfit lay on top, this time in blue. No weekend clothes. On top lay a toothbrush wrapped in toilet paper and a stuffed hairless animal that might once have been a brown mouse. I stared at the things for what seemed like a long time, then looked up at her. She was rubbing an invisible spot on her knee.

"You can wear my stuff," I said.

"It won't fit."

"Don't worry." It seemed important that she not worry. "My mother'll make you something. She designs clothes. She won second place once in a big sewing contest. On Sundays, she makes banana fritters," I added, in case the sewing wasn't enough. I wanted her to like my mother. Maybe then she'd like me, too.

Martine's eyes were fastened on the phony window. "I guess she wanted to make sure it never rains in your room."

"What do you mean?"

"Blue sky, sunshine. All the time."

I had never thought of it that way, but Mimi had painted blue sky in all four of the panes and, in one, a tree with a red robin in its branches. Martine was right—whenever I looked out my bedroom window, I saw blue sky.

"Why do you call your mother Mimi?" she asked.

"I don't know. One day I just started calling her that."

"My mother's name was Vivian," she said. "But if she was still here, I would call her Mom."

"I bet she was very nice." I put her things inside my drawer. I didn't want her to feel sad; not for one second.

Martine nodded. "She was."

She brightened when I pulled my Bonne Bell Bubble Gum Lip Smacker from my pocket. I was always the first to have cool drugstore stuff, a benefit of having Mimi for a mother and a trade-off for all the clothes she'd sewn me. Martine applied the lip gloss, then tried on my puka shells and sniffed my bottle of Love's Baby Soft. Finally, I said, "Come on. Let's eat."

In the kitchen, my mother was putting a hot dog in front of Theo, who ate only hot dogs, peanut butter, no jelly, and grilled cheese with maple syrup. Yesterday, dressed as Jesus, he'd dipped a piece of Wonder bread into his grape juice and my mother went through the roof.

My father walked in the door and slung his raincoat over the chair. To Martine, we must have looked like the perfect family— Theo and I hugging him and my mother tilting her cheek for his kiss.

My father looked surprised to see Martine there; I rarely invited friends over. "Dad," I said proudly. "This is Martine."

"Hi, Martine. Nice to have you."

Pleased at my manners, my mother smiled and held out a plate. "Tuna fish sandwiches with fresh dill and watercress."

"Watercress, Martine, is fancy lettuce," my father explained, sitting next to Theo, who was eating his hot dog, his upper lip smeared with grape juice.

Martine looked doubtful.

"Delish," Mimi said. "You'll like it, I promise. If not, I know you'll like my homemade lemonade and brownies."

She brought out plates of sandwiches, a pitcher of lemonade, and a big bag of potato chips. We sat down.

"Martine, you wanna listen to *Jesus Christ Superstar* with me when you're done?" Theo asked.

"No, Theo, she doesn't," I said. "Mom, Martine needs some clothes for relaxing." I spoke with my mouth full of peppery watercress—I was used to it.

"Only have glad rags, do you, Martine?" My father looked up from his sandwich.

Martine smiled shyly.

"I can trim your hair, too, honey," my mother said.

I glanced at Martine. I hoped she wasn't insulted. Mimi cut

everybody's hair, even my father's. She spread an old sheet under a chair in the kitchen and you had to hold still. She taped your bangs for an even line, and when she was through, she yanked the tape off, tapping her fingers against your forehead to quiet the sting.

"You don't have to if you don't want to," I said.

Martine shrugged. "I want to."

By Sunday afternoon, we both had a pair of matching bell bottoms and short bangs, like sisters, and we'd each played Judas and Mary to Theo's Jesus about a hundred times, holding tall candles for microphones.

Sunday night, Theo tattooed the insides of his wrists with red Magic Marker nail holes and my parents hid the *Jesus Christ Superstar* album in the cabinet above the refrigerator, next to the dusty bottle of vodka. Theo was like Mimi, the way he jumped in head-first and didn't come back up; but for once, I didn't care to dwell on my mother. I had a friend.

◆ ◆ ◆

Over time, I understood why I'd been so attracted to Martine. There was something open in the way she hung her sadness out on her sleeve, while I pushed mine down into that tight little bead no one could see, filling the space with emptiness, nothingness. Behind her sadness were energy and spunk and something I feared I lacked—a *self*.

We became inseparable.

◆ ◆ ◆

At her house, the summer we turned thirteen, we smoked. Martine dug out a pack of cigarettes buried in the toe of a pair of her father's old black shoes. We practiced inhaling and blowing smoke rings, safe in the garage, where the smell wouldn't waft into the house. We only coughed a little.

"Isn't this fun?" Martine murmured. "I think it's very satisfying."

"Yes," I answered gravely, trying not to cough, feeling mature. "I see why people smoke."

"From now on, we'll smoke, okay?"

"Okay." Something not to tell Mimi.

After we smoked down to our fingertips, we went out the garage door to her backyard. Martine dug a hole in the dirt by the bushes with the toe of her brown shoes and buried the butts.

"My mother was a beautiful actress," Martine said, staring down at the mound of dirt. "And a dancer. She danced in *Guys and Dolls* and *No, No, Nanette* at the Shubert Theatre in Chicago."

"Wow."

"She met my father in Evanston. He was in law school at Northwestern. Vivian had the most beautiful wavy red hair. And she loved dogs. Before I was born, she had a Yorkie named Isadora Duncan." She kicked at the dirt with her toe. "She got pregnant with me just when *South Pacific* went into rehearsals. She used to throw up backstage, then go do the play. When I grow up, I'm moving to Chicago to be an actress. Whatever talent I have, I get from my mother. At least, I hope I have talent." Martine had a way of telling me things that made me feel it was okay to tell her things, too.

"I'm gonna be an artist." I liked to sing, too, and I'd been practicing in my room, prancing around in only a baby-doll pajama top and white shiny vinyl go-go boots, eyelids sparkling with Mimi's blue-frosted eye shadow, mouth smeared with lipstick from an old tube of Ripe. On this stage, I was the star.

"I miss my mother. Every day of my life. Isn't that stupid?"

"No," I said quietly, my eyes resting on three bicycles in the back of the garage. One must have been Vivian's. "Want to listen to *Sgt. Pepper's* and I can do your makeup?" I tried to imagine what it would be like not having a mother, but it was like driving a car on empty. I didn't get very far. As horrible as Mimi could be, I couldn't imagine her gone.

◆ ◆ ◆

Sometimes, Mimi asked what Martine and I did together.

"Um, we listen to her forty-fives or watch *Lost in Space*. Martine likes to make Jell-O One-Two-Three."

"What else?" Mimi wrapped her hand around her bent knee.

"One day we decoupaged all her old Holly Hobbie paper dolls. I don't know. Stuff." I didn't tell her about the smoking or about the albums her father had given her—the Beatles, Bob Dylan, the Rolling Stones. We knew all the lyrics.

Our friendship puzzled Mimi. She hadn't known anything like it with her mother or her sisters, although she was growing closer to Sweet Nina Baby as she got older. "Well, you girls certainly seem to have fun together." I realized that except for Betty, who Mimi was always quarreling with, I was my mother's only friend.

◆ ◆ ◆

The morning was noisy, a regular school morning; I was a jittery seventh-grader, and Theo possessed a third-grader's swagger. It came, I guessed, from spending all that time dressed as Jesus.

Mimi stood under the fat hood of the stove frying eggs and po-tatoes. My father paced the linoleum, a piece of toast in one hand, the sports section in the other. Theo had poured the whole box of Cap'n Crunch into a mixing bowl and was plunging in with both hands to look for the prize. Mimi brought the eggs to the table on a platter. I dipped my toast in the runny yolk and tried to read my book, the gentle whir of the refrigerator steady as the sound of Misty lapping water.

"Dan, that meeting is tonight. At Silvie's school." Mimi eased into a chair. "Can you get home early?"

My heart started hammering. Would Mimi stand up in front of my teachers in her blue suede shoes bragging about how she'd dated Elvis? After Mimi had gone public with her tale at the dinner party, I found out that Eric Sloan, a guy at school, was Larry and Bev's son. Eric had turned me into the school joke—Girl Whose Mother Claims to Have Dated Elvis. That one night was ruining my life, as it almost had my father's career. Roger had eventually dismissed the incident with a wave of his hand, saying that Tina had told him he drank too much and that *he* was the rude one, but I might not be so lucky.

"I can certainly try." My father sat down next to my mother, reaching over to ruffle Theo's hair and then rubbing Mimi's back in small circles, probably making up for something.

The bead in my stomach hardened; if I didn't soften it with food, it would grow bigger and crawl up my throat like a hand and choke me dead. I shoved down the rest of my eggs and turned a page in my book, but I wasn't really reading, just looking at the pictures. I couldn't stop her from going to my school tonight; I could only pity the other mothers, drab in the glare of her lilting southern accent, her cheekbones, red lips, and blue suede shoes, sucking every eyeball away from their polyester dresses like a gaudy, overstuffed chair in a room full of wooden ones. Since I'd been friends with Martine, I could laugh things off, but not *everything*.

"Kids, PB and J, right?" My mother rose to make our lunches.

I gave a vigorous nod.

"No weird junk, okay, Mom?" Theo said.

Both Theo and I had begged: no specially seasoned fillets of sole wrapped in wax paper or margarine tubs filled with noodles and marinara; no sandwich bag filled with a few tablespoons of Parmesan cheese to sprinkle, no sprig of parsley to freshen my breath afterward. She'd grudgingly agreed to give us the bologna and cheese or peanut butter and jelly sandwiches that everyone else ate, but sometimes she smuggled a dark green shred of arugula onto the bologna. And that was before anyone had heard of arugula. She read exotic cookbooks. Ordinary came hard.

The kettle was steaming. Mimi made our sandwiches, poured a

cup of tea, and ate her egg standing up. On the counter behind her, a brick of lamb chops melted slowly beside a mound of unwashed potatoes, skins as leathery-brown and spotted as Granny's hands. That would be dinner.

Slipping off my chair, I mumbled that I'd forgotten my homework and padded out of the kitchen and down the hall, knowing exactly what to do. I had to encourage my mother to wear something presentable to the meeting, something *tame*. And—an idea blazed inside my brain—I had to hide the shoes.

Outside her room, I leaned against the wall to gather strength. My eye was twitching; I remember that. Scattered on the olive-green bedspread were velvet throw pillows that other mothers would call orange. She called them paprika, cumin, mace.

I flung open her closet doors and ran my hand over all the clothes on hangers, plucking through dresses smashed together, dresses covered in plastic bags to keep them "nice." I was looking for something plain, quiet, an ordinary outfit that might rein her in, bring her down to earth, stop her from bragging about Elvis.

There weren't many options—red? No, nothing red! My hands riffled on, fast and agile as a thief's, past the batch of mini-dresses. I touched the high neckline of a scratchy black funeral dress. Almost. My hand stopped—yes. Here was the dark brown crepe with the creamy lace collar and bow, a dress she'd bought on sale and worn only once. It hit at midcalf—not short, not bright, a little drab. This was the kind of store-bought stuff the other mothers wore. I stroked the plastic cover. Perfect.

"Silvie, hurry up," Mimi called from the kitchen.

I lay the brown crepe dress on her bed, the wire hanger sticking out of the neckline like a question mark. Darting back to the closet for a pair of brown pumps, I spotted the blue suede pumps and scooped them up, amazed by their condition. They looked almost new. Of course, she rarely wore them outside, and she'd had them resoled a few times. They felt heavy in my arms, and I wanted to throw them out the window. But I'd settle for hiding them. In the bathroom, under the sink. Then I arranged the brown shoes on the floor under the dress so that they looked like real feet. Maybe she'd see how pretty the brown outfit was, complete with matching pumps, and she'd forget the blue suede shoes. Stepping back to admire the display, I imagined someone's mother in that outfit. My mother.

I trudged off to school with my fingers crossed. In chorus, when we sang for Miss Easterbrook with our heads back and our eyes closed, I pictured Mimi wearing the brown dress that night. In electives—art—I tore colored tissue for a collage, ripped the brown stump of a tree, saw in it the shape of the brown dress. In the frilled golden leaves lived my wish for her hair to be set in prim and proper curls, like other mothers'. Not blunt at the chin like Mimi's—sleek, shiny, modern.

When I came home from school, Mimi was waiting for me at the door. "Follow me," she said cheerfully, leading me to her room. We stood at the bottom of the bed staring at the brown dress splayed out on the bedspread like a body without a person inside.

"Now, about this brown. Isn't it a little *dull*? I'm not even going to ask what you were doing in my closet." She shoved the dress to the edge of the bed and headed to her closet, her hands flying expertly through the clothes, dancing along, delighting in the weight and texture of silk, wool, crepe, cotton. Emerging pink in the face and a little breathless, she held up several outfits. Every person has their idea of paradise, and Mimi's was doing what she did now, padding in bare feet to her closet, slipping things off hangers, trying this scarf with that jacket.

"How about this?" She held up an electric-blue dress she'd trimmed with a black feathered collar. "Or this?" A deep yellow skirt and jacket she wore over a patterned scarflike thing she called a dickey. "Look, this suit's the color of squash! Modern, fresh; I just made it. Autumn-ish, conservative. Add the blue shoes and—

powee! I want to impress the teachers and other moms, let them know that *your* mom knows how to put herself together."

We both tilted our heads up to the yellow suit that fluttered like a flag between us. I lowered my eyes, feeling guilty that my own mother embarrassed me.

Suddenly, she put the suit down on the bed and beckoned. "Come here." Comprehension seemed to dawn on her face, slowly. She was a little exasperated. "You're embarrassed because of Elvis, aren't you? Just like your father. Is that it?"

Holding her gaze, I bit my lip hard.

"I don't understand why y'all are not proud of something that makes me special, why you want me to be like all the other mothers." But she wasn't yelling the way I'd expected; she was speaking softly, glancing down at the suit, watching me.

My lower lip trembled, but we both knew I'd never cry. Standing and looking at the floor, rubbing my finger along the cord that bordered her bedspread, I stiffened. I shifted my weight away from her arms, but I wouldn't let her hug me. She probably hadn't noticed that her shoes were gone. But she would.

"Well." She folded her arms across her chest, sinking back into herself again, young, stubborn, proud. "You're lucky your mother has such good taste. But for you, I'll wear the brown."

I hardly heard her. Then it sank in, flooding me with surprise and relief. "You will? And the brown shoes?"

She shut her eyes a moment, and I imagined her feeling the weight of this agreement. "Go on, now. Let Mom get ready." She turned to the mirror, holding orange-and-gold earrings up to her ears, long, dangly ones that glinted in the lamplight.

I knew I should say something. "Thank you, Mimi," I said, my words shooting out more stiffly than I had meant them to, like the spitballs Billy Gowan was always sailing into Kimberly Ray's back during geography.

After a while, Mimi came down to the kitchen in her robe and stockings, makeup done, bangs curled under with pink tape. She broiled the meat and fried potatoes, adding spices that rose up and parted the heavy kitchen air. My father walked in, loosening his tie. We ate hurriedly, because she had to finish getting dressed. My stomach was in knots. Even if she wore the brown dress, I couldn't control what she'd say.

A while later, I looked up from the couch and there was Mimi, in her bright yellow suit, the blue suede shoes strapped proudly on her feet. Her earrings twinkled as she waltzed by, then she disappeared in a cloud of perfume, hand in hand with my father. I gaped at her, wondering if she had ever worn those shoes to dance with my father. I hoped not.

"You look pretty, Mom," Theo said, knowing nothing of our battle. "Just like one of Charlie's Angels." I gave him a dark look and followed my parents to the door.

My father turned, letting his hand fall away from hers. He gathered me into a hug, whispering, "Good night, princess."

Hearing his gentle voice, I had to swallow tears. "You l-l-look nice," I whispered to him, and some understanding passed between us. My father didn't call attention to himself in his navy-blue suit. He looked like all the other fathers, except younger and a little more handsome. People noticed only Mimi's stormy beauty, but once, in third grade, Mrs. Shane had said my father had eyes as blue as the Caribbean. Mimi had teased him, "Dan, I believe your daughter's teacher has a crush on you." His pink, unlined face had spread open and crinkled into a smile and I knew he liked being the one singled out for a change.

Now as my father walked outside, Mimi turned to me and waved. "Tootle-oo." Her voice sounded imperiously cool and flat. Then she said, "Under the sink? Silvie, really! You might have thought of a better hiding place." And her blue pumps clicked across the threshold. Watching them, I hated her, and myself. She didn't care what I wanted. She would stand up at that meeting and say whatever came out of her mouth. My hands shook, and my belly felt as if it were on fire. Go ahead, tell the Elvis story, I thought, in your yellow squash suit, in your blue suede shoes.

From the living room window, I watched until the car disappeared down the street, then went back to Mimi's room. A thick fog of perfume lingered and one brown pump stuck halfway out from under the bed like a forgotten toy.

I looked into her closet. There was a whole army of shoes, organized and ranked by color, lined up on metal shoe trees. I started to throw the sensible pair she'd rejected back in when I stopped and stared down at the neat rows of shoes. Never did they end up in a tangled mass like mine, the quarter-inch heel of a black dressy shoe stuck in the round saucer mouth of a summer-white Keds.

I lifted the shoe tree and shook it as hard as I could. Shoes tumbled off, but still I shook and shook. Shoes scattered in a messy pile, a black patent leather on top of a paisley velvet slipper, a strappy gold sandal inside a loafer. More and more shoes flew through the air as I shook and shook, as if it were a toy box full of dolls, pulled apart and strewn everywhere, some with the wrong head on the wrong body, some with no head at all. In my mind, a sudden, vivid picture bloomed of my old Barbie, poor Barbie, her head twisted all the way around so that her breasts seemed to stand taut and high on her back.

I wanted those shoes ravaged, plundered. One tear fell on the toe of a red pump. Hiccuping, I wiped it away. Sitting on the floor, breathing hard, I gazed in shock at the disarray around me. In an instant, I'd turned her closet to chaos and now fear threatened to shake the pride right out of me. But I wouldn't let it and I sat for a minute, feeling amazed that I'd found a way to make her invisible.

A scratching sound at the door made me whirl around. I expected to see Wolfie, but it was Theo, ankles sticking out of his too-small Batman pajamas. "Holy shit! What the hell are you doing?"

He'd emerged from his Jesus phase swearing a blue streak. His eyes bugged out when he saw the mess.

"I . . . I'm . . ."

"Mom is gonna have a cow."

"Yeah, well, I don't care. I hate her."

"Why?" With his hands on his hips, he looked like a tiny lord.

"You'll see. When you get older. She's crazy . . ."

He regarded me patiently. "Silvie, *all* mothers are crazy. It's their job to be crazy. Anyway, Mom's not that bad. String Bean's mother is way worse. She makes him drink her homemade root beer that tastes like licorice. I almost barfed when I tried it. You're gonna clean this up, right?"

"No! I hate her!"

He took my hand in his little one. "Okay," he said. "Wanna play?" He'd just gotten the new G.I. Joe with the kung fu grip.

"You're supposed to be in bed."

"How about Clue? You can be Professor Plum."

"All right." At ten o'clock, when we heard the car in the drive-way, we scrambled into our beds. I lay staring tensely at the ceiling and listened as my father took out the garbage and my mother put-tered around the kitchen. Then I heard her tread on the stairs. Against my pillow, my head lay like an airless ball; my breathing was shallow.

"Silvie! Get in here."

Terrified, I got out of bed and went to her room.

She was standing inside her closet, cheeks pale, one hand on her hip. "Don't cower in the doorway like Wolfie when she wets the rug. Get in here." She pointed to the mess. "Well?"

I stared, then closed my eyes against the jumble of shoes and clothes at her feet. My head felt light and swimmy. I hoped I was coming down with something.

"I was going to let it go about your hiding my shoes, but now this! Well, I'll have you know, I am the mother around here. I wear what I want when I want. And you don't punish *me;* I punish *you.*"

The mirror on her closet door distorted her body so that she appeared large and looming, while I, tiny in the background, jittering from foot to foot in the old pink nightgown, looked like a little kid who had to pee.

"Most daughters would kill for a mother who puts herself together the way I do. But not you." Her voice went up. "You want *dull;* you want *boring.* Well, you can have it. *Be* it. Here." She thrust out the brown pumps. "For you. They're yours now. La-di-da. Old-lady shoes. If you like them so much, you wear them, Miss Mouse." She yanked off the dangling earrings. "On a shoestring, all the sewing I do to have nice things. And you're embarrassed."

My hand lay lifeless on the bedspread, the wrist exposed, a vein throbbing large and snakelike. I didn't trust the power pulsing in that blue vein, a long river that led somewhere, anywhere, away . . .

"I'm sorry," I said, our eyes meeting in the smooth surface of glass. Her high cheekbones now seemed a threat of what my own wide face might someday be chiseled into, becoming not my father's but hers.

My mother glared at me in the mirror. "Whatever you do, miss, you're stuck with me."

Lowering my eyes from her mirror eyes, I eased back into my face, into my own skin and bones and limbs, which carried my two feet back to my room, to my bed, to the old dollhouse I never played with anymore, to that dull, *d-u-l-l,* mother inside, wearing her painted-on pearls.

◆ ◆ ◆

The next day, my mother refused to speak to me, and in the evening, when she was making dinner, I dreamed, for the hundredth time, of leaving her. I got as far as the rock at the end of our driveway, where I sat in plain sight with my back to the house, waiting for my father to come home from work. The weather was mild, but it could have been raining, windy, or freezing, and even if Mimi had been yelling for me to get sensible and come inside, I wouldn't have budged. I just sat reading my book until the gleaming silver nose of my father's car inched into the driveway. Then I dashed to the car door, opening it for him, rubbing my cheek over his rough whiskers and letting him sweep me into a wonderful warm hug.

In the house behind me, I heard Mimi in the dark kitchen, stirring the air alive, chopping potatoes, humming a meandering tune. She alone would tunnel the night into a dark hollow I couldn't enter, clouds in her hair, daggers for bones, as alone in her tempest as I was on the rock.

I knew the truth. Vandalizing her closet had been nothing more than an ineffective gust of rebellion, like the moment when a small flag rises up and waves in the breeze and one person is watching.

CHAPTER 10

Shortly after Thanksgiving, Scottie planned a trip for us in Montreal. He was so excited about our taking a vacation together that I couldn't say no, although I was afraid I would be too preoccupied with Mimi to be any fun and would ruin things with Scottie. I was plagued with ambivalence—I thought I shouldn't be happy and having a life when my mother was losing hers, and yet here was Scottie, set down gently in my path. Did I really want to turn around, walk the other way?

My job had been going well, but as my mother deteriorated, I made mistakes, handing Florence the wrong layouts, misplacing the sketches for the February issue.

When I brought in a contract with a whole section untyped, Florence said, "Silvie, you're a mess. You're too preoccupied. Maybe you need to go home for a while, stay with your mother."

I lifted my chin. "But I have a job, a boyfriend. I signed up for that class . . ."

"Silvie, your life will be here for you when you get back. Your mother may not." She said all this without an upward glance from her magnifying glass and contact sheets, same as on the day I'd first met her. Steady Florence, with her stern posture, her hidden kindness, her practical wisdom.

All day, tiny wings fluttered in my shoulders, against my skin. By night, I felt bruised. My back hurt in a dull ache. I didn't want to go home. I have a life here, I reminded myself. I have a *life*.

◆ ◆ ◆

That weekend, in Montreal with Scottie, I ate everything in the large fruit basket on the table near the bed in our hotel room. People who never touch the fruit basket in their hotel room are the people who always *get* one. Scottie didn't go near it. I ate every last apple, pear, and grape. I ate and ate, until my fingers touched crackling plastic, then the soft tissue paper that lined the bottom. Sitting on the hard hotel bed, I slurped and swallowed, grape stems between my fingers.

On our next-to-last day, walking down a tree-lined street at midnight, Scottie asked me to marry him. My head went dizzy; my breath wheezed out so short and fast I thought I might faint. "Yes" contained revolution, freedom, possibility, and I couldn't say it; I just stood next to him, close but not touching, fighting tears.

"Shit," Scottie said, trying to smile. "You're scaring me. Is it yes or no?"

"Yes, yes. *Yes!*"

When we got back to our hotel, I called my mother, even though it was late. "I knew what was up when the phone rang!" Henry said. I heard Mimi demanding the phone, confused, thinking that something terrible had happened.

"Silvie, you're not sick, are you?"

"Mimi, I'm fine. I'm great. I'm, um, we're engaged."

"How wonderful! Congratulations." Her voice sounded threadbare as an old rug.

Lying on the bed near me, Scottie stroked my hand with his bare toes. Lifting his glass, he swallowed the last drops of champagne. I gripped the phone receiver hard. It was real, not like marriage, which suddenly felt like a party that other people attended in gardens with paper lanterns hanging from the trees.

"We have a lot to do if this wedding's tomorrow," Mimi said.

"Not that soon." It took me a second to remember the morphine. "Mimi, we're going to get you a dress, remember?"

"A mother-of-the-bride dress?" she asked, perplexed.

It was no use. Henry took the phone back, and we said goodbye. I looked up at Scottie, my fiancé, and smiled through a rainbow of tears.

That night, we called my father, Theo, and Martine. I sliced open the only fruit left—a pineapple. We sat down cross-legged on the bed, white-plush hotel towels spread on our laps, and we ate, juice dripping down our chins. And while I ate, I concluded that I was as ready as I'd ever be. I had to go home. Stay with my mother. Help her die.

Having made that decision, I slept deeply, holding on to Scottie's shoulder blade, that beautiful bone that lifted us on its wing, all night.

◆ ◆ ◆

Back at *Country House,* I asked Florence for a leave of absence. "Oh, Silvie, take as long as you need," she said. I thanked her, my hands twisting in slow circles in front of my skirt, until she finally put her arms around me. I stood there, wishing I could cry.

◆ ◆ ◆

And so I went home to stay with Mimi, and after dinner, it became our custom to hunker down on the couch in the family room for the evening, to talk and plan the wedding. Through French doors, the porch light glowed against the drab, tarnished sky. Cold air, heavy as breath, gathered around the door like smoke, snaking its way inside our house, spreading its long, inky sigh into every corner. Every time I looked at my mother, I was stunned by how gaunt she was, how big and fake the wig appeared against her hollow cheeks.

We were too quiet. I wanted to talk—not about dying. I wanted to narrate our story, the story of us, to find out why she was the way she was and to render all the difficulties somehow meaningful—and meaningless. But it wasn't easy to start. Opportunities dwindled down to something less, leaving the raw truth between us: There was so much to say and not enough time to say it. The morphine didn't help matters, either, hovering between us like a third person.

We looked at magazines, making a study of wedding dresses on other girls—girls with no circles under their eyes, no worry lines around their mouths, their smiles not sticky-sweet with stress. Dr. Tilden had told Henry that even four months was optimistic. Mimi could go sooner, so Scottie and I moved up the wedding. We had only six weeks to plan.

When we grew tired of looking at the beautiful brides in their beautiful gowns, Mimi waved scissors around and cut out the pictures. We were good at cutting and pasting—all those S&H Green Stamps when I was young, and later, all those articles on women who love men who don't. Now, we clipped magazine pages—the only sound the soft grating of the scissors, a muted wheeze as the blades opened and closed—and pasted the shimmering photos of smiling women in white into a scrapbook.

Silvie's Wedding, she wrote on the cover. That way, she could be there too.

◆ ◆ ◆

I was afraid of the air in the house, its odd, dense smell of sickness, like wet wool, and afraid of the sight of her, stiff and bowed. Theo and I had grown better at knowing when Mimi was strung out on morphine, her mind like burned sugar. Henry stood outside us; understanding and true comprehension passed among souls by blood, not marriage. I came to believe it was because Theo and I were better at letting our minds go as limp as hers, free, accepting that words don't have to be logical to mean something. She just talked, from some invisible place. Sometimes the morphine made her funny; always, honest.

On Tuesday, we were going over *Modern Bride* and I was pretending to read an article on necklines—jewel, boat, vee—but really I was staring at the page, guilt shaping itself over and over in my mind. I had come home with my sleeves rolled high, as Granny used to say. How could I be bothering with details like this? Dresses, flowers, menus, music. I had imagined her dying differently—richer, more obstinate, accompanied by more circumstance. I hadn't expected this surge of mundane ambition.

Because it was Letty's cleaning day, Mimi asked her to bring the old wedding album up from the basement and we sat with it on our laps. It was large, of white leather, with the words *Our Wedding* and a bouquet of flowers embossed on the cover. When you opened it, you'd hear a sweet, tinny rendition of "Here Comes the Bride." I used to beg Mimi to wind it and play that magic song.

We sat together, turning the pages of the large black-and-white photographs. In them, my mother glittered with happiness and hope. A yellowed newspaper clipping fell out. Mimi picked it up and began to read.

" 'The bride was radiant in a waltz-length gown of silk peau de soie and re-embroidered Chantilly lace in magnolia white. Her dress featured a molded bodice, with scallops of lace outlining the scoop neckline, and bracelet-length sleeves. From the back of the dome-shaped bouffant skirt a bow fell from the Empire waistline with a panel ending at the hemline.' " She lowered the article. We'd been discussing trains. "That's what I had instead of a train—a panel."

I sat close, her words catching me up in their spell.

" 'A veil of imported silk illusion flowed from a band of silk peau de soie fastened with tiny seed pearls. The bride wore short magnolia-white kid gloves and carried a colonial bouquet made of white roses.' "

"Sounds pretty. They didn't leave anything out, did they?" I said. "How did you wear your hair?"

Mimi lowered the clipping, remembering. "Chin-length, with short bangs. Connie and I had an appointment at Beulah's that morning, but Beulah was sick and we didn't trust anybody else, so we set each other's hair on pink rollers. It was more fun that way anyway. We locked ourselves in our old room and giggled about being old married ladies.

"What was the name of the woman who played the organ? Stokes? Yes. Mrs. Fred Stokes. And the photographer. Can you believe after all these years I still remember these names? Wimbish Blue, Walter Blue's daddy and the closest thing Biloxi had to an eccentric artist. He liked to take pictures of cemeteries at night." She pointed to a picture of a graffitied car, my father in a regular suit, and herself dressed in a skirt and jacket. "Look! My going-away outfit. That's what you put on when you ride off into the sunset. Mine was a two-piece emerald-green shantung suit with a bolero jacket and three-quarter sleeves, fashioned with a slim skirt. Spectacular. I only wish they'd had color photos then. I wore a green pillbox hat with matching shoes and bag." She looked up. "Silvie, I could do a few sketches, whip you up something."

I opened my mouth, shut it, thinking of Mimi's creations—vivid color, voluminous fabric, midi-skirts and fringed vests she'd sewn for me long after the other girls were wearing Levi's and Organically Grown sweaters and earth shoes.

Fortunately, she turned back to the wedding album, remembering something else. "Just hours before the ceremony, Connie and I realized I didn't have something blue—you know the old rhyme, something old, something new. We ran all over the house looking for something blue. We'd been wearing our robes all day so we wouldn't have to pull anything over our hair and we kept tripping on them and giggling. Connie, always the wit, raced around, picking up a huge blue vase, a blue ashtray, saying, 'How about this?'

"Shelby came in, watched us a minute, then slunk away, as he always did. But this time, he came back, holding out his hand. 'Simone, I have something,' he said. He had the softest voice, like something in water. 'I don't know if it's right, but it's small. And it's blue.' He held out a piece of blue plastic. Tiny, tear-shaped. I couldn't tell what it was until I went over to him.

" 'It's my favorite guitar pick.'

" 'Oh, Shel, it's perfect,' I cried, throwing my arms around him. He never hugged back. He just stood there stiff as a board, and his sadness passed between us like a current. Then I let him go." A sound like a sob escaped her. "I wish now I'd held on tight, but I let him go. 'I'll put it in my shoe,' I told him. And I did. Later, at the reception, we danced together and I felt that little blue teardrop rubbing against my heel. Shelby whispered to me that it was just like the pick Elvis used. I whispered back, 'I found my king, Shel. Now you have to find your queen.' "

Slowly, my mother turned to me, her face soft under the veil of memory. "I don't remember the something old or new or borrowed, but I remember that something blue."

♦ ♦ ♦

"When I married him, Henry was a holistic dentist who didn't drive," she announced. She was having a good day and we were in the car. She'd taken the long way home, thinking we might stop at the health food store. Lilting sounds from a Mozart tape Theo had made for her filled the car.

"Now he just loves to go, go, go." She gestured expansively before clamping her hand firmly back on the wheel. "Who would have ever dreamed what old Henry on that beat-up Schwinn really wanted? A hard-traveling hit-the-highway kind of gal with her makeup case packed. Me, I can't even leave the house without a purseful of M&M's in a vitamin bottle . . ." Mimi glanced at the car beside her and gasped. "Oh, those fool kids. What do they think they're doing?"

I whirled around and saw, behind us, a group of guys in a rusty car whose bumper kissed ours. Mimi, who usually stopped at yellow lights, gunned it through, this daring act raising a blush of rosy color in her cheeks and a sparkle to her eyes. She didn't look sick at all.

The boys followed us, weaving in and out of traffic. At the next red light, they pulled their car dangerously close to ours. The driver rolled down his window and the air filled with whistled hoots and catcalls.

"Hey, pretty baby!" The driver had greasy blond hair and a carefully tended shadow of stubble across his cheeks and chin.

I groaned and looked skyward, dimly aware that Mimi was staring straight ahead, her knuckles white on the steering wheel. Normally, she flirted back, throwing a construction worker an easy grin while I skulked behind, giving them the finger.

"What's the matter, Silvie? Think I can't handle this?" Mimi slowed down, turned toward her window, and flashed them a big, easy smile. The boys' eyes grew large as saucers. Suddenly, Mimi's hand moved up to her head and, in a rush of air I felt across my face, she whipped the wig off and dangled it above the steering wheel. She turned slowly toward them and grinned, the wig swinging gently back and forth.

The guys took one look at her nearly bald head, covered with a flesh-colored stocking, and gunned the gas. I gaped at her, my stomach cold as ice.

She glanced at me. "Oh, you're surprised. Well, the last strand fell out this morning." Her voice was flat, matter-of-fact.

I gulped. "It doesn't look bad."

"That's a load of shit." Her hands got busy, ejecting the tape, turning on the radio. Theo, who worked in the classical section at the record store, had given her a dozen tapes. All our gifts reeked of hope, cure.

"Fuck Mozart," she said, hands firmly back on the wheel. Turning off Woodward, she drove toward the health food co-op. As we crossed the railroad tracks, we lifted our feet without a word, both of us in unison, wishing, not out of faith but habit. Near the store, she braked hard and made a U-turn.

"Fuck carrot juice," she said, her hands tighter on the wheel.

◆ ◆ ◆

With wedding music Theo had brought from the store playing in the background, I addressed invitations and Mimi, armed with magazine clippings, called several florists specializing in unusual flowers. She was set on something tropical, called bouvardia. We forged ahead, crossing off our list. In the midst of all the planning, I asked her how she and my father had met.

"Haven't I told you that story?" She let the magazine flowers rest in her lap like a bouquet.

"You told me you met at a gas station."

She scrunched up her face, playacting at remembering. "He was wearing a uniform—probably a Keesler guy, I thought—and the way he leaned toward his car with the gas pump made me hungry and I thought, *Fuel.* Sounds silly now, but I did."

"It doesn't sound silly," I said.

"Yep, I stared at him until I felt him stare back with those eyes, the most penetrating blue eyes I'd ever seen. He seemed to look right inside me. And he had this calm, the calm of a normal heart. On impulse, I rolled down the window of the little red roadster I shared with Connie, waved and called out, 'Hello there! I'm Simone.' And I watched him wave back and go on pumping gas and I thought, *This* is the way out. I had to take a deep breath or else I would have slumped over the steering wheel just dreaming how I'd marry him and move up north, where they don't say *y'all* and *nekkid* and I'd have his children."

"And you did," I said, finally impressed by one of Mimi's stories. She'd been looking for a way out, too. We had something in common, my mother and I. This thought stunned me, and I forgot there was a wedding to plan at all.

"I looked into his face and my heart stopped hammering," she said. "Just stopped. As if I'd come *home*. And my mind got busy having an adventure with this new man. Busy melding beauty and love and security and adventure into one great thing." Mimi shot me a severe look. "Sometimes it is, Silvie, and sometimes it isn't."

I saw her then, twirling into my father's arms on the beach, her mouth wide, his closed as a fist, tilting back for a kiss, not knowing that in nineteen years, she'd divorce him and die, cell by cell, of sorrow, that inherited song.

"We were married six months later," she went on. "It was a whirlwind of excitement and necessity—the Air Force had transferred Dan to Ohio. The night of our wedding, we loaded his car and drove from Biloxi to Columbus, Ohio, our new home. Dan carried me over the threshold into that cheap hotel room, and without ever bringing our things in from the car, we did what newlyweds do and then just fell asleep, our wedding clothes rumpled on the floor."

An image of my parents floated up, the two who gave Theo and me flesh, who pulled us from their separate skins, fragile as paper flowers on parade floats.

"When we woke up the next morning, the sun was shining down and there was our car. When we went outside, we saw that someone had picked the locks and plucked every last inch of the car dry as a chicken bone, stolen our whole lives. Dan didn't want to go back to Mama and Daddy's; he said we were on our own now, and he was right—they would have made a big deal and bribed us to stay.

"And so I arrived in Columbus, my first trip above the Mason-Dixon Line, in my shantung suit and satin pumps, without even a change of underpants, toothbrush, or hairbrush, without my box of family photos. Nothing. Just those silly cans tied to the bumper, the graffiti saying JUST HITCHED, a stupid invitation for anyone to steal."

"So you had to start over."

"From scratch. But we didn't mind. Life was good. We made banana fritters every Sunday. We went to antiques fairs and listened to show music. He read and I sewed and the dreams came back."

"What dreams?"

"When I was around twelve or so, I stopped dreaming. Mama and Daddy were always arguing, and . . . I don't know. I just stopped dreaming. And I didn't start again until after Dan and I were married, and then they rushed out like a river after a storm, rich, vivid dreams."

"Wow." I gulped. My father had given her back her dreams.

Her eyes met mine. "You like that old story?"

"It's great," I said, glancing at my watch. I was due at my father's house for dinner in an hour.

Mimi shook her head slowly. "I guess it is."

◆ ◆ ◆

"You and your mother were never the best of friends," my father said. I was at his house, a ranch house in a neighborhood of ranch houses, each as long and narrow and close to the earth as the next, like boxcars on a train. Theo had left after dinner, and Laura, my father's wife, had served my father and me coffee and lemon bars in front of the fireplace before disappearing to another room.

"What do you mean?" I said. My father's dark brown hair had only a shot of gray in the sideburns. He still had the ruddy, handsome face of youth, the strong jaw and the bright blue eyes, but now they were rimmed with red when he was tired. When he smiled, the brown skin around his eyes creased like a crumpled paper bag, then smoothed out.

"You two always went at it. Sometimes she would yell, 'I hate you, I hate you.' She was hard on you."

"That's an understatement," I said dryly, feeling a stab of self-pity. What fierce thing had I nurtured inside me to survive Mimi as a mother?

"She didn't really hate you. She just . . ." Shaking his head, he stared into the unused fireplace. "You were good with me, smart and sweet, but with her you were just so headstrong and stubborn. I didn't know what to do about it." He wiped a mustache of coffee from his upper lip. "She wasn't as tough on Theo. He was an easy baby. And he was a boy. There just wasn't the competition. That's it, really. She was always competitive with you."

Now we both stared into the fireplace. A terra-cotta pot sat there, seeming oddly at home, as if it had grown inside the brick walls, out of soot and black ash. I thought about my spirit back then, my vigor that, over the years, she had whittled away like a tiny bar of hotel soap. I was angry about that. How should I stop being angry about that?

My father spread my five fingers and pointed to a fine white mark I'd never noticed, across the back of two fingers, tiny, as narrow as an eyelash. "Happened early one morning in Biloxi when we were visiting. You stood by the window with your hands on the sill. A train went by and the window slammed down on your fingers." He rubbed his thumb and index fingers over the scar, as if he could make it disappear. "That was the summer Paw Paw wanted us to stay, wanted me to work with him. But I knew he would swallow me whole."

We sipped coffee and bit into the lemon bars. "I remember the first time I saw your mother," my father said. "She was at the gas station, in her little car. She was beautiful and vivacious and a little wild, with some sensible thing at the core that bobbed up then sank back down. Your mother thought I was going to be something I'm not, some version of her father—powerful, ambitious. Where do people get the crazy idea that they can mold the people they love? It just isn't true. For the most part, people are what they are. Remember that, Silvie."

"I will."

"Remember when you used to sit on the rock at the foot of the driveway and wait for me to come home? Sometimes I felt like I was the one sitting on that rock, like I was outside the house looking in," my father said. "Like I didn't belong somehow, like I was living in some other man's house." He shook his head, chuckling, then growing sober. "The Elvis house. There just wasn't room for me. And that's not a good feeling."

"But I felt the same way!" I said.

"She was difficult, your mother." Here it was, the polished gem of truth we'd long hidden. To have said it out loud then would have made living with her all those years unbearable. "I'm sorry, Silvie. I'd give anything to go back to that time and be a different person, a stronger person." He took my hand in his again, and tears sprang to my eyes.

His eyes filled, too, and he squeezed my hand. My father was a practical man, an honest man, as constant as mail, and I believed him. The fact that I understood him in a way I had not understood Mimi, that I had had at least that much understanding in my life, was reason enough to forgive him, to allow the anger to leave my body.

I looked at my father and around the warm living room and saw that the terra-cotta pot inside the fireplace was filled, inexplicably, somehow joyously, with flowers. Everything was in its place, but he still hadn't made peace with his past, not completely.

"I don't want her to die," I choked out. "No matter how hard it's been, I don't want her to go."

"I don't, either."

"I still love her."

"Of course you do. She's your mother. I still love her, too." He blinked, like someone going from darkness into light. After a while, he spoke again. "Your mother is at peace knowing you've found someone. I'm happy for you, too. I know you'll have a good life. Remember—the key to happiness is being happy with what you have." He patted my hand, and that pat would be all. There were no more words.

◆ ◆ ◆

The next day on the couch, I turned to Mimi. "Why didn't you teach me to sew?" I had never wanted to learn, but the idea of my mother handing down this piece of our past appealed to me now. More than wanting to know how to sew, I suddenly wanted to be a person who sewed, who was calmed by sewing.

My mother's answer flowed out as if she'd been holding it on the tip of her tongue for years. "Because I was afraid you'd be good at it. Sewing was the only thing I could do. I wanted to be the artist, but you were better than I was, more natural. So I held on to the sewing, for me." She paused. "I didn't even like it, exactly. I just wanted all the pretty things." She glanced at me. "Maybe I should teach you now."

But later, when she tried to thread the needle, her hands shook and she missed the eye a half dozen times. "I'm a little rusty," she said wistfully, lowering her hands. "Let's try again after lunch."

◆ ◆ ◆

A paper with her scribble fell out of one of the magazines. I looked at it until I stopped seeing it. In a sharp, agitated scrawl, like a schoolgirl with a crush, she'd doodled my father's name in rows: *Daniel Page, Daniel Page, Dan Page.* In my mind, I heard a loudspeaker bleating my father's name, over and over, as if someone had lost him. The skin under the collar of my shirt tingled and I wondered if all life was a long look back, wishing you'd done things differently.

◆ ◆ ◆

One day, Mimi peered over her glasses and said mildly, "Maybe I shouldn't have left your father, but I did."

"What?" I lowered *Modern Bride.* I was tired: nights on the phone with Scottie; my whole life back in New York. Everything at Mimi's house blurred together.

She furrowed her brow. "Nineteen seventy-eight, seventy-nine, everyone was doing it. I was restless. You kids were up in Theo's room watching one of your shows on that little black-and-white TV—*The Brady Bunch* or *Emergency!*—and your father was on one of his business trips and I just stared out the window at the patches of brown grass under the dirty snow. And that swing set with the broken swing. He never fixed that swing. Hanging low on one side like that. Like a man with a limp."

"That's why you . . ." I stopped. My brain was foggy. I could hardly shape the words.

"A marriage can dissolve for reasons that have nothing to do with love. Despite love. Money. Religion. Child rearing. Toothpaste."

I studied my fingernails, thinking of Scottie and me, married, blending our lives, fighting over toothpaste. Would we dissolve, poof, after nineteen years, like my parents had?

She inhaled deeply. "I don't know. Maybe we could have seen a counselor."

"You could have worked things out? And you didn't try?" I stared at her, furious, years of anger coursing through my veins.

"I always say, if you're going to make a mistake, make it a big one." She laughed bitterly. "Not that I made a mistake, exactly. I do love Henry. But the grass that's always greener somewhere else? It's just grass. If you count each minute, you'll want to leave a thousand times. Count only the days, only the years."

My mother closed her eyes, leaving me there absorbing her wisdom. There had been so many lies. I wanted to remember her truths.

◆ ◆ ◆

When I returned to the couch one afternoon after Scottie and I had spent nearly an hour on the phone, Mimi leaned toward me conspiratorially. "Remember when I told you there was more to the Elvis story than met the eye? And that someday I'd tell you *everything*?" She pushed aside her magazine. She didn't need it anymore. When she was telling her story, she didn't need a thing. She fixed me with a look. A mad sparkle danced in her eyes. I braced myself.

"We did it, Silvie. We did! Just once, and that was the only man I was with before your father, but oh, Silvie, I lost my virginity to Elvis!" She reached for my hand, her eyes wide and round. For a moment, but just a moment, she looked ashamed.

I jerked my hand away like a fish, hooked, and gasped for air. She'd waited her whole life to play this trump card. Why now? Well, of course now. With her illness stripping away her power and her body breaking down, she was losing her grip and she knew it.

An impish smile curled her lips and she sat up tall in her seat. "It's high time you knew that your old mama and Elvis . . ."

"Does Henry know? Did Dad?"

"No, just us girls." She exhaled happily, as if a huge brick had tumbled from her shoulders. And landed on mine. "Now you know *all* your mother's secrets. Well, maybe not *all*." She laughed merrily. "But enough for now. What do you think?"

I gnawed at a cuticle.

"Think of it this way." She took a sip of Sustacal. "Always order a large. There. That's my advice in life—always order a large."

I stared at her.

"I thought you'd be proud, but no. You don't even believe me."

"I believe you," I said. What counted was that she believed it; in the face of death, she was still flaunting this one pitiful fantasy as her truth, her glittering self. Trotting out the box, opening the lid—here I am everyone, this is me, who I am is *here*.

◆ ◆ ◆

"A present?" I asked. "What for?" We were on the couch again.

"I don't need a what for. You're my daughter. You're getting married." Mimi felt around under the cushions. I watched her for a minute with mild amusement. "Whatcha doin'?"

"Getting your present," she said haughtily. "It's here somewhere." More fumbling. "Damn."

"Why did you put it . . . under . . ."

"Oh, here it is," she said brightly, sitting back. Her wig was askew. Annoyed, she tugged it straight. "I hid it in the couch so no one would steal it. Wasn't that smart?" She held out a large Ziploc bag that contained two lumps swathed in something soft and white and bordered by flowers. "Ta-da."

"Pretty fabric." I squinted.

"Yes." Her voice was far-off, dreamy. "Isn't it?"

On closer inspection, I saw that the fabric was actually a paper towel stamped with blue tulips. Unzipping the bag, I pulled out the small bumpy objects. They felt good resting on my knees, not heavy, but weighty and solid.

"Wait! Where are my glasses?" She patted the couch around her.

"You're wearing them."

She touched her face. "Right. Go ahead."

Each item was smaller than an egg and, like an egg, smooth and cool to the touch, made of a shiny gray material mottled with clouds of white. One was completely round, the other shaped like a chess pawn. I saw by the holes on each that they were salt and pepper shakers.

"They're beautiful." I stroked them.

"Unusual, aren't they? And old. Your father and I used them in our first apartment. I thought you might enjoy having them."

I tilted the small round one and a thin stream of salt poured into my palm. I imagined my parents starting their lives, years ago, with a set of nice salt and pepper shakers, talking over dinner, their voices rich with potential. Passing them on to me was a gesture of faith, a belief in my own marriage. "Mimi, I love these."

"Quick! Throw some over your left shoulder for good luck."

I poured a little salt in my hand, pretending to toss it over my head. Instead, I turned the head of the shaker and, with a crunching sound, a spray of pepper mixed with the salt in my hand. I stared down, fascinated at this union.

"For a long time, I liked being married, the routine, the security." Mimi's eyes were cast downward, as if she were looking for something. "But then it was the late sixties, with the sexual revolution and the music and the hair and burning your bra and civil rights, and there I was in the suburbs, just planning a week of dinners and making them."

A bolt of comprehension hit me and I understood her discontent, the discontent of all women caught between the work of staying home and raising children and the larger work of the world. It would happen to me, I thought. Here is where we would intersect, my mother and I, where our lives would meet, collide, and split apart, careening backward like cartoon characters, each for the very first time a whole person, with the other nestled inside.

"The key to happiness," she said, "is routine. Doing the same thing day after day builds muscle. It took me a long time to learn. I want these shakers to remind you."

"Thank you, Mimi." I hugged her, a fast glide toward her thin bones and a float away.

She lowered her glasses to observe me. "You really like those old things? I've got more stuff." As she turned back to her magazine, her leg took up its bounce, fragile as hope.

◆ ◆ ◆

The December air outside the family room window grew cold, murky with snow, dense as ice. One night, Mimi and I sat on the couch watching a storm, the air in the room, our silence, shaping itself around her pain. By the way she held her hands in her lap, I knew that even the bones in her wrists ached and I wanted to reach over, shut the throb inside my palm. The sky went green, then dark, seeming to hold its breath before a cloud burst, spattering the backyard, and we exhaled too.

"Showers in December," she said, and slowly rose, sliding open the door and setting a blue chipped bowl on the back porch. "Collect drizzle. Wait for time to fill it up."

"Then what?"

"I'll rinse my scalp in soft water and grow my hair back again." Wet fingers tapped the window. "We waste time, valuable time," she said.

I looked up from my book, startled, noticing her perfect makeup, her wig askew.

"Soap operas, home shopping." She gestured toward the television set. It wasn't on. "Don't we have anything better to do?"

In a low voice, I said, "We could talk. Mimi, maybe this isn't the right time, but we could try. So much happened . . ."

"Connie and I made brownies once, only she ran off to talk to Del Carey on the phone while I was mixing the batter. Well, the recipe called for a *dash* of salt and I put in a *dish*. Granny and Connie teased me forever. They always needed to feel better than me."

"How old were you?" I asked.

"Fourteen or fifteen, I think. Ah yes. People disappoint." She was staring into a small circle of space in front of her, her eyes set, stern, already gone.

A minute later, I heard a whisper. "Ah, Elvis," she said. I leaned close. "The King. He was in uniform. At the gas station. Bluest eyes I'd ever seen." The morphine was kicking in, slurring her words.

I was confused. "Elvis wore a uniform?"

"Yep. Air Force. Navigator."

"Mimi, Elvis wasn't in the Air Force."

"Elvis was pumping his own gas," she said stubbornly, her eyes opening wide, like a doll's. "He was my hero."

"He was your hero because he pumped his own gas?"

"Well, yes. No one did that then. It seemed—exotic."

"Okay," I said slowly. "I can see that. But I thought you met Elvis at Paw Paw's pool."

Her mouth curled into a mischievous grin. "No, I spotted that one at the gas station. I knew he was my ticket out."

"Mimi, you always told me you met Dad at the gas station."

"Yes, at the gas station. And he took me away—but then I left him. Why did I leave him?"

I sat in bewildered silence. "Are you talking about Dad?"

Her face grew slack and her eyes fluttered shut. I had my answer.

"I might think, oh, this is for over my thin shirts when they aren't enough." Her eyes, open again, were silent and as uninhabited as an empty closet. "Right?"

I bent over her, mind whirling, saying only, "Isn't your shirt warm enough? Do you want me to get you a sweater?"

She stared straight ahead, dull-eyed. I listened to her slow, muted breath, my eyes fastened on the white ceiling, where there was no mark of her at all. There would be no more talk tonight.

◆ ◆ ◆

Sunday afternoon, she tapped me on the shoulder. "Do you take baths, dear? Don't answer!" She held up her hand to stop me. "I know you; it's just a quick shower, then, *pffffttt,* you're out the door."

"Yes, Mimi," I lied, my voice rich with complicity. "I take baths."

"Oh pooh. You do not." Her voice was strong and chatty. "Baths get you clean, you know. A quick shower does not get the water up there. You should take more baths."

Our eyes met. "Okay. I'll take more baths." I could see that she was telling me to take care of my body so it wouldn't turn on me, as hers had.

By the time Henry came in and sat on the other side of Mimi, flicking on the TV, she was asleep on the couch, her head nearly touching her chest. A blaring horn sounded on the TV, and she stirred, mumbling, "Get the ring, Henry, get the ring." That's what she called the phone these days.

"That's just the TV, baby. Do you need anything?" Henry asked absently, his eyes darting to her and then back to the screen. He slouched on the sofa, legs crossed at the knee, swinging one foot in small circles. His finger was hooked around the high ridge of his sharp nose, resting there, but every once in a while he touched Mimi's wrist and kept on stroking. Henry bore the burden of her illness, the enormous weight of living its reality, day after day. What had I done?

A faint noise made me look down at her hands. They were moving fluently, eloquently, in a curious sign language. Then it dawned on me—she was sewing, without a needle, without thread, her hands lifting and dipping in a language all their own.

"Whatcha doin' there?" I asked.

"Sewing," she said. "For the babies."

"Mimi, you don't have . . ."

"For the babies, Silvie," she said indignantly. "For you and Theo. You'll need clothes."

Her hands continued to move swiftly, small white boats plunging down a raging river. Abruptly, they stopped, and I looked at the transparent skin, yellowed from chemo, the blue veins showing through, her once-perfect nails now ragged.

"I was sewing for my babies, but I think I'm too drunk." Her leg took up its nervous jitter.

Outside, in the gathering dark, a light snow fell. Flakes gathered and stuck. Soon, a thin white crust would cover the grass like a skin.

"They're moving. The trees are dancing, see?" Mimi said, her mouth slack and her eyes heavy, glazed. A smile came from nowhere, beamed from another planet.

I looked. I didn't know then that morphine sometimes made things kinetic. There was no wind. The dry winter branches were still.

She shook her head to clear it. "Don't ask me if anything I say is true—tonight I'm lying like crazy." She covered one hand with the other and held them both in her lap. "Not to mention the fact that I'm a bit of a pest."

"Never," Henry murmured, without taking his eyes off the screen.

"Mimi," I said a while later, knowing it wasn't the right time, but it was never the right time and I'd soon lose her to sleep. There was something I had to know. "Once, a long time ago, you told me my name was an anagram of Elvis."

"What's an anagram again?"

"You said you unscrambled the letters of Elvis's name to get Silvie. . . ."

"Aunt Omega-May had the most beautiful ruby earrings," she whispered. "She called them earbobs. Look in my jewelry box. Maybe that's where they are."

"Mimi, please."

"Can't a mother name her daughter a beautiful name?"

"Then why not Silvia?" I'd long wished for that last syllable, that feminine, lilting *a,* which would assure that I wasn't named for anyone but me.

"I liked Silvie."

"But, Mimi . . ."

"Okay, yes. You were named for Elvis. But I found the name first. *Silvie.* A musical name. French-sounding, which I thought Paw Paw would like. In the hospital, I was doodling, writing *Silvie* over and over, and then I started writing *Elvis*—you know, *Elvis Presley, Mrs. Elvis Presley,* that sort of thing—and I looked at his name and I looked at your name and I about fell out of my chair. It was *Elvis* backwards. I loved that." She sat up abruptly, seemingly not sleepy. "I think I'm hungry. Oh, I hope so! Could you make us a bread, butter, and sugar sandwich?"

Eager to get her to eat, I flew into the kitchen, settling back into myself, reclaiming my name, happy to have made some crazy sense of this piece of my life.

Mimi ate only a bite of the sandwich, followed by tiny sips of vanilla Sustacal. "Silvie, let's stop reading these silly magazines and go shopping. Tomorrow. For your dress."

"Oh, Mimi, I don't think so. You're not up to it." Visions of the earth tones she'd dressed me in as a child filled my eyes. It was my wedding day. For once, I wanted to dress myself. I wanted to be the one to shine.

She looked at me haughtily. "I most certainly am."

"I just meant there's time. We could go in a day or two. Later."

"Later? Why later? When later?"

Her face was pale as wax tonight, with an eerie glow, as if a lit candle were inside, in her cheeks. "Okay, we'll go," I said.

She dozed a minute. "Silvie." Her eyes opened. "Let's put some orange juice in our pockets and take a long walk."

"Orange juice in our . . . oh, Mimi." I giggled for her sake, wishing my voice didn't sound hollow.

A look of sudden clarity passed over her face. She spoke evenly, sadly, "I seem to talk, Silvie, and I just don't make sense."

"Don't worry. I understand you."

"You do?"

I smiled and squeezed her hand. "Yeah, I do."

"Isn't most of what I say out-to-lunch?"

"There's no one I'd rather go out to lunch with." At the moment, those words felt true.

"And shopping—don't forget shopping."

Ever the queen. Despite everything. "That too."

CHAPTER II

Almost every summer, we visited Biloxi. Trips to visit my father's family in Baltimore were few, and my knowledge of that side of my family was dim, hazy, like staring off at distant water where nothing floats up to the surface. It wasn't Grandpa or Grandma Page's fault. Next to the Reismans, anyone would seem small and less vivid. This year, I came armed with my pink vinyl suitcase of bookmobile books. I was thirteen, and although I enjoyed this annual trip, when we were in Mimi's hometown, she turned into a stranger. Here, her personality seemed tamped down, diminished, almost dull. Mimi made the annual pilgrimage to try to reconnect with her family. I traveled this year with a goal—to find some evidence of who, exactly, my mother, my family, were.

Behind my grandparents' house you could walk a long time without seeing anyone. Under my feet, the ground grew scratchy, twisted with raggedy old monkey grass, stiff weeds, flattened Coke cans and beer bottles full of piss, as Aunt Connie would say. Mimi didn't want me to go as far as the railroad tracks, where my grandfather's property ended and old Glenn Godchaux's began. But I loved kicking flattened cigarette packages all the way there.

Today, a penny glistened in the sun on the metal track. I imagined two young boys laying the penny on the gleaming metal, waiting breathlessly to watch the train roar by in a screeching rush, crushing the coin, laughing and running away, forgetting to take their flattened penny with them. Maybe Mimi had once found a penny like this on the tracks. Had she wanted it as badly as I did? Because, suddenly, I craved that smashed copper piece; I had to have its courage and luck.

Glancing around—no one was there—I leaned down and scooped up the shiny penny, putting it into the pocket of my shorts, running my fingers over it a few times. I'd defied her and nothing had happened—the sky was still the same hushed blue, stripped of clouds, the air so hot it felt solid, the damp smell of warm earth and the sticky spice of dried weeds tickling my nose.

A wave of panic sent a shiver through me and I broke into a run across the field. The hot sun beating into the top of my head made me woozy. I ran and ran until the Saint Augustine grass became crabgrass, and the toe of my sneaker caught the edge of something white, and for a second, I was excited, thinking it was a small animal, a rabbit or a kitten. I fished my hand down into the tall grass and brought it up, but it wasn't a pet at all; it was a pair of ladies' underwear, rumpled, the elastic torn. The label said *Nadine's Intimates,* in fancy script, size 6. I let them dangle off my finger, knowing I should throw them back. But I didn't. I stuffed them in my pocket with the penny and ran to the front porch of the big house.

My grandparents' house accommodated its bulk well, spreading gracefully over an acre of land, standing proud and tall in the hot

Mississippi sun, grateful for some shade from fig and pear trees. It faced the West Beach Highway but sat far enough away from the road that you forgot it was a highway. Dignified, full of secrets, the old house Paw Paw had built himself seemed to stare into the dark green waters of the Gulf of Mexico, all the secrets of the South churning there.

I leaned against the white wrought-iron railing, panting. The porch floor was made of green mosaic tiles speckled with bits of colored glass that sparkled and shone like jewels. A tired-looking birdbath sat under a fig tree close to the porch. Leaning over, I touched the warm syrupy water, thickened with fallen leaves and underripe figs hard as walnuts, overripe ones soft as butter, letting the water run through my fingers like sun-drenched honey.

My head was heavy with thoughts about Mimi: Who had she been when she dated Elvis? Was the story true? I was standing on the very same porch Elvis had stood on, asking Paw Paw if he could kiss the girl who was now my mother, the air filled with the sweet scent of Granny's camellias, azaleas, and begonias. A scrappy potato bug curled into itself on my finger. I flicked it off and reached gingerly into my pocket, touching first the penny, then the underwear. Pulling the panties out, I noticed they were stained with a few faint spots of blood at the crotch. Hastily, I stuffed them back into my pocket and ran into the house to ask Shelby for a card trick.

Instead, I ran smack into my grandmother, who was sitting at the large wooden kitchen table. Granny was smaller than Mimi, with heavily powdered wrinkles, a pile of brown hair on top of her head, and glasses that hung from a gold chain around her neck. She shared Mimi's affection for shoes, and today she wore sandals decorated with real shells.

She motioned to me to sit down and put her hand over the mouthpiece of the phone. "I just walked in, honey child, and the phone was ringing off the wall. Do you think Shelby could answer it? No. He's still sleeping and it's past one o'clock." She said this every day, and every day he slept late.

On a chair by the table were Uncle Shelby's Marlboros, his guitar, a deck of cards, and a full ashtray, shaped like a crab and reading I LOVE BILOXI, littered with butts. Thirty years old, living at home, no job, no girlfriend, he was a mystery. My mother, despite her love for him, acted as if he were a hot stove she was afraid to touch. But I couldn't take my eyes off him. I sensed that he knew things, things we all felt but couldn't see. Sometimes he looked at me so slow and long, I was sure his heart had used up all its secrets and the pure truth was ready to lift off his skin and float out in the air until my own skin absorbed it.

"Well, doodlebug," Granny was saying to me. She'd tucked the phone under her chin. "Your mama's shopping with Connie—they seem to be getting along all right—and your daddy got tired of hearing Theo beg and took him down to play at the Goofy Golf. . . . Oh, tarnation. Emery's got me on hold, damnit. He doesn't know doodley-squat about property." She snapped the receiver back to her face.

"Emery, is that you? You've got me on hold a damn hour and I don't like it one bit. Leon and I aren't gonna sell the Marina property and you know it. I've told you for years and I'm tellin' you now, so stop throwin' a hissy fit and . . . what? Pass Christian? You planning to tell me you had someone interested in Pass Christian? Sure, now that's another story . . ."

I hugged her neck and sat down at the long wooden table, twirling the lazy Susan faster and faster, daring the salt, pepper, ketchup, and sugar to fly off the orbit of their small planet.

Granny tucked the phone again. "This damn Emery Wyman. Calls every six months or so." When she or Paw Paw talked business, it sounded like a foreign language, strange and intriguing. "A real pain in the booty."

I giggled. That much I understood. I could see why Mimi

thought Granny never loved her; she was so absorbed in her work, far away always, but to me, maybe because my expectations were lower, she had her own kind of magic. When you had a bad cold, Granny stuck some Vicks right up your nose, even though the label said you weren't supposed to.

"Come and give your granny some sugar," she said now.

I sprang up and kissed her lips. They were soft but waxy-tasting, and I wondered why it was easier to kiss her than to kiss my own mother.

"How'd you get so sweet?" She lit a cigarette, the phone still tucked under her chin. "Oh, to hell with this. I'm hanging up." And she did, with a click, just as the door to Uncle Shelby's room opened and he shuffled out, looking disheveled, his jeans hanging loosely and his shirt buttoned wrong.

"So nice of you to join the living," my grandmother said, pursing her lips. "Now I suppose you'll be wanting coffee." The phone rang, and Granny snatched it up with a hearty, "I said *maybe*, Emery Wyman."

"I'll make it, Mama," Shelby said wearily, walking so slowly to the cabinet that I imagined his feet caught in the sticky maple syrup we poured on banana fritters.

I raised my palm and waved it around like a darting fish. This was our secret greeting. He managed a kind of bleary-eyed wink, his face pale, unshaven, his brown shaggy hair matted. It looked like he'd hardly slept at all. He wasn't especially tall and he never stood straight, which made him look shorter than he was. His shoulders were rounded and his long-sleeved shirt, which he wore even in summer, hung on him. He looked as though his body belonged to someone else and he was only borrowing it for a while.

Sitting down at the table, Shelby lit a cigarette with a shaky hand, slowly drinking his coffee and smoking. Granny held her hand out and took a drag of his cigarette, her other hand never leaving the phone. When she finished, she gave the cigarette back to her son and put a pencil between her teeth.

Shelby's eyes moved from the ceiling to the window and landed on me. "How old are you now, Silvie? Twelve? Thirteen? Has your mama bragged to you about Elvis yet?"

"Shelby!" Granny said, slipping the pencil out of her mouth and writing something on a scrap of paper. "Now, you be minding your business."

Alert now, caught in Shelby's gaze, I sat up like a dog, ears pricked. "She told me . . ."

"Geez, she's gonna ruin your life, too." Shelby shook his head, brought his cigarette slowly to his lips, and inhaled so deeply that I thought his body might rise above the table.

"What do you mean?"

"How about some gumbo, son?" Granny slammed down the phone. Despite her grousing, she would never fail to feed one of her own. "Just made a steaming pot this morning. Gumbo's as good a breakfast as anything else." Yesterday morning, she'd fried up some catfish and served it with hush puppies.

"It's lunchtime," Shelby said.

"You've got nothing in your stomach, boy. I call that breakfast."

She jumped up to fill a bowl. I sat close to my uncle, watching him smoke, waiting for him to tell me more. Shelby's green eyes were the color of a 7-UP bottle and turned suddenly clear, then cloudy again, like the mood ring I wore in school. He had the long, thin jaw of a Modigliani figure (the artist Mimi was currently obsessed with), a deep melancholy etched under dark eyebrows and above dark lashes. He had high cheekbones that made his face all angles, a crooked nose like Mimi's, and strong, robust features, which made me think that everything that should be strong inside of him was seized and gathered externally, here, on his angular face.

"Shelby, tell me about my mother and Elvis."

But Granny's hand came down in front of Shelby's face, setting down a big steaming bowl of gumbo and a plate of hot bread. Shelby jumped up to attend to his ritual before eating.

I followed him to the bathroom, where he stood in front of the sink, methodically rolling up his sleeves past his elbows.

"Hi," I offered, waving. "Remember me? Your niece?"

No answer, just a rush of water from the faucet and his hands dipping under, then the thick white lather of soap up to his elbows, and the scrub, over and over, like Dr. Marcus Welby on TV. I watched for a while, until I heard the front door open and the rustle of bags and loud voices. Mimi and Connie were home. Darn. I'd lost my chance to hear about Elvis.

"Silvie," Mimi was calling. "Where are you?" And in a flash she was standing at the end of the hall, watching me watch Shelby wash his hands. She was wearing flowered culottes I'd never seen before and a white sleeveless top. Even her lipstick looked softer, more pink than red, more the color of her real lips. I stared at her, and for the first time in a long time, I wanted to hug her.

"Silvie, come here, darlin'." Then she was next to me, her hand on my shoulder, and we stood together watching Shelby hold his arms under the faucet, watching the mounds of frothy bubbles collect, staring in fascination as he rinsed sin down the drain.

"Y'all," Sweet Nina Baby hollered, jolting us alert. "Time for lunch." Despite her quiet nature, her pleasing disposition, no one could bark an order like Sweet Nina Baby. I guessed she just wanted to be heard every now and then, loud and clear. Still, her name suited her, because she always had a shy smile on her face and was quick to offer a word of encouragement in that musical voice of hers, which sounded like singing.

Sweet Nina Baby had long brown hair and was pretty and plump and pale like the women in the Renoir paintings in Mimi's book. When she was born, Granny and Paw Paw were in their forties and my mother was sixteen. Now, at eighteen, she had a certain dignity that commanded attention. But underneath that dreamy little smile was something you couldn't reach, some part of her that she'd locked away. Most nights, she stood in front of the bathroom mirror, rolling her hair on jumbo orange juice cans before retreating to her room, where she talked on the phone and polished her toenails.

Granny had spooned out bowls of soup for everyone. Her gumbo was a thick and spicy mix of chicken, shrimp, hot sausage, okra, and fresh tomatoes, served over white rice. She got a kick out of the fact that my father, the Yankee, loved it more than anyone. We all loved the food in Biloxi, great steaming bowls of boiled shrimp with Granny's remoulade sauce or black-eyed peas and gravy and corn bread.

Now Connie was busy cutting the thick slab of bread Paw Paw had bought the day before in the French Quarter and Mimi was placing a butter dish on the lazy Susan. Soon, Theo and my father came in with the stuffed animals they'd won at the Goofy Golf and Paw Paw came home wearing his hard hat.

"Sil, I got a hole in one!" Theo's face was flushed from excitement.

"A regular Jack Nicklaus." My father ruffled his hair.

"Neat," I said. It was hard to pay attention to my father and brother in Biloxi; other people were louder, and my mind was busy figuring them all out.

"*Bonjour, famille,*" Paw Paw boomed, removing his hat and running his hand over his whiskery jaw. He was broad-shouldered, barrel-chested, puffed and proud. He wore tiny wire-rimmed glasses held together at the left temple with masking tape, although his daughters begged him to get them fixed. "They look so poor, Daddy," Connie would say, but Paw Paw would shake his head. "They work fine."

"Saw my men down at the site of the future Gulf Stream Shopping Mall," he boasted now, his accent a mix of French and Deep South. "Dan, it's gonna be a beauty." When he wasn't pressuring

Shelby, he was trying to entice my father into moving down South to work for him, manage his buildings. Sometimes he took my father with him to a site or a meeting. Someone, Paw Paw always said, was stealing his land out from under his feet. He always thought someone was robbing him blind, but no one ever did.

Anyway, he owned lots and lots of properties now. Sometimes we all piled into the car and drove by them, one by one, Paw Paw leaning half his body out the window, one hand on the steering wheel. He'd point out the movie theater, where we got to see the movies for free, several motels, a restaurant called Catfish Daddy's, famous for its fried dill pickles, a handful of parking lots, and the Goofy Golf, which Theo adored and which, until this more grown-up summer, had also been a favorite of mine. "I am *genuine* American," Paw Paw bragged while we drove. "I *own* land. Not bad for a little boy from a tiny village in France."

Now everyone sat around the table, Mimi fretting that Theo had gotten overheated in the sun. His face was flushed a bright red.

"Now, Simone, calm yourself," Paw Paw said. "That boy just had a nice afternoon with his father and you go on trying to dampen his fun."

"You're right, Daddy," Mimi said, laughing prettily. "I just forget how stiflin' it gets down here."

Connie looked up from her bowl and mimed a yawn. "Ho-hum, darlin'. Hard for me to believe you could forget this heat. Can't make a Yankee overnight out of a little girl who lived in Biloxi for twenty years." Connie was taller than my mother, with darker eyes and wild, curly hair, beautiful, as all the Reisman women were, but with a wide mouth always set in a tense line. She had not yet been able to have children. Maybe because Uncle Phil was never around, Mimi had commented under her breath one night.

"Nineteen," Mimi said to Connie now, with a little eyebrow lift.

"Simone, better count," Granny said.

Connie nodded. "Now, darlin', I know for a fact that you were married a week before your twentieth birthday." Once she started, Aunt Connie wouldn't stop. That was just the self she was born with, Mimi often said.

Mimi glanced at Paw Paw for support, but he was chomping a large bite of bread, his head so low over his soup bowl that he seemed to be praying. She had to settle for looking daggers at Connie and resuming her meal.

Shelby wouldn't eat while we ate. He stood by Granny's sweets cabinet; inside were bags and bags of delicious, mouth-watering candy—Mr. Goodbars in their shiny yellow wrappers, Heath bars, quarter-pound bags of M&M's, half-eaten pralines in their crinkly cellophane wrappers. But Shelby wouldn't touch a thing. He'd just survey the candy while we were eating dinner, shake another cigarette from a nearly empty pack, raise it to his mouth with a trembling hand, light it, inhale, slowly exhale, and repeat the process a half-dozen times, staring silently into the sunny day beyond the kitchen window.

"Simone, what do you call those things you're wearing?" Paw Paw growled.

"Culottes, Daddy. I designed them myself."

"Stand up," Paw Paw boomed.

Mimi hesitated.

"Stand up! I want to take a look."

She stood, awkwardly, hands smoothing her hips.

"Looks like they can't make up their mind to be shorts or a skirt," Connie sniffed.

"They're pretty, Simone. Would you make me a pair?" Sweet Nina Baby said.

"Now, child, I made you a perfectly good pair of culottes," Granny said.

"They make me look fat, Mama," Nina said softly. "Simone's don't flare out as much."

"Walk," Paw Paw ordered my mother. She did. "Turn. *Bon*."

"Eat, child, eat," Granny said to Sweet Nina Baby, who had refused gumbo and now sat hunched over the same meal I'd seen her
eat all week—a small salad and a Tab with ice. Mimi said that Nina
had gone off to college and stopped eating, and for once, she wasn't
exaggerating.

"You should have won that sewing contest," Paw Paw bellowed.
"Did you do your best, Simone?"

"Leon, second place is nothing to scoff at," my father said.

"It's not first. In this family, we come in first." My grandfather
slapped the table. "I didn't come all the way over here from France
on that boat to be a nobody! I don't expect my children to be no-
bodies, either. As far as I can see, that's exactly what they are. Connie's wasting her brains taking care of that good-for-nothing
husband of hers. Simone dropped out of Ole Miss to get married.
Shelby here never gets out of bed. And Sweet Nina, well, the ver-
dict's not in yet."

"Simone got out of this goddamn house," Shelby said. "That's
an accomplishment." He fished around for his cigarettes in the
pocket of his shirt and sat down at the table.

Everyone stopped eating, so rarely did Shelby speak.

"Don't you light that cigarette at my table, boy," Paw Paw
warned, his bread poised above his gumbo. "Now, you listen. I sold
my stamp collection, left France, and landed on Ellis Island with
not a cent in my pocket. A total stranger lent me twenty-five dollars to pay the landing fee if I'd work in his clothing store. Later,
my father, my pregnant sister, my brother-in-law were herded off
like wild animals to concentration camps. They all perished except
my sweet Maman. Maman was moved down on the Nazis' list because she sewed like an angel. How did she do it? Fine, even
stitches despite her quaking hands? I don't know, but don't y'all sit
there eating pie and talk to me about trouble."

"Hush up, old man," Granny said.

"All the money I've spent to feed you, educate you, and what do you give me back? Nothing." He dropped his head into his hands, then peered out from behind his fingers.

After that trip, my father would tell me that the same kind of strength it took to overcome negative circumstances could make you tyrannical, which meant bossy, I found out when I looked it up. He said that although I had my mother to thank for my artistic gifts—and she had a real eye for line, for color, just like her father did for business and her brother for music—there was sometimes a price to pay. In families like that, pain and tragedy are handed down along with sensitivity and depth. These people live on the edge with their gifts, my father said. They have to hold on extra tight to keep from falling off. He seemed, by saying this, to set himself apart from Mimi and me.

"Tell me one thing, Dan!" Paw Paw was saying. "Are you taking care of my daughter and her precious children in the way she was accustomed?"

"I'm doing my best," my father said, smiling affably.

"But is your best good enough? Do you have the extras?"

My father swallowed. "What kind of extras do you mean?"

"No one's talkin' about extras, Leon," Granny said.

"I work for a good company," my father said.

"A good company?" Paw Paw said. "Who's the *me* in your company? Hmm? Who's the boss? Does he know you exist? Does he know that my beautiful daughter or her beautiful children exist? Have you had the hotshot over for dinner, like I've been telling you to?"

Mimi perked right up. "Oh yes, Daddy. We had a wonderful dinner party. We invited Roger, Dan's boss, and . . ."

"Simone . . ." my father said.

"It was lovely." Mimi shot him a look.

"They had shrimp," Theo put in. "With a yucky sauce."

"It was not yucky, son," my father said.

"If you worked for me, Dan, you'd be a real hotshot," Paw Paw continued. "When you're the boss, when you're the big man, you say, 'Hop,' and the little people say, 'How high?' "

"Not everyone can be the boss, Leon," my father said quietly.

"Bah! Why don't you at least ride over with me after lunch and take a look at this property I plan to turn around and lease to Walgreen's?"

"All right. I'll go," my father said.

"Dan!" Mimi turned on him. "You can be a boss! It just takes time. We're doing very well where we are . . ."

"Simone," Paw Paw bellowed. "You think you belong some place better than here?"

"No, Daddy. We just like to do things on our own."

Paw Paw pushed his chair back and folded his arms across his thick chest. "Better to be a big fish in a small pond than a little fish in a—how do you say—big pond."

My mother stood up, trembling, hands on hips. "I am *not* a little fish," she said, stalking out of the room. My father pushed back his chair and went after her.

We sat in the gust of silence Mimi had left. Theo slipped out of his chair and stood so close to me that I felt his breath on my cheek. "It's okay," I whispered. "Go sit down."

"What's she doing in Michigan anyway?" Connie said. "Old Tallulah should have moved to Hollywood."

Everyone but Nina had finished eating. Now Shelby moved to the sink, where he washed a clean bowl, then a spoon and knife, and the glass for his Coke. Then he served himself some gumbo, sat back down and began to eat.

Shelby chewed each bite twenty-six times, because he'd read somewhere that it was healthy to do so. "Masticating properly," he had explained to me. Back at home, I'd coached Theo and we'd tried masticating, practicing over and over. We gave up after about ten chews, because by that time, the food had disintegrated to nothingness in our mouths.

"I made pee-can pie, y'all," Granny announced, plunking the pie down on the table, the nuts such a rich brown that they smelled like caramel.

"Nora, not everyone at this table is finished eating, can't you see? You, little girl," Paw Paw said gruffly to Sweet Nina Baby. "You haven't eaten a thing." He jumped up and stood over his youngest child, dangling a piece of lettuce in front of her. Her salad looked untouched. "Rabbit food. Why can't you eat bread and gumbo like the rest of us?" He grabbed his last bite of bread and pressed it into her face. Sweet Nina Baby clenched her teeth. "Eat it!" Paw Paw barked. Nina responded with a defiant shake of her head.

Paw Paw threw the bread down in disgust and turned to Shelby. "And as for you, son, swallow! Swallow your goddamn food." Paw Paw stood behind Shelby's chair now, shouting. Shelby didn't answer, just looked out the window and went on chewing.

Paw Paw sat back down in his seat, on his way stopping to cup Nina's chin in his hand. "I don't worry about you for long, little girl, you're so sweet. But this one gives me pain. Right here." He tapped his heart, then leaned over and tapped Shelby's cheek lightly. *"Petit perdu garçon."*

Years later, I learned what the French words meant: "Little lost boy."

Paw Paw pointed at his son. "You. Shelby. Why don't you ride over with me after lunch and take a look at the Finch property? Corner of Hill and Bayou. Prime location."

Shelby, who had pushed his food away and lit a cigarette, jerked it to his lips, looked at his father, and blew out the smoke.

"Bah!" Paw Paw's hand sliced the air. "Go back to bed."

My parents came back to the table, my father steering Mimi toward a seat.

"So happy you could join us, little girl." Granny looked around at her children. "I do hope you're proud. Y'all have behaved so ugly."

"All y'all are angry because I left, because I got out of this, this . . ." Mimi stopped, her voice hot and indignant, like a teenager's. "You could at least try to be nice when I've traveled all this way."

"Why'd you leave in the first place . . ." Connie started.

"I told you," Shelby spoke up. "She left because this house is a loony bin, that's why." He glanced at his father.

"Shelby's the only one who tells the truth around here," Mimi said.

"*Fini!* Enough!" Paw Paw roared, and soon everyone went silent. Theo said he wanted to get another hole in one tomorrow, and we moved on, chattering about lighter things. Every now and then, I reached into my pocket and touched the penny and the underpants nestled there, my secret rebellion.

◆ ◆ ◆

At my grandparents' house, the four of us, my father, Theo, me, and Mimi, in that arrangement, slept in Granny's king-size bed. Mimi had told me that Paw Paw and Granny hadn't slept in the same bed for years. My father and Theo always fell asleep within a minute of lying down, while Mimi and I lay in the darkness, staring at the ceiling and the white walls, the gentle hum of a table fan moving the air around. Thick curtains blocked out the moonlight, and that night, I felt the darkness sucking us in.

"They hate me, Silvie. Always have." Mimi's voice came out haltingly, filled with tears. "Because I had stars in my eyes. But it was Paw Paw himself who put them there! He says all those things about success, but he doesn't want his children to have any, to be better than he is, to leave him. Not one mile away. You know that old rhyme?" she whispered. "Sticks and stones may break my bones . . ."

"But words will never hurt me," I finished, holding her hand.

"But it's not true, Silvie!" she cried out in anguish. "Words *do* hurt. The most."

I held on to her hand, surprised she was saying this, she who had hurt me so with her words, her looks. I felt happy, happier than I'd been in a long time. Then she snuggled up to my back, giving off the sullied female power that burned like a spear inside her, handing it over to me.

◆ ◆ ◆

In the mornings, my grandparents' empty living room looked pale, startled, as if its inhabitants had dropped everything and left unexpectedly. I tried to imagine Mimi's days in this room as a child, unfolding as a play unfolds—the talk, the arguments, the love so close to hate that the house itself now possessed the stories, etched into the mortar that held the brick together. Here was the closet, with its thrilling jumble of old toys—Nina's Mystery Date game and Barbie Dream House, Shelby's Chinese checkers and paint-by-number kits. A steep staircase led to the attic room where my grandfather slept.

Nights, we gathered in the living room after dinner, under a large bay window overlooking the water, the baby-grand piano in the corner. "Listen up, y'all," Sweet Nina Baby shouted one night, clapping her hands. "Shelby's gonna play his music. Go ahead, baby." She called Shelby baby, although he was older than she.

We all scrambled to find a seat on the rattan love seat and chairs as Shelby lifted his sleeping guitar from its case and without hesitation made it sing, nicotine-stained fingers racing over the strings, strumming, left knee bouncing in perfect rhythm, feet tapping, shoulders straighter than I'd seen them all week. Relieved, I thought he'd discovered some trick, some magic way to be happy. As he launched into "Long Distance Information" and "House of the Rising Sun," in a raspy, unused voice, perspiration stood out on his forehead, giving his whole face a sheen. His eyes grew increasingly alert and animated, his hands almost steady, a rare smile flashing across his face.

I ran my hand across the round glass table trimmed in rattan and brought away a dust-covered finger. Granny, although she loved to cook, had never done a lick of housework in her life—another one of Mimi's smug revelations. And Rosie Rose, the maid, whom we all adored, was known to miss things, because she watched soap operas while she worked and every few minutes settled her ample frame into the sofa, letting her tears trickle out, wiping her face with a dust rag, two round spots of pink flushing her cheeks. Once, I tugged her arm and said, "Rosie Rose, don't cry. It's not real, it's just TV." And she lifted her face and gathered me into one of the deep hugs I loved, shaking her head ruefully. "Miss Silvie, you just too young to know. All life sad, you see, honey chile. You see when you old like me."

I settled back next to Paw Paw, who put his arm around me. Theo was already snuggled under his other arm.

In the middle of the "House of the Rising Sun," Shelby pointed to me and I joined in. I'd been working on my voice at home, singing "Bridge over Troubled Water" and "Let It Be" into candlesticks with Martine, transforming my bed into a stage, the pillows acting as an audience of admiring boyfriends.

My father beamed. "Thata girl! Not half bad."

Mimi leaned toward Granny. "Hear her, Mama? Has a pretty voice, doesn't she?"

I'd never heard her so proud of me, even after she once put mayonnaise in my hair to make it shiny and it came out slick as oil and we had to rinse and rinse, six or more times, until the film was gone and finally my hair was how she wanted it, golden brown and smooth, like honey.

Connie smiled at me; music could always reach her.

Sweet Nina Baby sipped her Tab and stroked my hair, whispering when the song was over, "Silvie, want me to braid your hair before I go out?"

We started another song, Nina sitting behind me gently weaving my hair while I sang. Shelby had said I was an alto, and he lowered the notes a whole scale so I could reach them. "You have a good voice, low and clean," he said softly during the part with no words. "You're still free enough to sing real simply and sound good."

I just smiled and went on singing, directly at my uncle, the most handsome, talented creature on earth. I thought about the nights we sat up late together, watching old movies on television, *The Birds, Funny Face, Days of Wine and Roses.* Shelby was good with cards and a yo-yo; he taught me to shuffle fast, the way grown-ups did. For Theo, he pulled a penny out of his ear, guessed jack of diamonds from a whole deck, burped and tooted on cue. He was also an expert joke teller, perfecting accents and pausing for emphasis. Paw Paw howled at one that involved a rabbi, a priest, and an Indian. It was strange how much Shelby, who rarely laughed, loved jokes. He responded with a whisper-laugh, so soft you could barely hear him.

When I came back to earth, the concert was over and everyone was clapping and Theo clamored for his turn and Shelby, face flushed, eyes shining, hauled him up on his knee and showed him some chords, teaching him about blues music, how the tunes were based on variations of one pattern.

Connie jumped up, saying she had to run—Uncle Phil would be home from Mobile by now—and Paw Paw yawned and retreated to his attic room. Granny went to get Nina off the phone and never returned. I pictured them both sprawled on her bed, Nina's feet up on her dresser, a Tab in one hand, the phone in the other, Granny greasing her whole head with Dippity-Do to make pin curls for her big date later with Bo Corco, whose mama, Nina said, had won first place in the annual Gulf Coast Chicken Fry. When I started dating, I wondered, would Mimi help me improve my hair? No, she'd be jealous.

Now, perched on Shelby's knee, Theo sang "Hound Dog," twice, with Shelby accompanying him. Mimi didn't say a word, although both my father and I glanced at her several times. She just sat there, lost in the music, which seemed to have no connection to her other than once having been a popular song on the radio. When they finished singing, she jumped up and hugged Shelby. "I'm proud of both my boys. Shel, you're so talented."

Shelby stayed limp while she hugged him, looking down at his hands, but he flashed her a shy smile as he smashed out his cigarette. "I'm outta cigs. Gotta run to the store."

"Can I go with you? Please?" I looked from him to Mimi to my father. Mimi had a pained expression on her face, but my father said, "Sure. But don't be gone long."

The air had cooled some, and the big oak from which my mother's childhood swing still hung stood tall and strong, bathed in moonlight. Backing the white 1966 Mustang out of the driveway, Shelby drove down the highway along the beach toward Willie's Market. The windows were open and the trees hung low as a canopy over the highway. The humid air seeped in, warm as Mimi's bathwater, heavy with the perfume of sweat and magnolia blossoms.

At a red light, he pointed to the letters printed on the dashboard: L1, L2, and L3. "Know what that L-Two means?" I shook my head. "Means leap over two cars. If you put it in second gear, we'll leap right over those cars in front of us."

"Can I try?"

"When the light turns." We waited for the light to turn, and when it did, he said quietly, "Best shade of green we're gonna get," put his hand over mine, and guided it to second. I shifted the stick and we seemed to fly, and I barely heard his voice, like spitting gravel, saying, "Next time, maybe next time," because it seemed to me we leaped over at least two cars on the highway.

When we pulled back into the driveway, I rubbed my fingers over the panties in my pocket, then over the penny, for good luck. Now. Now he'd tell me about Paw Paw, about my mother, about what he'd meant when he said she'd ruin my life.

Shelby turned off the ignition, but he didn't get out, just flexed his arms on the steering wheel and turned to me in the purple dusk. He'd left the radio on, and "Sweet Caroline" trickled out softly.

"I was surprised your mama let you come with me."

"Why?"

"She thinks I'm nuts."

Horrified, I said, "No she doesn't."

He laughed, a harsh, dry sound, and clicked the radio off. "Truth is, this whole family's nuts. It's like living inside a pressure cooker. You think you're going to explode. But you never do. You just go on cooking."

"What do you mean?"

He didn't respond. Finally, he said, "Ever hear about Louise?"

"Louise? No."

"Lou was a girl I used to know. Nice. Real pretty. She sang at the Bayou Club. Boy, she could sing. Voice like butter. She made strong men cry."

"Did you like her?"

He looked straight ahead, out the windshield. "We were friends. Paw Paw didn't like her coming around."

"Why?"

"She was a black girl."

"Oh."

"I haven't seen her in a while."

"Why don't you call her up?"

"I don't know." He lit a cigarette.

"Do you have a picture of her?" I persisted.

"Yeah, somewhere." He made a vague gesture with his cigarette and an arc of light from the glowing tip sped through the car. "I put it away special, but I can't find it."

I fell silent. "Why did Paw Paw care that she was black?"

"Don't think he would have liked her if she were white, either. She didn't come from much. Shouldn't matter. Color of your skin, how much you got in your wallet—we're all just souls dressed up in bags of bones and flesh." His voice was weak, as if he had hardly enough energy to push the words out. "So your mama told you the Elvis story?"

I tried to laugh. "About a million times."

"Yeah, but has she told you the facts, I wonder." His tone rendered the Elvis story cheap, tawdry, perhaps a bald lie, the truth blinking behind it like a diner's old neon sign that read the same on both sides—she was a nobody, a rich man's pretty daughter in a small town.

"This is B. B. King." Shelby pushed a tape into the eight-track. "Ever hear of him?"

"No." I liked the deep voice that boomed out.

"That was 'Caldonia,' " he said. "And this is 'Nobody Loves Me but My Mother.' Now, *there* was a king. Elvis learned from him. Know why everybody loves Elvis?"

"No."

"Because he sings and moves like a black man but he's white." Shelby stared off into the distance, his long face pinched and sad. "About your mama, you should know the truth or else it will hurt you later," he said, in a voice that seemed to come from another planet.

Finally. The truth was here. I gripped the vinyl seat cushion.

But without another word Shelby turned off the tape, climbed out of the car, and began moving toward the house in his gentle shuffle.

Desperately, I ran after him, bargaining. "Shelby, wait! I want to show you something."

At the top of the driveway, he turned, his pale skin tinged with green under the garage light.

Touching the underwear in my pocket, I said, "I found these, out back." I pulled them out and thrust them toward him. Maybe he'd tell me something now.

He stared down at them. "You'd better throw them away."

I held them out, eyes steady and hopeful.

He took them, rolling the panties into a ball, hands trembling. But they had always trembled, hadn't they? "She'll tell you lies," he said, very quietly. I had to move closer to hear him. "She'll exaggerate. She'll ruin your life with it. She'll make you reach, then slap your hand when you try."

"But did they go out? Did she really go out with Elvis?"

"Well, he came to pick your mama up. I don't know what went on after that, but he was here on that very porch." He pointed. "I happened to be sitting out here with my guitar around my neck—I was only fourteen—and he taught me a few licks while he was waiting for her to get ready. And later, he wrote me a letter. Told me to keep my music heart alive. So they did go out, but she was home early. I know because I waited up, hoping to see Elvis again. But I never did. I guess I shouldn't have told you." He held out the underwear.

"You can keep them," I whispered. He seemed to need them more than I did.

He shrugged and took them. We stood and looked up at the night sky, empty of stars.

"Will you show me the letter Elvis wrote you?"

"Yeah. Sometime." He paused, figuring something. "See, up there in the North, your mama can stretch the truth and make people follow her. Like a queen."

"But why does she want that?"

He jerked his head up. Something that had been simmering a long time bubbled over. "Because Paw Paw taught us to want that. So your mama reaches for the stars when not a thing's in the sky. But watch out, she'll destroy her life. Everyone in this family destroys things. She'll destroy her life, because she doesn't carry any trust around inside her."

It all rang true. "How do you know?"

"People who wreck their lives recognize each other." He laughed harshly. "Down at the Winn-Dixie, rotting away between the bananas and the cantaloupe." Raising his palm, he scooped the air—our fish salutation. Then, he turned and walked with his sweet languor into the house, stuffing the stained underwear into the pocket of his jeans.

I hoped my gift would bring him luck. Louise. I hoped it would bring back pretty Louise. Instinctively, my hand flew to my own pocket, to the flattened coin there, my own lucky charm to help me once I was home again.

◆ ◆ ◆

The next day, in a whirl of hugs and kisses, we said good-bye to Paw Paw, Granny, Connie, Shelby, and Sweet Nina Baby. Paw Paw stood with his hands behind his back, kissing us roughly and slipping one ten-dollar bill into my hand, then one into Theo's. Shelby promised to write, and I envisioned his tiny, cramped writing growing bigger and bolder across a page, freed with the good fortune the underwear had brought him, bursting forth with all the news about new music, a return to love. But I knew he wouldn't write. And even though I left Biloxi armed with a bundle of new knowledge in my little pink suitcase, Mimi would go on being whoever she wanted to be and Shelby would choose one day out of every other day and jump off the tallest building in Biloxi.

CHAPTER 12

I had hoped my mother would forget about shopping, but the next morning, when I came upstairs, she was dressed and sitting very straight in her chair at the kitchen table, pushing the poached egg and dry toast around on her plate. Henry brought her a glass of Sustacal, which she sipped, her mouth set in a determined line. She wore a purple velour sweat suit and, on her feet, little black flats covered with multicolored buttons. Her wig was shining. "We're going to find the perfect dress for you," she announced. "I'm having a good day. Let's go."

Henry held her by the elbow and steered her out the door, his thick black brows knitted together. My mother walked slowly to the car, taking careful breaths. She slapped his hand away when he tried to buckle her seat belt, saying, "I can do it." Henry dropped us off at the bridal salon, like two teenage girls going to the mall.

In the dressing room, spacious, lushly carpeted, with a small round podium in front of a brightly lit three-way mirror, Mimi blinked when I faced her in the first dress. A magazine phrase

floated through my head: *the lovely bride in white*. I thought her eyes
would fill or that she'd gasp, but she didn't. "Turn," was all she said.

I turned. The stiff fabric rustled. "Just wait till you have to take a
whiz, dragging that thing around," Mimi said.

"I don't like puffed sleeves on me." I wrinkled my nose.

"Hideous. On anyone. Once, Granny bought me a dress with
puffs for the Debuteen Ball and I whacked them off with scissors.
Oh, Evelyn . . ." Mimi's hand, as she called to the salesgirl, rose
helplessly and fluttered down, landing on the chair's armrest. Normally, we were independent shoppers, rolling up our sleeves and
plunging in. "Where are you, Evelyn?"

"It's Evangelina." A salesgirl appeared in the doorway, correcting
Mimi's mistake with a precise movement of her blunt auburn hair
and a pursing of her glossy lips. She already had another batch of
dresses over her arm.

"We are not fond of the puffed sleeve," Mimi said, then stopped
abruptly and gave her wig a tug of annoyance.

Evangelina nodded. "Cap maybe, or sleeveless." She studied us
in the mirror, taking in my mother's gaunt frame, the velour sweat
suit that hung in folds, the incongruously bright buttons decorat-
ing her shoes. Mimi had the watery, distracted look of the sick,
busy in her head, adding and subtracting, remembering multiplication tables.

I caught Evangelina's eye, but she looked down at her fingernails, long, polished, the color of eggplant. She was the kind of joyless girl who smiled with her mouth closed, as if trying to convince
herself that things really mattered. "Now, girls, you mustn't overlook the sequins," she said grimly. "Dazzling, aren't they?"

Mimi and I turned to the sequins, each tiny disk containing
some portent, like a cell or a cloud. Evangelina left to gather more
dresses, and my mother mimicked her, "*Girls, mustn't overlook the sequins. We can do better.*"

We ran our hands over them, rough as fish scales. Usually, Mimi liked things shiny, luminous; once sequins would have appealed to her, with their flash of color and surprise, like a drop of gasoline in a puddle. All the radiant grace and splendor that seemed absent from the regular world, she'd found in a textured linen or in hand-painted china buttons. It didn't take an expensive thing to catch her eye, a bargain would do, but it had to be quirky, interesting, hand-made by an artiste, who had put some heart and soul into it, like the collage purses she collected. I carried a black backpack. She called my taste classic, but we both knew what she really meant. Boring. *D-u-l-l.*

From her chair, Mimi lifted her arms to unzip me but couldn't muster the strength. Evangelina came in, cradling the unwieldy new dresses. "I'll get that," she said.

I pressed my elbows against my ribs, a silly twenty-six-year-old longing for her mother's touch. There was no poetry in Evan-gelina's resolute tug on the zipper, only the practiced aplomb of a salesperson who, when you weren't looking, sneaked glances at her watch. The dress fell heavily to the floor, and Evangelina swept it away; I stood shivering in my bra and underwear, feeling my mother's eyes on me.

"You have my arms exactly," my mother observed, head cocked.

I smiled, raising them in the mirror, and imagined lifting off high above this tiny room and flying far away. I hadn't realized how much my arms were like hers, slender and tapered as two candle-sticks. But my eyes, my jaw, were all my father.

Evangelina slipped another dress over my head and fastened it roughly. I felt anger in her, deep down, that hard cold kernel you sometimes feel from people. She spoke in clipped tones, all busi-ness. "Now, this next one is *more* than a dress—it's a work of art. Cutting-edge for fall, most definitely. Cap sleeves, no sequins, the thing here is the color. Not white but pink, a new shade called blush. Big, big, big at Carolina Herrera in New York." It was funny, really, a dour girl selling fluffy dresses.

One more "big" and I would have socked her. I studied myself in the mirror. The pink satin had a magnifying effect; I looked like a huge, overdecorated wedding cake. Behind me in her chair, Mimi gave a starry-eyed sigh, as if it were 1958 and she were the bride. "Dreamy," she said, wadding the tissue in her fist into a ball.

"Yeah," I muttered. "A real nightmare." I tugged at it.

"Silvie, don't be negative. I think it's dreamy."

"Well, I don't like it." When she opened her purse for another tissue, I made a face at her.

"Ladies, ladies, how about this?" Evangelina interrupted, holding out a boat-necked mountain of lace.

"No lace," I said.

"We'll try it," Mimi said, at precisely the same time.

We looked at each other and giggled.

"Don't let's give up," Evangelina said soberly. "Remember, we're on a quest for perfection. We're on love's voyage." She trudged off to a white room I imagined filled with tiers of dresses. If you tipped your head back, they'd be standing stiff and tall on hangers, so heavy that if one fell, you might be crushed by folds of chiffon and silk.

"Did she just say we were on *love's voyage*?" Mimi asked.

"I believe she did."

"Maybe we should sneak out the back door." Mimi let out a sharp bark that with more air might have been a laugh. In the mirror, her face was gray as newspaper.

"Mimi, let's stop for the day," I said. Here we were, *shopping*. It was painful to look at her, lips pale and cracked from dehydration and vomiting. I'd been spared the ugly details, since Henry pulled over to the side of the road on the way home from chemotherapy. I felt a familiar stab of guilt about not having come home earlier, about being home only when she felt well enough to shop. I should be sitting on a park bench with her, holding hands, summing things up, saying good-bye. But it was hard to say good-bye to someone who insisted she wasn't going anywhere.

"Are you kidding?" she said slowly, with effort. "I haven't had a chance to try on my mother-of-the-bride dress yet. Remember what I always said: You get the ring, I'll get the dress. This is a big day for me."

"It's a big day for *me*."

"Something in fuchsia, maybe, or white."

I looked at her. Here it was, pushing in, the reason I hadn't wanted to do this. "Mimi, the bride wears white."

At that moment, Evangelina came back and helped me into the last dress—satin with long, fitted sleeves that ended in a point on the hand. The dress was a perfect white, soft, not the blue-white of snow or paper but a sweet, rich cream; it was off-the-shoulder, fitted at the waist, with a row of satin-covered buttons down the back. The neckline was adorned with a narrow band of pearls, a delicate wreath.

Mimi gave a weak whistle. "And you vowed to be married in a black pantsuit."

I lifted the full skirt and turned slowly toward the mirror, letting it drop, drawing my breath in sharply.

"The pearls are spectacular," said Evangelina, who smiled in spite of herself, revealing a mouthful of silver braces. No wonder she'd been stingy with her smile. Suddenly, I felt sorry for her, working in this place of inflated dreams, with jittery, self-indulgent girls trying on gossamer dresses, smugly making one day the centerpiece of a lifetime.

"The handwork," my mother exclaimed, fumbling in her purse for her glasses so she could examine the gleaming bud of a pearl. Good seams and basting could always make her cry. "It's a Silvie dress, all right. Quiet, tailored, yet with a bit of *powee*."

"This dress will knock the groom out cold, honey," Evangelina said, showing more spunk than she had all day.

"He's a *doctor*," Mimi jumped in.

Evangelina took in this information with a grave nod. I was busy admiring my reflection. This was the first time in my life that I'd ever felt beautiful with my mother in the room. My cheeks seemed rosy, my hair, thick and glossy.

Evangelina arranged a long veil over my face and down my back. "Veils are all the rage this season . . ."

Mimi sat up, spine rigid, haughty. "Now, why would you go and hide a pretty face?"

"I like a veil." I peeked out from behind it, attempting to conjure mystery and romance right here in the dressing room, but the mood was slipping away and the room was just a room, filled with Mimi's wavering voice.

"Evangelina, what is the price of this whole to-do?" Mimi asked. "How much is this whole getup?"

Evangelina lifted the veil from my face and quoted the price, as if I were the thing for sale.

"And that's before alterations, shoes, headpiece, stockings," Mimi said, ticking off a detailed list on her fingers. "It's a little high. You could wear my dress," she offered.

"Which one?" I asked sarcastically, imagining all the bad stuff passing through the fabric, through the thin wall of cells between us, catching and sticking, spoiling first one life, then another. Anyway, I'd have to hold my breath to fit into her first wedding dress, and the second one, the weird beige lace number she'd designed herself, with the high collar and cape, looked like some outtake from *Dr. Zhivago*.

After Evangelina had whisked off my dress and carried the last pile out of the room, Mimi said, "Did I tell you about my visualizations?" Closing her eyes, she leaned back, resting her head on the back of the chair.

I shook my head. I was standing in just my underwear.

"Well, I imagine all the people who love me—you, Theo, Henry, Aunt Nina, Aunt Connie, Letty, even Loretta, the woman up at Vanities who does my nails—as a team of Pac-Man creatures.

They all come in with little vacuum mouths and swoosh the cancer away. Next, I visualize Theo when he was young, invading my body in full Batman attire, avenging the cancer. Remember the costume I made him? He absolutely *lived* in it, never once took it off." She opened her eyes and bit her lip. "Every day I went to the grocery store with a little creature in black tights and a cape and— what did he call that mask? A cowl?" Her eyes misted over and she shrugged, a little embarrassed. "So."

"Those are great." I reached for my clothes but didn't put them on. She'd created these defenses against her cancer while I'd been in New York, falling in love.

"One more. This one involves your father. He's playing one of our old musicals on the stereo, *My Fair Lady* or *Camelot,* and we're both singing 'Wouldn't It Be Loverly' or 'What Do the Simple Folk Do?' Our voices get louder and louder until, finally, we're shouting the lyrics at the top of our lungs, singing and laughing, drowning out the cancer with our happiness."

That jolted me. I looked at Mimi's reflection in the mirror, close and yet far away, her shape outlined in bright light. She made a fist and shook it high. "Yep. I can lick this."

I stood there, my arms wrapped around my waist, wondering if she really believed that.

There was a tap on the door and Evangelina walked in.

Mimi sat forward in her chair. "Evelyn—Evangelina, what do you have for the mother of the bride? Something in hot pink, maybe, or white, a soft, creamy white like Mississippi magnolias."

Evangelina looked puzzled. "White? I don't know if you want..."

"Mimi, I told you, the *bride* wears white, not the mother."

"Old rules don't always apply today."

"Do too." I bent over my jeans, sounding, even to myself, like a petulant child.

Evangelina began fluttering around the room, gathering an armful of padded hangers.

Mimi turned to Evangelina. "Bring a real knockout, will you?" she said. Evangelina nodded and practically ran out of the room. Mimi glanced at me in the mirror. I looked away and yanked my jeans up around my waist.

"Maybe my hair will grow back in time for the wedding," Mimi said. She was staring straight ahead, like a blind person.

I stood there, half-dressed. The air had changed. We were coming up against a fact—that she might not make it to the wedding at all.

Evangelina returned with three frothy dresses for Mimi, a peach, a yellow, and a pale blue.

Mimi eyed them with disgust. She hated pastels. "Evangelina . . . do your parents call you that?" she snapped. "Surely you don't expect me to wear *peach*?"

"I'm afraid we're loaded down with pastels this year."

"Pastels simply won't do. We'll have to look around." Mimi struggled to her feet, gathering her coat, scarf, and purse.

Evangelina cocked her head. "You need something bright to liven you up a little. I'll keep my eyes open. Here's my card. The bride has seen some truly exquisite looks today. Call if you want me to put something aside for you." She regarded us solemnly and lumbered off.

Groping in my purse for my glasses, I saw in the mirror that I was just me—far from glamorous: hollow-cheeked, pale, my thin, wispy brown hair looking almost gray under this light. I suddenly felt naked and adrift. All this effort seemed vain and small and ridiculous. My bra dangled over the shoulder of Mimi's chair and I snapped it on, fastening the hooks around my back. "How about red? You've always liked red."

"Maybe. Or gold brocade." Her voice trailed off as she looked past me in the mirror. She'd normally take a full five minutes fixing her makeup, stretching her lips into a wide O to apply fresh lipstick, but a frown passed across her pallid features when she saw her

wig, and her thin hand drifted up to straighten it. Underneath that
wig were the last few stubborn strands of her hair.

"I liked that pink on you." Mimi followed me out of the dressing room. "Evangelina called it *blush*." She made her voice all
jaunty and bright as we passed the salesgirls at the cash register.

"I hate pink. Anyway, brides wear white," I said stubbornly.

"Why be like everybody else?" She pushed her weight against
the glass door. Bells tinkled, and the two saleswomen called out,
"Good-bye!" in unison.

"How about cream?" Mimi said. "I could wear cream."

We stood under the awning side by side, waiting for Henry to
pick us up. We talked straight out in front of us without looking at
each other. "You can't wear cream or white or oyster . . ."

Mimi ignored me. I ignored her right back, but shakily, without
the usual secret thrill.

A playful wind had picked up and a few leaves skittered across
the parking lot. The temperature had dropped ten degrees in a span
of hours, the sudden bite in the air reminding me again of the ex-
traordinary circumstances. Pretending was strenuous. Winter was
here—somber rains that turned to snow; cold sunshine. We should
be at the kitchen table drinking hot cups of Mimi's favorite almond tea.

"Silvie. If for some reason . . ." She stopped.

I rubbed my thumb over a callus on my middle finger. I'd been
gripping the pencil too hard lately while drawing.

"You should get the dress you really want, that last one. It was
special on you." Mimi pulled her coat around her tightly, clutching
the collar.

The way she gripped the fabric made me afraid. "Mimi . . ." I
said and flapped my jeans jacket open, my hands, in my pockets,
acting as hinges. The air rushed in, cool and plush at the same time,
like a velvet egg, I thought, wanting to paint that bizarre image.

"Come on," she said. "I'm freezing." We ducked into a shop that turned out to be a sporting goods store, not a place my mother and I would normally find ourselves. Footballs, basketballs, soccer balls, and baseballs lined the high shelves, sharpening the air with their tangy scent. Mimi gestured to the stacks of catcher's gloves and gripped my arm, whispering, "I haven't seen this much leather since Shoe Stop."

I giggled, and the hard thing between us dissolved.

"I'm glad you have someone special in your life." She held my gaze.

We didn't often look into each other's eyes. I looked away, rubbing my finger over a stiff, waxy baseball mitt.

"Thanks," I said.

"You wear the white. I'll think of something. Used to be I could whip up something on my old Singer," Mimi said, her face ashen. "You know, create my own look."

I swallowed hard. There was no graceful way to do this, lose your mother. "Mimi, did you really hack off your puffed sleeves?"

"Sure did. With Granny's kitchen shears." We laughed. "Connie thought I'd lost my mind. But Granny just took the dress out of my hands and said, 'Let me see what you've done, little girl. I'll just turn the edges under and stitch them up, good as new.' "

"And yours was the prettiest gown at the ball."

"And mine was the prettiest gown at the ball."

We walked to the store window. Standing side by side, we gazed out. Dark clouds scuttled across the sky on pockets of wind like a million breaths. Rain started; slowly, then fast. But to the east, there was a far-off pocket of golden light. "Move over," Mimi said, nudging me.

I had positioned myself right next to her, our coats touching, my body almost on top of hers, as if I could protect her. I moved over, remembering that she felt claustrophobic lately. Dying must be like going blind, I thought, all the darkness closing in.

"You know what I do?" she said, wistful. She took my hand.

"Whenever I think about you all grown up and getting married? I just think of Misty, in *Misty of Chincoteague,* who had to go away from her mom." That was a book we'd borrowed from the bookmobile when I was little, one of our favorites, about a horse that had to leave home.

Her thin hand felt sharp in mine. I tried my voice. A searing lump had thickened my throat. "I'm not going anywhere, Mimi. I'm getting married, that's all. We'll still talk on the phone."

"Yes."

"Except I'll be married. That will be the only difference."

"Yes." Her breath gathered around us like an old woman's shawl. "I like Scottie, you know. He has big teeth. That's an asset."

I smiled. "He does have big teeth."

"And he's . . . resilient. He'll hold you close."

"But he'll take me away."

"Yes. That too."

I listened to her gentle breathing beside me, my eyes fastened on the cars streaming in and out of the parking lot. For a moment, I imagined capturing her breath inside a small glass jar, the way, as a child, I'd kept fireflies by my bed, to guide me through the night.

Henry's car appeared and, squeezing my hand, Mimi said, "Let's make a dash for it."

We ran to the car, slowly at first, then picking up speed, as if just now remembering how to run. We held hands, but we still got wet.

She didn't leave the house again until we took her to the hospital. I called Scottie that same day and told him to come and get fitted for his tux. And I ordered the dress I loved.

CHAPTER 13

Back from Biloxi, Theo, emulating Shelby, performed concerts on the hearth, singing into a candlestick. I sat next to my mother, scowling, as she clapped with her hands high in the air. My own clapping seemed stiff and hollow, my hands only a few inches above my lap. It was impossible to know what I liked with her grand appreciation seeping right through the air and into my skin. I never seemed to have enough padding on my bones to keep her out.

She rubbed her hand over my knee and down my shin. I tried to pull away, but she kept on. Then her hand stopped. "Silvie! When did I say you could shave your legs?" After my grumbled reply, she said, "I would have liked to have been consulted, that's all."

"They're not your legs," I mumbled, rubbing my hand over my smooth shins. My skin seemed prickly, unfamiliar, and for a moment I wanted the soft, downy hairs of childhood back.

"What did you say, young lady?"

"I said, Martine and I bought razors." I raised my chin defiantly.

"Hmmph. I should have known this was Martine's idea."

"Don't you think I'm capable of deciding to shave my own legs? I'm almost fourteen. God."

Mimi set her jaw. "You're supposed to ask your mother first."

I wouldn't look at her. Gazing at my smooth skin, I felt the weight of her love like a piece of furniture on my bones. I shifted another inch away.

◆ ◆ ◆

A month or so later, my mother and I stood in the laundry room, folding mounds of laundry. Gripping the ends of a towel, we walked toward each other. We were supposed to follow that motion with a kiss—a family tradition, handed down from Granny.

Today, instead of meeting her lips, I froze and turned my face away. "I got it," I mumbled, not looking at her. Instead of feeling excited, I felt ashamed, sheepish that my body was changing and that I needed to tell her. For an instant, I was swallowed up by a deep wish to know everything—about breasts, about periods, about sex, about *her* first period. I'd learned everything I knew from *Are You There, God? It's Me, Margaret.*

"You got what? . . . Oh, my sweetheart," she said, smoothing the folded square and blinking, raising damp eyes to mine.

She'd never called me that before, "my sweetheart."

"Come on, let's go up." She held out her hand. "I've got things upstairs."

I pulled my hand back. "I have things." My voice felt heavy, sodden with desire. To allow her to touch me would be to admit my longing for closeness.

"You do? Where did you get them?" She picked up another towel and folded it alone, no kiss, her eyes misty.

"Um, Martine and I rode our bikes to Seven-Eleven and bought stuff."

"You and Martine seem to have the whole world figured out," she said softly, doubling the towel over her arm, patting the warm, clean cloth with the same small circles I'd felt on my back when I was small and couldn't sleep.

"Well," Mimi said. "If you need anything, just let me know."

I did, I needed . . . my mind swam with questions. Would it happen in a strange place? Would I walk out of algebra and down the hall with people pointing at the large red poppy blooming on my pants? I swallowed hard, not knowing where to start. "Okay," I promised, cringing as her hand settled on my wrist like cement.

I began marking the first day with an X in a small date book I carried in my purse and showed to no one. Then I counted twenty-eight days from there and marked the next month with a question mark on the day I expected it, to be changed to an X when it came. Every month from the age of thirteen. Fourteen years of months. Each only twenty-eight days long.

One Saturday when Theo was outside helping Mimi wash her car, I snuck to her bathroom to steal tampons. I stopped short outside the door. There was my father, standing in front of the mirror, bare-chested, flexing first one bicep, then the other. He didn't see me as I watched him thrust his face toward the mirror, turning each cheek until his sideburns came into view, sizing himself up. On tiptoe, I hurried away, feeling nothing—wasted, maybe, empty. Pushing it down, on to the next thing.

I'd have to ride my bike to 7-Eleven for tampons or stuff my underwear with a wad of toilet paper. I just couldn't bring myself to tell her I needed something, to ask her to buy it for me.

♦ ♦ ♦

By the time I was fifteen, it was evident that I had grown, more or less, into my adult face. Mimi seemed secretly pleased that I was plainer than her, shorter, more subdued. She concealed her pleasure by offering to help me improve myself, as though the self I was

on my own wasn't enough. Maybe growing older made me a potential rival—for my father's attention, for all the lovers I might
someday have that she would not have had.

My mother sewed wide-legged pants and long tunic tops, which
she wore with Candies sandals. She sewed the same weird outfits
for me, which I wore with earth shoes, dreaming of stuff the other
kids wore—Organically Grown sweaters with painters' pants. We
each slung a large macramé bag over our shoulders, a jumble of lip-
sticks, tampons, and gum inside. On the eight-track in the car,
Mimi listened not just to Elvis but to "Bare Trees," by Fleetwood
Mac, and "(You Make Me Feel Like) A Natural Woman," by Car-
ole King. She no longer wore red lipstick; she now favored a shade
called Coffee Bean. She followed me around, dropping tortoise-
shell lipstick tubes into my open palm, one at a time. "You should
have these. One, two, three—here, I'll keep one, Revlon Coffee
Bean. One day, don't you just *know* they'll stop making it. Happened with Cherries in the Snow. It's back again, but still, all those
years."

Obligingly, I smeared some on, checking my lips in a mirror.
"Too deep."

She whistled. "Gorgeous-ity. That mauve you wear is weak. I
myself think you could use a little color."

I refused to wear it.

For days, Mimi's mournful gaze burned a hole in my back. But
when I turned around, she seemed to be looking at someone else.

◆ ◆ ◆

The summer I was sixteen, two deaths shook my family, plucked us
off the road like a car in a tornado, and set us down again, only this
time facing the opposite direction.

Paw Paw's death from cancer was like the opening volley in a series of shots that would shatter Mimi's family, blasting them apart
in ways they would never mend. My mother spent weeks at Paw

Paw's bedside, unable to save him, and when he was gone, Shelby grew thinner and paler, until he seemed a faint impression of himself, as though without the combat between him and his father, he had no purpose in life. Granny called to say that he'd been spending whole days in bed and that he refused to play his guitar. Sometimes Mimi sat on the couch, clutching a gray, knotted tissue, her chin in her hand, eyes pensive because she was worrying about Shelby. When she pressed the tissue to her lips, her face sagged at the mere mention of her brother.

Early one Saturday morning a few months after Paw Paw's death, when we, a thousand miles away from Biloxi, were cleaning out the basement, the cool cement walls and floor steeped in murky darkness, throwing away our old toys, paint cans, outgrown clothes, books, Shelby jumped from a building and threw away his life. Suicide, only we didn't use the word. Mimi screamed, a ghostly wail, when Connie called with the news. She hung up the phone and ripped the newspaper she'd been holding to shreds, threw the tiny pieces up into the air and sobbed, floating that day's news down around us.

I thought of Shelby's clean hands, his sad, determined chewing, the weight of his long-sleeved shirts on his shoulders. I was numb and stiff and mute, yet I wasn't surprised. Not really.

My parents flew down for the funeral and then back home; not another word was spoken. For months I was seized with terror, lying awake at night wondering where Shelby jumped from, how tall the building was. Was there a black steel fire escape knotted up the outside wall like a shoelace? Did he take the elevator or climb the stairs, his hand resting on the smooth knob of the door that opened on the roof? Was his first step tentative, like a baby's, on the soft black stomach of the tar, oozing in the early-morning sun, his footprint like the one of the first man on the moon, except he carried a guitar and a carton of Marlboros? Did he empty his last thought out of his head right there on that roof; did he drain his body of all fluids before he went, his soul an empty bottle? Did he walk toward the edge? Did he run? Did he hoist his breath over his shoulders like a sack of used feathers; did he carry his breath into the next life? Did he say out loud: "Fly"?

Now there were more afternoons when Mimi climbed into bed, shades drawn, a cold rag on her forehead, battling a migraine. I grazed my knuckles against her bedroom door, just a small tap to let her know I was there, tiptoed across the carpet to where she lay in the darkened room, one arm dangling off the bed. "I should have done more for him," she whispered. I felt sick inside when I heard that. "I knew he needed help." Her voice cracked. "Silvie, I didn't get him help."

Again and again, I saw the black street stained by Shelby's leap, his voiceless rage denting the earth, the tender bone under the skin of pavement cratered like the moon when he landed. I wondered who witnessed him hurl his spent body through space, who saw him land, a broken piece?

Loss set us apart from other families, and we stood on the edge of a new unhappiness, white and endless and swirling.

◆ ◆ ◆

After several weeks, Mimi got up out of bed and stood in front of the mirror holding strands of her hair in front of her eyes. "Drab Number Nine, I call it," she fretted. "In high school, I used to beg my daddy to let me color this twine. He never would. I should have just gone ahead."

Comparing a strand of mine to hers, I found it, to my chagrin, almost indistinguishable. But I was happy that this new concern had jolted her out of her grief.

A week or so later, she came home in a floppy hat and not until we were all seated at the dinner table did she shyly yet with a great flourish take the hat off, unveiling vivid Brigitte Bardot–blond hair.

My father stole apprehensive glances at her throughout the meal, clearing his throat a number of times but not speaking, at a loss. I sneaked glances, too; her new hair was the color of margarine and cut in a modified shag, with winged bangs.

It was Theo who spoke first, observing sadly, "Gee, Mom, you look like Farrah Fawcett."

"Yes, do you like it?" She smiled expectantly.

No one said a word.

"It's cool," I managed, thinking that brown was not a flashy color; it didn't yell soul, like red or yellow. Brown was the color of lumber, strong as skin.

Theo said to me in a small voice, "Hey, Sil, Mom had brown hair when you were little. You were lucky."

"Get used to it," Mimi said sharply, taking a bite of mashed potatoes.

My father attempted humor. "Well, Blondie, is my suit ready for tomorrow? The navy? I've got that presentation first thing in the morning and then straight to the airport for Hong Kong."

"Picked it up today," my mother said woodenly. "It's on the bed. I pressed the white shirt, too."

"Thank you," my father said. "Theo, how are you getting along with that math? Let's take a look tonight . . ."

Later, Theo would say that something changed then. Mimi stopped sewing and, when she had her new blond hair and store-bought clothes, my parents fought. Checks came in the mail, because my grandfather's properties were making money, but the more money Mimi had, the more dissatisfied she seemed with her life. She bought miniskirts and high white-vinyl boots. Mimi wanted my father to grow his sideburns, but he refused. She bought him a pair of bell-bottoms. He wore them once, but he looked lost in them, as if he were wearing an enormous raincoat or a suit two sizes too big.

◆ ◆ ◆

All it takes is one or two memories to be a family. Long after things had disintegrated, I held on to the notion that we were happy. But at a certain time of night, when the sky deepened and the air grew cooler, we could be found in separate rooms, this quartet—Mimi in the dark kitchen, a new recipe up her sleeve; my father with his briefcase in the den, cozying up to a computer; Theo, outside practicing grinds on his skateboard ramp as a trumpet played in his head; and me, on my bed with my drawings, floating above the stairway, quiet in the small spaces. No matter where I went, inside each room, there I was, seventeen years old, hungry.

The leaving happened slowly, gradually, as these things do, and before we knew it, we were lost to each other, as if a magician had whisked a cloth off a table, leaving the dishes there, jolted. And when we looked back it was all a blur, time on fast forward, hurtling to an inevitable conclusion.

◆ ◆ ◆

The noise of my father's car crashing into our house seemed to signal a foray into new, inevitable territory, and when it was over, the front fender grazed the lip of the toilet in the small half-bath off the laundry room.

Theo and I ran down the steps in our pajamas. Our mother ran after us, gripping the sides of her fuchsia bathrobe closed. When we reached the garage, Mimi thrust her arm out like a traffic cop, as if blocking us from crossing the street. Across from where we stood was a huge hole in the garage wall, jagged as a monster's mouth. We stared straight through it into the laundry room. As for the car, the left front fender was mangled, the metal twisted and hanging down a few inches, like a boxer's fat lip.

Red-faced and panting, my father shifted on the balls of his feet, his tie loose and the pockets of his suit jacket hanging heavy and sad. He looked at us and then back at the dark blue Cutlass, currently kissing the toilet. Besides the fender, the car was scratch-free, sternly impassive, proud of loosening one family's foundation from its moorings on a still night.

Mimi pointed to the hole in the wall and screamed.

My mind raced. True, my father's complicated ear surgery a week ago had upset his balance. He wasn't supposed to be up and about and certainly wasn't supposed to drive, but she didn't have to *scream*. Still, I knew it would be worse when she stopped.

Theo smacked the side of his head, eyes wide in frank admiration, and said, "Dad, ya did *that*?" He gripped Wolfie.

My father winced, a sweat mustache surfacing. He seemed dazed, and he stood across from us jangling his keys in his hand, as if the whole damn thing were somehow their fault.

Mimi's hands were on her hips. "Explanation, please."

It scared me to look at her. She seemed madder than I'd ever seen her. Studying a splat of oil on the cement floor shaped like a stretched-out pancake, I looked up at a pair of my old ice skates, leaning to the side like an old couple walking down the street, holding each other up.

My father still hadn't said a word. He ran his fingers through his thick brown hair. "Goddamnit," he yelled finally. Then, more quietly, "I must have mistook the accelerator for the brake," he said.

I stuck my foot up inside my nightgown and scratched my calf with my toenails. The grease on the floor seemed to darken and twist, like sinister animals. Out of the corner of my eye, I saw Theo bury his face in Wolfie's fur. He gave her a loud smooch, and Mimi, who worried about dog germs, smacked him lightly.

"A dog's mouth is six times cleaner . . ." Theo started.

"You mistook the accelerator for the . . ." Mimi's hands fell to her side, and her sigh sounded strong enough to make the roof of the house cave in, too. The air filled with the powdery silt of plaster and blame and something dangerous—disappointment, disillusion.

Later, in the hall outside our rooms, Theo asked in a forlorn voice, "Are Mom and Dad gonna get the big D?"

"No, silly," I said. "Parents argue."

Lying in bed, I heard muffled voices for a long time before I fell asleep, the pillow over my head. I would move away, but I would never leave this house. I would go back again and again, suck the kitchen air out with a straw until it was flat, an empty balloon, dead as my doll's skin.

◆ ◆ ◆

The next morning, while I stood in the kitchen pouring out Grape Nuts, my dad was on the phone with Sidney Shaw, the insurance man. When he hung up, the skin around his eyes looked loose, and he grabbed his toast from the toaster, slathered on grape jelly, then returned to the table to crack open the newspaper.

I was feeling optimistic until my father lowered his paper and brought his eyes to mine in a level gaze. "Silvie, I . . . I'm afraid I'm failing."

My heart seemed to leap up into my head and seal my ears. Afraid to hear what he had to say, I jumped out of my chair, ran to the bathroom, and looked in the mirror, liking what I saw. My hair was a soft, lustrous fan, each strand folded, bent wide on either side of my jaw. Last night when I couldn't sleep, I'd braided my damp hair in a dozen skinny braids and now it was big and beautifully crimped. Noticing the hole in the wall, which still gaped, uncovered, I touched my velvet hair as I slowly returned to the kitchen, preparing myself to hear what my father had to say.

But Mimi and Theo were now at the table, Theo in just his underwear.

My father raised his eyebrows above the newspaper. "Whattya doin' in your skivvies, boy?"

"Mom's getting my pants from the dryer." Theo poured himself a glass of milk. Just seeing his underwear droop on his small frame made me sad.

"Hey, Sil, stick your finger in a light socket?" Theo asked, referring to my hair.

"Shut up," I said, crunching cereal. My father shifted from the sports page to the editorials.

"Pass the salt," Mimi said to one of us, to no one, forking her yellow yolk eye on our family china, white and fine as bone.

◆ ◆ ◆

A week passed, then came the night my parents sat Theo and me down to tell us they were breaking up. They had shepherded us downstairs to the basement, and later I would think it was fitting that this conversation should take place underground, where secrets grow and all life begins and ends. We sat on the old baggy couch among suitcases, canvases Mimi had bought to paint on and never did, hockey skates my father and Theo wore when the driveway froze over, and an old dressmaker's mannequin Mimi no longer used. From the concrete walls came a damp, cold odor, faintly sweet, like old grapes.

Mimi did most of the talking. What I remember is how stiff she sounded: "We feel it's no longer in the best interests of our family to stay together." She wore deep purplish lipstick the color of a bruise, her new blond bangs combed flat against her forehead. One bell-bottomed denim leg crossed over the other, her foot, in black platforms, swinging a little, almost free. My father nodded silently beside her, his hands twisted in his lap, his expression weary, a strange mixture of defeat and relief.

My hair in a long braid, blue eye shadow shimmering on my lids, I stared at the flat basement carpet, hearing as words rolled slowly out of their mouths, vague flutters of sound, which rumbled and echoed like vibrations deep beneath my fingertips.

Theo stroked the dog's fur so hard and fast that she nipped at him, but he just hugged her harder and watched me for a sign. I didn't have one to give. It would be a while before the truth reached my head: In a few months, I would graduate from high school and my parents would be divorced.

"Do we have to leave our house?" Theo asked, eyes filling with tears.

Mimi's face was falsely composed; any minute now I expected her eyes or nose or mouth to unlatch and send a million tiny birds flying out.

"Sport," my father said, clearing his throat. My parents looked at each other. He bowed his head. "I'm going to live somewhere else, and you'll stay here with Mom and Silvie."

"But, Dad, you belong here." That was Theo, strong and true, next to me, boarded up and dumb, wishing my own tongue didn't feel as stiff as an ironing board.

"Well, sugar, of course you feel that way, it's only natural. But sometimes, even when parents still love each other, they just can't . . ." That was Mimi.

"Sometimes parents love each other but they . . . they, um, can't live together." My father spoke in a grave voice, tripping over his next words. "And then it's better for everybody if they live apart."

"It was a mutual decision. Right, Dan? It's important that you children understand that."

My father nodded, steepling his fingers against his mouth.

I jumped up and ran out of the room, screaming, "I'm never getting married."

Upstairs, I lay on my bed. I flipped my pillow to the cool side. After an hour or so, I rose up out of bed like a ghost, gooseflesh rising on my arms, the hair on my scalp tingling, and crept to my parents' room, pressing my ear against their door. The people inside, whom I'd once known, now slept heavily, and distant and deep as thunder.

♦ ♦ ♦

The next morning, I was ready for my father to drive me to school as usual. I averted my eyes from the gaping hole in the wall, which had been covered with garbage bags and masking tape.

My father, a man I'd seen crying only at parades, spoke in husky tones, fighting tears. "I feel bad for you guys." He took one hand off the steering wheel and held it over mine, and I knew he wanted to protect me from the rest of my life.

"Lots of kids have divorced parents."

"It's a funny world we live in, isn't it, Silvie? All these people ordering divorce like the finest entrée on the menu."

"Yeah." We had turned onto West Lake Road. "Would you want to try if Mimi wanted to?"

My father stopped at the light across from my school and rolled his thumbs on the steering wheel. He smelled of Chapstick and Wrigley's Doublemint. "Well, honey, the divorce was her idea. But some part of me wonders if I won't be happier, too."

She won't be happy, I thought. She thinks she will be, but she won't. *Seventeen* magazine said that you had to like yourself first before you could love anyone else. Mimi carried happiness outside herself, like a little purse, an accessory; she would never hold it inside her, like breath.

My father pulled the car to a slow stop at the circle where the buses lined up and we sat in silence, our thoughts crowding the small space with all we couldn't say.

He gave my hand a squeeze and lifted it to his jaw. "How about a knuckle sandwich? My father used to say that."

God, there was Eddie Cullum in the distance, climbing off the bus, in mirrored shades and those dirty green-and-white-striped Adidas sneakers with the laces undone that made my heart start up. Eddie sat in back of me in humanities. Sometimes we passed notes back and forth; sometimes Eddie just poked me in the back with his pencil. The dark hair on his arms made my stomach flip. I kissed my father's cheek. "Gotta go, Dad. I'm late."

◆ ◆ ◆

My father moved out on a cold February day. With each suitcase, box of books, and carton of record albums that Theo and I helped him carry to the U-Haul, I'd gather up what was left of my breath and help carry the next load. Mimi, who had been upstairs in her room, met us in the kitchen after everything was packed and made tuna salad sandwiches, which made me feel as if I were choking down sawdust. How many meals had we eaten as a family at this round oak table? Today we ate in silence, Mimi's expression harsh and joyless, puzzled, like a person who wakes up after sleepwalking in a room she's never seen; I couldn't read my father's face. He whisked his keys and loose change off the kitchen desk and I pondered the many orbits the stuff in his pocket had made, from the kitchen to work and back home to this house again. Now it would live on a new desk somewhere, in another kitchen.

His new apartment building was a lonely beige structure about twenty minutes away from our house, inhabited by single people and divorcées. He shifted into his new life there armed with the albums from Broadway shows that they'd divided—*Oliver, West Side Story,* and *Company* for him. Mimi kept *Camelot, My Fair Lady,* and *Funny Girl.* Later, when we'd visit him on weekends, his furniture, mostly bits and pieces ransacked from our basement, was dusty and his toilet had a ring of rust around it.

He'd bought a single bed for the small bedroom, which had a sliding glass door that made you think it opened onto a patio or deck, but there was no patio or deck, just miles of air. On the floor by the bed was an oval rug I'd never seen before, hooked, like one of the pot holders I'd woven in second grade. When I asked where he'd gotten it, he said it was only three dollars at the True Value hardware store on Old Orchard, as if I might want to run over there and get one for myself. On the nightstand lay a book, *How to Survive a Loss of a Love,* and on the old console stereo he'd taken from the basement was a 45 of "Send in the Clowns."

"The men always remarry first," Mimi said that night after our first dinner without my father. "Just wait and see."

That night, Mimi passed me in the dark hall outside our bedrooms. We'd woken up at the same time and walked toward each other silently, our faces still, our breathing deep and regular. She stopped and faced me head-on, her face sad and open, with an apology there, or something like it. But instead of speaking, she made a motion of zipping her lip, turned away from me, and walked back to her bedroom, her nightgown fluttering around her ankles above an old pair of my father's thick athletic socks. Talking would bring us wide-awake. And what was there to talk about? Our fate was sealed, and so we craved sleep, empty and void of dreams. She closed the door to her room. I was alone.

◆ ◆ ◆

I carried my dollhouse to the basement, putting it on a rusty metal shelf by Theo's beloved catcher's mitt.

The next time I looked, the shelves on which our childhood had dwindled away were empty. Sarah Prudence, my doll, gone. The dollhouse my mother had labored over, the little doll family of four, a father, mother, and a girl and boy like us, all the miniature beds and tables and lamps, the tiny stove and refrigerator, the porch swing—gone. Theo's small cast, smudged with black-inked autographs from Vida Blue and Willie Mays—gone. I thought about its snow-white underbelly with the black line where the doctor had cut it off. And his catcher's mitt, soft with the hours he'd spent in the backyard catching my father's pitches—gone; even his beloved hockey skates were gone. I thought about my brother, how skinny he looked, his collarbone and shoulder blades fragile as Tinker Toys. I thought about Mimi, how she'd left depth behind, gliding now on thin ice, wanting to be light, rich, happy, executing easy jumps and twirls.

Now, this to never forgive—how in frantic, disorderly haste she'd opened a garbage bag, filled it with air, and thrown all our childhood inside, a restless sigh in her heart, her new skin.

◆ ◆ ◆

Every night after dinner, my mother and I sat at the kitchen table eating caramel-crunch ice cream from the carton.

Theo had gulped his food and was on his way outside to skateboard. For my benefit, he stood quietly next to my chair a second before fleeing. "Ask me if I'm an airplane," he said, with the nonchalance of an expert joke teller.

"Are you an airplane?"

"Yes. Ask me if I'm a boat." His constant motion seemed to hint at some rage that we all carried inside us but had been unable to express, some bitter thing that had long been out of balance.

"Stop that. Are you a boat?"

"No, stupid. I just told you I was an airplane."

I laughed so hard I dropped to the floor and, spying Wolfie, scooped her up, nuzzling her gray hair mid-gasp. If I stopped laughing, I'd cry.

Rolling his eyes, Theo left. Mimi leaned over the table and looked at me on the floor. "Your father wasn't always easy to live with, either," she said. "At least I come out with whatever's bothering me."

I got up, returned to the ice cream, and our spoons collided as we dived for the crunchy pieces.

"Do you know what passive-aggressive is, sugar? I read about it in one of my self-help books." She clinked her spoon against mine as if in a toast and giggled, not her normal quicksilver laugh, but a laugh of a different color, a darker sound, deeper, the color of wheat instead of butter. "Well, that's your father to a T."

I studied her as she gobbled ice cream; her cheeks were pale and she wore no lipstick, like a little girl who'd waited a long time for dessert.

"We had some good years together, but he was never enough man for me. I'm all woman. That's something I'm getting in touch with now."

She looked all woman, all right, here at the kitchen table, stabbing at the ice cream furiously, the satin arm of her robe brushing the carton, coming away sticky and white.

"Sure I'm scared of being alone. And with you wanting to go off to college in the fall." She gave me a plaintive look. "You know, Silvie, I was thinking, you could postpone school a year, wait awhile until you go running off, let us get our lives settled."

"My life is settled."

"You're not even eighteen, sugar. You have time."

"Fuck you." I'd never used that word with her; in fact, I never used that word. I closed my eyes, waiting for her to jump up and throw her spoon in my face.

But she acted as if she hadn't heard me. "Would you look at this mess I made?" She swiped at a spot of ice cream on her sleeve, desperate to get the robe clean again.

Hadn't she always carried this divorce inside her, from the day they were married, holding back a hand, a foot, an arm, a piece of her heart? What about the land they agreed to travel, only to find no map, loose change? I saw her alone now, holding her old Elvis story up to the light, seeing all its holes.

Shaken, I got up and left the table, left her rubbing away at the stain. I felt hollow, as I had since my father had moved out. Nothing made sense.

"I'm taking the car," I muttered.

"Just where do you think you're going?"

"Out," I said.

I got into the old gold Cutlass and drove the half mile to Little

Caesars, where Eddie Cullum worked. I'd stopped by a few times that summer at the warm, fluorescent-bright place, dense with a hot, yeasty fragrance that made my mouth water.

A bell tinkled when I walked in the door, and Eddie looked up and smiled his slow smile. "Hiya," he said. Particles of flour floated in the air and tickled our noses. At Little Ceasars, we were always on the verge of sneezing, and much later, whenever my mind would wander back to Eddie, I'd feel like sneezing.

"Wanna watch?" he asked, and I nodded while he tossed the white spongy dough, patting it down with strong arms on round aluminum pie sheets, his long fingers wrapping around the spoon that spread the sauce, the black hairs on his strong wrist almost shining as he flicked a spray of mozzarella, pressed on pepperoni, and sprinkled diced mushrooms. Then he turned his back to me and shoveled it into the huge square oven, big as a child's playhouse. With a sly smile, he said, "Twenty minutes, some lucky soul is gonna have a kick-ass za." *Za*. I loved that. Because he said so little, everything that came out of his mouth seemed lofty and filled me with awe, reminding me somehow of Uncle Shelby.

Eventually, Eddie put on a huge oven mitt, heaved the Jolly Green Giant–size metal spatula, and hauled the small pizza out of the oven, sliding it with a miraculous scraping sound onto a round cardboard, like a baby sliding out of the womb. Then he slipped it into a cardboard box, which was hot to the touch. "Finished," he said, leaning over the counter. He kissed me then, my first real kiss, and I froze, my knees turning rubbery as day-old mozzarella. But I did it. I kissed him back.

♦ ♦ ♦

Eddie and I were naked, sprawled across a lime-green beanbag chair in my basement. Sex was a balm for me, an exciting new place where my mother couldn't find me, and I wanted to be there all the time. I didn't fall in love with Eddie that summer; I fell in love with having sex. All summer, we made small pizzas with pepperoni and double cheese, tearing into them, then locking the store and fucking on the floor. We rarely talked, just licked flour dust off each other's arms.

◆ ◆ ◆

Theo and I heard the news on a warm afternoon in August, the grass brown from thirst because my mother kept forgetting to turn on the sprinklers, the sky a blue so cloudless it looked like the skies I had colored as a child and still liked to color sometimes, a dense, viscous blue, like eye shadow or a cerulean glaze awaiting the kiln. Theo, Martine, and I sat on our front porch listlessly breathing hot, sticky air and watching the dog, who was dashing wildly from one end of the lawn to another. We burst into peals of laughter at the sight of Wolfie's small body gaining speed, her ears pinned back, fur plastered against her small frame as she hurled herself into the belly of the dry wind. Spread before us was a plastic pitcher of Kool-Aid, a carton of Dixie cups, and a bag of oatmeal cookies; three pairs of eyes searched for raisins.

There was a small, strangled sob behind us. I turned my head in a slow swivel, hoping I could blink my mother away, with her unbrushed hair, her pasty skin. She stood in the doorway, in jeans and an old white shirt that my father had left behind, no shoes, no toenail polish, but it was her face I didn't want to see, the sunken eyes and vertical lines that had dented the sides of her mouth since the deaths of Paw Paw and Shelby.

"Children, the King is gone," she announced, voice breaking.

We gave her blank looks.

"Elvis has died." Mimi looked hard at us.

I blinked, feeling a kind of paralysis settle in. I watched Theo's face register shock. Martine's mouth hung open, her lips wet and shiny from her lip gloss, until she clamped her hands over them, trying to cork either surprise or laughter.

Behind Mimi's blue eyes a light went out. She looked at us dully, her fingers moving gingerly to her hair, which she fluffed and re-arranged before blinking and walking back inside.

Martine watched me. "Does she really care that much about Elvis?" I had never told anyone the Elvis story, not even Martine.

Theo and I locked eyes. Wolfie jumped off his lap and ran off again, racing passionately around and around the maple tree.

"Mom's always been a special fan," I said finally, and Theo and I broke out laughing, both holding our sides and sputtering. In that moment, Theo and I shared some understanding, some awareness we hadn't spoken about before.

Mimi continued to mourn, but it was a quiet sadness. There were days when she didn't get dressed and her mouth would get tighter and tighter, until, by night, her whole face crumpled.

"As if Dad had died," Theo said.

But it was Elvis himself, God bless his soul, just a good old boy from Tupelo. It seemed he had extinguished himself like a match, his infamous pelvis spread in excess fame, whittled himself away from too much of the wrong kind of success, his bloated death spawning millions of imitators in white spangled jumpsuits and scarves around their necks. The facts surrounding his death embar-rassed Mimi, let her down, tarnished her long-held fantasy until the whole broken-down dream was like a rusty car that refused to move another mile.

◆ ◆ ◆

Late one night, Mimi walked into my room, singing. "Lazy Mary will you get up . . ."

"What are you doing? It's the middle of the night."

"I can't sleep. This silly diet you dreamed up has me famished all the time. Come to the kitchen. I've got to have a snack."

I groaned. "No snacks, Mimi." We'd both gained weight since the divorce—seven pounds.

I joined her at the table. On a night when we longed for hot fudge sundaes, we silently, with sharp resolve, ate lettuce out of mixing bowls and bit into crunchy carrots. As the sun rose, we sat, a row of tiny hearts bordering the sleeves of my mother's nightgown, until two clocks turned, one inside her, one inside me.

◆ ◆ ◆

Despite Mimi's plea, I went off to college and on to the rest of my life. Some things won't change, I remember thinking. Or everything will.

CHAPTER 14

My mother lies in the hospital bed, looking beautiful. She lies there with fuzz for hair in the greenish glow of light. In the small circular gleam, her hair is as beautiful as a fawn's, dark brown, with tufts of blond and silver, short as a rug, damp with perspiration. I sit clinging to the arms of a vinyl-cushioned chair as if it's a life raft. I'm marveling at the shape of her skull—a perfect oval and breathtakingly beautiful. Her forehead is higher now that there's no hair to confine it, her nose a bumpy line a kid would draw with a crayon in the center of a wobbly oval. Her skin is flawless, the color of milk, her blue eyes dark and hungry, somehow luminous, calm.

There's no weather in this room; the curtains are tightly drawn, and the temperature is neither hot nor cold. In the corridors, there is the dense hospital smell of hot dryers and yesterday's cooking, but in my mother's room, there's a curious, sweet smell, some cross between ether and medicine and wilted flowers. The faucet in the bathroom drips steadily, like a heartbeat. The walls never brighten except at night, when the lamp goes on and shadows appear on the ceiling, and the long corridor outside her room, with the brightly lit nurses' station, buzzes like a machine, so that if you open her door, you are jarred into a false coziness.

Her first day there, she lies on her hospital bed, on top of the covers, holding her arms stiffly at her sides. She has refused to put on the hospital gown, refused to ease her body between the sheets and under the blanket. I sit beside her.

"You said we should talk," she says. "You know what I want to talk about? Remember when you were little and you and Theo would hand me your chewed-up gum? 'Here,' you'd say. 'Here, Mom. Hold.' " Instead of a hospital gown, she sleeps with one of my T-shirts over her nightgown and a pair of Theo's thick athletic socks on her feet. She borrows our clothes now, wanting us as close as possible, next to her skin.

"Yeah." I try to smile.

"That was when you still called me Mom."

"Yeah." I think a minute. "Do you want me to call you Mom again?"

"If you don't mind."

"I don't mind." I swallow, a floodgate opening inside me; so many things to say.

She lifts my hand and kisses it. "Don't talk. I have to go soon."

"Where? Where are you going?"

"To sleep." She leans back against the pillow and her eyes drift shut. On her feet, the pale socks glow; her head is a halo of light.

◆ ◆ ◆

Because she has asked me not to, I no longer call her Mimi. The old name slips away like childhood. Neither of us blinks now that Mimi is gone; we do not look for her or speak of her at all; the name has outgrown its usefulness. But calling her Mom stings a little, brings back the irony of a little girl standing over a mother who has taken a bite of a fake apple and is pretending to die.

◆ ◆ ◆

Henry has shelled out the bucks for her room—private, not small: the bed, a bathroom, a chair by the bed, and a couch opposite, arranged, as in a hotel room, around a wooden coffee table and two side tables with reading lamps whose glass globes hold small ships. A television hangs from the ceiling. We don't watch it; it watches us, like a god. What you notice when you enter the room are the high white bed and the light above it, its one small piece of day shining down and my mother lying small under it. When I first saw her small figure lost in the starched white hospital sheets, I knew that black isn't the color of death; white is—the colorless nothingness of white.

I lift the blanket off her and watch her whole body sleep. Her shoulders drink the lotion I rub in, but they still remain withered and tight, as do her feet, the transparent skin barely covering the curved bones. How easily they might break, like shells, in my fingers! How strange that this odd, gentle receding of her toes is the closest I've been to death. Her breasts under the cotton nightgown that I brought from home are shrunken hills. When I was very small, I called them "peerpeaks"—and when the nurses change her nightgown, I can see the skin puckered around bluish nipples.

My mother and I don't talk about the fact that she is in the hospital to die. The knowledge passes between us swaddled in thick cotton. It doesn't bruise or even shock us. It just *is*.

◆ ◆ ◆

From the hospital pay phone, I call Martine and tell her I doubt my mother's going to make it to my wedding, and that I can't imagine getting married without her.

Martine is adamant. "This is the first time in your life you ever

had anything that was all yours. Don't let the ghosts move you off
your path, Sil. You have to be firm. You need to tell the ghosts they
can't disrupt you. Goddamnit, tell them they can't intrude."

"I wish I could. It's not that simple."

"Did you ever think of this? That maybe your being unhappy
enables you to keep Mimi alive and well?"

She has to invert the statement before I get it.

"Maybe you feel that if you're happy, she'll die."

◆ ◆ ◆

"Hello, Perlita," my mother calls without lifting her head. She can
tell each nurse by sound: the spritely, hopeful step means Perlita;
the flat, realistic tread brings Eunice. She turns her head almost im-
perceptibly in my direction, says, "Perlita prays for me on the
couch."

She loves each nurse separately, desperately—Eunice, for her
big, soft hands that massage her at night; Perlita, for the gold fila-
gree cross she wears around her neck, for her optimism. When I
meet Eunice, she says, "This one, my Eunice, does a rat-a-tat-tat on
my spine."

◆ ◆ ◆

In this room where she is busy dying, I am alive; I am electric. Even
as the mind digs its boring little ruts about what to have for lunch,
the heart deepens, until it seizes upon a thought that lodges itself in
my spine, possessing me with the idea that I have tried to mend
everything that stands between my mother and me, everything that
keeps us from love, that has ever kept us from love.

But there are whole days without talking, thinking, whole days
behind the dark curtain that clings to people and makes them
break. There is a pain in my chest as if I'd swallowed wrong. Outside, it's snowing faintly, small, light flakes that seem to disappear on

their downward flight but mysteriously leave the pavement wet and glistening.

◆ ◆ ◆

One busy day, Theo brings Claire to visit, and Martine, in town to visit her father, drops by. By the end of the day, my mother is exhausted.

"Bring my jewelry box tomorrow. You know where it is, top drawer." Her words sound garbled, like when she held a threaded needle between her teeth during the years she sewed.

I close my eyes so that I can open them and see her there.

"Heard that surviving cancer obligates a person to do something transcendent," she murmurs on her way to sleep.

But the next day, when I show her the jewelry box I've brought from home, she waves me away. She's propped up against an extra pillow, holding the hand mirror she brought from home for just this purpose—brushing on blush. Every day her eyeliner is shakier, like skywriting done by a drunken pilot.

"You don't want it?" I ask, surveying her. Her face glows and her eyes glitter blue and bright.

"Later," she says.

"Look at that," she says, raising her head an inch off the pillow to scan the room, unoccupied except for Henry and me, sitting in silence over magazines we don't read. "Perlita's still praying on the couch."

◆ ◆ ◆

Scottie flies to Michigan and comes to the hospital. "You've never seen my mother without a wig," I say. "I mean, when you met her, she was already sick."

We're sitting on a wooden bench in the chapel, a high-ceilinged room, small, with wood-paneled walls so dark that it's like being inside an envelope. There is an odor of cheap men's cologne, flowers, week-old prayers. I feel I should pray but realize I don't know how.

"I'm not sure what I'm supposed to do." I breathe in so sharply it sounds like a word escaping.

"You're doing it."

"I'm not. There are lots of books and movies and plays about people who sit by the person's bedside and hold hands until the dying person says a profound word or two and a great white light appears and whisks them off."

"Those are books and movies and plays."

Maybe this is both the strength and the weakness of doctors, that they turn on every experience the dry eye of science, that they are not sodden with hope like the rest of us.

"I can't even tell her good-bye, because she's so fucking high."

"You're telling her good-bye, every day that you see her."

"But I want to do something!"

"That's not what she needs now. Just touch her, hold her hand. Words don't matter at the end."

The end. We lean together, rubbing the toes of our shoes.

◆ ◆ ◆

Aunt Nina comes from Biloxi for a week. She spends the days at my mother's side, clinging to her hand. She says very little, and sometimes I forget she's there. Aunt Connie, who has a fear of flying, calls every day.

Henry, Theo, Nina, Scottie, and I sit around her hospital bed until we can't stay another minute, then we migrate down to the gift shop on the main floor, dodging the people who wear labels reading VISITOR, looking away from the patients going home, in wheelchairs, with balloons and vases of flowers on their laps. Three, four, five times a day we traipse down, and are bombarded by the green and red tinsel, the multicolored blinking Christmas

lights, the tinny nostalgic strain of carols. Today, I sit on a bench in
the hospital lobby, my hands hanging between my knees. A woman
bursts through the revolving doors, stomping snow off her boots.
Underneath her coat, she's wearing a bright green sweater that features a fuzzy reindeer with a red pom-pom nose. I sit awhile and
watch all the people come and go in their dumb, cheerful sweaters,
and I'm struck by their aliveness, their glazed, tenacious human-
ness. None of us knows a thing, I think. Not one thing. We aren't
prepared for this life. This is all we are: people, in our dumb, cheerful sweaters, trying too hard, stumbling through.

◆ ◆ ◆

I walk down to the fourth floor to see the nursery. When I tell the
OB/GYN nurses that I'm staying with my mother on the fifth
floor, they let me stand outside the glass and watch the squalling
newborns with bloodred faces. My fingers tingle; I want so badly
to pick up a warm pink or blue bundle and smell the sweet, fresh
baby powder, the milky breath, the sour diaper. Anything besides
her smell of wet leaves, mold, dust.

That night, Henry brings food from McDonald's, which Theo
and Scottie and I wolf down without talking. Henry plays with his
fries and Nina doesn't eat at all, just lies facedown on what has become her place on the couch, her head buried in a pillow, her hand
dangling to the floor, gripping a Styrofoam cup of Diet Coke.

I sit on the floor, my head against the couch, reading my book.
After a while, when the guys have scattered, I hear Nina's voice behind me. "Every morning when I take my bath I think of what it
would be like to just slip down the drain."

"I've felt that way," I said. Her voice is soft; I turn around to face
her.

"But not every day," she whispered. "You don't feel that way
every day."

"No. Do you? Every day?"

"Since I was a little girl." She takes my hand in her small, cold one and I hold it, feeling, for just a second, as if she's the one who's dying.

"You know, everyone said Shelby was weak. But I think it took guts to jump like that." Aunt Nina, Sweet Nina, with her sad little smile, is scaring me.

I reach to hug her and she slides her thin self into my arms like a baby. I hold her for a long time, feel the sharp edges of her shoulder blades under my hands.

◆ ◆ ◆

The next day, my mother lifts her head off the pillow and calls out, "Eunice, shush those squeaking shoes. Listen, now. I'm going to read to you from this book about my life." She peeks around the bed at me, holding up *Love, Medicine and Miracles.* A few pages are turned down, her morphine-shaky handwriting drifting in the margins. Mostly, the book sits on the windowsill, dusty and beseeching, a platform for the Styrofoam head that holds her blond wig.

"I've come to believe that 'all sickness is homesickness,' " she says, quoting one of her self-help books. "The longing. For a home, a safe haven. I left Biloxi, I left the home I'd created with Dan, I destroyed everything I ever built. I stopped sewing—why did I stop? Somewhere along the way, I lost my center." She gestured toward infinity. "That yearning for something, for some place to call my own, is why I got sick."

I feel myself holding my breath. Today, the morphine has loosened something inside her, unknotted memories that flow out like silk scarves.

"I worshipped my daddy. In him, I saw only goodness, but now I see that he was filled with rage. He could not love. Not really. I guess I inherited his temper, too, his black moods, terrible, oppressive moods where you could almost see his breath leave his chest.

That melancholy was underneath all our skin, cast over us like a spell. And that spell was etched faintly in the ceiling, walls, and floor of our house, the house my father built with his own hands when he longed to put something between himself and the world. I see now that Daddy made us all feel bad about who we were because he felt bad about who he was. Really, Mama and Daddy's focus on achievement and competition and success drained us all of our connection to our hearts.

"But, oh, how his rough accent could play a strange kind of music in my chest. Little girls love their daddies. I think of Silvie, how she waited on the rock on the driveway for her dad. You know, Eunice, I have my father's nose, big with a bump in the middle, and even though it's nowhere near perfect, it's the feature I'm most proud of.

"Mama and Daddy really screwed up Shelby, all that pressure, the only son. Last day of Shelby's life, he pulled up the old Buick in front of Sweet Nina Baby's tiny house—she was married to T.J. then—and stayed all day, eating a tuna sandwich for lunch and taking a long nap on the sofa while Nina watched one of those awful soaps she loves. I always tell her, 'Real life's so painful, who needs another dose?' Anyway, Shelby asked her to take him down to Gayfer's at Edgewater Mall. Odd, she thought, but being Sweet Nina Baby, she asked no questions. The next morning, he jumped.

"Sure enough, it was Sweet Nina who got the call a month later. They said the negatives were back; did Shelby want to come in and order his prints? She had to think back to the day she drove him to the mall, not knowing he was getting his last portrait done. Nina drove back to Gayfer's to choose from the prints. She never told the salesperson that her brother was dead, just that he'd sent her to choose. I have a copy of the one she picked in my wallet. So does Connie."

"I know that picture," I said. In it, Shelby's skin seems unnaturally moist, with an almost eerie glow, making him seem more alive on his last day of life than he'd been the other thirty-odd years. He wears a blue denim shirt buttoned all the way up, so that his neck juts out like a strange bird. His lips turn up in a big, tight smile like a kid hiding braces.

"I should have done more for him," my mother said softly. "Mama has never been the same since he died. I'll never forget her saying, over and over, that day they called with the news, that he'd brushed his teeth that morning, shaved. Nothing that day had led her to believe he would do what he did. He had his guitar at the kitchen table, and a huge bowl of cereal. The fact of his clothes." She paused, licked her lips. I held her water glass and she sipped from the straw.

"My mama was hard on me, but life was hard on her. Then I go and hand that right on down to Silvie. If there's one thing I've figured out, it's that the mother is a road map. If you can't read her, you can't read yourself."

All afternoon, I listen to my mother's memories. She never stops calling me Eunice. I want to scream and keep on screaming until someone wakes me, and at the same time I want to remember every word.

◆ ◆ ◆

Nina flees home to Biloxi, pale and shaken, clutching me in the airport, sobbing. "I know I'll never see my sister again." I just hug my aunt, and try not to cry.

Theo, Scottie, and I arrange our chairs into a semicircle at the foot of her bed, to weave a web around her. Henry sits, the newspaper in his lap, and twirls his hair—he has enough to twirl; he keeps missing his barbershop appointments.

"Bones are used in some bands as percussion instruments," Theo whispers when she's fallen asleep. "They're tied on a string and hit, like cymbals."

Scottie nods. "In med school, I learned the names of bones as if they were poetry. Just the sound of some of them—clavicle, fibula, femur."

I listen to my almost-husband, the sound of his voice. Low, steady.

Henry rustles his newspaper. We all turn to look at him, but he just raises his eyebrows in an almost imperceptible movement and burrows back into his papers.

◆ ◆ ◆

I find myself in the hospital basement one day, donating blood. The walls are gray and the air cool. I follow a long, meandering hallway to the blood bank, where a nurse eases me into a recliner and ties a giant rubber band around my upper arm, prodding a flimsy, recalcitrant vein. She talks in a sweet, fat voice, tap-tapping the blue lines at my wrist. She feels around the inside crook of my arm, looking for a vein, finally finding and jabbing one. I feel every drop trickle out. As the two pints leave my body, I begin to shiver. My legs are quaking so violently, the nurse covers me with blankets.

"Almost done, almost done."

I stare up at the ceiling, ashamed at how selfish I am, at how they had to drag my blood from my body. The nurse hands me an oatmeal cookie and a tiny cup of orange juice. In a few minutes, she touches my toes. "You can go now. You'll be fine. Now we send this nice red blood of yours along and they radiate it."

"What?" I'm standing now, swaying slightly.

"They make it so it contains the same level of radiation as your mom's." Her voice is gentle but closed. That's it. That's all I'll get from her.

I nod dumbly, breathing more freely knowing that I've relinquished everything inside me to my mother.

The next morning, because my blood has dripped into her all night, a faint wash of color blooms in my mother's cheeks. I whisper, "You have my blood, Mom. How do you feel?"

"Like a good student." Her lips curve and she holds an imaginary pen, layering the air with flowing strokes. "A good artist."

"Are you scared?" This pops out without warning.

"No and yes. Together."

I take her hand, thinking my blood is too late. Inside her, my blood is water when the baby needs milk.

◆ ◆ ◆

"For some damn reason, that Elvis story isn't as much fun as it used to be." My mother's face sags as if, without the old story, it can't quite hold itself up.

"Did Elvis have something to do with the divorce?"

"You want to talk about Elvis?"

"Yeah. I want to talk about Elvis."

"Why? God knows, you never wanted to before."

"Not when you were always in those blue suede shoes dancing in front of the stove."

An odd smile plays at her lips. "We're just kitchen witches, you know, you and me."

Before I can ask what she means or say, "Not me, I'm not a kitchen witch," she goes on.

"One night does not a life make, Silvie. I let one silly thing like that rule my life. I don't want you to do the same."

"You put yourself through hell. Living in the pain of something that would never be."

She bows her head, speaking after a moment of deep silence. "Now, why do you suppose I did that?"

"I don't know, Mom. Why did you?"

"You get used to pain. Then you want to jiggle it all the time, like a loose tooth." She goes very still, thinking about . . . I don't know, her next breath. "I couldn't see past wanting some symbol of importance. I had the shoes but no place to go, I guess. I felt so small when I left Biloxi and moved up north, and Daddy was always pushing. I wanted something to set me apart. But I was just stupid. And blind. Elvis wasn't the most important person in my life. You were. You and Dan and Theo."

Now I was quiet.

"Wanna know the truth, Silvie?" she says after a minute. "I only went out with Elvis three times."

"Did you sleep together?" I ask nonchalantly, but my palms, to my dismay, are slick with sweat. I'm amazed by how much I want her to say yes, and not just so she won't be a liar. My whole life, I'd imagined it, my mother with Elvis. It was her myth, our myth, and to let it go completely would be to strip the veil off our lives and see them as empty as they were.

"Well . . ."

"Mom, you have to tell me."

She bites her lip, hesitating. "What did I say before?"

"You told me you had sex . . ."

"I did?"

"Yes! Did you?"

"Nah, but in my mind we did."

"Mom! I've slept with a lot of people in my mind."

She frowns, a mother's frown, mock-stern. "How many?"

That makes us laugh.

"No, I never slept with him. We just spent the whole night talking. He was a big talker. I've been bragging about this my whole life, and he only wanted to talk. He did write a letter to Shelby, though."

"Why did you lie to me?"

"The story just grew and grew, like a tumor." We are quiet at this. "Sooner or later, I believed it myself. Shelby knew the truth. I'm surprised he didn't tell you." She looks at me.

"He told me stuff. But I wanted to know more. And he went and killed himself before I could."

Her eyelids droop. "I was angry my whole life, Silvie. I don't want you to be. Anger wreaks havoc on your relationships. Just call it a day and move on. And don't live in a dream of better things. Nothing's better than what you have right now. The trick is to know when you're happy—to not be looking out the window at the moment when it comes."

◆ ◆ ◆

After lunch, she says, "I have one bit of advice for you, dear. Chew off all your lipstick." A smile plays around my mother's lips. This is the most lucid she's been in days.

"Chew off . . ." I stop, confused.

"Chew off all your lipstick. Women try too hard. Just be yourself."

"Here's the jewelry box you asked for."

"That old thing?" She looks perplexed.

"You wanted it."

"I did?" She's in the chair by the window. Someone, maybe Henry, has helped her into her red robe.

"Something about Elvis?" I sit beside her. Scottie is at the pay phone; Henry and Theo are somewhere in the hospital, like soldiers waiting to learn their destinations.

"Ah, yes. There's one thing we forgot to do." She wags her finger to bring me closer and lifts the pendant off the crimson velvet. "See this?" The necklace sways, as it had so many times before, in her hand.

"Mom, I don't want it . . ."

"Toss it."

"Excuse me?"

"In the garbage. The picture, too."

My jaw drops. "You want me to throw away Elvis's locket, along with a picture of the two of you by the pool?"

"That's what it is, garbage. Just toss it." She sits very still in her chair.

I walk over to the wastebasket and hold it over. "You're sure."

"Very."

I let it drop. Outside the window is a dingy blue, no clouds, just the blue of ash, a sky on the edge of night.

After she's asleep, I tiptoe to the wastebasket and lift out the necklace. The weight of its thin chain feels scant in my palm. I open it, look at it closely, rub the two small faces, wanting to erase their easy, weightless grins. The picture looks smaller to me now, the idol whittled down to a glitter speck. Then I snap it closed and put it in my pocket. Some secrets are secret so long that they turn into truths.

♦ ♦ ♦

I walk into her room after getting coffee late the next day and two nurses are holding my mother, who crouches halfway between her bed and the bathroom. Evidently, she's tried to make it there. She's wearing the nightgown I'd brought from home; white cotton sprigged with tiny red tulips, damp now and wrinkled. She sways between them, Eunice on one side and Perlita on the other, like a scarecrow in a strong wind.

"I'm going on the floor," she moans.

"No you're not, sweetie," Eunice says, holding her. "You've got a catheter."

"I am," she shrieks.

"Honey, it's okay." Eunice grips her tighter. "You've got a catheter in. Do you remember what a catheter is? It's a little tube . . ."

"I'm going on the floor!"

I flee down the hall, sobbing.

♦ ♦ ♦

"Where you been, Simone?" Calvin, a black technician about twenty years old, my mother's friend from radiology, walks right into her room wearing baggy jeans and black sneakers, big as boats, and stands by her bed. His job is to prep the radiation machine and draw a target range on the patient's body with a thick marker, but his gift is his special brand of warmth and good humor, his ability to keep people comfortable. "It's Calvin, ma'am. Today's my day off, but I thought I'd . . ."

"Oh, Calvin!" My mother's face lights up. Henry smiles and touches her hand. Theo and Scottie and I are at the other end of the room just watching the show.

"I wanted to come by and say hey. I've missed you down in radiation. How's my favorite patient doin'?"

Mimi shakes her head sadly.

"Well, don't you worry. I remembered you was havin' some trouble eatin' and I asked you your favorite food and you said red beans and rice. Well, that's mine, too. Good Mississippi red beans and rice. My mama taught me how to make it real good. This mornin', my day off, I was doin' some cookin' and I said to Chantel, I have to make an extra batch for someone special, and I did, special for you. I brought a big batch that's bound to get you hummin' and singin'." He looks around. "Chantel," he calls.

A young woman enters the room as if on cue, holding out a large Tupperware container. When she catches sight of the pale, withered figure on the bed, the bald head like a baby chick's peeking out from the blankets, she slows to a dead halt in the middle of the room. She looks from me to Theo to Henry and back to Mimi. Then she lets out a long shuddering sigh and crosses herself.

"*Chantel,* where is that *food*?" Calvin dashes over, lifts the container out of her hands, and places it lovingly on my mother's nightstand. "I made it myself, didn't I, Chantel? Just for you, Ms. Levy."

"Who's this Chantel?" she whispers. "I can't see her."

"She's my fiancée."

"We have another fiancée in here someplace," Mimi says. "Sil-vie, where are you?"

"I'm right here." I give a little wave from the couch, then resume my latest position, my hand cupped on my shoulder holding the knob of bone attached to my clavicle. I didn't even know I was sit-ting like that until I thought back later and saw myself that way, holding myself.

Calvin smiles at me and pushes his girlfriend toward the bed. "Show yourself, Chantel."

Chantel stumbles and rights herself, inching across the room until she, too, is right by my mother's side. "I'm Chantel Williams, ma'am." Her voice is sweet and clear.

Mimi makes a motion of lifting her head, but I don't think she looks. "Pretty."

"Yeah, but she can't cook." Calvin grins. "I do all the cookin'." He pats the Tupperware container.

My mother licks her lips in the slow, exaggerated movements of a dream. "Ummm, red beans and rice. A good southern lunch. Calvin, thank you."

He squeezes her hand, bending down to give her a gentle hug.

"Okay, Ms. Levy, I best be goin' now. Now, you enjoy that food. And you take care, you hear?" He seems to have a tight grip on her hand.

"Do you have to go?" she whispers.

"I better go, Ms. Levy. I'll come back soon, I promise."

My mother nods. "Please." Her eyes fix on the ceiling.

"Good-bye, ma'am," Chantel says. "Nice to meet you." She fol-lows Calvin to the door. Then she steals a quick look at Calvin and, as if she can't hold it in another second, speaks up loudly. "Ms. Levy, you're gonna get yourself up outta that bed, now aren't you, ma'am? You've gotta try, you can't give up . . ." Calvin pulls her out the door.

Henry and Scottie spoon red beans and rice on plates that Perlita brings from the cafeteria and we all dig in. Best meal we've eaten in weeks.

◆ ◆ ◆

Later that day, Eunice sends in first a priest, then a rabbi, covering all her bases. "As long as God gets the message, it doesn't matter who the messenger is," she says.

The rabbi knocks twice, two sharp raps, walks in, and hovers over Mimi's bed. He's a sturdy man with a thick beard. He shifts his weight every few minutes and makes unconvincing gestures with his hands. Every now and then, he leans close and mumbles into her ear.

"Speak up," she croaks, looking confused and miserable.

Again, Theo, Henry, Scottie, and I watch from the couch. "Henry," I whisper. "He's making things worse."

Henry nods. He pads across the room and touches the man's shoulder. The rabbi turns and studies him, turning his hat over in his hands, glancing down one last time at my mother as if he knows he's failed her.

Her eyes flutter open. "Don't care much for the rabbi, but I sure love that Calvin."

◆ ◆ ◆

"Silvie! Theo! Are you listening? I want to apologize." My mother leans up in bed, her voice strong today. The morphine dulls the pain and leaves her skin pure, smooth, unlined, as if all life's tragedies have passed right through her, kissing her lightly but not lingering.

"For what?" I actually sound cheerful.

Theo's head bobs up from where he's sitting on the floor by her bed sifting through the pile of cassettes he's brought her. He still works in the music store, but now his band is playing gigs.

"I'm sorry I didn't give you guys religion." Theo and I look at each other. We'd rarely talked about God in our house. "Jewish, not Jewish. It was all so confusing. Now here I am, at my age, talking to God. I give him our address, we've moved around so much. I think of all the chewed-up gum I've handed him. Do you guys believe?"

"Do *you*?" Theo says. He puts the tapes down, hands idle, eyes inquisitive.

"I'm trying, Theo. What choice do I have?" Her voice reminds me of something faded, some little trinket you've let hang in the window too long.

"God's in my music."

"God's in some people's eyes, but not all," Mimi says. "Is Scottie here?"

"Yes," I say.

"Ah. Where he should be." Here is permission, exoneration, I realize, just a low rumble you could miss if your ear wasn't to the ground.

"I brought you some music, Mom," Theo says quietly.

"No sad Billie Holiday. Or Chopin. Or Mozart."

"Not even Mozart?" He smiles, shuffles through the little plastic boxes. "Rolling Stones. John Lennon, solo after the Beatles. Dylan. Zappa."

"Nope." She shakes her head, a small smile creeping over her face. "None of that."

I nod vigorously, suddenly getting it.

"What then?" Theo asks.

"I want Elvis."

Theo's face falls. "Mom, I didn't bring any . . ."

"Love Me Tender."

"I don't have . . ."

"Sing it. Like when you were little. I loved that." And she sinks back into her pillow. Still a queen. Theo looks like he's just swallowed a jug of water in one gulp.

"Go for it," I say.

"There are few times in life when a request is *not* to be turned down," Mimi says weakly, her eyes shining. She claps her hands twice, with enthusiasm, like a schoolteacher.

Theo shrugs and in his pure, sweet tenor, starts in. " 'Love me tender, love me sweet . . .' "

She relaxes into the pillow, her eyes at half mast, around her head again that shimmering halo of light.

" '. . . never let me go.' " His voice wavers, but never quits. " 'You have made my life complete and I love you so.' "

If it weren't for the smile playing at her lips, I'd think she was asleep.

My brother's memory doesn't fail him. " 'For my darlin', I love you . . .' "

She doesn't move, but her face is tilted on the pillow and I can feel her listening.

" '. . . and I always will.' "

He finishes. Mimi doesn't open her eyes or applaud or say one word. I look at Theo, my eyes brimming over. I am filled with an immense love for him, and fear; we will soon be alone in the world together, alone the way you are when you have no mother.

We think that she's fallen asleep for real and that we'll sneak out for candy or a Coke, but then her voice comes, thin but oddly content, "Okay, I believe."

♦ ♦ ♦

Scottie goes back to his hospital in New York; I stay here at mine. One afternoon before dinner, I run errands, worrying about being away from the hospital for even twenty minutes. I'm crazy just thinking that I might not be there when she dies. Waiting in line under the fluorescent lights at the bank, sweating and itchy in my long wool coat, I watch a woman in front of me. Her baby is wrapped so tightly in a blanket that I see only its face and the tiny

body, wrapped like a mummy, not moving at all, and I keep imagining the baby dead. But the mother just keeps on holding it, patting its back now and then. She could stand in line at the bank for
a long time waiting for a teller, not knowing her baby has died.
Maybe in the deli, when she stopped for orange juice and paper
towels and diapers, her baby took a last breath and went to sleep
for good; it could happen and she wouldn't even know.

Mimi; Mom. Her names blaze in my head, and I'm afraid I've
screamed them out loud. Sweating, breathless, I have to hurry back
to her pain, its faces, all of those she has ever loved; me, whom she
also hated.

I begin walking and soon I break into a guilty run, my footsteps
pounding back to her, and as I count them, I know I'm losing, by
degrees, little by little. I race across the hospital parking lot, past the
information desk to the south elevators and down the corridor to
her room, open the door, think drunkenly that she's leaving me before we can forgive, talk about love, say good-bye.

◆ ◆ ◆

In the doorway, I stop short, my eyes jumping all around, looking
for her. I can't find her. The room is dark and extravagantly quiet.
My eyes roam over her bed, the chair by the window, the bathroom door, which is ajar, an amber stripe of light underneath. I
stand in the doorway, afraid that she's dead, that she died while I
was in line at the bank. Then I see her; she is in the chair by the
window. She's turned it around—or Henry has—so she can look at
the sky.

Her voice, when she speaks, is a smoky whisper. "Please just
apologize for me. Tell the kids I don't always act like this."

I kneel beside her chair, take her hand in mine, stroking it. Cau-
tiously, I try my voice. "It's just me, Mom."

"Tell her then. Tell her."

"Okay, I'll tell her."

Her mouth goes slack; her hands unknot themselves. "I think Henry likes me better when I'm part of the party."

"I think he likes you fine."

"Where is he?" She's impatient now, restless, moving her head back and forth in a pantomime of looking around.

"He probably went downstairs for coffee. He'll be back."

"He drinks herbal tea. You'll have to help me order."

"Order?"

"Our lunch for the party, Chinese food. I'll have the strawberry shrimp and the pineapple noodles."

"Ummm. Sounds delish." I don't know what to say; this is what comes out.

"Yes, delish." Her eyes wide as a child's, earnest. "But if the rabbits get scared, they won't come."

I hesitate. "Do you want to have a party?"

"No." She bows her head. "But I think I'll take a bath and make the water real soft." And then, in a barely audible whisper, "Hi, Silvie. Hi, Silvie. Please just tell Silvie I'm sorry."

I cradle that apology in my arms like a newborn; I stretch it to cover our whole lives, until it seems enough. In the end, isn't any small thing enough?

◆ ◆ ◆

Some softness has descended, blurred and fuzzy, all around her. I sit in the dark room listening to the stillness under her wrists, the faint beat of her pulse, wondering what time it is until, finally, I grope for the thin gold watch by her bed and put it on.

"Call Florence," she says without opening her eyes. "Tell her you're coming back."

"What?" I haven't thought of my boss in weeks. I've barely noticed the flowers she sent to the hospital.

"Call her."

"Okay."

We are so quiet that I think she's fallen asleep. Then her fingers start stroking—my thumb, my pinkie, and each finger in between, like a blind person thinking: *hand*.

"I like it when you're here next to me." Her whisper is gray now, flimsy, a slight voice I've only dreamed before. When she speaks, she turns her head slowly toward me, wigless, bald.

"It's harder than I thought," she whispers. Her eyes have a stunned, milky look.

"What is?"

"Dying. I thought maybe you just closed your eyes and drifted away. But it's not smooth at all. It's like sliding down a slide in the summer when your legs are hot and sticky."

"You don't have to hold on anymore." My voice is husky with tears. "Not for us. We'll be okay."

She nods. "Go back there and buy that pretty dress." A whisper, paper-thin. "That's what I want."

"Okay, Mom." A hand squeeze; a sigh. I lean over her face; her lips brush against my hair. She sleeps, or stares up into space with her eyes closed.

A while later, she plucks at my sleeve. "Loved his hands." Her voice is raspy, like a knife scraping burnt toast.

"Whose hands, Mom?" My own voice shatters; I feel my heart's desperate surge. The stars outside her window are just tiny lights pushing through the sky.

And then I swear I hear her say, "I need better shoes."

♦ ♦ ♦

As quiet as that day is, the next day is noisy. Her breathing, now nothing more than a ragged rasp, stuns Henry and Theo and me to silence, makes us think of the rusted rattle and clank of heavy machinery.

Henry beckons us away from her side. We huddle miserably by the couch. "There's a machine we can put her on . . ."

"No," we say, one beat away from each other.

♦ ♦ ♦

While she dies, I hold her hand, a tiny sack of bones inside a velvet glove. I stroke her hair and whisper, "Don't be scared, don't be scared," over and over. There is no sign that she hears me, but I keep lifting her hand to my nose so that I might smell death plainly, hold her hand until her skin blends with mine. The brain is stronger than skin, I think, the way it holds a scent forever.

♦ ♦ ♦

Theo and I cross the sidewalk to the hospital parking lot without stepping on the cracks. I clutch her black purse, pieces of her tissue inside. We weave by the cars, the snow banked on the side of the road, the sun staring like a lover, me with my arms in the sleeves of her wool coat, Theo, who, despite the wall of music he's built between himself and the world, doesn't hum or whistle or sing.

My hand freezes on the car door. A terrifying thought pushes all the air out of my lungs: It will be easier now that she's gone. In our deepest moments we were in a tangle so thick that I couldn't see, like after a building is torn down, suddenly there are *lake, sky, trees.*

CHAPTER 15

Standing inside my mother's closet, I feel almost good enough to hum. I pause by the window, snap the shade up, and watch the sky unfold, layers of light breaking in waves that will swallow the darkness until morning comes. I turn and place the items inside the purse I am packing to go beside her—the black alligator wallet, the tiny bottle of Pheromone, the small hairbrush with the boar bristles—no, no, the wallet on top, the brush in the corner here, the perfume snug in the other corner. My hand strokes the purse's embroidery: a picture of a woman, a hat shadowing her face.

The list the funeral home gave me hasn't mentioned a purse, but I can't stop picturing it slung over her shoulder, a tiny transportable home. Without knowing I will, I empty the purse out on my mother's bed and calmly sweep its contents to the floor. I have put in the wrong things, silly things.

I start over. I open closet doors, drawers, a box where she kept her keys. Moving more swiftly now, I know what I want without thinking. No perfume or wallet or hairbrush. When I've gathered the items, laid them out on the bed, rushed and panting, I can't fill the small purse fast enough.

1. Glasses with large pearly-white frames
2. Lipstick, #40, Mostly Mauve
3. Oriental hand fan
4. Powder in a black Deco compact with gold trim
5. Two heart-shaped paper clips for important papers
6. Several half sticks of Wrigley's Doublemint gum
7. Tissues
8. Blank address book
9. Key to the front door

What doesn't go in:

1. Quartz crystal
2. Vitamins
3. Safety pins
4. 4-by-8 piece of paper on which she had scribbled: I decide to get well. The pressure of her underlining ripped the paper.

I take a pen and in the child-size address book write *home* under "H," her address, phone number, and the names of the people she loved: Theo, Henry, me. Aunt Nina. Aunt Connie. I hesitate; the pencil flutters above the miniature page like a wing on a tiny insect. Who am I forgetting? Oh. I must be crazy. My father. *Dan.* I write his name. There.

The packed purse against my hip, flat, rectangular, solid. I walk back and forth in front of the mirror, savoring the feel of it, then catch a glimpse of my face in the glass. My mother's face stares back. I blink; she blinks. Stare until it's my face again, my skin sallow, my tongue spicy as her perfume. My hands are ice, my legs water; I have no feet. I don't know what I'm standing on.

The room is growing brighter now. She wouldn't approve of this radiant winter morning bullying its way in. "Light is overrated," she always said, drawing the drapes.

I snap a grocery bag open with a crack of my wrist and fill it with air. She didn't like to pack. We always hated leaving a place; we were alike in this. I riffle through blouses and skirts, until I spot the perfect dress, black sweatshirt material with floral patches and a ruffled hem; informal, not at all stiff. Whimsical, she'd said. She'd made it herself.

I bury my face in the fabric, trying to smell her perfume. My fingers fumble with the dress; I can't seem to pull it off the hanger and drop it into the bag. When I finally release the dress, I catch a flicker of perfume, a twinkle of sweet, heady spice, and I see her sashay by, proudly modeling.

Why do we bury people in shoes? But she loved shoes, and shoes are on the list. On the floor of the closet, perched on shoe trees, toes pointed, are black shoes, several pairs, perky, expectant. I reach for a pair until I see, in the corner, the blue suede pumps. I lift them to my chest, running my finger over one heel, cradling the worn leather as it digs hard into my palm. They're dingy but still blue. I arrange them on top of the dress in the bag.

What about a slip, bra, underwear? Jesus; God. And stockings. I open a drawer and touch everything; every pair, I lift gently and put down. Some new, unopened, crackling in the plastic sleeve, some worn, with a long run she'd dabbed near the knee with clear nail polish now hardened to a rigid glaze. Finally, I choose a pair sheer as silk, the color of skin.

A cosmetics case. Black sea-mud soap, face cream, makeup. My fingers stumble over the round plastic cases for a good fresh one: Warm Toast. Brown eyeliner—no. Too dreary with all that black;

better make it plum. An eyelash curler. Flirtin' Rose blush. Coffee Bean lipstick.

At the jewelry box, I tilt open a torn envelope and out fall the rings from my father, an engagement ring with a modest diamond, a thin silver band—but it isn't right. . . . No, but they are beautiful. The ring from Henry, I can't find. She doesn't cling to propriety anyway. It is Theo and I, children of divorce, who crave custom, and I slip my father's rings into my pocket thinking that I'll show them to Scottie; maybe I could wear them.

Wig. Quickly, I scalp the Styrofoam head and the wig squeaks past my fingers, landing with a flop on the floor. Picking it up, I stroke the wig back in place, the strands like real hair, smooth, thick as rope, just as her hair had felt. Or had it? I can't remember if I've ever touched my mother's hair.

I arrange the wig on top of the dress in the bag. Done. Finished. What about lint on the dress? Black shows everything. I stand in her closet, the bag heavy in my arms, the purse still over my shoulder, thinking about lint, and the Egyptians, how they went with food, dogs, servants. All I can fill are a brown paper bag and a small embroidered purse.

◆ ◆ ◆

"Not a grocery bag," says Henry when I meet him downstairs with the bag full of clothes. I grab a coat out of the closet. He hands me the canvas carryall where she'd kept her art supplies.

I stare at him blankly. "Not a grocery bag," I repeat.

◆ ◆ ◆

The sky is wide and shining now, a sunny Thursday morning somewhere between Christmas and New Year's. Persistent, clamorous cold, snow bright as metal. In the car, I grope for the seat belt, my fingers thick.

I shove my hands into my pockets and find a wadded-up tissue, a half piece of gum, a small appointment card. I pull it out. A word scrawled on the back in my mother's loopy writing. CHEMO.

I am wearing her coat.

At the funeral home, we stand in a long hallway studded with doors. A man shakes my hand, offering condolences. "These are her things?" he asks. He reaches for the canvas bag.

"Just a minute," I say, placing the bag beside my feet and opening the embroidered purse with its half-smiling woman. My fingers rummage through . . . have I packed everything she'd need? I clutch the purse tighter. Oh God. The man's face is kind, patient, but his hand is outstretched, uncompromising.

Out of the corner of my eye, I see someone open a door across the hall and slip soundlessly into another room. Words tumble from my mouth. "Nothing prepared me. Gathering her clothes, filling her purse . . ." I feel Henry's hand on my shoulder, soft as a leaf.

Panting, I look away from the man's startled face. He would zip her dress, feather her face with powder, but I would be the one to clasp my index finger and thumb around the bone of her wrist, cry into her mouth.

Raising my eyes to the man, I nudge the bag forward with the toe of my sneaker. "Yes," I whisper. "These are her things."

CHAPTER 16

On the Sunday after the funeral, I fly home to New York, fall into bed, and sleep for sixteen hours. I wake to a bright and cloudless sky above Riverside Park.

I get up and wash my face. It startles me to see on my finger my engagement ring; I'd almost forgotten I was getting married. I get dressed, pad to my jewelry box, and take out the Elvis necklace, slipping it into my pocket.

Heading toward Eighty-sixth Street, I stop at a Korean market, where a homeless guy opens the door for me and holds out a tattered cup. I give him a few coins and he veers away. I buy a bag of M&M's, put it in my pocket next to the necklace, and continue my walk down Broadway, thinking that death could be anything—a river where all you do is float on your back all day or the Beatles playing for the last time on a summer's night in Central Park. As my mother contracted, I expanded, filled up and up, like a balloon, for once without her breath inside.

The sun is shining, but the air is cold; the sidewalk, crowded with people who walk fast, breath puffing out in little clouds of white smoke. At the bus stop, a dense knot of people waiting for the next bus; they crane their necks and check their watches. Suddenly, through the grit in my eyes, I see them.

They walk single file, twelve, maybe thirteen children, the wavering line dissolving into a wobbly circle. A long string loops around each small waist, connecting them one to another. They all wear a bright yellow sign around their neck, hanging low, like an oversize bib, all the way to their ankles. In large, friendly block letters the sign says KIDS ON THE MOVE.

A woman I presume to be the teacher jerks the end of the long string. I'd never liked those leashes parents held, their squirming, red-faced toddler straining on the other end like a dog, but in this case, there are so many kids and only one of her. At the corner, she claps her hands. "Children, what does the light say?"

A loud chorus sings out: *"Walk."*

"And what does that mean?"

"Cross." This motley group yanks itself into a semblance of a line and makes its way across the street.

Only, not one of them walks. One boy runs, a girl skips, one does a little jig, one hopscotches. A few stick out their tongues or hold their arms out like airplanes to fly. One small soldier in front leads the others on a march, his knees high. Another girl stops to pick up a rock and examine it, readjusting the sign that bumps her chest so that she can sneak the pebble into her pocket.

I am transfixed by their disorder, their chaos, their freedom. With all that rope, they could be frozen, stiff, unable to move. But nothing breaks their spirit. They all move in their own way. And they all make it safely across the street.

Theo was right: I've spent too long trying to get her right, sketching her, painting her, carrying around that hard bead of anger, furious at how much of my own life I had to throw away to be her daughter. Now I realize that I can hate her and love her and still miss her, still sit down next to her memory at the movies or a restaurant, keep her in my palm afterward, small change from a large bill. I have a lot to look forward to—the wedding, the art class I signed up for, returning to my job. Florence called to say that Mindy Carson was leaving and she was promoting me to the art department, where I would arrange spreads of beautiful houses photographed in scenic small towns. And Scottie is looking for a new apartment for us.

A hard bump into a garbage can pulls me out of my reverie. I peer down inside it—McDonald's bags, Coke cans, a half-eaten bagel. A man walks by, studying me curiously—a woman holding a bag of M&M's, almost letting it drop, then tearing the bag open and dropping a handful into her mouth. I touch the necklace in my pocket. Still there.

I feel light, weightless, turning the corner at a jaunty pace, glancing at my watch. A man with a sad face trudges past, his Indian-print backpack heavy with books, and I imagine that his books are about grieving; there's some hint in his thin, gauzy pants, his sculpted head, which he carries carefully, like a trophy on his graceful neck.

Sprinting off down the street, munching M&M's, I stop at a pay phone, fumbling for a quarter. I want to hear Scottie's voice. Now. This instant. My soul seems to rush right up to my head and beat in my ears. Maybe it isn't the heart when we hear beating. Maybe it's the soul.

"Hello?" Scottie sounds out of breath. But it's his voice, his voice. A thread in my stomach knots all by itself.

"Hi." I fish up the Elvis locket, let it sway in the cold air. She stays with you. Whether you want her or not. In her blue suede shoes, with that dream. That's the one. Go to him, she'd said. Go to him.

Words tumble out. "I—I love you." *Look, Ma, no hands.*

"And I love you. Is everything okay? Where are you?"

"Broadway and Eighty-sixth." The whole noisy day pounds into my ears. She was a landscape, a frontier; she went farther than the horizon, farther than a daughter's eye could see. I had to take her death and spiral toward a higher place. I had to pull myself out of the depths of her and into the height of something else.

"Marry me quick," I say. "And take me off my hands."

We both laugh, and I sink back against the metal pay phone, panting. I'd reached the ledge, jumped, and here was high ground.

I put the old necklace around my neck and walk on, chomping the last of my M&M's. This time, I skip.

EPILOGUE

My hands are steady. Putting in, taking out, taking my time. Humming that hum of hers. Packing my honeymoon suitcase. Over Riverside Park light is breaking up the darkness. Soon morning will come, my wedding day. Sunglasses. Lingerie. Jeans, sneakers.

How like hers my hands are—square-tipped fingers, knob-knuckled. Men, damn them, Mimi used to say. They throw in socks, a half-dozen T-shirts, sneakers, pack their pockets with keys and a wallet, don sunglasses, and they're out the door, while women sit on swelling suitcases, praying they'll shut.

I sit on mine a long time, thinking. It must be in the bones, the white hour where mothers and daughters meet, stretch to each other, become one person—mother, child, a whole angry heart. Over the years she played her games, writing on my flesh like paper, dense ropy-veined words that told me who not to be. And from her fine white bones she chiseled stories, weaving them into tight scarves that crowded around our skin like weather.

Later, in the bathroom of the restaurant where I will be married, I take a shower, dry my hair, put on my dress. Martine is coming soon to help me with my hair. She's good with hair, gentle yet strong. She did hers for her wedding. The dress floats over my head soft and easy. Martine will zip me. I sit on the couch and put on my white satin ankle boots, lacing the white shoelaces and buttoning each white satin button. I allow myself a glance in the mirror. My face, her face. She loves me, she loves me not. I love her, I love her not. I love me.

What has she taught me? What has she left me with? In my head I hear her last words, a strange mix of things she'd said over the years and things I want her to have said: "Cut your hair. Take up space. Speak up. Chew off all your lipstick. Always order a large. Mail yourself out to the whole world. Express."

It's late when I remember something old, something new. Martine's here and we scramble, tripping over each other in our long dresses. Hers is a deep blue velvet. She is my matron of honor.

"Okay," Martine says, her red hair bright against the dark fabric, her dark eyes luminous. "Your dress is new."

"And my engagement ring is old."

"Something borrowed." Martine's eyes roam frantically around the room, resting on her black velvet purse. She pulls from it an embroidered handkerchief. "Put this in your bra."

"In my bra? Are you crazy?"

"Tuck it in. No time to argue."

"It's beautiful." I look at the linen square, cream-colored, with the letter *V*, surrounded by violets.

"It was my mother's. I was going to cry into it when you came down the aisle, but I'll just let my mascara run."

"Thank you." I hug her. Outside, a strong winter sun sparkles on the snow-covered trees.

"You look beautiful, Sil," she says. "Mimi would be so proud."

"Or jealous." We laugh, but my throat catches.

"God, I gotta be out there to line up." She gives my hand a squeeze. "Next time we talk, you'll be married." She runs out and just as she disappears, I think, Something blue. I paw frantically through my jewelry box, then through Mimi's, both of which I've lugged here. Nothing blue. Except. That old blue guitar pick from Uncle Shelby. Surely she'd saved it. Yes, here. I slip it into my shoe. I will dance on that small blue piece all night, to slow songs, borrowed, blue.

◆ ◆ ◆

Ready. The music swells. Dressed in white, I am supposed to take my father's elbow and begin the long walk up the aisle toward Scottie. But I don't take his elbow. I put my hand in his, and we walk like that, holding on to each other. Scottie seems far away yet near in his black tux, holding out his smile. Outside the tall windows, the black night collects, unrolling around us like a carpet. I walk toward the candles, tiny flickering lights whose liquid glow fills the corners of the room. An ache lodges itself high underneath my rib cage; I miss my mother. But I keep walking. One foot in front of the other, holding sadness and joy, death and life, at the same time, in a little bouquet, as my father, tears in his eyes, walks me into another man's arms.

At the end of the aisle, my father kisses me and our hands fall away and now my hands are my own and I deliver myself to Scottie, my shy wrists rising, a blue guitar pick in my shoe.

We face each other. Our eyes meet as if for the first time. My heart whispers, *Here is my baggage, Scottie. Here are my things.*

He slips the ring on my finger, takes both my hands in his. *Here is your husband, holding you home.*

ACKNOWLEDGMENTS

For their encouragement, support, and friendship: David Breskin, Leah Callahan, Gloria Gregory, Amy Koppelman, Laura Pintchik (who rescued my manuscript from the back of a New York City taxicab), Renee Rosen, Susan Shapiro, Mima Viera.

To every member of the Novel Workshop—your sound literary criticism is a constant source of inspiration.

For careful, honest readings and music that lights the way, my brother, Michael Glasgow.

For faith, for love, for always showing up at the rock, my father, Page Glasgow.

For sturdiness, for steady hearts, Richard and Judy Stern, and all the Sterns.

Special thanks to my editor, Kate Medina, who patiently helped structure and deepen this book, and to Veronica Windholz and Meaghan Rady.

For saying yes, my agent and friend Jane Gelfman, whose generosity of intelligence and spirit, sense of humor, and keen intuition have steered me along.

To the other Kate, without whom there would be no Jane.

And especially to my guardian angel. She alone opened the box and finished the book. And opened the door.

My deepest gratitude to my teacher, Fred Shafer, who guided me toward the path and lit the way with his wisdom.

For taking long naps, my daughter.

And above all to Jim, for shelter, for sustenance, for always.

Another Song About the King

Kathryn Stern

A Reader's Guide

A Conversation with Kathryn Stern

Fred Shafer *was an editor for several years with* TriQuarterly, *the international literary journal published by Northwestern University, where he has taught fiction writing in the English and Radio-TV-Film departments and the School of Continuing Education. His stories, essays, and interviews have appeared in several journals. He also leads private workshops in story writing and novel writing, of one of which Kathryn Stern is a member.*

FS: At a time when many fiction writers and poets have been publishing memoirs drawn from their lives, you chose to write a novel based on your relationship with your mother. Why did you decide to write a novel, rather than a memoir?

KS: My mother was diagnosed with cancer before a number of things between us could be resolved. She died just as I was becoming engaged to be married, and there I was, falling in love inside a space of great loss, forced to close one door when another door was being flung wide open. This novel began as an attempt to explore everything that had been left unsaid about our complex relationship, and to make peace with losing her so soon. But it never occurred to me to write a memoir. I didn't have the confidence to blatantly expose the emotional truths of my life, or the arrogance to assume they would be interesting. It takes courage to say, "This happened to me and I'd like to tell you about it." I guess that's because we are ashamed of our weaknesses and flaws, even though they are what makes us human.

Writing a novel, rather than a memoir, gave me a license with language and imagery that was utterly compelling. And it was the best way I could find of trying to understand the things that had always puzzled me about my mother's personality. I wanted to write a version of our story. As it turned out, that didn't keep me from feeling guilty about using the people I love for the sake of art or for my own personal catharsis. But the need to hold my life up to the light, in order to study it and find meaning in the struggle we'd gone through, somehow outweighed all other concerns.

FS: **From a writer's standpoint, what distinctions have you found between memoirs and fiction based on autobiography? Does a work of fiction give the writer more of a sense of being protected?**

KS: It only seems easier to hide behind a work of fiction than a memoir. I have found that it's impossible to hide behind any writing that strives to reach a deep place. But the line between fact and fiction is always indistinct, and even a memoirist must, at times, be forced to invent. I don't see how anyone can remember entire paragraphs of dialogue from her childhood. I know I can't. A weakness in my character, but perhaps one of my strengths as a writer, is that I rarely tell the whole truth. If I come home and say to my husband that I was involved in a fender bender, the minor scrape on the bumper will invariably lengthen and deepen, and the time it took the police to arrive will grow from twenty minutes to forty-five. Conversely, if I set out to write a novel based entirely on things I've imagined, I suspect I'd be unable to resist throwing in a character who resembles someone from my family, or a few lines of dialogue lifted from last year's Thanksgiving dinner when Aunt Pearl drank too much wine and began cursing her dead husband. The impulse to liven things up, to embellish, to make the world a more profound and interesting place, is what separates art from life and makes a person a storyteller.

FS: **John Irving, in an interview published several years ago in *The Paris Review*, said that he starts out by writing about real people, then invents and exaggerates until he has produced "autobiography on its way to becoming lie," and the lie interests him more. Is this what you're talking about?**

KS: Yes. Looking back, I'm not always sure which things I made up and which are true. When she was a teenager, my mother had a date with Elvis Presley, but she rarely talked about it while I was growing up, and I was left to color in what was shrouded in mystery. It always intrigued me that my mother was so hush-hush about the dates she'd had with men. She was the kind of person who you'd expect to shout it from the rooftops.

Elvis was nowhere to be found in any of the early drafts; it was primarily a book about a stormy mother/daughter relationship, ending in loss and grief. But as I wrestled with it, one line kept popping up: "Silvie, did you know your mama dated the King?" It hung over me, and I didn't know what to make of those words. It wasn't until I went to a neighborhood barbecue, where a woman actually drove home to get a scrapbook she kept of the time she met the Beatles, that I began to pay attention to the Elvis theme in my novel. I was struck by the air of discontent this thirty-year-old woman wore like a cloak, and how it dissipated only when she launched into her story, holding court in that tiny backyard, recounting her fifteen minutes of fame. It was clear that nothing in her life had equaled, or ever would equal, the experience she was describing. And I thought, "That's what Simone has been trying to tell me!" Unlike my mother, Simone had been holding herself and her family hostage to a story about the date with Elvis. I was on my way to loving the lie I'd invented, and I couldn't turn back from the sense of freedom it brought to my writing.

FS: **Does this mean that you made up many of the things that people say or do to each other in the book? What limitations or boundaries did you set in regard to inventing action or dialogue?**

KS: I invented almost everything the characters say or do to each other. Which doesn't mean that I didn't live in New York City or meet my husband there, or that I didn't have a difficult relationship with my mother, that she didn't date Elvis Presley, or that she didn't die and I didn't sit beside her on the couch while it was happening. But not one of the events in the book happens as it did in real life, and very few lines of dialogue were actually spoken. Isn't it a writer's duty to carry a conversation a step further than might have happened in life, to unveil hidden truths so that a reader has no choice but to respond deeply?

I didn't consciously set boundaries. The only guideline I followed was to stay true to the characters I had created on the page and to the action that was taking shape. In chapter two, for example, Simone sends Silvie a manila envelope full of perfume samples torn from magazines. I was never the recipient of such a gift, but I seized upon the idea one day while leafing through a magazine in a doctor's office. It was exactly the kind of project Simone would undertake, collecting those samples for her daughter, and the kind of unspoken message she would send: "All you need to have in order to succeed in the big city is your femininity and a good perfume." After I'd written a monstrous first draft, the characters gradually became entities in their own right, separate from my personal history. And whenever I used situations from my life, I'd always ask myself whether the characters would behave differently than the real people did under those circumstances.

FS: **The novel is structured with chapters that describe incidents from Silvie's childhood are interspersed with chapters concerning her mother's illness and death. How far into the writing did you decide on the structure of the novel? Did your choice of this structure have any impact on your understanding of the story?**

KS: I wrote several drafts in chronological order, and that helped me to get in touch with my story. In the course of producing a later draft, I realized that the structure itself would help carry the issues of the plot forward. By juxtaposing Silvie's childhood self with her adult self, I found that I could create suspense and make connections that might not be apparent otherwise, because, of course, the past influences and, at times, foreshadows the future. Once I'd rearranged the structure, some of the connections surprised me. For instance, the chapter that follows the Thanksgiving scene, in which Simone misbehaves when Silvie brings home Scottie, begins with the line, "My new friend, Martine LaRue, gave me courage." What I realized in putting the two together was that, just as Silvie's friendship with Martine helped her to gain a measure of independence, her relationship with Scottie is bound to grant her a life beyond her mother's grasp.

FS: **Did the need for introducing a plot enable you to learn anything about the characters?**

KS: It's astounding how much a writer can, and must, learn about her characters as she watches them respond to situations into which she has thrust them. How will they behave when a new person enters their lives? How will they react when someone they know well does something unusual? A writer's reward for all the grueling hours spent in isolation struggling with one sentence occurs when characters surprise you by acting in ways you never dreamed possible or by saying things you never expected them to say. You just shake your head and exclaim, "Wow, I didn't know they had it in them."

One area of the plot where the characters continually surprised me is what I came to think of as the Simone and Silvie dance; it's a kind of love versus hate, dependence versus independence two-step. In order to sustain the ebb and flow of this dance, I invented many scenes in which the characters draw together, but then fall back, due to insensitivity on the part of one or the other. For instance, after Simone bites into the apple, Silvie stops calling her "Mom" and eventually renames her "Mimi," as a way of gaining distance from behavior that has become increasingly confusing. Later in the book, following her own failure in the sewing contest, Simone criticizes Silvie when she wins the art prize, then Silvie sets out to destroy her mother's carefully organized closet.

In writing these scenes, I wanted to create tensions that would lead the characters to react strongly to each other, to the point that both of them might become capable of changing and growing. What I realized, instead, was that this mother is the major impediment to Silvie's being able to find her own identity. With each small act of rebellion, the girl moves a step closer to the independence she seeks, but also fears. I was like a surrogate parent, cheering for Silvie whenever she quietly fought back.

FS: **Did you ever feel the urge to make things happen between Silvie and Mimi that you wish had taken place between you and your mother? Is there ever a place for wish fulfillment in an autobiographical novel?**

KS: In writing the hospital scenes, I often felt the urge to compose a farewell that my mother and I did not actually share. Those were the first scenes I wrote, beginning only a month after she died. That room was still vivid in my mind, and the dialogue came easily. It was often stitched around a single line that my mother said, but that, because of limitations imposed by her illness, our shared denial that she was dying, and my usual tongue-tied response to her, did not go any further. The Hollywood deathbed ending, with the apologies and white lies and good-byes, rarely happens. People die, and very little is said. That was certainly my experience, and at first it may have fueled my need to make the final chapter happen as I wished my real life experience had.

Like dreams, wishes are potent, and very much a product of our imaginations. I believe that anything that comes from such a deep place is valid territory for a writer to explore. But there is no place for wish fulfillment in a novel, unless the words or details fit with the story you're telling. You have to be true to the story. You can't just get your ya-yas out, in terms of wishes or revenge, because the possibility of engaging in self-indulgence is too great.

FS: **Speaking of dreams, one of the most powerful and disturbing moments, apart from the deathbed scenes, occurs at the end of chapter four when Silvie, soon after she arrives in New York, has a nightmare about riding the subway with her mother. Did you actually have that dream?**

KS: It started with a dream I had before beginning to write the novel. My mother was a few weeks from death. I woke up and jotted a note on an index card: "Riding the subway with Mom in NYC. She is turning round and round, crying, confused, like a dog, and I am trying to hold her by the shoulders." That was the central image, and I built the entire sequence around it, just letting my imagination go. I rewrote that section countless times, and with each new draft tried to get closer to the characters' deepest need, which, at that time in their lives, was to connect, really connect, before it was too late.

FS: **Do you feel that Simone and Silvie have achieved closure by the time Simone dies?**

KS: If closure means accepting the most basic truths about a relationship and letting go of things that shouldn't matter, I'd say, yes, they do achieve closure, and they find peace. When Simone asks Silvie to drop the Elvis locket in the wastebasket, it shows that she recognizes the extent to which she's hidden behind the myth, and is finally able to set it aside. Elvis is a symbol of the ambition and desire that were very much a part of my mother's personality, but we never talked about Elvis when she was dying; there wasn't room for him in our conversations.

However, it seemed right that, on the threshold of Sylvie's and

Simone's marriage, the two of them would gain closure through talking about him. I have trouble reading those scenes aloud now. They transport me back to my own experience so completely: the feel of the room, the smell of death, the longing to keep my mother alive. I used the present tense in chapter fourteen to convey the fact that the dying ends only for the person who closes her eyes; death lives with the survivor forever.

FS: **In the last few years of revising the novel, you gave birth, first to a daughter and then a son. Did becoming a parent have any impact on decisions that you made about Silvie and Simone? Have you learned anything from writing about those characters that has influenced the approach you and your husband take in raising your own children?**

KS: I feel that I have a lot more sympathy for Simone now. Being a mother is hard, and until you have children of your own, you can't fully appreciate how hard it is. After my daughter was born, I saw Simone as a fellow mother, and I was concerned about making sure that she seemed sympathetic, even likable. I felt I truly understood how a woman like Simone could be pushed, out of tedium over endless loads of laundry and drives to and from school, to invent a glamorous counterlife for herself and to behave in ways that are unpredictable and, at times, cruel. And when I began to see Silvie as having an identity separate from my own, I was able to regard my daughter as separate from me, something Simone was never able to do with Silvie.

As a parent, I try to look the other way when my daughter, at four, refuses to brush her hair or insists on wearing her pink tutu over her overalls. I am not, by nature, overbearing and competitive in the way Simone is, but I am much more aware now that the role assumed by a parent can stifle a child's creativity and identity. By the time I revised the final scenes in the book, I cherished my own budding relationship with my daughter, and I wanted Simone and Silvie to come as close as possible to forgiveness, understanding, and a kind of mutual respect. It was painful to let Simone die. I kept wanting to keep her alive, through another paragraph, another page, so that Silvie wouldn't be left without a mother at her wedding or when she, someday, had a child of her own.

FS: What do you think would have happened in their relationship if Simone had lived?

KS: In some ways I find it difficult to imagine what Silvie's married life would be like if Simone were still around, because the premise of the novel has to do with the sense of freedom that Simone's death brings Silvie. But it is a writer's job to learn more about her characters' lives than goes onto the page, and that may even include speculating about the roads that were not taken. Once Silvie was married, I think that Simone might have felt jealous of the happiness and love that she'd attained with Scottie. The tension might have kept building between them until Silvie had children, and Simone began to acknowledge her daughter's new role as a mother. But I don't think that Simone would have been pleased to find that she'd become a grandmother. She certainly wouldn't have allowed herself to be called Granny. They would have needed to come up with a more glamorous name for her, perhaps something like Mimi!

FS: Have you ever wondered how your mother would have felt if she'd been able to read the scenes from your book that describe Silvie's childhood?

KS: I've thought long and hard about that. Her pride at my accomplishment in writing and publishing the book, I know, would have been filtered through a sense of competitiveness. She would have regarded the story itself as a black-and-white picture of our relationship, without the subtle shadings that I see there. And I'm sure that she would have been unhappy with the portrayal of Simone, whereas I regard Simone's shortcomings as human and real and often lovable. Would I have written this book if my mother were alive now? I don't think so. Not this book. If she were still actively making an imprint on my consciousness, I would have felt too restricted.

FS: You said earlier that, following your mother's death, you wanted to solve the puzzles of your relationship with her. What have you learned through writing the book?

KS: It has been part of my journey as a woman to come to terms with my mother. Many women have an opportunity to do this face to face as they grow older, but I was denied that luxury. Writing this book enabled me to grow into myself as an individual, with an identity separate from the one I had with my mother. What took place between us was so powerful that I could not easily let go of it. I had to stick my hands into it, all the way up to the elbows. That deep digging has been tremendously therapeutic for me, and that's why writing a memoir would have been insufficient: I needed the freedom to take conversations into places where they never had a chance to go. What I've come away with is the understanding that those conversations did not go further in real life because I was too weak and passive; as a fiction writer, I am far more courageous. But I was young then, and I shrank from challenging her, without realizing that confrontation might very well have led us into the dark night that precedes the day.

Although some readers may not believe it, this book is intended to be a love letter to my mother, an offering of tremendous potency, and I feel certain that, at her very best, she would have seen it that way. The book honors her by saying that ours was the most difficult but also the most important relationship of my life. Our lives gain meaning from sorrow and pain, not from comfort and ease, and often the people who affect us indelibly are those against whom we have struggled but ultimately loved.

Reading Group Questions and Topics for Discussion

1. The central event in Simone's life, she keeps reminding her family, was the date she had with Elvis Presley, "the most famous—and the greatest—singer who ever lived. . . . They don't call Frank Sinatra the King, do they?" People commonly hold on to memories of their encounters with well-known personalities, no matter how brief those encounters were. What does the extent to which Simone relies on the memory of her evening with Elvis suggest about her needs, fears, and longings?

2. When Silvie is a little girl, Simone throws a scare into her by taking a bite out of an apple and collapsing on the floor as if dead. Silvie stands beside her, gasping in horror, until Simone jumps up and announces that she was simply playing a trick, "To make you feel something, to feel *passion*." Has Simone genuinely discovered something that Silvie needs to learn? Can you read motives into Simone's behavior that she may be unable to acknowledge, even to herself?

3. The right to name someone else is usually reserved for parents, and, in commemoration of her date with the famous rock star, Simone has given her daughter a name formed out of the letters of Elvis's name. Silvie assumes power over her mother's name, first by calling her Mom, and then by refusing to call her by any name, before settling on Mimi, a name she is still using at the time her mother becomes ill. Can you describe the gratification that often accompanies the act of choosing a name? Why would having this power appeal to a child like Silvie? How does her mother feel about the names Silvie chooses?

4. When Silvie is almost ten years old, she paints a picture that shows her mother "smiling, in a blue silk jacket, one eye cocked to heaven, a blue kite soaring from her head." Silvie's brother Theo reproaches her, saying, "You've got her all wrong." What does Theo understand about their mother that Silvie has failed to perceive? What is it about his position in the family, as a boy, that enables him to form a different perspective on Simone?

5. The way the novel is structured, with chapters about Silvie's childhood interwoven with ones describing her early adult years, the reader learns about Simone's final illness and the claims it makes on Silvie as early as chapter four. What effect does this knowledge have on your reading of subsequent chapters, in which the girl is shown struggling to break free of her mother's domination? Can you think of specific insights and

ironies that are made possible by the juxtaposition of chapters showing events that take place at different points in Silvie's life?

6. Simone's attitude toward Silvie's growth as an artist often seems to be marked by contradictions. She encourages her daughter to set high goals for herself, but in a voice that appears to say, "I'm the artist in the family." When Silvie wins the drawing prize in grade school, Simone lapses into silence and shortly afterward, following her own failure in the sewing contest, she angrily dumps a container of sour cream on Silvie's head. What does Simone's behavior suggest about her feelings about her daughter's artistic gifts? Does she want her daughter to fail?

7. When Simone sums up her view of her personal tragedy by saying "I wasn't always a suburban nobody driving around in a white station wagon," she seems to imply that she is suffering under circumstances that are beyond her control. How accurate does this assessment seem to be? Can Simone's problems be traced to the fact that she was married at the age of twenty in the early 1960s, a time when middle-class wives usually were expected to stay at home with their children? Is there anything that she could have done to shape a life that would have made her feel better about herself? When Silvie begins to pursue her career as a commercial artist in the late 1980s, does it seem that new opportunities have opened up for women? How different are the women she meets in New York, in terms of their sense of themselves, from her mother?

8. After her Elvis routine drives the guests away from a dinner party she's given for her husband's friends and associates, Simone justifies her behavior by telling him, "You're better than them all, Dan. You could be a great man . . . you just need a little push." To what extent do these remarks coincide with her usual feelings about him? How different is his personality from Simone's? What are some of the devices he uses in coping with her behavior? In what ways does his treatment of Silvie differ from Simone's?

9. What does Silvie learn about her mother's background through the visits the family makes to Biloxi, Mississippi? Is she able to conclude anything about the source of the flaws in Simone's personality through observing her mother's parents, Granny and Paw Paw? What similarities or differences does she find when comparing her mother's values, beliefs, and dreams with those of her uncle Shelby, a man with "a deep melancholy etched under dark eyebrows and above dark lashes," who stays in Biloxi, only to commit suicide before he reaches the age of forty?

10. After learning that her mother's Elvis stories have made her the butt of jokes in middle school, Silvie vandalizes Simone's closet, scattering shoes and clothing. Of all the rooms in the house where Simone spends time, why does Silvie choose the closet as a site for expressing her anger? Several years later, she enters her mother's closet again, in search of clothing in which to bury her. Do her feelings about being inside that closet change?

11. When Simone lies dying in the hospital and Silvie stays by her bedside and begins "to feel that she was the child and the mother," does Simone, as she nears death, sense that the dynamics of their relationship have changed? Does she relax any of the pressure that she has always exerted on Silvie? What does Simone's request that Silvie throw the Elvis necklace into the wastebasket signify about her feelings in regard to the story that has dominated her life? To what extent do their final conversations enable Simone and Silvie to draw close to each other?

12. In the weeks following Simone's death, what does Silvie decide that she has learned from her relationship with her mother? Have any of Simone's words of advice stayed with Silvie? What insights into life has Silvie gained that go against her mother's teachings? When Silvie watches the play of several children who are linked to each other by a string held at one end by their teacher, what does she realize about her own life?